RJ

David Boyle is the author of a number of books about history, including *Blondel's Song* and *Toward the Setting Sun*. He lives in the South Downs.

Regicide

Peter Abelard and the Great Jewel

David Boyle

THE REAL PRESS
www.therealpress.co.uk

For Zoe and Zoe

Published in 2016 by the Real Press.
www.therealpress.co.uk © David Boyle
Kindle edition by Endeavour Press

ISBN 978-1535440417

Contents

Prologue

The New Forest, 2 August 1100

It was one of those long, lazy summer's evenings in southern England, with the dry undergrowth rasping together in a haze of crickets and pollen. The shadows were lengthening, but the sun was still high and the forest glowed with the heavy heat of a waning afternoon. The trees were only one generation old then.

In the murky shadows of the woods were watchers. Some remembered this wooded track when it snaked between villages, hovels and farms, but those places had disappeared in the fifty years since the Norman invaders had imposed their ferocious Forest Laws. It was forbidden to hunt here now, and those caught lost their hands or even their lives, which would be forfeited in the slow, agonising ways favoured by the Normans for their Saxon victims. The forest teemed with game, but families around it had to starve before they could take so much as a rabbit.

That was why the woods were now left empty and echoing, with only the odd mound of stones to remind anybody that this was once a thriving community.

Occasionally the pounding of thundering hooves rang out, with the jingling of spurs, the baying of hounds, and the sound of the horn, but hunting was the preserve of those with the privileges of rank and wealth: the knights and barons who served the king, the churchmen not too fat to mount a horse, and, of course, the king himself.

There were people, though, brave enough to disobey the law and enter the forbidden territory. With their forest skills, they knew how to leave no trail, how to move silently through the undergrowth and how to melt away into the green darkness. Also perhaps a favoured few, licensed to live and ply their trade in the forest, blackened creatures of the woods, the rank smell of charcoal on their clothes who lived off the forest and its fruits.

Today the king was coming to hunt, as he did when in residence at Castle Malwood on the edge of the forest. The day was drawing to a close. He would be here soon. The watchers in the woods were invisible in the shadows, waiting, and one man in blackened leather jacket, his face tar-black from smoke, leaned in the shadows against his charcoal cart.

The sounds of the approach came first – the tramping through the bracken, the slashing of foliage – then the beaters and servants appeared, silent but breathing hard, their eyes focused on the undergrowth, intent on reading the signs there that the quarry might have passed by. In their muddy jerkins and old leathers, they were dressed in the colours of the forest, dull and drab in comparison to the small group who followed behind.

French voices were heard declaiming loudly, and then the Norman lords came sauntering into sight, a vision of bright colour and sumptuous fabrics, glinting with gold and jewels, looking like curious fantastical birds against the murky undergrowth. Their horses, magnificent beasts which probably saw more oats in one evening than a Saxon family did in a month, were held back by the grooms as the lords dispersed into small groups for the ritual business of seeking out the elusive stag. This part of the hunt would be undertaken on foot.

From the general crowd, one man emerged. He was as richly dressed as the others but by his confidence and swagger it was evident that this was the King, the son of the Conqueror himself. He was short, red-haired and pot-bellied, and a little pale, as if he had recently been ill and come out hunting for reasons other than strict enjoyment. He held himself apart from those around him, and issued orders in a rough, barking Norman tongue, sending the groups of lords off in different directions with a flourish of his hand. The noblemen obeyed him without question, and within moments the king was left alone with his hunting partner, a man whose ease with the handling of his bow showed him to be a practiced marksman. The grooms hung back with the horses, waiting until their masters should deign to return.

The King turned to his partner and spoke in a low voice, indicating with a gesture of his hand where he thought they should begin their stalking. The other man nodded, pulling an arrow from his quiver in readiness. The King barked another order and a groom brought forward two horses. The marksman took their reins and the two men set off through the undergrowth together.

Within a few minutes, they approached a clearing, as silent and deserted as the rest of the wood. A light breeze ruffled through the branches, shafts of golden evening sunlight fell through the forest canopy in places, and all was quiet. The two men had a quick muttered conversation, then the marksman looped the horses' reins over a tree branch to tether the beasts while the men walked on into the clearing, where they trod with more care. Beyond the line of trees was, at last, some wetness, and they stepped delicately across the marshy ground. The sun was beginning to dip below the tops of the trees and the first hint of evening chill came from the shadows. The King took up his bow in readiness as he stared into the dimness on the other side of the clearing, and pulled out an arrow. Beyond him, on the edge of the trees, the marksman played his fingers over the string of his bow, already taut in case they should spy their quarry. They were evidently of the mind that the stag was close by now, and did not speak. The King stepped silently into the clearing, out of the boggy ground ready for whatever might emerge from the trees.

Suddenly, there was a rustle in the undergrowth and the sound of cracking wood. The two men swung round separately, the King fumbling his arrow onto the string, the marksman pulling back his elbow and dropping into stance as the stag suddenly burst from the cover behind and skittered between them. The marksman followed its path with his body and let fly his arrow. The string twanged and the arrow hummed through the air. Startled birds fluttered up into the sky in panic, chirruping and beating their wings.

The stag raced free into the undergrowth. A loud, human groan echoed out in the evening air. The King staggered forward, dropping his bow as he clawed desperately at an arrow lodged into his chest. He broke it off as he fell to the ground, first to his knees and then forward, onto the dusty ground, crashing down onto his front, his face buried in the dust. His laboured breathing stopped and there was an eerie silence.

The marksman stared in horror, then ran to the prone body of the King. He spoke rapidly in French, breathless with appalled disbelief. Could the arrow that had struck the King really been his own? He stared at it, too terrified to touch it, unsure whether this was the very shaft that he had been handed earlier. Then the panic came. Sheer terror possessed him and he began to shake, his face dead white. In the distance were the voices of the other Norman lords. They were approaching, no doubt led to the spot by the appearance of the fluttering birds.

As his nerve deserted him utterly, the marksman dropped his bow, slipped off his quiver, turned his back on the dead man and ran across the clearing to where the horses waited in the undergrowth. There was his mount. He took the reins, hauled himself onto its back and turned its head away from the clearing and in the opposite direction to the approaching voices. He kicked his heels to its flanks, and urged it off at speed. In the dark shadows, the watchers began to melt away. They must leave before it became known that they had witnessed this dark corner of history. One darted forward towards the clearing and from the leafy ferns, broken by the stag's flight, he scrabbled for a moment before lifting out an arrow, then hurried back to join the others as they fell back into the depths of the forest. The man with the blackened face moved carefully back into shadows. They were invisible when the first shouts and cries were heard.

The dead King had been found.

PART I

1/Alys

Beaugency, 8 December 1119

It was indecent, that was all there was to it. Indecent.

Now, Hilary, he rebuked himself, *you ought not to be thinking of yourself and the way you are being treated. You should be thinking about Alys.*

He called her face to mind: thin, inquisitive, intelligent, with pale blue eyes and slender expressive lips. But the memory was already fuzzy at the edges, not quite realised in his mind's eye. Blurring. How was it possible to forget so quickly?

Poor Alys. Dead only one day, and already he couldn't quite recall the exact colour of her hair. He had seen her coffin committed to the ground that very afternoon, the gravediggers shivering as they waited for the burial rites to be completed, leaning on their shovels against the frozen, rutted ground, and eager to resume work filling in the hole they had made, so that they could get warm with the effort. Poor Alys. So sweet natured, so clever, so unreachable. And now – so utterly gone. No amount of poetry could draw her back.

He had loved her… or at least, he had certainly tried his best to. He had strained to develop a powerful passion for his pupil, to make the long days in the castle at Beaugency more lively, and to make sure she made the case for his continued employment. And, of course, wandering scholars did have a certain reputation that had to be upheld: Hilary knew his own weaknesses. He had even penned a series of secret poems dedicated to her, in which he had written: 'Can Sapientia blossom unless the sap of Venus flow?'

He envisaged what would happen when she read them, that cool young lady with her pale face and lofty bearing. She would look on him differently, those chilly eyes would soften and, rather than a dishevelled, slightly portly tutor, his monkish tonsure framing a round field of stubble, she would see a romantic hero and they would fall in love, and then...

What awaited them beyond the dangerous revelation of his love for her, he had never really considered. He was sure he would begin to love her if she would only unbend a little and smile once or twice, and perhaps talk of something other than the classics, which seemed to be all that interested her. As her father said, with her nose in the masters of Latin and Greek prose, she was certainly a modern girl.

But before she could read his poems and understand his feelings, Alys had sickened. She became ill at around nones on St Clement's Day, and within hours she was raving that she was being bitten. A physician from the nearby monastery had attended and, after hearing her delirious shrieks of her skin crawling with a thousand ants and witnessing her spasms, announced that she was suffering from St Anthony's Fire. She died a few days later without recognising anyone – paler than ever but scarred with livid blisters – in the depths of Saturday night.

Hilary, merely her tutor, had not been allowed to see her once she had become ill and separated from the rest of the household. He had endured the stories from the maids who waited on the sickroom about her sores and her drenching sweats in the frozen nights; he'd seen the ghastly wads of pus-encrusted linen taken from her bedchamber and carried away to be burnt. He had been powerless to help but, then, so had everyone else. There was no cure for the Fire.

She was buried quickly to contain the sickness, even though

the ground was so hard it had taken the diggers a full day and night to make enough of a grave to put her in. And after the funeral, as they began to make their way back towards the Great Hall, Alys's father, the Lord of Beaugency, had turned to him and said: 'We shall be sorry to say goodbye to you, Hilary, but you may have an escort as far as the river, if that is any help to you. The cart will be ready whenever you wish to get on your way.'

Hilary had blinked, gaped at him, tucking his icy cold fingers into his sleeves but unable to stop a great chill creeping over his chest. 'My lord?'

'You are a wandering scholar, Hilary. Isn't that what they call you?' said Alys' father. 'Your work here is done. You can hardly stay on without a pupil. It is time for you to go off and ... wander again.'

The afternoon was already beginning to fade. The rushes were burning with an acrid smell, and the outline of the Great Hall of Beaugency, his home for the past two years, was beginning to darken to a silhouette in the winter light. Late afternoon seemed to be merging imperceptibly with dusk, as if the day had never quite carried enough conviction. There were bent figures moving in the distance, pall-bearers back from the chapel, and the distant sound of ladies weeping as they returned to the castle, still shocked at the extinction of Alys. The Lord gives and takes away. Sometimes he just seems to take away.

It was only when his position seemed to slip out of reach that Hilary knew for certain that he hadn't really loved Alys. He had loved his life at the castle, with its food, lamps, firelight and clean straw. He had loved his tiny cell with its iron sconce and writing desk, where he was able to lose himself in poetry, all the while knowing that the aroma drifting up from the kitchens meant that dinner was a certainty. He had loved his pints of ale, and the evenings where stories were told by the fire in the Great Hall, when he might be asked to stand up and entertain them all with a poem or a song. He would pretend reluctance and then perform, declaiming a courtly romance or a comical verse tale, his audience leaning back on stools and trestles and benches.

'Where will I go?' he had said piteously.

'You'll find another pupil,' Alys's father answered. 'A scholar of Ste Genevieve should have no difficulty at all in securing a place. You are well regarded, are you not?'

'Yes,' Hilary replied miserably. That was what he had told him at the beginning, when he had first arrived at the castle. He had been delighted to be believed. It was rare enough for the great lords to employ tutors in their households, and to employ tutors for their daughters was almost unheard of. It was a lazy, fed and magnificent existence and he had very much enjoyed teaching Alys too, despite her preference for books.

'There you are. Now, you will need to be gone before supper, Hilary. I've promised your cell to the clerk.'

That was the indecency of it. Alys was barely cold and here he was, out on his ear. The funeral bell was still tolling as he dragged his box of books and belongings across the cobbles of the courtyard, out to the waiting cart.

The servant who was to drive him to the river lifted up the box and flung it on.

'Careful!' shouted Hilary. 'There's a lifetime of copying in that chest.'

The servant, a man he had always disliked, said nothing but gave him a malevolent glance and climbed up into the driving seat. Hilary took his place behind him and wrapped himself as deeply into his woollen cloak as he could. It was freezing and almost dark. Why on earth couldn't they have left tomorrow when it was light? He imagined his cosy cell now with that distressingly self-satisfied clerk settling down in it, no doubt delighted to have won it from Hilary. He tried to think of where he might be spending the night but could see nothing in his mind's eye but a vast blankness. All he was sure of was that it would be cold and unpleasant.

There are moments in any life when there is no going back, and when the future is still completely shrouded from view. That is where I am, said Hilary to himself. He tried to nurture that forlorn hope that something better awaited him, but it refused to spark into life.

That's the problem with wandering, he thought. You never quite belong anywhere. And if there's no pupil to teach, then it means squires or minor princelings to entertain in return for board, lodging, and maybe a generous change of clothes, and then back on the rutted tracks for the nearest monastery or cathedral. Oh yes, there are worse places to be than in castles and manors, but where will it all lead? Will the day come when I'll find nowhere to lay my head? *Foxes have holes, birds of the air have nests* – no, he must not compare himself to Our Lord. This was no time for blasphemy.

Neither of the gate keepers acknowledged him as the cart swayed through the stone portal, clattering a little on the stones. There was hardly anyone to be seen now, and no one seemed to care much that he was leaving. It was true that the household had never really taken to him. Some had disapproved of his poetry, or shared the irritation that servants reserve for those household dependents who consider themselves above menial work. Neither one thing nor the other, that was the fate of tutors everywhere. Hilary liked people to like him and he had fondly imagined that he would win everyone over with his songs and poems, his late night turns in front of the fire. Evidently not.

Or perhaps it was worse than that. He was an Englishman, after all, and although he had trained in Paris and was as fluent a French speaker as any native, there was still a trace of his Hampshire accent, and something about him that set him apart. He hadn't spread the fact widely, but Alys had known of it and her father, when in his cups, had jokingly insulted Hilary for his Englishness (or perhaps not so jokingly), so no doubt they all knew it. The fact of being English was not such a crime in itself. It was being different that was the thing.

Still. He tried to put his dejection to one side and think of his future plans, but the bells that had tolled all day still echoed in his head. At least five miles lay between him and the river, an hour's journey in the company of this taciturn servant and the back of a disapproving head, bent slightly over the reins of the horse. He could barely think of anything, as if a huge bruise had covered his available thoughts, too painful to touch, but he pulled himself together and began to ponder his prospects. He had enough money for a few days. He would take a boat into Orléans and offer his services at the college again. There was often work for wandering scholars, especially scholars from the great colleges of Paris, in these rival and provincial seats of learning – though 'provincial' was a word he agreed with himself not to use in the city that considered itself the royal throne of kings.

Orléans was stricter about theology, or so it was said – none of your logic was allowed here – but he could deal with that. If they had no space for him as an assistant, he might have to beg some meals from the monks and then seek out some new master. If that wasn't possible, he might even have to go home to Hampshire to be a hedge-priest or a hayward, or something equally hopeless. But it wasn't as if this was a new predicament. He had been lucky at Beaugency, he knew that, and he might yet be lucky again.

It was vespers before they began to approach a small village, with a magnificent castle in the distance and a large inn by the bank of the river. The cart came to a halt.

'Beaugency-sur-Loire,' said his moody guide. 'That's it.'

Mist was rising off the river and obscuring the woods. Nobody was about. The travelling season had been over for more than a month.

'Can't you at least take me to the wharf?' Hilary asked. 'My box is no featherweight.'

Ignoring him, the servant manhandled his chest off the back of the cart. The tension had been in the air since they left the castle. For a moment, Hilary wondered if he was in for some kind of beating. If he was, he calculated he would come off by far the worst in the encounter. It was moments like this when he might just have his throat slit and his body tossed into the Loire. It took another effort of will to rise to his feet and summon up some effort of command.

'All right. Just leave it there. You can go now.'

The servant stared for a moment and seemed to be making up his mind. Then he climbed onto the cart. 'No more boats tonight,' he said, grasping the reins. Then he clicked to urge the horses on and the cart began to pull away. With a sinking sense of abandonment, Hilary watched the cart lurch through the potholes in the gathering gloom. Despite what he had felt about the servant, he would have happily joined him on the journey back to Beaugency and the security of his little cell.

But that life was over now, snuffed out with Alys's existence. He imagined her slender body in its rough coffin, now buried under mounds of icy earth, and sent up a prayer for her soul as he set to work and dragged his box the few hundred yards to the riverside. There was a barge there but, sure enough, the crew were hauling down the sails, and had the definite air of going home about them. Apart from them, there seemed to be nobody around. The only signs of life came from the inn, where lamplight flickered in that peculiarly welcoming hue of gold through the low windows. He thought of a trencher of something hot, a tankard of something comforting, and a warm corner where he could sleep. He had barely enough money to pay for such luxuries and hardly enough energy to speak, let alone to perform in return for them. But he had to find some kind of shelter. He hauled his box towards the inn door.

The door was unlatched and he pushed it open to reveal a murky interior clouded with smoke from the fire. A few other travellers sat about on the great benches, or at the trestles, supping on something that set his mouth watering with its thick, meaty smell. Hilary realised he was famished. When cheap inn slop looked appetising, it was a good sign that a meal was overdue.

A woman approached, sour-faced and carrying a large pitcher of ale.

'Good evening. I am a scholar of Ste-Genevieve,' he said hopefully. 'Might I crave your hospitality this one night?' He drew aside his cloak, and lowered his head to reveal what remained of his tonsure and his semi-monastic status. Surely this was as God-fearing a place as Rouen or Reims, where he had often cadged a bed on the basis of his holy orders.

'Nope,' said the woman. 'We'll have no holy scholars here. No wandering poets neither. No doubt you're about to tell me you'll sing or recite for your supper. Well, we don't want anything of that kind here, thank you.' She stood in front of him, put the pitcher of ale on the table, and then her hands on her ample hips. 'You should see what happened to the last one who sang. Out you go. Go on.'

Hilary felt too tired to argue. It was going to be one of those nights when he slept in his monastic cape under the stars. He began to calculate his chances outside on a freezing night, wondering if he could double back and sneak into the stable. He was too tired even to be angry, wondering where he had hidden his few coins in his luggage.

'You heard me! Shift your arse!' snapped the woman.

A voice came from somewhere in the gloom. 'Leave him be. I'll pay for his supper.'

Hilary looked down the bench, trying to make out who had spoken through the smoke from the tallow candles and lamps. The wind was whispering through the window and making the lamps dance in their pots. Then he saw a pair of bright eyes staring at him in the gloom. The speaker was a man, well wrapped in a travelling cloak, with a dark greying beard and a weathered face. Hilary was too relieved at the unexpected offer even to wonder what had prompted this act of charity. Praise be. I shall eat at least, he thought, gratefully.

The woman shrugged. 'As you wish. But I'll take the money now, if you don't mind.'

As the traveller unwrapped his cloak to reach his purse, Hilary said: 'Who are you, sir? My thanks are due to you. I am in your debt.'

'Say nothing of it,' said the man. His voice was rough and yet had a sing-song lilt, the trace of some accent Hilary could not identify. 'We are riding the same cart, you and I.'

Hilary blinked. 'You're a scholar too?'

The stranger laughed. 'Do I look like a scholar?'

Hilary peered harder. He said nothing but thought to himself that true scholars tended to look more bedraggled than this man, and less energetic. Nor did they usually carry expensive blades like the one that Hilary could see hanging from his belt.

The landlady stretched her hand out towards the traveller and beckoned rudely for the money. He reached into the red leather pouch that hung around his neck, extracted two coins and pressed them into the rough palm. The landlady looked at them suspiciously for a moment, eyed the two men and then was gone, muttering that she would return presently.

'Come, my friend, eat with me. You look like a cornered stag. We have that in common. I *feel* like a cornered stag. Keep me company tonight and tomorrow we will voyage into Orléans. I'll wager that's where you are going?'

'Yes, that's right...'

'Good. Then sit!' The stranger laughed and Hilary trusted him a little more. He sat down on the bench which was empty apart from his new friend. His eyes had adjusted now, and he could see that the stranger was dressed beneath his cloak in a short tunic over leggings bound with criss-crossed bandages above a pair of stout, short leather boots. He looked as though he had been on the move for many days and was still far from wherever he was going. He gave Hilary a keen glance and said: 'Now, my good clerk-in-holy-orders. Why are you here exactly and with such a forlorn look about you? I know you wandering scholars. Now, let me guess. Gluttony? You stole the wine? I believe the Swedes, a barbaric northern race, think themselves blessed if they drink themselves to death at the holy mass. Come, let us have no secrets between us. We will be companions on the road.'

Hilary stared at him for a moment, taking in everything about the other man. Despite his ease of manner, he seemed to be alert, like a hare in the middle of a field. There was something taut about him, as if he was aware of every noise inside the inn and outside it.

What's he afraid of? Hilary wondered, suspicion prickling on his skin. But, glad of the meal to come at his benefactor's expense, he decided to be friendly and said in a jovial tone: 'I am not quite the wandering scholar you take me for. I am in search of a new place, by God's will. I am a teacher. They call me Hilary the Englishman. As you guessed, I'm on my way to Orléans.'

'Aha. Are you perhaps Hilary the Englishman the poet?'

Hilary blinked at him, astonished. 'You know my poems?'

'I heard them sung at Rouen. I liked them very much and asked who had written something so fine.'

A glow of pleasure spread down Hilary's back and he smiled for the first time that day. He wasn't used to being recognised, and – however exhausting the night, however distant the hope of employment – it cheered his soul. 'I am glad of it, truly. Perhaps you would do me the honour of telling me your own name?'

The stranger laughed again. He nonchalantly flicked something off his tunic. 'Ah, well, that depends who you talk to.'

'Oh yes? And me? What if you're talking to me?'

'To my friends I am usually known as John.'

'John?' Hilary blinked. So that was the accent he had half identified. 'You're English? John of where?'

John looked immediately serious. 'At this moment, I am English, yes. If another were to join us, I might be someone else and from somewhere else. It all depends.'

'What do you mean by that?'

'Come, my friend, how long since you were a plain and simple Englishman, no matter what they called you? You've lived here in France for long enough to know that you can be whatever it suits you to be, whatever it's expedient to be. Isn't that right? You and I are lucky, perhaps, that we can take on the colours that serve us best when necessary.' John smiled and Hilary had the distinct impression that he was supposed to understand what the man was talking about. 'Now, here is our supper. Thanks be to heaven.'

The landlady put down two wooden bowls of stew that seemed to contain hunks of pork and slices of turnip in a murky liquid strongly favoured with dried sage. Dry bread was provided to soak the stew up and Hilary fell on it, ravenous after the long, freezing day, shovelling it in and revelling as the savoury warmth hit his stomach and eased the empty feeling in his blood.

'At least you'll make quick work of it,' the landlady remarked, watching him. 'It isn't godly to burn tallow into the night.' She left them to their meal. John ate too, a little less frantically but with relish, and then called for ale and cheese, which the landlady brought over with her usual grumpiness. When the platters were cleared, Hilary sat back against the wall, satisfied.

'I needed that,' he said sincerely. 'Thank you, friend.'

'You'd have done the same for me, no doubt, if our situations were reversed. Now, we have an hour or so before I can sleep, if we can persuade the good lady to light another tallow. What do you say to a little gaming?'

'Gaming is a wicked pursuit,' Hilary said piously.

'Come on, indulge me. You may have taken holy orders but you look like a man who has lived to me. I'd bet my cloak you've had your fair share of the gaming table in your time.'

Hillary shrugged. This fellow was perceptive, he'd give him that. It was true that he enjoyed a game or two. Only occasionally, of course. He said lightly: 'Well... perhaps. ...What's your fancy?'

'You can choose. Chess? Tables? Nine-men's morris?'

'You *are* English,' said Hilary. 'Nobody here calls it that.'

John ignored him. 'Excellent, tables it is!'

Hilary wrinkled his nose. He had developed an aversion to tables during his student days in Paris when, for a while, it seemed to be all he did. And it had cost him dear, too.

John reached into the red leather purse at his neck, and Hilary noticed that he had two other large pouches hanging from strings around his neck. Then he banged down a handful of coins on the table. 'I can't stake money,' Hilary said at once. 'I don't have any.

Well, hardly any.'

'Never mind. Here. I'll advance you some. And if we can't play for money, we'll play for something else.'

Before Hilary could protest, John had pushed some coins towards him, produced a pair of dice and the game had begun. Although Hilary hadn't played for a long time, the rules quickly returned to him, for all the good it did him. Within a few throws, he had lost all the coins John had lent him.

'Bad luck, my good clerk-in-holy-orders,' John laughed. 'I'll give you another chance. Here's some more metal.'

The game was on almost at once, and this time Hilary seemed to have a little more luck. He won a few throws and John called for more ale, and they played again. But his fortunes turned once more, and he swiftly lost all the money to his benefactor.

'Ah, you're Fortune's fool tonight, my good Hilary.'

'I think your dice are badly made,' Hilary returned sulkily. He could feel the pull of the game exerting its hold on him. He was hungry to play more even though he knew the futility of it.

'I've another set of dice here, would you perhaps prefer these?'

'No, no more dice!' said Hilary, a little louder than he had intended. He felt unsure of his words and volume. The ale had certainly taken hold.

John leaned towards him, his flinty eyes shining in the firelight. 'Come on, I can see you want to continue. We don't have to play for money, my friend. How about we play for promises?'

'Promises?'

John nodded. 'Here's my promise to you. If you win the next game, I'll fund your journey to Orleans with a little over for you to enjoy when you get there. But if I win...'

'Yes?' Hilary said suspiciously. He had the sense of having fallen into a trap whose true nature he was yet to discover.

John lifted one of the pouches at his neck. It was large and bulky, made of animal skin, deer by the look of it. 'I've been charged to deliver this to Count Fulk of Anjou, but I've other business I must attend to first and frankly I've managed to get myself into a difficult situation. I can't be in two places at once. If I win, you undertake to deliver the contents of this pouch to Count Fulk, thus freeing me of my obligation.'

'Who? What? All the way to Anjou?' Hilary was indignant.

John smiled. 'It's not so far.' He shrugged. 'Besides, I hear that Count Fulk is looking for a tutor for his sons. You might find that God's hand is in this, guiding you towards Anjou for his purpose.'

'*Your* purpose, more like,' grumbled Hilary but he could see something in what John said. Perhaps a spell in the delightful environs of Anjou might be rather welcome, especially if there were the prospect of a job. He rather fancied a Christmas in the count's castle; no doubt the wine flowed more freely there than in the monastery of Orleans, where there would be more praying than playing. So, he reflected, if I win I get a journey to Orleans, and if I lose I take the road to Anjou instead. A thought occurred to him and he said craftily. 'If I'm freeing you of your obligation, then it's only right you fund my journey to Anjou, if I end up losing.'

John threw back his head and guffawed. 'You like to try your luck, don't you, friend Hilary? Very well – I agree. You will have money to feed you all the way to Anjou – if you lose, of course. After all, you may win.' John fixed him with an amused look.

'Yes, I may win,' Hilary said, but secretly he was thinking that he had cleverly engineered things so that it was win-win either way as far as he was concerned. He would get a game of tables, and money, win or lose. And if he lost but happened to get a better offer on the way to Anjou and accidentally mislaid the pouch over a hedge, then who would ever know or care? He was unlikely to meet John again, after all.

'Good.' John clashed his tankard against Hilary's and both men drained their ale. 'Here's to the lure of the dice, Hilary!' He held the pair of black pocked cubes out on his palm. 'Shall we play?'

'Play!' declared Hilary, and he watched as they flew from John's hand towards the table, carrying his fate on their spinning faces.

2/Orleans

Beaugency-sur-Loire, 9 December 1119

Hilary awoke, stiff and uncomfortable. Light seeped into the darkness of the room, illuminating the dust floating thickly in the air. The noises of dawn were filtering in from outside. He sniffed the unmistakeable aroma of straw that had been used as a bed many times and by many different travellers, with its layered scents of sweat and urine, and remembered that he was in the back room of the inn, one that was no doubt used as stable when it wasn't providing a cheap bed for the inn's poorer guests.

He groaned and shifted, recalling how he had followed John in late last night, his head swimming with ale. He had overindulged as usual. What made him imbibe so heavily when the ale was free? He knew it always gave him a sore head and a bad thirst in the morning. A large and awkward shape was prodding into his neck and chest. Putting one hand to it, he felt the bulky leather pouch he had seen around John's neck the previous evening. What on earth was it doing around his own?

God's curses, he must have lost every game of tables last night. The memory of the promise he had made came crawling back into his mind.

His heart sank. By the Lord's name, I swore to go to Anjou! I said I'd deliver this blessed pouch to Count Fulk... I must be seven kinds of fool to put my word to such a promise. Well, I shall just have to tell him that I was gone in ale and can't be held to an oath made that way. I'm not going to Anjou, and that's that.

Now he recalled John's laughing face as he pressed the pouch around Hilary's neck, pulling the leather string over his head so that it sat heavily on his chest. 'I know you'll see this task complete,' he had said, his eyes merry. 'After all, if I can't trust a man of God – and a famous poet at that – who can I trust?'

Hilary groaned again, remembering how they had come back here together the previous night, John carrying a lamp to light the way, and how the other man had sat down and pulled off his boots, releasing the smell of dirty, well-used feet into the stable room. His face had been lit by curious shadows as he had said in a low voice: 'Now, Hilary, tomorrow we'll set out together on our journey and, who knows, I may be able to come some or even all of the way with you. But if I cannot, will you swear to me that you will take this pouch to Count Fulk? It contains a number of important documents which must reach him. Will you do that for me? Will you solemnly promise, on the authority of your holy orders?'

Did I promise? Hilary stared up at the gaps in the thatch above him where daylights gleamed through. I must have. But what else did he say? Oh, that's right...

John had said: 'My name is John of Muchelney. Remember that. You may need it. And something else. I want you to say it after me. Are you listening?'

Hilary had grunted as he wrapped his cloak about him in preparation for the sleep which he now craved.

'Listen. *Hit waes geara iu.* Did you hear that? Say it.'

'*Hit waes...*'

'*Geara iu.*'

'*Geara iu.*'

'Again. From the beginning.'

'*Hit waes geara iu.*' It meant nothing and yet... there was something familiar in the cadence, in the pattern of sounds, like an old nonsense song remembered, or a poem once learned in another language that now meant nothing. Images of his home flashed before his eyes. He saw his mother, bent over the fire, raking out ashes to help it draw. Oh, but he was tired. He wanted suddenly and with all his heart to be at home but was too exhausted to do anything about it.

'Very good.' John had blown out the lamp and they were left in the darkness together. 'Remember it, Hilary. Do I have your word?'

But Hilary's eyes had fallen shut with the darkness that enveloped him and he had slept almost at once.

Now wide awake, he reached out his hand and patted the straw on either side of him. On his right, it was flattened but empty. His new friend must have gone outside to relieve himself. Hilary felt the first pangs of stiffness that afflicted him after a night on a bed of old, squashed straw, and a chill as his cloak fell away from him, letting in cool morning air. There was a muffled chink as a smaller leather purse fell from inside his cloak and on to the straw. He stared at it, then picked it up and examined it. Inside, it was a quarter full of silver coins.

I certainly did not have this yesterday, he thought with surprise, and then remembered that John of Muchelney had talked of funding the journey. These must be the funds, and very generous they were too. But why slide the money inside Hilary's cloak like this, instead of handing it over in the morning? And hadn't John said he might come some of the way to Anjou? Perhaps, with this much money to spend on food and lodging, and with the company of an amusing friend, the mission might be pleasant rather than otherwise.

Hilary felt his own call of nature, and decided to venture outside to find a likely place to relieve himself and see if he could spot his friend. Perhaps John was already in the inn taking his breakfast. Hilary hauled himself to his feet, blinked in the lightening gloom and made his way out into the frosty morning air. He stepped into a filthy yard thick with chicken shit and kicked a hen out of his path, making the whole flock protest with deafening screech of raucous chatter, then headed towards the gate that led into a field behind the inn. To his right, he could see a squadron of crows swooping over something lying in the vegetable garden through the next gate.

'What's pricking their fancy?' he muttered, watching the great black birds dive and flutter. 'Have they found a dead rabbit? They don't usually get so excited over a carrot or two.'

He glanced idly into the vegetable patch as he walked by, but he was too eager to be free of his water to stop and look. He found a ditch at the far edge of the field and let go a stream of warm urine that arched satisfyingly over the weeds and landed with a splatter in the mud. On the way back, he noticed the birds were in even more uproar and, curious, he strolled over the field and let himself in at the gate. The crows were thick around a large dark shape on the ground. A sack, he wondered? A fallen sack of grain that would be like bounty from heaven to the starved winter crows.

But as he approached, Hilary realised it was nothing like a sack. It was a man, lying spread-eagled on the ground, impaled through the stomach by a massive wooden stake. His body was black with sodden blood and the ground around him was wet with it. The birds were busy at his face, and already one eye socket was empty, stringy trails of scarlet meat hanging from it. Nevertheless, Hilary could see easily that it was John of Muchelney who lay there in a brutal death.

Hilary gasped, then muttered, 'Holy Christ...', crossing himself quickly. 'Blessed saviour, have pity on his unshriven soul...' He closed his eyes, feeling dizzy with horror. He knew the blood had drained from his face at this frightful sight. Nausea rolled in his stomach but he fought it. What did this mean? His friend was slain, murdered with vicious cruelty. How long did it take a man to leach out his life in this manner? Not long, he hoped, though his friend's twisted mouth seemed to speak of deep agony endured over terrible minutes.

Hilary approached, fighting the sickness in his stomach, pressing one hand against his mouth to stop himself retching. Pity filled his heart as he gazed down at the body before him. His poor friend, butchered! Who had done this? And why?

He stood there in the gathering dawn, the morning breeze on his cheeks, as he stared at the terrible scene before him. He felt as if he had inadvertently stepped out of God's world and into an unpredictable, ungovernable universe pervaded by horror. How had he come to be here, in this bloody garden in the icy dawn? Had he gone against God's will and been allowed to wander into the Devil's peril? Or had God led him here for a purpose yet unrevealed?

But this was not God's work. This was evil, practised by man in Satan's possession.

'I must do something,' Hilary told himself. 'I must bring God's will to bear.' He tried to keep calm and think. What should he do? He must, of course, tell someone that this wicked murder had been perpetrated. And they must begin at once to look for the murderer.

At once, a scene enacted itself before his mind's eye, in which he showed the landlady this awful scene and she looked at him with her contemptuous expression and noticed the pouch about his neck that last night had been around John's, and saw the purse of silver coins that John had taken his payment from, and at once she gave him an accusing look and pointed the finger of guilt at him.

They will think *I* did it! Hilary felt the rise of sudden panic, as he clutched at the deerskin pouch at his chest. And the longer I stand here to be seen by any passer-by, the harder I will find it to explain all of this.

He glanced frantically about. It was absolutely quiet, save for the swish of the wind through the empty trees. There were a few early risers working in the fields in the distance, but otherwise he was alone with his mangled friend. It would be just his luck if the landlady called her husband, and together they summoned the peasants, and the whole ignorant gang of them decided to enact summary justice on him right here. They might very well string him up from the nearest oak.

A crow squawked and jumped a little closer, emboldened by the lure of carrion to risk approaching Hilary. Others watched to see how the first fared. Hilary kicked out at it, sending it scuttering a few paces off.

'Be off, you bloodthirsty wretches!' he cried, forgetting for a moment that he was attempting not to draw attention to himself. He froze in panic but there was no sound on the still air but the indignant croaking of the crows. Perhaps no one had heard.

But even if they don't lynch me, he thought, then they will turn me over to the authorities. How will I explain all this? That bitter wretch of a landlady will say she saw me lose at tables last night, saw me lose every last coin, and that I must have killed my friend in a drunken rage and taken his money.

Appalled, he put his hand to the pouch about his neck with its awkward cargo of documents and then a thought of such icy horror possessed him that it felt as though a pail of frozen water had been tossed over him. Someone had killed John of Muchelney, that was certain. And why? Not for that purse of silver coins, surely. Such brutality for so little? No. Perhaps it was because of the very things that hung around his neck at this moment. He glanced down at the corpse on the ground, where crows were now stalking closer again, determined to get back to the prize. Around John's neck were knife marks and the front of his jerkin was slashed as though it had been opened in search of something thought to lie beneath.

Hilary drew in a shuddering breath. A man had been killed and very likely for the things that he now had in his possession, the cargo John had asked him to convey to Anjou. And who was to say that the killer was not at this very minute lurking about, ready to enact the same slaughter on whoever had his prize?

Hilary nearly howled out loud in terror. Only the thought of a bloody villain ready to pounce from behind a wall or a hedge kept him from making a sound.

Christ's wounds, he thought, almost faint with fear. I'm certainly in mortal danger. If I don't get hanged for a murderer, I'll be gutted on the ground next to this man for the sake of this cursed pouch.

He looked wildly about again, then wrapped his cloak tightly around him, muttered a prayer and made the sign of the cross over his friend's body, then began to walk as quickly as he could towards the road beyond the inn. All he could think of was to get away as fast as possible and with as few people seeing him as he could manage. The road was the best way and he made for it at a rapid trot, wanting only to put as much distance as he could between him and the awful fate that surely awaited him if he stayed in that cursed place. His precious box of writings was just too heavy. His very life depended on leaving it at the inn. With a sad heart, he bid it adieu and hurried away as quickly as he could.

Hilary walked in a dream, terrified of what might be on his tail, horrified at the demise of his new friend, reminding himself constantly to make more haste. He moved swiftly along the wide muddy track that served as a road, hoping that he was going in the right direction, towards Orléans. He knew that the city lay to the east, and by the path of the sun as it climbed steadily upwards into the sky he could tell that he was heading roughly that way, with the river on his right – though some distance away. As the day brightened, he thought of the landlady of the inn. She would be getting up by now, starting her day's work. She might not wonder where her customers were immediately; it could be some time before she thought to peer into the stable, but perhaps, before then, the busy crows would alert her or she would need a turnip for the pot and would venture out to the garden, only to make the gruesome discovery of John's body.

And not long after she found that, they would begin seeking him out. His flight would look like guilt, he knew that, but really what else was he supposed to do? Staying there would be just as perilous. He would never be able to convince them of his innocence. He congratulated himself for refraining from mentioning his name to the landlady the previous evening. Or had he?

What an absolute fool I am. Hilary settled down into a steady trudge along the path. I have managed to get myself into a pretty mess in less than a day. God knows I have only utmost pity for my poor companion, and desire justice for him, but I daren't risk sharing his fate. What good would it do? Besides, everything points to me as the guilty party, even I can see that. If I didn't know better, I would think I did it myself. Only the church will give me a fair hearing, so there's but one remedy: I'll seek sanctuary as soon as possible, in Orléans. I have a good start. As long as I can reach the city, I'll be safe.

He thought nervously of a watching murderer, creeping after him, waiting for his chance to pounce, slit Hilary open and take the pouch for himself, and at once peered into the bushes and undergrowth that lined the road, as though he might see a pair of malevolent eyes glinting there, and the flash of the knife.

Don't be silly, he told himself as bravely as he could. If the murderer was still about, he could have done his foul business before now. I'm alone, I'm sure of that. I must just get there as quickly as I can. It's my only chance.

But it was a long and slow journey on foot, even if he didn't have his box with him to hamper him. He thought with a dull pang of his life's work of manuscripts sitting in the stable of the inn and wondered what would become of it. Perhaps it would be found after his death and his genius finally recognized. He remembered his poem to Alys that would be found in there.

'What do they know of wisdom, who only wisdom know?
Can Sapientia blossom unless the sap of Venus flow?
O Virgin, I can lead you towards true Sapiens divine:
If only you would take my hand and wrap your legs in mine.'

He didn't have to worry about his designs on Alys being found out now. He would probably be dead for a murderer long before anyone discovered he had once tried to entertain a passion in one of his female pupils. He shrugged off thoughts of his writings. He may as well forget them for now. Every step took him further away from them, after all.

The morning warmed slightly with the advent of the sun, and he thought again of home as he had last night. Was it time to go home? Or perhaps to enter one of the monasteries in Paris and submit to the rule, at least to keep still, to try and discipline his unruly mind a little. These days, you hardly ever met a churchman who was married, and maybe only the rigid rhythm of monastic life could keep him on the path to paradise. He could never have stayed at Beaugency, even if Alys had lived. His soul required some kind of backbone. No more wandering. No more fleeting bouts of passion, even if they were only in the mind.

He seemed to have been walking for hours when he heard a cart rolling roughly along the road, and turned to see an old peasant couple in a battered wagon pulled along by a scrawny nag. He waved them down and the old man clicked the horse to a standstill on the road. 'Are you going to Orléans?' asked Hilary hopefully.

The man nodded and his wife said: 'To market. Winter cabbages.' She gestured at a few dozen yellowish heads in the back of the cart.

'May I beg a ride in your cart?' Hilary said, trying to sound as gentlemanly and scholarly as he could. 'I'm a humble churchman making his way to the monastery there.'

The couple exchanged glances and then the man gave a brief nod to show that Hilary could climb up into the back of the cart.

'When do you expect to reach the city?' he asked, a little relieved for the first time that morning as he settled down among the sad-looking vegetables and the rough sacks that covered the cart bottom.

'By nones perhaps?' said the peasant woman. Her husband appeared to leave all the talking to her. 'The road is dry and that's a blessing.'

They rumbled off again and Hilary relaxed a little further into a nervous, watchful rest, the road passing by without his having to tramp every wearisome step of it. Then he thought of John of Muchelney and his recovering mood evaporated at once. No matter what the consequences for him, nothing would change the fact that a man had been killed. John had shown him nothing but kindness and a stranger had cruelly murdered him. Now that Hilary felt relatively safe, he began to ponder the mystery. Why had John been killed? Was it really for whatever was in the pouch around his neck? What was there? He considered emptying it out but, on reflection, decided that now was not the moment: he needed privacy and quiet. And in all of the uproar of this morning, he had almost forgotten that he had sworn to take the pouch to Anjou and deliver it to Count Fulk.

That promise is void now, he told himself. I'm at risk of a false accusation of murder. I must first save my skin before I keep my word. Nonetheless he felt uneasy. He had sworn an oath. And oaths had a very annoying way of making a man live by them and keep them even when he knew rationally that doing so was extremely stupid.

It was with relief that he saw the outline of Orléans in the distance with its great walls, and noticed that the traffic on the road was becoming heavier. The cart passed country folk loaded with goods and tramping towards the great city. The gates were open now and people streamed towards them.

At that moment that he heard the unmistakable rhythm of hoof beats behind them. This was it; they are here. Whoever was on his trail from the inn had caught up with him. Sick with fear, he strained round to get a better look before realising that it was more sensible to take no notice at all. He glimpsed a flash of chain mail as they went by, one, two, four of them, with blank, serious faces. How long would it have taken to ride from the inn? An hour perhaps? Two at most. He looked away and they were lost among the crowds ahead. Hilary's heartbeat rang loudly in his chest. Perhaps they're nothing to do with me. I mustn't let my imagination run away with me.

'Dear God in Christ, don't squirm about so,' said the woman. 'What's the matter with you?'

Hilary ignored her. The best way of hiding, he thought, is to say nothing and just *feel* invisible. He shrank inside his cloak, as they reached the outside of the crowd, pulling the edge over his head to conceal his tonsure, rubbing dirt into his face to make sure he couldn't be seen. Moments later, he felt the wind as two more riders rushed by on either side, shouting at the people in the crowd.

'Make way, make way!' shouted one of them, with the arrogance of the aristocracy. The other followed at a trot now towards the gates as they swung back to let in the crowd, looking to right and to left and, for one terrifying moment, Hilary felt his gaze swing across him like a burning candle flame. For a second, they locked glances. Hilary felt a kind of horror. The man was dressed in grey, with chain mail beneath his grey shirt, and deep passionless grey eyes. His face was thin and aristocratic. He looked watchful and intelligent, but also deeply malevolent. There seemed to be nothing behind the eyes at all: a terrifying ungodly nothingness. Hilary felt utterly certain that this man was connected to the gruesome events of earlier in the day.

I must think nothing, he said to himself. A frightening thought occurred to him. *This man can read minds.*

Then a moment later, the stony gaze had moved on, and the riders were inside the city and the old cart was trundling slowly, laboriously after them with its vegetable cargo.

Hilary breathed a deep, silent sigh of relief. He had escaped this time, but they - whoever they were - were surely on his trail. I must beware. Whatever happens, they must not find me before I reach sanctuary.

Once inside the city walls, Hilary thanked his hosts and quietly slipped away from the main thoroughfare, into a mud-spattered back street. Feeling conspicuous, he found to his surprise that the even the alleyways were now filled with frenetic activity – women selling potatoes, pigs eating intestines, children playing with buckets of slops, goats relieving themselves in the gutter, and the stalls in the market beginning to fill with produce. He had not been in the city for a year, though there was a time that he had known it well. He racked his brains about how to reach round behind the cathedral without marching out into the main crowds, when his eye was caught by a boy selling pasties from under a white muslin sheet, just as if it was Paris. Even at a moment like this, he told himself – his mouth watering – he seemed consumed with unmonkish and ever so earthly desires. In any case, he had no time to waste – and there were people who would know his face only too well in this neighbourhood, if he was where he thought he was.

He was careful to avert his eyes from everyone he passed, for fear of being recognised, either as himself or as a man with the unmistakable air of a clergyman on the run. But every new street brought him a little closer towards what he thought was the city's North Gate, edging through courtyards to avoid the main thoroughfares, where those searching for him would almost certainly be waiting. He crossed one courtyard with rotting marrows and weeds, went over a small wall and out into another street. Bearded, black-robed figures peered at him from windows. Of course, it was the Jewish quarter. There would be nobody he knew round here. It might just be safe to linger there for a moment.

Then out again past the gateway of the Grande Ecole, Alys' *alma mater*, where she had first tasted the freedom of mental inquiry, before the purity campaigners decided to remove women from the premises. Then round a winding narrow street towards the unmistakable stench of Tanner's Wharf. It was the wrong way, but at least he knew where he was.

If he was going to make a dash for sanctuary in the cathedral, then it really had to be now. But, now that safety was almost within sight, Hilary found his doubts were growing. Questions poured into his mind as he made his way through the stinking streets. Was Orléans really the best or safest place to seek sanctuary, at least for him? His survival or otherwise would then depend not just on the church, but on the local lords – his former master, the Lord of Beaugency would be highly influential, and would he throw his weight behind him? If he ever caught sight of Hilary's poems to his late daughter, now rather obviously in his abandoned box of papers, almost certainly not.

Will they really look in my box? Will they understand it, if they do? Who in that household understands Latin? Am I really going to rely on nobody grasping who that poem was for, when I quite clearly wrote her name on it? Why did I pay so little attention to anybody else in the lord's entourage?

No, there was no doubt about it: familiarity did not help him – they knew his more disreputable side around Orléans just too well. Chartres was the place, less than a day's journey away. As soon as this thought occurred to him, he was certain. Orléans was no good. It had to be Chartres Cathedral: it was near enough to reach, powerful enough to protect him and still far enough away for no rumours about his poetry to have reached the clergy, or anything else that might make them doubt his wholesomeness as a clerk-in-holy-orders. But that meant getting out of the city, as soon as he possibly could.

I never seem to make things easy for myself, Hilary thought with a sigh. Leaving meant braving the city gates again, and his skin prickled clammily at the thought that he might see that man once more, the one dressed in grey with the granite stare of terrifying emptiness. A man who seemed so determined to find him that somewhere, somehow, their paths seemed to have been fated to cross.

But not today, I hope, he said to himself determinedly. Today, I go to Chartres, the saints be willing. Let the man in grey find me there – if he can.

Doubling back through the narrow side streets, through the pigs and geese again, Hilary quickly made his way back across the city. He panted as he went, unaccustomed to such exercise. It seemed an age before he had last found himself at the great north gate of the city, now busy with people coming and going, and there – in a back street around the corner – he found what he was looking for. In a haze of cabbage was a large cart of straw, with an unhealthy looking driver sitting picking his fingernails with what looked like a dagger. The horse and driver seemed almost indistinguishable. They could almost have swapped places.

Hilary walked towards him, smiling in a friendly manner, hoping his travel-worn clothes and the cloak still concealing his tonsure might make him seem like a peasant traveller himself.

'*Ho-là*,' he said in what he hoped was a cheerful, friendly way. 'Are you heading out the gate, by any chance? Can I suffer you for a ride?'

The man glanced up, put down his dagger, and gave him a look of such miserable contempt that, for a moment, Hilary was nonplussed.

Why is it so difficult to get lifts in the weeks before Christmas, thought Hilary? People might be expected to discover a bonhomie within that is absent so much of the rest of the year. Had that not been so in the past? He remembered a number of Advent lifts in carts along the lanes of Normandy from his student days, but no – this man was glaring back suspiciously. He was now eating a chicken in a most disgusting way. A quick glance in both directions confirmed that he was really the only candidate available. 'Running away, are you?' The man spat into the dust and leered horribly. A red dribble of saliva crept out of the side of his mouth. Was the chicken raw?

Hilary tried to guffaw in the manner of man of the people. 'I don't think so! Just having a wander, that's all. I fancy getting out of the city for a bit.'

The man grunted, looking him up and down sceptically. He clearly wasn't convinced for a moment by the peasant routine. 'Are you this Hilary the Englishman they're looking for?'

Hilary felt the blood drain from his face. How on earth was his name known already?

It is just as I feared! Hilary's mind raced. I must have spoken my name in the inn after all. Now the constable is on my trail and I will be hanged. How on earth did the news get around the city so fast? Did they send someone by river? Surely it's the only way, when poor John has only been dead a few hours.

Hilary struggled with the purse around his neck and extracted a silver coin with a shaking finger. The man's demeanour changed immediately when he saw it, and there was a whiff of something like lust.

'Get in then,' he said with a grotesque attempt at a smile. 'I'll take you as far as Cercottes.'

Hilary heaved himself with difficulty onto the back of the cart and inserted himself, as far as he could, between two straw bales. He was horribly aware of the dampness seeping down his back. The man looked down with ill-suppressed amusement.

'Well, go on, then,' said Hilary, his irritation overcoming his fear for a moment. 'Cover me up and get on with it.'

The man sniggered and threw a few wads of straw over him, and at once Hilary's view was reduced to all he could see – rather distantly – through a small air hole at his side. To his great relief, he heard a shout at the old nag and the cart juddered out towards the main road and the gate. For the second time that terrible day, Hilary breathed a sigh of relief.

It's all very well, he thought, as the cart swayed and jolted, the fetid straw making his nostrils twitch, but this whole situation is bitterly unfair. Yes, I've sinned, certainly. I won't deny it. I've been guilty of drunkenness, lust, aimlessness and quite hopeless love, and too many times in recent years. But I've never harmed anyone. I've done nothing to deserve this – on the run from the law, and probably pursued by the murderer as well. It would be ridiculous if it wasn't so terrifying.

To his shame and surprise, hot tears of self-pity flooded his eyes at the awful situation he was in.

This is no time for self-sorrow, he told himself sternly, blinking hard. If I can fight off the cold and despair and just keep my head, I will get to Chartres and cling to the high altar like a limpet. I will *make* them believe the truth.

But how many hours were there to Chartres and the safety of the cathedral? Could he get there by evensong perhaps or would it take another day? It was an exhausting prospect and a great deal could happen on the road if his pursuers guessed where he was heading.

The gates to cities had their own distinctive smell, of urine and manure and rotting vegetation, from all the detritus dumped just outside the jurisdiction of the walls. As the cart hobbled towards this familiar odour, Hilary shut his eyes, realising as he did so how childish this gesture was – as if somehow the man in grey, whoever he was, would not then see him. As they rumbled over the cobbles, he felt a convulsive shiver through him. What if that man were the murderer himself, the one who had slain John so brutally? Perhaps he was not the constable but the agent of dark forces, on Hilary's trail to find the pouch and shut his mouth for good.

Hilary whimpered fearfully, screwing his eyes shut even tighter. That was it, he was certain. Suddenly the strings of the pouch around his neck felt like a noose and at any second he expected the straw bales to be plucked away to reveal those cold, malevolent grey eyes staring down at him with death in them.

He mumbled a prayer to St Martin the Horseman, and – a minute or so later – the rumble of the cobbles turned to the usual uneven wobble of the road. Hilary opened his eyes, drenched by relief. They were through the gate, and on their way.

'You're a lucky man today,' guffawed the repulsive driver on whose meagre goodwill Hilary's life now depended. 'They were sniffing your arse back there, weren't they? We'll see later how grateful an Englishman can be...'

Hilary left his friend with the chicken on the edge of a dark forest in the pale winter sunshine, some hours later. From the driver's slumped position and heavy breathing – and the occasional snore – it seemed he had fallen asleep and was letting the donkey do the work. Hilary slipped quietly off the back of the cart and scuttled off the road. It was all the better that his driver wouldn't know exactly where his passenger had alighted.

He set off on foot through the forest, keeping off the road but making sure he could see it through the gloom of the foliage.

What were his chances of escape, even in Chartres? On the plus side, he would be safe once inside the cathedral, and in any case ought to have the protection of the church as a graduate of Ste-Geneviève. They would expect him to hand all his belongings to the church in return, but since he had none that was hardly a disadvantage. On the other side, he knew very well that he was not a fully-fledged member of the church, and giving him sanctuary for such a brutal murder would require determination on the part of the church authorities – and once he had revealed his identity, there was the little matter of his reputation. It was one thing to have had his love songs to nuns passed around Paris and sniggered over, but even the Chartres clergy would hardly snigger over his love songs to novice monks.

Hilary considered his career again as his feet pounded rhythmically on the track. It wasn't that he liked writing suggestive verse, heaven knows. Yet something strange seemed to happen when he picked up his pen. It didn't matter how noble the opening lines, how beautiful the original sentiment – after a couple of lines, the pleasures of the flesh found a way of worming their way back in.

Pull yourself together, Hilary. Concentrate. Yes, he was articulate and would be a powerful advocate in his own defence, but he had to be realistic. He was a serious outsider. Not just English, but a former scholar. Not just a scholar, but a wandering scholar with a reputation for some of the most erudite risqué verse in the Latin language. Not just that, but – like his comrades in Paris – a former student prankster with a long line of successful stunts in Notre Dame. Jeering the bishop, wearing mitres in the congregation at mass, giving out fake wafers – he and his friends had certainly given those pompous church authorities something to rage about. Pranks that would be remembered for decades. Drinking bouts that would echo down the centuries. Of course, news of these might well have reached Chartres, long before his arrival as a clerk begging for mercy at their high altar.

I am truly repentant, he thought, *but will it do me any good? The provincial clergy are so easily shocked.*

The sky was beginning to darken and the cold began to intensify. It became clearer to Hilary that Chartres might not actually be the right place to go either. Could he rely on the church authorities to defend him? Defending any churchman accused of murder meant difficulties, inconvenience and serious trouble for any senior cleric. The chances were that, in this case at least, he would hardly be worth the trouble? At the very least, it wouldn't be definite. You did hear about monks getting away with murder, after a full public confession, but they were fully-fledged monks. The authorities might equally well hand him over and have done with it. Having spent much of his short adult life making fun of the church, was simply asking for sanctuary was enough to save him? The answer, he accepted miserably, was almost certainly not.

No, there is a mystery at the heart of this, he thought. And it is almost certainly contained in whatever documents hang around my neck. Hilary touched them to make sure they were still there, and as he did so, a thought came into his mind with a lucid intensity.

Of course! I know what I must do. I need someone to help me, someone absolutely fearless, someone whose grasp of the truth is fierce and without rival. Someone who knows me and will fight for me, and who can pull strings high in the French court if he has to. Somebody who is so aggressive, so hungry for public controversy, that he would never let any problem go, intellectual, logical or moral. And I know exactly who that is.

Why have I not thought of him before? My honoured mentor, my noble teacher, Peter Abelard.

In a flash, he had abandoned the idea of making for Chartres, with the hue-and-cry on his heels. He would find his way somehow to Paris, seek out Master Abelard and beg for his help and protection, and – from what he knew of his teacher – Master Peter would be the most ferocious protector in the whole of Christendom.

The moment Hilary made his decision, walking along the very

edge of the road, he heard the telltale sound of an excited horse. Then the rattle of hooves, picking their way through the rutted trackway at speed.

The dark had not quite fallen, but his vision was obscured by a peculiar wintry mist rising from the damp ground. There was no time to dash into the trees and Hilary leapt into the ditch. It was wet and he prayed again, as he had done so fervently that morning. Then he tried to turn off his thoughts and clear his mind, in case the Man in Grey could hear them somehow gibbering away in the ether. Alys, if you can hear me now, please pray for me. Ask for my forgiveness, if you can intercede. Protect me from the terror by night and the arrow by day.

Peering out, he could see two horses passing by. Their pace never slackened. Hilary was just relaxing again when there was again that faint rhythm in the distance. He ducked back down into the wet. Another horse was coming, not nearly so fast and, again, Hilary peered out of his hiding place.

The horse trotted slowly past. The man on the back was dressed in grey and was looking around him, almost sniffing the air. It seemed to be seeking out some scent, and it seemed to Hilary that the man was sniffing for him – like a hound, as if this apparition was not entirely human. His mouth went dry and something shivered down his back. This was the Man in Grey indeed, and he seemed to draw around him an aura of fear, which rippled into the fields on either side of the road. Yet outwardly he was calm and possessed. Hilary had imagined him then as if he was Satan himself, sniffing out his imperfections and lust and coming down to greet him personally.

Despite the cold and damp, sweat trickled down Hilary's brow. It was as if this man knew he was there and was waiting in his own time when he would simply pluck his victim from the bushes and drag him straight to the underworld. From his hiding place, struggling to control his panic, Hilary knew that the mist he could see was simply steam from the damp in the gloaming but, for a brief second, it looked like the very vapours of hell.

It was an awful night. Hilary soon found it too dark to travel by the forest tracks and feared crossing the path of wild boar, but the road was just as dangerous. He could barely see an inch ahead and besides, he feared the reappearance of his grey pursuer, who seemed to have almost supernatural powers and could no doubt materialise noiselessly beside him at any moment.

Hilary gave up attempting to continue his journey and settled into a wet, black, slug-infested pit beside the road, where he tried to sleep despite shivering like a St Vitus dancer. Somehow he managed to doze fitfully, waking with frightened starts at the forest noises all about him. It was almost a relief when he guessed that morning was coming, and he crawled out of the pit, muddy and sopping, to continue his trudge northwards as the sun rose reluctantly to hang low in the winter sky.

How long can I survive like this? His stomach ached with emptiness. He had managed to eat nothing but a crust passed to him by his wagon driver the day before. *This is no time of year to be on the road.* A sudden feeling of being utterly tired of the wandering life seized him; surely he'd reached the apotheosis of wandering now – he was without a home, possessions, and food. All he had were his clothes, and they were in a frightful state.

And the pouch belonging to John of Mulchaney, he remembered. And, perversely, money. There was the silver John had given him. He laughed hollowly. He had more money than he'd ever owned at one time, and no earthly way to spend it.

What's in that pouch? Whatever it is must be to blame for this parlous state I find myself in. But I've not had a chance to look inside since I found it round my neck yesterday.

Now was not the time, in this damp air and with his fingers stiff with chill, but he resolved to look as soon as he was somewhere warm and dry, if that ever happened again. Until then, all he could do was continue northwards to Paris and Peter Abelard.

Ah yes, Master Peter Abelard, Hilary's old tutor, and the one man in Europe, the one man in Christendom, who could assist him, and help him disentangle himself from this terrifying misunderstanding.

Hilary would set the problem at the feet of Master Peter, and watch him live up to his aggressive nickname, the Indomitable Rhinoceros. It wasn't that Master Peter approved of wandering scholars or their jokes at the expense of the poor benighted church authorities in Paris. He was far too busy for that, winning his intellectual jousts in the great schools of the city, Ste-Genevieve, St-Victor and Notre-Dame, when Hilary was just one among the hundreds of students who crowded into the cloisters to hear his famous demolition of Roscellinus or Alberic of Reims.

But Hilary had grown to love him in those days, partly because of his sheer exuberance and the way he was prepared to confront the most famous masters of his generation, especially the most pompous, with those dramatic put-downs, those flights of rhetoric. Privately, like most of his more serious contemporaries, Hilary had doubts about Abelard's teaching and the way it flew in the face of the accepted wisdom of the scriptures, and precisely what the scriptures said in every case. But he had been inspired by the idea that that God made people with human urges, and with consciences too. 'Surely he meant us to use our conscience, to his glory,' he remembered Master Peter declaiming across the cloister. 'Men wrote the Bible, but God made our consciences. Does he want them to gather dust?'

There were those who feared for Abelard's soul for such ideas, but they loved him for them as well. And Hilary loved him for something else as well. There had been a little trouble with his poems to a fellow student when he had been a scholar in Paris, which had somehow ended up in the hands of the bishop. Master Peter had intervened on his side and prevented him from being expelled. He had defended his songs, even the risqué ones; they had even once, memorably, performed together in the cloister of Ste-Genevieve, to the horror of the church authorities. Hilary had corresponded with him over the years since he had been a student, apprising his tutor of his progress and asking questions on theological matters, but it was well over a year since there had been any contact – perhaps more. But he would at least remember, wouldn't he?

Yes, Master Peter has defended me before and, if I can reach Paris, he will defend me again. The thought drove his exhausted feet onwards, tripping over roots and brambles on the forest floor, keeping the track always in sight as he travelled north and remained alert for any sign of his pursuers.

It was a relief when he managed to get a lift from a passing cart, where he also begged a little water from the driver's flask, and he slept for three jolting hours in the back, regaining some strength. When the cart eventually turned off the road towards a village, Hilary found himself alone on the road again, still miles from Paris and night coming on apace. That was the worst of winter days – there was so little light to travel by.

And such long nights. He groaned at the thought of another freezing night out here in the forest. *I can't do it!* he thought helplessly. *How on earth did I get into this situation? I've not slept a decent night since I left Beaugency. I can't face another in a pit.*

He prayed to St Christopher, the patron saint of travellers, as he stumbled onwards along the forest tracks. It wasn't long before he sniffed the acrid scent of smoke.

A fire? There must be someone close. He sent up thanks to St Christopher and hurried on as the scent grew stronger. A moment later, he saw a clearing and in the middle the hut of a charcoal burner. Flooded with relief, he hurried over and knocked at the door. The charcoal burner listened to his carefully worded tale, nodded wordlessly and ushered him in. Compared to the ditch where Hilary had spent the previous night, the hut was a bower of luxury, with a dry dirt floor, crude wooden furniture and some old straw for a bed. A fire burned in the middle, providing warmth and light, the smoke drifting upwards to the hole in the roof, leaving a grey choking mist.

'There's soup there,' muttered his host, indicating a battered iron pot at the side of the fire. 'And a bit of bread on the table. Eat if you like. A little ale in the flagon.'

'Thank you,' Hilary said weakly. 'God bless you.'

'I'm going out for a bit,' his host said gruffly without elaborating. Hilary nodded gratefully. As soon as the hut door was shut behind the charcoal burner, Hilary stripped off his wet clothes and hung them up to dry. He would brush off the mud when it had caked. Wrapping himself in a bit of old sacking, he sat down the fire, helped himself to a bowlful of soup and devoured it. When he had also polished off a hunk of bread and slurped down some ale, he felt more human again, and could think of something else besides his stomach and his freezing feet.

He fingered the purse and pouch around his neck. The silver in the purse was welcome but awkward – he could hardly buy a meal with a piece of silver – but what was in this pouch that Count Fulk needed so badly? With an ear cocked for the return of the burner, Hilary tugged open the strings at the pouch's neck and put his hand inside. Stiff smooth paper met his touch. He pulled out two folded documents, laid them open on the floor in front of him and knelt over them.

The first one was clearly a letter, written in Latin and addressed to Count Baldwin of Flanders. *Not Count Fulk? How mysterious.* Hilary read hurriedly, but it referred to another letter without which that one was almost incoherent. There was a confusing reference to 'the Great Jewel', which he did not understand. It had an impatient tone to it, apparently offering Count Baldwin something which he must want, but had not committed to. Hilary struggled to skim it before stuffing it back before it could be seen, unless somehow the smell of it attracted the Man in Grey.

The second document was also in Latin but it was no letter. It appeared to have been torn from a valuable book, copied in a beautiful monkish hand. Again, Hilary read as fast as he could. It seemed to be from a history of England and referred to events some eighteen years before, when King William Rufus had met his mysterious death in the New Forest. According to the text, the King had received warnings of imminent danger to his life and refused to heed them.

Hilary released a breath he had not realised he had been holding. A sudden memory flashed vivid and arresting in his mind: he was eleven years old, harvesting barley under a powerful sun, along with the other boys and men from the village. There was a shout and they all stopped working and turned to hear the news. Young Oswine, the boy from the manor, red-faced with running, and perhaps with a hint of fear – everyone knew that when their rulers fell on bad times, those bad times spread. The king was dead, shot accidentally by an arrow in the New Forest, and now there was a new king. Rufus had no son, so his younger brother Henry, the first of that name, was now on the throne.

Hilary could still remember the shock by which his village had received the news. It was hard to believe a king so powerful and unchallenged as Rufus could have died so ignominiously. It was unnerving. Rufus had been popular among ordinary people simply because he was known to be so unpopular with the church. There was a lasting grievance that he had been taken from them, and mutterings for years about his unexpected end.

But who on earth cares now? Hilary stared at the dark flowing script. *And why does Count Fulk need to know about it?*

There was a sound of cracking twigs outside the hut, and Hilary struggled to stuff the cutting away. His host entered, bringing a blast of cold air in with him, shaking off the cold mist from his clothes with a shiver. He was followed by a bulky dark four-legged shape, larger and rounder than a dog, snuffling and grunting as it came. Hilary stared at it.

'Will you mind the pig joining us?' his host asked, taking himself to the fire glowing in the middle of the room. 'He gets fair cold at this time of year.'

'Er – no, of course not.'

The pig, evidently familiar with the hut, trotted over to a pile of old sacking in the corner and settled down on it, still snuffling loudly. It looked over at Hilary with small bright eyes and blinked at him.

As the fire died down into glowing embers, they ate a little more of the mutton soup and talked. The charcoal burner seemed a man of few words.

'I'm most grateful to you for your hospitality,' Hilary ventured, after his last few attempts to start a conversation had ended unsuccessfully. He wondered if he might have more luck with the pig, who seemed a friendly soul.

The charcoal burner shrugged. 'I don't mind helping a man down on his luck, a man of God too. There's no saying when we might require a good turn from someone. There's enough suffering in these parts without lack of charity adding to our misery.'

It was the longest utterance he had yet made. Hilary gazed at him, bewildered. 'Suffering?'

'Yes, sir. The war, of course.'

'Oh, yes... of course.' Hilary had forgotten for a moment that the whole area had seen incursions by Flemish and English troops over the previous summer in the endless conflict between the English and the Franks – this time over who had the right to be Duke of Normandy. 'Has it caused you much hardship?'

'We've been lucky, Sir. But the next village was burned by the English, white-faced bastards, as stupid as their little tails.' Hilary said nothing. He was familiar with the accusation that the English had tails. 'They say the ghosts of the villagers stalk the forest in these parts. I've heard strange shrieks in the night, even here.'

Hilary stared into the fire, glad that his Englishness was so difficult to spot. He reflected on those warlike demi-gods, Henry I of England, King Louis the Fat, Baldwin of Flanders – and little William Clito, nephew of the English king, whose claim to Normandy lay behind the latest squabble – and how their Olympian disorder, their endless disputes here between Normandy and France, laid waste the lives of those little people below them on earth. They seemed so far away, so unreachably distant, and yet...

He thought of the papers in the pouch and their reference to the death of William Rufus. Was it possible for an ordinary man such as himself to become embroiled in the affairs of kings? A rush of fright went through him. Whatever those papers meant, it was obvious they were dangerous. John had been killed for them, he was sure of it. And whoever sought them would not simply give up.

If I had any sense, I'd throw them into the fire this minute and have done with this whole miserable business!

The embers glowed red and gold, eager to blaze up again and feed off the stiff paper and the death-bringing words it held.

But he would not do that. He was bound by an oath and its power over him seemed to be much greater than he'd anticipated. He owed it to John of Muchelney, who had helped him in a time of desperate need, to see the task through to completion. As soon as Master Peter had ensured his safety from a murder charge, Hilary would make his way to Anjou and discharge his promise.

He sighed, overwhelmed with exhaustion, settled down on the old sacking by the fire and was at once asleep.

The next morning, Hilary shared a plain breakfast of bread and ale with his host, brushed down his now-dry clothes so that the worst of the mud was off, dressed and prepared to set off again. He was at least two days' walk from Paris but he felt better now that he'd had some food and a decent sleep.

All I need to do is carry on – and make sure that I keep my eyes peeled for anyone on my trail.

He hoped that his path was sufficiently obscure to prevent anyone tracking him – the forces of law or whoever wanted the documents – and he had decided that he would adopt a new identity while on the road. Hilary had always wondered about the life of a travelling carpenter. Nobody wants a wandering scholar at a feast, as he had discovered over the years – sometimes to his cost – but anyone who can mend a door frame or construct a table leg is always welcome to a bowl of stew by the fire. It was risky but, as long as nobody actually asked him to wield a lathe, he should be all right.

As he trudged along the track, seeing barely a soul, he went through the possible names he might call himself.

Harold sounded too English. Not Jacques either: too French. No, the answer was Ambrose, the saint that scholars pray to. Ambrose the Carpenter, Ambrose of Sarum, perhaps. It seemed sensible to remain English to explain his ignorance about the surrounding geography and the local dialect, and trust to good luck that he managed to avoid stumbling into a village which had been burned by his fellow-countrymen.

Feeling more secure in his newly acquired identity, he decided to risk an inn for his evening meal. *I've got money after all. It seems ridiculous to sleep in ditches when I can well afford a warm bed.* The bread and ale in the charcoal burner's hut seemed like a distant memory and his stomach was rolling and growling with emptiness.

He sought out the landlord and asked for a meal and a bed for the night. The landlord was built like an ox, with a swarthy countenance, as if he had only recently come home from the Crusades. He looked Hilary up and down with distaste, clearly taking in the detritus of mud and foliage from the forest that still clung to his robes. Hilary reached into his purse and withdrew a silver piece. He immediately realise his mistake.

The landlord looked greedy and then deeply suspicious, staring at Hilary as if he had a notion he'd robbed a cathedral. *How could I have been so stupid? Why is a carpenter in mud and wattle carrying a purse of silver pieces? I'm going to have to demonstrate I'm not rich somehow. I'm going to have to act stingy.*

'Alms from a man of the church. You have surely seen your share of silver pieces before now. But I have no other, so I would be grateful if you could return me the unspent portion.'

The landlord still stared from the coin, to Hilary and back to his torn and bloodied hose.

'Do you have some difficulty?' asked Hilary desperately. 'Have you not seen a carpenter down on his luck before?'

The landlord woke from his reverie, blew on the coin and rubbed it suspiciously, grunted and motioned for Hilary to follow.

'No tin coins here,' he said. 'No tin, no copper. Take it or leave it.'

Hilary gave an exhausted nod to say that he took it. He could practically have bought the inn with that coin, but what could he do? Once again, he regretted that John of Muchelney hadn't thought to provide him with small change.

The inn was full of well-to-do farmers and men in leather with the bright red faces from the fields. There were some raucous tinkers in one corner playing an incoherent game involving counters, which they kept knocking on the floor and roaring with laughter. Hilary realised they must be back on one of the trade routes to Paris. He was getting back into dangerous territory. There was an overwhelming odour of manure. The piglets and dogs were going from table to table around the room and the straw laid out below their feet was of a peculiarly pungent variety. Still exhausted, despite his rest by the fire in the cottage that morning, Hilary plunged a thick lump of bread into the platter of stew which was brought to him by a boy with long hair worn like the English. Hilary gave him a broad smile. He grinned back and moved on.

The smell of human and animal sweat rose up from the floor. It smelled safe, and he began to relax at last. Perhaps he was far enough from Orléans now. The Man in Grey must have known his general direction but even the cart-driver thought he was heading for Chartres. He began to feel sleepy.

He awoke to see two merchants staring at him. He felt horribly conspicuous. On the other side of the room, a man in a leather jerkin, who looked like some kind of rough and ready sheriff's officer, was moving slowly across the room. It was time to be gone, though the prospects of a night in the forest was a gloomy and frozen one. Where else could he go? He sidled out into the night.

3/Hubert

Towards the Seine, 11 December 1119

The forests between the Loire and the Seine are darker and more forbidding than most, especially without a moon, and there was no moon that night. There are tales about these forests which keep children awake. Hilary reminded himself that even grown men thought twice about entering this one after dusk, children left for the beasts, half men-half wolves stalking the woods, dead lovers who gouged at the eyes in the night.

But what could he do? He slept the night on the edge of the forest, not too far to get lost, but not too near the road for his presence to be suspected.

It was an uncomfortable and frozen experience. Roots dug into his back whatever way he lay down. He woke every hour or so as some beast subjected him to close inspection. As the night dragged on, and the musky smell of moss and rotting nettles seeped into his clothing, he could feel the warm breath of something much bigger. Hilary assumed in the darkness that it was a boar and stayed as still as he could. But he feared the sheriff's brutes, and their mysterious overlords in grey, more than the wolves, and kept them all at bay with the aid of some half-remembered prayers, until he saw a faint glimmering of light in the sky. Then he picked his way shivering back to the road. By the time the sun was peeping at the day, he had reached the Seine.

The world still seemed to be asleep, but the great ribbon of water powered past him towards the sea. He stood on the very edge feeling alone in the world, as if he was the first human being to discover such a sight, with the birds swooping low over the water and the trees floated by in the half light of dawn. He could not be more than thirty miles from Paris now. Not much more than that, surely?

Then a stroke of luck. There was a barge, carrying turnips, just preparing to leave after spending the night there. It hurt to offer the bargee a whole silver coin to speed him to Paris, and it was hardly a surprise when he said yes. The problem of small change was becoming acute. Hilary scanned his face for signs of greed – any indication that he might murder for more – but the bargee seemed to be a civilised man. Hilary settled down among the roots, amidst the rotten smell of soil, pulled his mud encrusted rags over his head and went to sleep.

When he woke, it took him a moment to remember where he was. There was a sinking sense of foreboding as it flooded back. But he looked ahead down the river, and there were the stumps of Notre-Dame, which always revived his spirits. Paris - he knew it well: the students with their books ragging by the river, the washerwomen on the beaches, the great processions, the street food in baskets down beside the Grand-pont. There were many downsides about spending time in Paris, of course. There was the gibbet, which he dreaded seeing, as a symbol of his likely demise if he was caught. There was also the snobbish atmosphere of luxury, the ridiculous vanity, the feathers arranged on the heads of the women, the aroma of spices from the expensive shops, the affectations in the queues by the cookshop in the morning. There were also some of the most ridiculous pointed shoes you could see anywhere in the world.

Yet Paris was always to him the great city of the soul, struggling rather painfully towards spiritual truth. There were those theological hothouses, those laboratories of spiritual research. There was Master Peter brandishing his weapons of logic and learning. There was William of Sens and Alberic of Reims slugging it out between them in the cloisters. It was a powerful prospect, and Hilary felt a strange mixture of contradictory emotions. *Will the news that I am wanted for murder have reached Paris? Will Master Peter take up my cause? Will anyone actually be interested?*

It occurred to him that the papers around his neck, though they weighed him down with their morbid memory of violent death, were intriguing. *Yes, I will show them to Master Peter. He won't be able to resist.*

It was dark before the barge had made fast alongside the wharf of the Right Bank, and there was nobody to help them unload and no officials to carry out the basic administration, and the barge crew bedded down for the night. Hilary listened to the watchman calling out the times by the stars. Sleepily, he rehearsed the shocks of the previous two days before the sky began to lighten, and he could hear the herald from the Chastelet announcing that the rim of the sun had risen above the horizon. Hilary gathered his possessions, climbed stiffly onto the wharf, and headed across the Grand-Pont, with its merchants setting up their benches, and into the city.

It was a relief to be somewhere familiar. The stones of the bridge felt almost friendly, as he walked carefully, warily across, glancing over through the morning mist towards the royal palace at the other end of the Ile-de-la-Cité. It crossed his mind that the King might be there, even now hearing the news of a murder outside Orléans.

It was only two weeks to Christmas. The sky was grey and spots of rain trickled down his face. The stall-holders were setting up as he arrived, piling their tables high with root vegetables and some doubtful cuttings of meat, on sale first for the poorest labourers. The rejected fish from the night before were still in the gutter, and a sour-faced slave was removing a skeletal corpse from the gibbet to make way for the next poor fellow. Hilary made the sign of the cross. An unpleasant thought occurred to him that they might have been making space for him.

Hilary knew that Master Peter Abelard's preferment had been rapid in the years since he had studied with him, and heard his dramatic lectures from the back and then the front of the crowd, before the fame of the man had taken him into the hallowed cloisters of Notre-Dame itself. The very prelates of learning had succumbed to his force and charm and invited them into their bosom. *Will he be welcoming?* Hilary wondered as he approached the door to the ancient cathedral. *One thing is sure. He won't have forgotten me.*

The Cathedral of St Etienne loomed in front of him in its familiar crumbing state, the weather-beaten statues still standing in the niches of its huge façade.. He pushed open the old oak door and stepped inside. The drizzle had begun again in earnest and there was already a crowd in the middle of the five naves sheltering from the rain, despite the echoing sound of the choir nearer the altar. Deals were being struck in the corner by the font and some lascivious laughter was coming from behind a pillar in front of him. Hilary remembered that some of the women of the street tended to transfer their trade into the back of the nave in bad weather, and he became aware that the rain had now transferred most of the street inside. There were men selling chickens on one side, and in the distance, in the outside naves, somebody appeared to be hawking horsemeat.

The naves were lit only by the light that seeped in through the slits in the walls, and they smelled of urine and body heat.. The warmth from the crowds was making the air fuggy. The sound of loud conversation was almost deafening. He had to push past a number of merchants and money-lenders, in red and blue silk, sitting at tables with bags of coins, before he could get to the North Transept and the door to the familiar academic calm of the cloister of Notre-Dame.

'Excuse me,' he said, as a passing monk bowed his head in greeting. 'I'm looking for Master Peter.'

'Peter Abelard?' he said. There was a curl of his lip, maybe a flicker of amusement. What did it mean? 'Oh, you won't find him here, I'm afraid.' He hurried off without any further explanation, his hands tucked into the sleeves of his robes. Hilary was puzzled. He understood Master Peter to be living and teaching here at Notre-Dame, a respected figure in the church hierarchy. Was he at some gathering of great theological minds? Was he ill, moved to the Infirmary, where the sick were cared for by monks? Or worse? Surely Hilary would have heard, somehow, if Master Peter had died. Unless it happened very swiftly, too swiftly to reach him as he trudged along the road out of touch with all the great happenings.

Oh God, I beg – don't let him dead now, not when I so need him!

Hilary immediately rebuked himself for his selfishness and tried to settle his fear. A gaggle of students in threadbare hose and stained tunics stood by the door to St-Jean-le-Rond, waiting for the morning lecture, wax slates and stylos in their hands. Hilary approached and asked one the same question. 'Could you tell me, has Master Peter gone away?'

The one nearest, a sullen youth with greasy hair, looked amused. 'You could put it that way,' he said in a strong Germanic accent. 'There's less of him about, anyway.'

'Sorry, I don't understand? Is he ill? Has he lost his position here?'

There were guffaws and some of the students turned away to hide their mirth. 'Well, he's certainly lost something,' said another, a pock-marked boy in a shabby red tunic. 'Some rather valuable things of his. He's probably searching for them now.' At this, the stifled amusement erupted in open hysteria. Students slapped themselves in mirth.

'What are you talking about?' Hilary demanded crossly but he could get no sense from them as they giggled and laughed at their obscure joke. He moved away, increasingly disturbed. *What can they mean? He must have lost his position. He's offended the authorities one too many times, I suppose. Well, I must find where he's gone, no matter what.*

A sudden inspiration came. *There's one person I can ask!*

He headed off past the clerestory down some stone passages, along the open drains that carried the blood and waste from the kitchens, past the piles of offal and ancient cabbage, and up a small flight of stairs. Some minutes later, feeling short of breath, and cursing the stairs, he knocked on a door and pushed.

A great stench of sweat, ale and fetid air hit him in the face. Hilary had once been warned that he would end up the size of Master Hubert of Huntington if he did not restrict his consumption of sack. But Master Hubert's problem had gone some way beyond that, after decades of eking out peculiar translations all by himself in his own room, away from his fellows and friends because he considered himself too fat to attempt the stairs to the library. There, in a tiny room, rendered even smaller by the bulk of the man inside it, surrounded by the detritus of scholarship – inkhorns, goose quills, penknives, ancient candles – sat the man himself, squashed against a small desk, a quill in his ink-stained hand.

'Not here, not in here – I look after my own slops!' bawled the voice inside. Master Hubert had been large when Hilary had last seen him, but now he had grown to a vast size, to a living cathedral of flesh. The two scholars stared at each other, Master Hubert's expression halfway between bewilderment and annoyance. Hilary remembered his rags and dishevelled appearance.

'Master Hubert, it is I – Hilary. It's been some time since last we met.'

'Hilary? Hilary the Englishman! I don't believe it! What are you doing here and dressed like a purveyor of turnips?' Hubert's chins wobbled in excitement. 'Forgive me if I don't get up. Come in, come in. Draw up that bench. It does me good to see you – it reminds me of the old days. You always did run me a merry dance. Now, tell me. How goes the good life in Orléans?'

Hilary was lost for words for a moment. The good life? His position at Beaugency now seemed like a dream. But he felt himself relaxing; he always used to relax with Master Hubert, as one Englishman to another.

Hubert eyed his filthy robe and held up a hand. 'Don't tell me, let me guess. You have fallen on hard times? From the smell of you, you've had to turn to humping turnips around. But hold on, let me have another go.' The vast face screwed up so that the bright eyes disappeared in folds of flesh as Hubert pretended to rack his brain. 'You made fun of the local clerics in one of your verses and have been sent back to Paris in disgrace? You always managed both to bait authority and to make it fully aware of your actions. I believe they call it asking for trouble.'

Hilary squirmed. This wasn't a moment to feel comfortable about his student pranks.

'Well, no, it's complicated...' Hilary realised he had not worked out exactly what he was going to tell of how he came to be back in Paris in this state. He tailed off.

'Hilary, you're incorrigible.' Master Hubert began to heave

with amusement. His great face creased and he slapped the top of his table, making the ink stands jump and froth. 'You have attempted to seduce the daughter of the house? No, don't tell me – the son?'

'Really, I'm much more respectable than I was when—'

'I knew it. You are a work of art! Why can't you learn to keep your pen in its pot?' Hubert began to enjoy his own humour a little too much and was soon coughing and fighting for breath.

'Well, I...'

'Still, it would be a great disappointment to me if you changed. It is too good to see you, Master Hilary, too good for my feeble frame to laugh this much. Now sit yourself down. Make yourself comfortable. Honestly, what is it with you philosophers? Always in difficulties. Always complications.' He laughed again. 'You and Master Peter!'

'Master Peter? That's why I've come to see you. No one seems to know where he is. At least, they're not telling me. Is he all right?' Hilary sat down on a stool as Hubert shifted himself around to face him. 'Why isn't he here?'

'What? You haven't heard? I thought the whole world was talking about it.' Hubert leaned forward confidingly, his knees disappearing beneath his huge stomach. 'Do you remember a canon here called Fulbert?'

'Fulbert? I know him. An old curmudgeon.'

'Master Peter fell in love with Fulbert's immensely intelligent, and absolutely delectable niece.'

Hilary frowned as he took this in, then the full import of what Hubert had said struck him between the eyes. 'But you don't mean Heloise? *Non credo!* She's only ten, isn't she?' But as he said this, he realised that it had been at least nine years since he had last seen her, and then she had indeed been ten.

'She's young, I grant you, but not that young. Master Peter

lived a while in Fulbert's house and tutored the girl. She was his most brilliant pupil, or so he said, skilled in Latin, Greek and Hebrew. But he taught her different arts as well. All the time, as it turned out, they were.... Well, you can guess. The poor girl became pregnant and they married secretly, but she found it intolerable living with that appalling old uncle.'

'Who can blame her for that?' Hilary shook his head, amazed at what he was hearing. 'I could hardly bear being in his company for ten minutes at a time. But Heloise was pregnant? By Peter? He *married* her?' Hilary blinked. His own misdemeanours were small fry compared to this.

Hubert nodded, turning his mouth down at the corners. 'Yes. Peter himself suggested the marriage to placate Fulbert when it became obvious the girl was with child. A pretty state of affairs. It all got very complicated, so Peter spirited her away and hid her. Fulbert was absolutely incandescent and the next thing we know, maybe a year ago now, he sent his brutes round in the middle of the night.'

'Not in *here*?' Hilary was shocked. 'In Notre-Dame?'

'Yes, in here. They beat him and...' Hubert trailed off staring at him, clearly searching for the right word.

Hilary hardly dared speak his fears. Was Abelard dead? Was he too late? Would he never see him again? 'Surely they didn't ... kill him?'

'Kill him, no. But it was worse in some ways. They neutered the man.'

'They *what?*' Hilary felt his eyes grow wide and a nasty chill gripped him. He felt the more intimate parts of his body clench in horror.

'They castrated him.' Hubert spoke the words with distaste, and glanced down in embarrassment, as if unable to face the full disaster.

As the horror of his old master being castrated like a beast sank in, Hilary realised that there were more implications than simply pain and humiliation. Master Peter was a teacher attached to Notre-Dame, a theologian and priest. It was one thing to be a married priest – there were such rarities, as he knew all too well, though hardly in the vicinity of Notre-Dame. But a priest had to be provably male. Was there not a special chair in Rome where newly-elected Popes were checked for testicles? That was the story that was whispered, at least. In his denuded state, Master Peter could be no more than a poor monk, perhaps not even a teacher. It could only mean the end of the Indomitable Rhinoceros.

'I don't believe it,' Hilary said, stunned. 'And he survived?'

'Oh yes. He has recovered his health outwardly.'

'But... is he destroyed?' Hilary hardly knew what he meant – whether destroyed as a priest, or destroyed as a man.

'To be honest, I don't know.' Hubert seemed relieved to move off the sheer indelicacy of the physical. 'No, I don't know where he is. Fulbert is still awaiting the decision about the punishment for his part in the crime. Those who actually carried it out were blinded. Master Peter has gone, somewhere, I know not where. Poor Heloise is taking her vows as a nun, on Peter's instructions I believe. There is a child, a son being brought up in Brittany by Abelard's family, or so I heard. It is a tragedy. *The* tragedy.'

Hilary shuddered again to think of the flashing blade of a knife, the robe tugged up, the exposed softness of flesh at the centre of a man's body, the seat of his earthly desires, soft, vulnerable, helpless. He felt suddenly the biting blade slice at himself, and winced. But how accurate would a gang of ruffians bother to be as they eagerly chopped away? 'When they say castrated...?'

Another look of distaste crossed Master Hubert's florid face. 'I don't know, Hilary. I believe it was only... you know... I did catch a glimpse of him afterwards and he seemed remarkably well. But you know what they say about pigs, don't you?'

Hilary didn't know, but decided not to let on. It was obvious to him why Abelard had fled. If Fulbert had been punished there was at least the risk that the Fulbert family would feel duty-bound to finish the task on his behalf. There was the danger of serious reprisals and a blood feud at least. Of course he had gone, and of course it was going to be a pretty secret where he had gone to.

'What about Fulbert's family?'

'The tongues do not tell, Hilary. I haven't heard.'

'And Master Peter? Where did he go?'

'Again, these things are kept secret.' Hubert shrugged. 'I wish I knew.'

Hilary stared at him, demoralised. *My old protector has clearly lost his powers – in more ways than one.*

His gaze travelled from the vast form of his old friend, who sat looking at him with sympathy, and over his impressive library. He was surrounded by the most brilliant books of the classical world, and was known to be a master of the ancient languages and many others besides. A sudden thought floated into Hilary's mind. The scrap of unknown tongue that John of Muchelney had asked him to memorise that night – it had stayed stubbornly in his brain, drifting occasionally to the front of his mind as he trudged the long road to Paris. *No harm in asking.*

'One other thing, Master Hubert. Do you know what language this is..? *Hit waes geara iu.* Have you any idea what it means?'

Hubert frowned. 'Some kind of Mohommedan? Say it again...' Hilary obliged and a huge frown crossed Hubert's great face as he considered. Then his expression cleared and he beamed like a great happy moon. 'No, I know what it is! It's Saxon, an old version of our own tongue, Master Hilary. You should have recognised it yourself.'

Hilary realised at once that Hubert spoke the truth, and that somehow he'd half understood it from the start. 'How stupid of me! I'm a dunce. Of course it is. I even know what it means – something like "in those days...".'

'More like "In bygone days". It's just a phrase.'

'Yes, yes, now I know it exactly.'

'And why do you wish to know?' Hubert's scholarly curiosity was pricked and he raised his sparse brows at Hilary.

'Oh, no reason, really. It's not important. Just something I heard and could not place.' Hilary looked at the floor, wondering hard. *Why would John of Muchelney force me to learn something so useless, so pointless? How stupid I am for not realising it was Saxon. I could have asked him at the time.*

'I should have known that, should I not?' said Hilary, only partly to himself. 'Don't they call me "Hilary the Englishman"? What's the matter with me that I don't recognise my own language?'

'Yes, but I believe that your name is intended as a little – how shall I say this – a little satirical, is it not? I seem to recall that it was a way of accusing you of combining the two quintessential English vices in one person.'

Hilary was irritated. Yes, he knew Master Hubert well enough for this banter, but after his ordeal of the past few days, he didn't feel like it. 'Oh yes, and what are they?'

'Beer and buggery,' said Hubert, laughing uproariously again.

'Oh, for goodness' sake. The second of those was purely the result of rather an outrageous poem I wrote. The first is perhaps more difficult to deny – but it was a long time ago. And none of this explains why John of Muchelney should have said anything in old English before he died.'

'John of who? He died?' Hubert made an irritated face. 'You're still talking in riddles, Hilary.'

But Hilary was thinking. John of Muchelney obviously knew by then that he was under some kind of threat. *Had he known he was about to hang those mysterious papers around my neck? I was the guardian of the documents, so he taught me the phrase to go with with it. Surely that means there is some connection between the papers and the phrase. But what is it? Why did he not tell me what I should do with my little snippet of Saxon?* Hilary stared unseeingly at Master Hubert, trying to puzzle it out. Even though he now understood the phrase, it still meant nothing. *Why should he have said 'in bygone days'?* It sounded little more than a rather melancholic password, typically, almost irritatingly, English? Or perhaps it was some kind of nervous tick of his to recite English before he went to sleep.

Hubert disturbed his thought. 'Hilary, you have gone into some kind of reverie. Please tell me what has been going on?'

Hilary realised he was staring straight at his old friend. Hubert's huge but kindly face gazed back, intrigued and puzzled at the same time. *Since I might never find Master Peter, I could perhaps test Hubert's intelligence instead.* The sudden desire to confide all his troubles to a sympathetic ear overwhelmed him and the next moment he was relating the whole story. He began with his encounter with John of Muchelney and omitted little until he had reached the wharves of Paris that very morning. 'So you see, Master Hubert – I have reason to believe that I'm pursued both by those who believe I committed the awful murder, and the actual perpetrators as well – presumably for the pouch that hangs around my neck.'

Master Hubert had rested his vast head on his arm and listened intently. Now he lifted his head and said: 'My dear Hilary, what an ordeal you describe. You interest me strangely, and I would like to see the contents of your pouch, if you would be so good. I hardly have time for a prolonged study now, but may I cast a glance?'

For the second time, Hilary pulled out the contents of his pouch and handed them over.

Hubert scanned them quickly, furrowing his brow. 'Strange, strange. Hard to judge, are they not?'

Hilary perused the letter again, reading the final peculiar line out loud: '*The Great Jewel will then be revealed from its holy hiding place...*' He looked up at Hubert. 'Do you know about this Great Jewel that is spoken of?'

Hubert brightened. 'Ah, well, I can help you there, Hilary. It sounds like the Great Jewel of King Alfred. It was a magnificent creation and the centrepiece of the crown he made, with which his successors were also crowned. If you believe it ever existed.'

'So it's gone? Lost?'

'Quite right, Hilary. One or the other. It was reputed to have spiritual power. After Alfred, all the kings of our country had it placed on their heads in the crown. But it has not been seen since King Harold's coronation in 1066. That hardly mattered to the Conqueror and his family, but King Henry thinks differently. He married a Saxon princess and knows something of our traditions. He wants to be a legitimate king of the English, not merely a conqueror. England is still a land divided between Saxon and Norman, and the king would like to mend it and make it one people. I have heard rumours that there are many who would like to find this jewel. It has worth far beyond its intrinsic value.'

'Does anyone have any idea where it is?' Hilary asked, intrigued. *There must be some connection between the Jewel mentioned in the letter and the death of the letter-carrier, and maybe even my own pursuit.*

Hubert looked mysterious. 'There are rumours of course. They say it is in Jerusalem, taken there by a monk called Saewulf to keep it from the Normans. I remember a Saxon master who taught here for some time told me so. But who knows? I certainly do not.'

Hilary frowned, puzzled. 'Jerusalem is a curious place for a jewel of Alfred's to end up. Perhaps that is why it is of interest to Count Fulk– and whoever wants this letter.' He took it and gazed at it again. 'There's no mention of where it might be here. Just that it will be revealed if Count Baldwin agrees to some obscure deal.

'Your tale interests me, Hilary,' said Hubert. 'I can quite see the sticky situation you're in. But if you're at all tempted to go haring about looking for this jewel, you ought to know that the Jewel of King Alfred casts a malign shadow. It's rumoured to be unlucky for anyone who holds it who is not a true king. Still, I suspect you are unlikely to find it, even if you looked.'

'I'm not about to go haring off to Jerusalem, don't worry about that,' Hilary said emphatically. 'The Holy Land has never held the attraction for me that it does for some. Besides, this jewel might not even exist.'

Hubert eyed him knowingly. 'And you're not the kind of man to expend unnecessary energy, I'm aware of that. I'm made of the same stuff.' He picked the piece of illuminated manuscript and handed it back to Hilary. 'This is as fine a hand as my own, I must admit it. I know someone here in Paris who might be able to shed some light on the doings of certain shadowy figures in this kingdom who might be concerned with this matter. I'm mightily intrigued myself by your mystery. I shall seek him out this very afternoon. Will you come back tomorrow? I may be able to help better than I can now.'

Hilary nodded gratefully. 'Thank you, Hubert. But there is still the small issue of proving my innocence of the murder of John of Muchelney. I still seek the protection of the church. Do you really have no idea where Master Peter is?'

At this, Master Hubert waved one arm in a theatrical gesture, his forearms wobbling, and stared out of the window, across the gargoyles and duckboards and the ancient roofs. 'Well, I could hazard a guess. I did hear the rather unbelievable rumour that the Abbot of St-Denis offered to take him in.'

'St-Denis!' Hilary was astounded. 'Surely not! The inhabitants of St-Denis are true believers.'

'Yes, and not so much in God, but in the royal line of France. They tend to worship the heirs of Charlemagne. A most regrettable form of blasphemy.' Hubert gave him a sideways glance. 'That's why I've found it hard to credit that Master Peter would be in such a place.'

Hilary's mind reeled. 'It is a place without a sense of the ridiculous. Master Peter would hardly last five minutes there.'

'You wouldn't think so, would you? But what choice did he have? Now, let us say our farewells, Hilary. I don't mind admitting it takes me a little while to manage the staircase so I'd best be leaving now.'

'Thank you, Hubert. I shan't forget this, really.' Hilary shook his hand with emotion.

Master Hubert began to struggle to his feet, his cheeks reddened with the effort. 'Now my dear Hilary, you must be extremely careful,' he said, admonishment sounding through his breathlessness. 'My advice is to go to St-Denis and see if you can find Master Peter. Come back tomorrow and let me know the outcome. I may have made some progress on the matter of the identities of those concerned with the Great Jewel. I wish to help you, my old friend, and I certainly don't want to see you swinging for something you did not do. In the meantime, God be with you, Hilary. God speed, my friend.'

'Thank you, Hubert,' Hilary said sincerely. 'I shall see you anon.' Feeling more hopeful, he slipped out of his room and away, determined to make for St-Denis immediately.

4/Abelard

The monastery of St-Denis, 12 December 1119

Hilary knew the geography of the muddy, rutted way to St-Denis only too well from his days as a scholar, and the whole of Paris from Ste-Genevieve to the Chastelet tower was his province. It was an easy journey, even on foot, even when some of the puddles had frozen, as they had today and despite the usual cart traffic to be dodged.

The pouch still hung about his neck but it felt lighter now that he had shared the contents with Master Hubert.

Apart from Master Peter, Hubert is definitely the man to help me. How lucky I thought to go to him. And I'm most interested in what he has to tell me tomorrow.

At the doors of St-Denis, Hilary announced himself as a traveller in search of shelter for the night, and was ushered with little ceremony into the Hospital and told to sit at a very rough table where, after a while, he was given a wooden platter with bread and some rather grisly stew. Another traveller, rough and emaciated, sat opposite him, slurping from his own stew.

'God be with you, my friend,' said Hilary, hoping to gain some knowledge at least. 'How go the monks here? I have been away some years.'

The man looked up, took another slurp but said nothing.

'The stew here is not quite as – how shall I say? – well, thick, as one might expect.'

Still the other traveller said nothing.

Hilary gave up. *Well, here I am in, in the Abbey. But how on earth I'm going to find out anything about Master Peter, I have no idea. If he's got a peck of wisdom, he'll keep his head down and lie very low.*

Hilary chewed another indigestible morsel of stew, depressed that the Indomitable Rhinoceros had slipped through his fingers.

A sudden commotion sounded next door, getting louder and louder. The next moment, there was the sound of running feet, and in burst three monks, dressed in their habitual black, all carrying large sticks. For a frightening moment, Hilary assumed they had come for him. But they looked about, ignoring him. 'Not here; he must be in the sacristy after all,' one of them muttered. They all ran out, leaving the door swinging on its hinges.

'That's exactly the kind of behaviour that makes people think so little of monks these days,' said his travelling companion slowly.

Hilary called over to the servant who had given him the stew. 'Hey! What's happening?'

The youth made a face as he poured out a flagon of well-watered ale. 'Oh, some stupid rumpus. One of our number, an eminent guest here, has angered the brothers over something he has been saying. It doesn't bother me, that kind of thing. I keep myself to myself. A squall in a bucket if you ask me.'

'Who is this guest?' asked Hilary, a spark of hope in his breast.

'I've no idea. The Hospitaller will know. He's over in the lodging where you'll stay tonight.'

'And where are they?'

The boy gestured through the door. 'Across the courtyard there.'

'Ah. Well, I've finished this delicious stew so I think I might go over now and introduce myself.' Hilary got up and left his taciturn companion to finish his stew in peace. Out in the cold courtyard, he was startled as another and larger group of monks ran past him shouting: 'Montjoie! St Denis!'

Goodness, they are in a state. There's only one man I know who can rile so many so effectively. Let's see what the Hospitaller can tell me.

But the door Hilary had been directed to was locked and no one answered his hammering. He searched around the side, and saw to his surprise that a large canvas sack appeared to be dangling out of a window about six feet off the ground. It dropped and landed on the hard earth with a heavy thump. Hilary looked back to the window where an arm was disappearing back inside. Then, to his surprise, a head poked out and a pair of bright dark eyes was staring straight at him.

'Hilary! Thank goodness, you've arrived just in time. Come over here and help me with these books.'

Hilary laughed to himself, not knowing whether to be delighted or irritated. So here he was, the man he'd been searching for, and exactly the same as ever: arrogant, infuriating and so self-centred that he assumed Hilary's whole purpose at the abbey was to help him.

But he's here! I'm saved! A feeling of elation coursed through him. Surely now, things were looking up.

'Come on, don't dawdle, I've really got to get a move on.' The figure had appeared at the window again, and now a second sack, heavy as a sack of potatoes, came down after the first.

'Don't let it down so fast, I'm not ready!' said Hilary in a suppressed shout. The furious monks with sticks very likely were the cause of this escape, if that's what Master Peter was up to. Hilary tried to catch the sack as it plummeted towards him but it slipped through his hands and something heavy enough to be a bible with metal edges landed on his right toe. He stifled a cry of pain.

The voice from above was reproachful. 'By heaven, Hilary, be careful – that's Aristotle you've got in there. Now, stand out of the way – I'm going to jump!'

Master Peter appeared on the window sill, skinny legs protruding from a brown robe. The next moment, there was another thud as his master hit the ground and managed to steady himself.

'That wasn't so far!' he said, evidently pleased with himself. 'I'll show them.' Then he seemed to become aware of Hilary again. 'Hilary, where have you been? I could have done with your support last night, I can tell you.'

Hilary stared at him, flooded with memories. Peter Abelard was as dark as ever, perhaps a little shorter, but that must be imagination, and just as infuriating as ever. He had no thought for anyone but himself. It was hard to imagine that he loved Heloise enough to risk everything. It seemed most uncharacteristic.

But, Hilary thought as Abelard finished inspecting his books and turned to him with a smile, *I forgive him. There's something very comforting about the way Master Peter never changes, especially when the forces of law and the forces of darkness are on my tail.*

'Master Hilary!' Abelard said, and reached to embrace him. 'What an opportune moment to arrive! Now, I'm in a rather a hurry so if you want to chat, you'd better come along with me. Where's the nearest way out?'

Hilary said quickly, 'Master Peter, I am just delighted to see you. I've been looking for you.'

'Yes,' Abelard said drily, looking around. 'You and a few others. Come on, I don't want that gang finding me. Let me just make sure my books are all right.'

Hilary watched him bend over his books again with a tenderness that others might have reserved for children. *It is strange, and no doubt blasphemous as well. But we sometimes love people for the very qualities that cast doubt on their entry into heaven.*

Abelard was murmuring almost to himself. 'Now, I have the classical philosophers in this one. Not the way they see things in this monastery, I can tell you.'

As Hilary observed him, he realised how little the years had marked his tutor. Abelard still had his dark Breton eyes and hair, only faintly threaded with silver, the same aggressive nose, and the same restless energy that meant he could never keep his rather short limbs still. He was even dressed exactly as Hilary remembered, in a tunic and an old-fashioned short cloak. Hilary stole a furtive glance at Abelard's hose in case somehow his injury would be obvious, but there was nothing to see. Surely an affair with a girl half his age and the loss of such vital body parts ought have to aged him a little, if not rendered in him a more spiritual air of resignation? Apparently not.

Abelard straightened up, apparently satisfied, and gestured to the sacks. 'Take these, Hilary, if you would be so good. Be careful, they're extremely precious. We are going to have to make haste if we are going to escape from this godforsaken bunch of ignorami.'

Hilary began to obey but felt it was time to broach the question, if he dared. 'Master Peter, it so happens that I have come to beg you for help. You see, I have become...

'Hah, Hilary, you shame me – and here was I assuming you had come to help me! Now shift your vast frame with those books, or we'll fall among the murderous monks who inhabit this lair.'

Abelard strode off, and Hilary had no choice but to lift both heavy sack and struggle after him, weighed down by Aristotle and the great classical philosophers. He made a second attempt to ask his favour.

'Master Peter, I wonder—'

Abelard was not listening. 'You would not believe it, Hilary, these spineless oafs at this abbey have taken objection – and in a somewhat violent way – to my simple question about the identity of their patron.'

'You mean St Denis?' Hilary breathed a sigh of resignation. It was absolutely typical. Master Peter wouldn't have been able to prevent himself casting doubt on the existence of St Denis himself, just when the monks dedicated to the memory of precisely that saint had offered to protect him. He can't be diplomatic to save his own life, let alone anyone else's. And this is the man I want to protect me. He can't even protect himself.

Hilary panted on behind, trying to keep up as Abelard made for the main gate, keeping in the shadows as much as possible. They were in luck, the gatekeeper was absent and they were able to slip through without being seen. Abelard led him down the small cobbled lane and then out into the road Hilary had come along earlier. 'This way!'

'Where are we going?' panted Hilary.

'There's a small inn less than a mile down the road to Paris, and I will explain everything once we're settled there. The argument will amuse you – it reminded me of my titanic clash with William of Champeaux, which I believe you witnessed, didn't you? Or the one with Anselm of Laon, for which I am still being pursued by my arch-enemy, Alberic of Reims.'

Hilary quickened his pace to keep up as Abelard walked briskly off into the gathering gloom, and wondering how to broach again his urgent predicament. 'First, may I ask you a question ... Master Peter, because it goes to the heart of the nightmare which ... has engulfed me?'

Abelard threw him an impatient look. 'Come along, Hilary, we must move quickly, it's nearly dark. I would prefer the monks not to get their hands on my manuscript. I have been beaten once too often in recent months. But yes, ask away. You know I will help if I can.'

'Then tell me – what is the meaning of the phrase '*hit waes geara iu*'?' Abelard stopped in the middle of the road, staring ahead. Then he turned towards Hilary for the first time and gave his full attention.

'It is Anglo-Saxon, I believe. It means 'In ancient times' or 'In bygone days'. Something like that. But, Hilary, you must tell me immediately why you use this phrase. Did you hear it somewhere?'

'It is Saxon, of course I knew that. But what is its significance?'

'Well, surely, Hilary, as a former student of mine, its main significance has presumably not escaped you?'

Hilary said nothing. He had clearly missed something obvious.

Abelard sighed. 'How disappointing. It is the opening line of Boethius' *Consolations of Philosophy*. Surely you recognised it immediately?'

Hilary flushed. He had of course read the famous book but could recall very little. 'Well....'

'It is Boethius in his most famous translation, as well – a translation into verse by Alfred they call 'the Great', the King of all England. But there is another significance, is there not?'

'Is there?' Hilary said cautiously. He frowned as though thinking hard, but his mind was a blank.

Abelard tutted. 'You an Englishman! Dear me. It is a famous phrase because it stands for Saxon scholarship and Saxon culture, now I fear long since forgotten under the Norman yoke that weighed down the necks of your forebears.'

Hilary began to understand. 'You mean, it's some kind of English watchword? Some kind of slogan of resistance?'

Abelard shrugged. 'That seems to be a reasonable hypothesis, don't you think? And why are you so interested in this little phrase with all the resonance it holds?'

'A man made me learn it, but he died before he could explain its significance.'

Abelard raised his eyebrows. 'Died? Well, this sounds like an interesting tale which I will swap for my own once we have reached the inn, now that the weather, the night and the monks are closing in. I will tell you then what else I know about this phrase. Now, give me one of those sacks; you're panting fit to burst.'

Despite these words of encouragement as they set off from St-Denis, Master Peter became moody and unresponsive the moment they reached the road out of the city and night wrapped itself around them. They trudged in silence along the rutted, frozen track until they at last reached an inn sufficiently far from the Paris road to put off any monks still in pursuit of Abelard.

'Those monks appeared to have murderous intent, Master Peter,' he said.

'Indeed.'

'I find it hard to believe that it was really you who was the object of their rage.'

'Nevertheless, it was.'

They were in an old stable behind the inn, with straw mattresses which had, once again, seen better days. Master Peter was examining the heavy sacks of books they had dragged along in the cold. He was irritatingly silent.

'Please enlighten me, Master Peter. I have helped you from the window, while all around us, bands of marauding Benedictines, vowed to poverty, chastity and obedience, were banging their weapons together. I can't help wondering what occurred to make them angry.'

'Hilary, you know as well as I do. Some people are enraged to hear the truth.'

'The truth about themselves?'

'Indeed. In this case, the truth about their patron, St-Denis.'

'I hope you don't mind me asking. I've been wondering what could possibly have been said to make you fear for your life.'

A look of intense irritation crossed his face, but he didn't look up. 'They would not have dared kill me, Hilary. I was fearful purely for my manuscript. I have been writing it now for two years.'

'Come, Master Peter,' said Hilary lightly. 'They looked ready to do you some lasting damage as well.'

Once more the look of intense annoyance. 'I'm no longer afraid of that,' he snapped. 'There are some kinds of damage that can only be inflicted once.'

Why did I say that? Hilary cursed himself for reminding his teacher that his last confrontation ended in losing more than his dignity. No, castration had not dimmed Abelard's spirit or his aggression, but it hurt him still – of course it did. How could he have allowed himself to raise the subject? No, this was no time for self-criticism.

Hilary was considering how to apologise when Abelard closed the dusty old book before him, checked that nobody was listening at the door and asked him to sit.

'Now, we haven't much time, and this fleapit is unfit for fleas, but they won't look for us here. I know you, Hilary. I can see you are concerned – more than concerned, frightened even – and I have had a bellyful of bullying in the last months, I can tell you. Also, I have reason to believe that the phrase you mentioned has a dangerous significance for those who use it. So tell me, how did you come by it? Tell me your story, Hilary, and pray, leave out no details. I will not have mysteries, certainly not mysteries that threaten my former pupils.'

Hilary outlined the story and, half way through, Abelard got to his feet and began to pace around. His eyes blazed. Hilary watched fascinated as Abelard's intellectual excitement began to stir itself again – perhaps, thought Hilary cynically, not so much for a mystery to unravel so much as an error to confront. But when it came to the contents of poor John of Muchelney's pouch, Abelard seemed to catch fire as he spread the documents out beside them in the moonlight.

'Open it up, Hilary. Get it out and open it up.'

For the third time, Hilary took out the two documents, written on velum, and unfolded them. He stared down at the letter in Latin but it still made little sense.

'Come, read it aloud, Hilary. Let's hear what this is all about.'

Peering closely at the letter, which was a little faint, Hilary translated from the Latin:

> *'Aelfgar, by God's grace abbot, to the esteemed and worthy prince and man of God, Baldwin, Count of Flanders, greetings.'*

That was pretty clear, and perhaps this Muchelney that John took his name from was some kind of abbey, but then the letter appeared to refer to previous correspondence and its meaning was obscure.

'Let me assure you, in the faith of Christ,' the letter continued, *'that the offer I conveyed to you in my previous letter remains true and honest, and one that is within my power to make, not from me but from the one whom I serve.'*

'Well, I don't know what you think, Master Peter, but it seems to me that the abbot had received only an acknowledgement to his last letter, rather than an enthusiastic acceptance of this offer and its conditions, whatever it was.'

'That much is obvious.'

'Nor is it clear who the abbot was acting as messenger for.'

'Quite so, quite so. Please read on, Hilary, or show the letter to me.'

The end of the letter, as it turned out, took on a more desperate tone:

'It is the belief of the one I serve that you, who are a root from the stump of our forefather Alfred, have the strength and will and the favour of God to receive my lord's blessing and anointing, and to restore the ancient liberties that have been stolen from us. Yet my lord requires an unequivocal answer, and that he is yet to receive, either by my messenger before you or by any other route. Time still passes. The hour is soon at hand. Do not delay, my lord, or the offer will be withdrawn. But convey by my messenger your acceptance and we will await your arrival, by the grace of God. The Great Jewel will then be revealed from its holy hiding place.'

'Is that all?' said Abelard tetchily.

'There's no seal. No other way of identifying it.' It was the first time Hilary had been able to read it when he had not been in a tearing hurry.

Abelard took it in his hand and examined it on both sides. 'It's interesting. This is a letter that would have conveyed everything to the correct recipient, but would have left anybody else who intercepted it as confused as a bat in daylight. Like us.'

'Well, it is apparently offering something to Count Baldwin of Flanders, isn't it? But look, Master Peter,' said Hilary, pointing at the scrawl at the bottom. Why hadn't he noticed it before? There, by itself at the foot of the page, were the words in Saxon: '*Hit waes geara iu*'.

'Ah,' said Master Peter enigmatically. 'King Alfred the Great again. The greatest piece of English literature until the invasion of your forefathers, Hilary. The reason I was so concerned when you first mentioned this phrase is that I believe it was incorporated into the coronation oath of Alfred's successors, the rulers that came after him – until King Harold's death of course. It is not a safe phrase today. Now, let us look at the other one.'

The other document seemed to be more straightforward. As Hilary had already discovered, it was a page of a book of English history and obviously cut from a larger volume.

'It appears to describe events before the strange death of William II, known as Rufus, just eighteen winters ago,' he said, handing it to Abelard. 'Do you remember it?'

'Of course. How could anyone forget?'

It began just where the page began, in mid-sentence:

'... assembled about him, a monk of Gloucester presented himself and delivered to the king a letter from his abbot. Having read it, the king burst out laughing, and said merrily to the knight just mentioned: 'Walter, do what I told you.' The knight replied: 'I will, my lord.' Slighting then the warnings of the elders, and forgetting that the heart is lifted up before a fall, he said respecting the letter he had received: 'I wonder what has induced the abbot to write to me in this strain, for I really believe he is a respectable old man. In the simplicity of his heart, he transmits to me, who have enough besides to attend to, the dreams of his snoring monks, and even takes the trouble to commit them to writing, and send them a long distance. Does he think that I follow the example of the English, who will defer their journey or their business on account of the dreams of a parcel of wheezing old women?' Thus speaking, he hastily rose, and mounting his horse, rode at full speed to the forest. His brother, Henry, with William de Breteuil and other distinguished persons followed him, and, having penetrated the woods, the hunters dispersed themselves in various directions according to custom. The King and Walter Tirel posted themselves with a few others in one part of the forest, and stood with...'

Hilary read it out again, uncomfortably reminded of his tutorials with Abelard all those years ago.

'Poor William Rufus,' said Hilary. 'We churchmen are supposed to have held him in contempt, but I have never quite managed to align my opinions with those of the church on almost any matter.'

'The fault of an expensive education, no doubt.'

The death of Rufus had been a shocking thing. Hilary and his generation never forgot what they were doing when they heard the news. It had seemed so impossible. Rufus dead, despite all his determination, his strength and his sheer *joie*. Now he remembered, his mother had wept when she heard the news. There had been special prayers in the village church. They had interrupted the harvest to pray.

'He was never a Christian, of course,' said Hilary, unaware that he had said it aloud.

'No, but since so many of our European rulers profess Christianity while they practise the most brutal kinds of bigotry, you might at least admire his consistency.'

Once more Hilary thanked God, silently, that Abelard was on his side, with all his trenchant, unconventional certainty. He exuded a sense of safety.

'It is true that I was never able to condemn a man, in quite the way I was supposed to, just because he preferred the company of young men in his bed,' said Hilary.

It hardly seemed possible that the death of Rufus, and the rise of his brother Henry, could have been as many as eighteen years before. It all came flooding back. How he had been shot so accidentally in the New Forest, while out hunting, by the great marksman Walter Tirel, lord of Poix, a man known for the sharpest eyes in Christendom. Of course, Hilary had heard rumours before that the King had been warned not to go hunting, and that he had dismissed those who warned him as superstitious rumour-mongering. This history seemed to confirm it.

'Is that all?' asked Master Peter, looking up from the page he had been reading.

'Yes. The page which set out the message is presumably still in the original book.' Hilary looked hopefully into the leather pouch again. It gave off a smell like ancient wisdom.

'Strange. The implication here appears to be that these messages – it mentions more than one warning, does it not? – were serious. Divine intervention. That God was on the side of Rufus as he battled against fate. Why tell that to Count Fulk of Anjou or Count Baldwin of Flanders? I confess, I don't understand.'

Hilary knew what an admission it was to wrench from the lips of the Indomitable Rhinoceros that he did not understand, and was respectfully silent for a moment. But he was worried too. There had been at least one death because of these papers so far, and his own had seemed imminent – and might still be the moment he left the safety of this stable – so the death of John of Muchelney must have had something to do with them. Hilary preferred not to hear that his old teacher was as confused as he was. It made him nervous.

Abelard put the papers carefully away, placing the pouch around Hilary's neck like a garland. 'Come, Hilary. We must sleep. There is some devilry here. You appear to have stepped into a dangerous place between those who hold England now and those who once ruled it, as you so rightly said, in bygone days. An uncomfortable place and I will not allow the devil's work to come to fruition again. Tomorrow, we will ride to Paris and consult Master Hubert, as he suggested. He knows more about the secret ways of our rulers and may shed some light on this conspiracy. Then, well, I will help you fulfil your promise.'

'My promise?' Hilary was nervous again. His main commitment was now to simple survival.

'The one you made to John of Muchelney, to deliver that letter to Anjou.'

Hilary's spirits sank. Of course, he had sworn solemnly. He must uphold his oath. It was going to be difficult and dangerous, even if he could get through the next few weeks intact, but he would have to do it.

5/Notre-Dame

Notre-Dame de Paris, 13 December 1119

There is something else I don't understand in this whole mess, said Hilary to himself as he picked his way through the giant potholes on the road to Paris. Some other confusion. I know it's there, he said to himself; I just can't trap it.

Then he knew. 'What I don't understand,' said Hilary, riding with increasing difficulty alongside Abelard, 'is why John should have been carrying a letter to the Count of Flanders when he actually told me it must be taken to the Count of Anjou.'

Hilary felt safer now they were on the road to Paris to make their assignation with Master Hubert. He had been puzzling over many things along the journey, but this was now what puzzled him most. All the rest seemed to be a matter of being in the wrong place at the wrong time, but this was just odd. One silver piece had secured two small palfreys, and a bundle of worthless tin coins as change, and Abelard had been silent since they had started along the road south. Now, as they negotiated a large muddy pit of grey water, he looked a little smug.

From long habit, Hilary examined his syntax. He had clearly overlooked a simple logical device. Again.

'Well, I don't think there's really any problem about that. Come, Hilary. You have presumably heard the news about Baldwin of Flanders, who was a descendent of your King Alfred I believe. He was badly wounded last year in a skirmish against English and Norman soldiers in the north, and it is widely believed that he will not recover. The man this letter is addressed to may even now be dead. We must assume, therefore, that your friend John left with the letter before this was known, and has had to fall back on some other plan which would direct the same letter to Fulk of Anjou.'

Of course, Hilary had heard about Baldwin's wounds. He berated himself for forgetting it. But it made sense: John of Muchelney had changed direction after he left England.

'Now, Hilary, what do you make of the two letters being together?' He gestured vaguely towards the pouch around Hilary's neck.

'What do I make of what?'

'Of these two letters being together in the same pouch. One of them has a phrase in Saxon that appears to imply a nostalgia for Saxon learning and civilisation, at least before William the Conqueror and your forebears arrived.'

Hilary felt a wave of irritation. 'I don't know about that,' he said. 'Saxon civilisation sometimes looks like a contradiction in terms to me. How can a society that keeps slaves be considered civilised? Even King Harold began his life as a slave-trader, I believe.'

Abelard made no attempt to conceal a familiar flash of exasperation. 'That may be the case, Hilary, but I'm asking something else now. What can we learn from the juxtaposition of these papers?'

Hilary wracked his brains. He knew he had never asked himself the question in quite that form before. He fingered the pouch, remembering details of the strange, uninformative letter and at the torn ragged edge of the history about William Rufus, ripped out of a valuable book.

'Well, I think we can say that he doesn't mind damaging books. The history book must have taken months to write, yet he has just torn the page out.'

'It means he was in a hurry, doesn't it. If he had more time he would have had it copied. No, your friend John left in a hurry, and all he could do was simply tear it out. If he just wanted to destroy the page, it wouldn't be included here. No, it carries a message in it which he wanted Baldwin or Fulk to understand. Let us run through the possibilities. Is it a warning? Is there an implication that God warned Rufus, and he didn't listen? Or is it perhaps a boast, that despite the warning – and the others – Rufus was killed? Are you following me?'

Hilary's mood had begun to lift. Not only was he following closely, but it felt exhilarating to have the greatest mind of the age focussed on his problem and the evidence he carried so dangerously around his neck.

'But then, look at the two pages together,' said Abelard, gesturing again towards his friend's neck. 'In one letter, there is an offer, a potential arrangement, from someone who hankers after the old Saxon ways in your country, Hilary. In the other, the description of a warning to the man who presides over its thraldom. And look at the ink.'

Hilary took the reins in one hand, opened the pouch with the other, pulled out the documents again and stared. It looked like any other ink.

'Come, Hilary. Hold it up to the light. Compare the ink used in this page of history with the ink used by the abbot. The history book is written with ink made of iron and acid, as you use yourself, I'm sure. The abbot's ink is made of charcoal. It is lighter, you see. Either this was written a century ago, or it was written by somebody remote from the world.'

'Maybe they just like using the ink of their forefathers.'

'Maybe they do, but it will fade faster, and this is an important letter. No, I think Abbot Aelfgar uses charcoal ink because he knows or can afford no better.'

Hilary stared at the letter again. It did look a little fainter.

'Tell me this,' said Abelard. 'Do we believe this warning?'

'What do you mean?'

'I mean, the history says that this monk had a warning dream from God. Did he really? Does God go around warning people who are going to die? Not in my experience, he doesn't. He has got more important tasks before him. So maybe this is what they simply *have* to say because they actually have evidence of a plot. Maybe that is what we have to take away from this torn document. That the death of your king William Rufus, those eighteen summers past, was not a terrible accident with an arrow, after all. It was a conspiracy, and the writer of this letter – this Abbot Aelfgar – implies that he knows this, maybe is even claiming that he knows who organised the killing. Maybe he organised it himself, though why a Saxon abbot should replace one Norman king with his brother, goodness knows.'

Yes, Hilary thought to himself, there was some message along these lines. The two documents together were telling Baldwin or Fulk that the Norman rule over England was not safe – perhaps it was even celebrating that fact. But Master Peter's blasphemous denial of God's role stuck in his throat. Surely, he thought, it could not be right to deny God's ability to intervene in the lives of men? Surely, even Master Peter would not go so far?

'That is correct. You are right, I feel sure. But do you really deny the monk's dream? Did not God appear in a dream to Samuel, to Joseph and to St Paul?'

Abelard held up one finger and indicated that Hilary should put the papers away again. He obeyed without thinking. He castigated himself for slipping into the old relationship far too smoothly.

'Maybe he did, maybe he didn't. But remember what I always say, Hilary. We can't just accept it – we must doubt it. For by doubting we come to inquiry, and from inquiry we come to the truth. We are in pursuit of the truth, you and I. That means we must doubt. And I doubt whether God would stir himself to issue quite so many warnings, would he?'

'Rufus was the King, Master Peter.'

'Do you not know the story of the Widow's Mite? The widow lost a small coin, almost worthless, but searched and searched and turned the whole house upside down to find it. Surely God's love and care extends equally to us all, Hilary?'

Hilary was silent for a while, unsure what to say, aware of his conscience but a little ashamed of it.

'Doubt, Hilary,' said his teacher, with passion. 'I'm just expressing creative doubt. When you get two explicit warnings, let alone a personal dream – brought on by the most abominable indigestion, I expect – then which is most likely? That God is stirring on your behalf or that there is actually some kind of plot which is known about but cannot, for obvious reasons, be spoken? They could hardly reveal what they actually knew, in case they were questioned too closely about *how* they knew, so they dressed the warnings up as dreams.

'But, as we know, the warnings did not work, and Rufus rode out with his friends – including his brother Henry, who was King by the following day. No, Tirel did not loose his arrow accidentally. He must have done it on behalf of a conspiracy. That's the implication of the sheet torn from the history book. You can't escape it. That is what the papers you carry imply: it implies not just that William Rufus was done to death, but that these Saxons have the power to do exactly the same again to another king.'

The bridges were in poorer states of repair than he remembered.

On one of them, they had been forced to dismount and pick their way past gaping holes with the Seine running beneath. On another, they had squeezed against the crumbling balustrade to let a heavy cart through.

'At times like these I really don't see why we should give way to carts,' said Abelard as it splashed them both with mud and ice.

Hilary realised that he had been so preoccupied making his way to St-Denis the afternoon before that he had barely noticed the crumbling state of the road, made all the worse for the latest freeze. But he was feeling more confidence now that he was with Abelard, and he felt another surge of relief as they crossed the Grand-Pont back into the great metropolis. Not only did he have the Indomitable Rhinoceros on his side, sadly reduced it was true, but he had the vast bulk of Master Hubert too.

Paris was familiar territory. Hilary knew it from the vineyards around the schools to the cookshop in the rue de la Hachette. He felt more secure there. Even the painful memory of Alys began to melt a little. He began to strut a little less like a man chased by demons, though – by the look of the Man in Grey at the city gates of Orléans– that is what he had been.

The drizzle was beginning again as they led their ponies down the street. It seeped into their undergarments and hose. But, despite the rain, there were now more people in the street: shepherds with mangy, bedraggled sheep, miserable poppy-oil sellers, expectant groups of peasants in damp smocks, looking overwhelmed at the sight of the ancient towers of Notre-Dame and St Etienne, as well they might be. In fact, there were definitely more people in the streets than there should have been for an ordinary day, and once they had lodged the ponies, they began to press about Hilary and Abelard on all sides – peasants, students, girls in virginal white, and squeezed into the muddy, pot-holed lanes, along with the ancient vegetables, the pools of urine and the detritus of city life.

'Of course. It's Santa Lucia,' said Master Peter. 'At least it will make us a little less conspicuous.'

A strange, sweaty mist rose above them in the peculiar heat that they produced all by themselves, part animal, part human, part faeces, running down the street in that refined Parisian way, and that familiar odour of cabbage, straw and pig manure that so reminded Hilary of home. It was time to see if Master Hubert had made any discoveries.

The Christmas procession was in full swing as they approached the ancient West Front of the cathedrals. '*Ut queant laxis, Resonare fibris,*' sang the crowd, already in their places outside, their candles burning brightly despite the weather: first the clergy brandishing crosses, then the cathedral monks, then the nuns, then the children. Hilary could hardly see them all, but in the distance he knew were the other processions – the laymen, the widows and the married couples, many of them probably still squabbling in the nave, knowing they would have to process around the city in the rain and be back there by dinner time.

They edged past the chapels – St-Denys-du-Pas, St-Aignan– and towards the twin entrance-ways. On procession days like this, the ruined Ste-Marie basilica next door was open to everyone, and they headed through there.

Suddenly, Abelard headed off at a pace by himself.

'Excuse me. I'll meet you at Master Hubert's room.'

'What? Where are you going?' shouted Hilary. Too late, he realised that Master Peter would hardly have relished arriving publicly at Notre-Dame for the first time since his attack. Hilary watched him slip in through the ruins and told himself he forgave this rare moment of shyness to lick his wounds.

An unfortunate expression, in the circumstances, though Hilary. I must not let my mind wander in this way, still less think about Master Peter as if he is a lesser man than he was...

From Ste-Marie, he carried on into the main cathedral, with the mosaics and marble pillars he knew so well, expecting the crowd to thin there. He was wrong. There were even more people in there than outside and their attention was obviously somewhere else, chattering nervously and excitedly, and with no obvious intention of joining the procession. Slowly Hilary began to be aware that they were agitated about something.

'What is it then?' said one woman as he passed.

'Don't know yet. I saw the sheriff. Six soldiers went in before the bell tolled just now.'

'It's shocking, shocking, and on the day of the procession too.'

Hilary tried to push past the nave and into the transept, and found his way blocked by a solid phalanx of peasants, townspeople and traders gawping expectantly with all the relish of a hanging.

It took him the equivalent of five rosaries to force his way into the same corridor where he had slipped through so easily some days before, and found that was almost as full, with a mass of monks, many of them in tears. He struggled on towards Hubert's room, aware that something rather unusual must be happening, but too intent to question too closely what it was. Nobody paid him much attention until he finally came to a complete standstill, this time amongst silent monks and other cathedral officials standing in the corridor, watching a hive of activity ahead.

'They're coming! Mother of God!' said an elderly monk. There was an audible sigh amongst the crowd and a couple of sobs.

Coming towards them, pushing with difficulty through the crowd, was what looked like some kind of funeral bier, surrounded by a group of struggling monks. There was suddenly much shhh-ing behind and then a stunned silence as the bier came closer. It was then that he overheard his own name, unmistakably, whispered some yards away. Hilary shot round but realised it had not been addressed either at him or towards him.

Then the bier was upon them, carried by eight hefty monks, and he could see the huge mound of flesh on it, and the grotesque twisted face of Hubert, his eyes staring out as if he had been strangled, with great red welts on his neck and his white pasty, puffy face. Hilary glanced down at his hands, which were always so delicate, and they were ribboned with lacerations. The smell of blood and faeces wafted up to him as the heavy bier went by.

He stood in horror as the remains of Hubert were carried by, his mind racing through the possibilities. It was hard to avoid the conclusion that his visit the previous day and this death were connected somehow. Hubert had warned him that there was danger. Hilary could barely face the thought, but it was impossible to set it aside, and it was far more likely than anything else. Had Hubert just happened to hang himself after their meeting? Or did he coincidentally face some hideous death at the hands of intruders soon afterwards? It just wasn't credible.

Hilary tried to compose his features to disguise his explosion of horror, but one glance at the ashen faces around him and he realised this was unnecessary. What scared him were the implications. He had to assume, if Hubert's horrible fate was linked to his own visit, that those who were seeking him were also responsible. Not the bovine sheriff's official perhaps, but the Man in Grey with the piercing eyes he had glimpsed from the turnip cart, and his minions.

The main question was why? Was Hubert being punished somehow for talking to him, or did they imagine that Hilary had shared these fearsome papers with him?

Then it struck him. Perhaps it wasn't the visit he had made to Hubert yesterday which had sealed his fate, but the visit they knew he was making *today*. Maybe Hubert was overheard mentioning it at Matins or Laud. Maybe they knew Hilary was coming back for more information. But why kill him, for the love of Christ? Hubert was loved like no other monk in the miserably competitive world of Notre-Dame, perhaps because he stayed rigidly in his own world between the cathedral, his room with his books and the refectory.

A possible answer nagged away at him but, to start with, Hilary dared not even articulate it to himself. Had Hubert had been killed deliberately to lure him into another compromising trap, one which he could almost certainly never escape from? But if so, why not simply wait until he had been with Hubert and then pounce? And if he had been killed because of their conversation, then who was not against him – even in Paris? Even in Notre Dame itself?

The bier carrying Hubert's mangled neck had been dragged only a few yards before Hilary had thought this through, and began edging back into the crowd. His first thought was about those murderous papers around his neck, so fatal to all those who carried them. Maybe he could just drop them into the Seine and have done with it. But even as he thought this, he knew it was impossible – his pursuers wouldn't know and would carry on after him. In any case, the papers might provide the only clues available to escape from this nightmare.

At that moment, Hilary heard the phrase he feared most. 'There he is!' shouted high-pitched shriek. 'The murderer!'

It came from some distance away towards the cloisters. The crowd snarled, and began searching first for the voice and then for Hilary. He took the opportunity of their momentary confusion to duck into a small doorway, banging his head on the lintel. Then the oak door behind him was flung open, a hand shoved over his mouth and he found himself dragged inside.

Hilary had been chased before in his life, mainly in the back streets of Paris. He knew what it felt to be the quarry, but never with quite so much at stake as there was now. When he felt himself grabbed from behind, for a moment, he gave himself up for lost. But the big door banged behind him and he found himself staring up into the face of Master Peter Abelard.

'Thank God!'

'A little premature, I think, Hilary. Somebody must have seen you. Help me barricade the door.'

Hilary felt his heart racing, and tried to put out of his mind the thought of what would happen if those monks got hold of him, bereft for the moment as they were of the peace of God.

'Come on, I can't do this alone!' Master Peter was seizing the topmost barrels from a stack, and was rolling them against the door, and wedging them under the latch. With difficulty and sweating profusely, Hilary rolled one of them over in the same way. 'How come you were there? What an extraordinary coincidence. I can't believe...'

'I've been following you since I realised what was happening.'

Then a sudden thought struck him. 'Where are we? Is there any way out?'

'I don't know, but I think there are some stairs over there.' Suddenly there was a bang on the door, and then a whole tumult. When Hilary turned back, Abelard was holding open the arras and the small door which lay behind it.

'Are you coming, Hilary? This is no time for philosophy.'

Hilary followed, ducking down into the darkness and nearly fell head first down a flight of narrow steps.

It was only a short flight, but the next room or corridor seemed to be in total darkness. Breathing quickly as the banging on the door above became deafening, he tripped over what felt and sounded like a bottle on the ground. There was the terrifying noise of splintering wood coming from upstairs.

A moment of panic and he realised there was in fact a little light filtering in from holes in the ceiling, presumably from the refectory where poor Hubert had enjoyed his last meal, and Hilary picked his way after his teacher towards the blackest part of the cellar, past the cobwebbed bottles of beer and wine, in the hope that there might prove to be some way back to the surface. Abelard paused occasionally ahead to hurry Hilary along behind him.

That corridor led to another, with great haunches of bacon and other meats, some of them which had evidently hanging there expectantly waiting to be consumed for decades, judging by the weight of dust and dirt which covered them, and at the end of that corridor was a door. The sound of pursuit was not far behind. Somehow the prospect of being dragged through the underground tunnels of Notre-Dame was too much for him. He panted desperately. Following Abelard through the darkness seemed almost as greater hazard as dodging his pursuers alone.

I'm done for, Hilary said to himself. I've run too far now. 'Leave me here, Master Peter. I have lost my breath. Let's take our chances alone. We'll be less conspicuous that way. They can't chase us both.' He breathed desperately.

Abelard ignored him, heaved at the door and, reluctantly, it gave way in a suffocating tangle of cobwebs. Breathing deeply, they set off again, down another set of steps, another dark corridor even darker than the one above, this one apparently forgotten. Then a fork.

After a moment's hesitation, aware of the footsteps and raucous shouting echoing around the stone behind them, Abelard turned left and came upon yet another small door. This one had evidently been used not very long before, because behind it was a small chapel, a stone altar, a cross with a carved figure of a triumphant Christ, and a single oil lamp, then another door. This time, it was Hilary's turn to be impatient. Abelard was searching the top of the altar and, for one sickening moment, Hilary thought he was going to pray. *Come on, come on...*

He hurried on to the next door. It was half wedged again, though he pulled it with all his might and heard a small yelp of frustration and fear, realising it had issued from his own mouth, before the door shot open again. Another cobweb covered his eyes and mouth. Beyond the door was complete blackness.

'What are you doing?' he hissed. 'They're not far behind!'

'Patience, Hilary. Just a moment...'

A faint, but comforting light filled the chamber. Abelard had found a half burned candle. Hilary could see his familiar features, strangely shadowed, in the candlelight. Praying to whichever saint the chapel was dedicated to – presumably the lady whose memory dominated the great institutions above – he plunged on after the long shadow that Abelard cast on the wall.

The sounds of angry voices behind them had been silenced briefly by the fork, but were after them again and Abelard and Hilary hurried on. This corridor seemed to be seriously disused. The cobwebs hung down like curtains, with dirt and grit which got into their mouths as Abelard manoeuvred the candle around each one.

'What is this place?' Hilary demanded in a loud whisper.

'I don't know, but I can guess.'

There was something under foot and Hilary looked down, trembling with fear and excitement, and saw it was a bone which looked disconcertingly human. It was far too big for a chicken, or for the rats which he could hear scurrying away ahead, fearful of what would be the sight of their first live human for centuries. Even Abelard, ahead, was treading more carefully, holding the lamp above him.

'Ugh!' said Hilary, in involuntary horror. They had stumbled, not so much into a charnel house, as into the catacombs.

'Yes, we're about to disturb the slumbers of the monks and abbots who have inhabited this place since the days of Pepin and Charlemagne,' said Abelard in a loud whisper. 'Not a good argument for the bodily resurrection, I fear.'

Sure enough, a moment or two later, the corridor narrowed and, on either side of them, lying awaiting judgement and in various stages of decomposition, in dirt encrusted rat-chewed vestments and mitres, were the corpses of the good and great of Notre-Dame, St-Etienne's and the previous temples on this site. Abelard lifted the candle. A small rat leaped out of the eye socket of a particularly gruesome corpse occupying the shelf next to them.

There was hardly time to consider their new predicament, still less to feel the horror they might have done had not the successors of these corpses been pursuing him. Bizarrely, at a moment of such peril, Hilary found himself wondering what these poor remains would be like at the Last Judgement. Then there was a crash behind. Their pursuers had ventured into this dungeon of the dead as well.

What a place to have to die, said Hilary to himself. For what seemed like hours, they blundered on, looking neither to the right nor to the left unless they had to, the sound of the footsteps of the living behind them, following Abelard's lamp blindly down every unlikely turning they happened upon, until the angry noises grew more distant and tentative. Perhaps not even the Man in Grey he had witnessed at the gates of Orléans would have had the nerve to pursue them quite so deep into purgatory.

'Master Peter,' Hilary whispered loudly. 'How do we get out?'

'I admit I'm not very certain,' Abelard said, stepping forward down another dark passageway. 'But I think the horror before us in the daylight is marginally worse. The same fate as poor Hubert or a slow death among the long dead? Which are you going to choose?'

At that moment, Hilary stubbed his toe on what seemed to be a human skull, moved there presumably by a detachment of the army of rats that watched their every move. Amidst the rank smell of death and decay, there were now tears of desperation pouring down his face, a rare human life in this Hades. It was a humiliating revelation of his own powerlessness.

'Hold on,' said Abelard ahead. 'This feels better.'

Sure enough, there seemed to be a slight breeze on his face, and Hilary followed as quickly and quietly as he could, again for what seemed like miles under the weight of the cathedrals above. The breeze grew stronger. Abelard increased his pace and Hilary found himself lagging behind, careful with each step where he put his foot.

'Come on, Hilary!' said Abelard with irritation. Hilary broke into a desperate run, kicking bones and dirt out of the way. At last, there was the chink of light he longed for. It was no more than a chink: another small chamber, and what seemed to be a tiny window high on the wall above layers of more ancient decomposing men of God.

Hilary looked at the small gap with horror. 'We will never make it through that hole. I am greater than you are.'

'I beg to differ, Hilary. Have a bit of faith.'

'Even if we could reach it, we will never fit through the window.'

'Yes, we will. Look.' Abelard climbed onto the ledge and motioned him to follow. Some blackened bones fell around them.

At least I have got another choice of death, thought Hilary to himself. I can die wedged half in, half out of a window between the living and the land of the dead. 'Perfect,' he said out loud in desperation. 'Stop prattling and give me your hand.'

Hilary reached up. He put one foot on the shelf of a blackened skeleton, and reached up towards his neighbour above. Then he closed his eyes. With one arm, he swept the remains of what appeared to be an ancient, long-forgotten abbot out of his resting place, blessing him as he did so. The abbot seemed disconcertingly light. He opened his eyes again. The skull and fly-blown headgear, and one arm remained. There was a clatter onto the stone ground as he pushed them away.

'In heaven's name, Hilary. Do you want us discovered again. Shhh!'

'Sorry.'

Hilary reached over and peered out of the small window. It was a wonderful glimpse of life again, of the river below, and he could see the procession of light in the distance crossing the bridge back to the city.

'Listen. I will go first and help you out onto the ledge the other side. Don't be afraid.' Hilary's heart was thumping, and thinking suddenly of Alys, decomposing in her new grave like these ancient corpses around them. Hilary took a deep breath and followed Abelard up onto the shelf. Abelard slipped through the window and stood outside on the ledge. Hilary contemplated the tiny aperture. Why had he taken so little care of what he ate and drank? Why had he exercised so little?

He put his head further through the window. Then his right arm, and then – wonder of wonder – he was squeezing through.

'Come on, Hilary. You can do it.'

Hilary put Alys and her books out of his mind and squeezed further. There really was no choice but something was awkwardly wrong. He stepped back again into the darkness. There were the handful of bones around his knees on the shelf again, awaiting judgement. He should have gone feet first. Again, his feet and legs slipped through easily. A moment later, his waist was through.

He struggled to organise his arms and shoulders, with his head still in darkness and then he could feel Abelard – God, let it be him – pulling from the other end. Hilary pushed again against the roof, imagining a magnificent death stuck in a small hole above the Seine. Even that may have been preferable to a lynching at the hands of a posse of bloodthirsty monks. And then he was out, banging his head on the stone window lintel, and balancing next to Abelard on the ledge, hidden from view by tall weeds and grasses.

The damp air hit him full in the face. 'What did I tell you?' said Abelard. 'We have emerged like Jonah from the belly of the whale.'

Hilary panted on the ledge, trying to remove the image of the remains he had swept aside to allow him to escape, and listening for the sounds that would reveal that their exit from Notre-Dame had been seen. God seemed to have allowed them to escape.

'Now, we are not clear yet,' said Abelard next to him, speaking a little too fast, and indicating down to the river bank below. 'The monks are looking for two men, so we must divide our forces. I am not under suspicion, so I will return through Notre-Dame. You will be safer going alone. Go down to one of those barges and I will meet you upstream at Provins at this time in exactly three days. I will go ahead and organise the protection of Count Hugh. Do you understand? This whole business reeks of the devil: I believe poor Master Hubert may have been killed for no better reason than to trap you. Be on your guard until we meet again.'

'Wait!' shouted Hilary, struggling to his feet. But Abelard was gone.

6/South

Provins, 16 December 1119

'In heaven's name, where have you been? I expected you hours ago.'

Abelard stood in the stone gateway of Provins, with the bespattered straw around his feet, and looked relieved. Hilary recognised the relief and felt gratified. Of course he didn't want to upset or irritate his old teacher, but he was pleased to see at least that evidence of continuing interest in him. You never quite knew with Master Peter. It wasn't that he was self-centred, just that he carried a great deal in his head, including perhaps an unnecessarily detailed memory of his intellectual jousts with the masters of the past generation, and goodness knows what else, or what painful memories now clouded his greyhound mind.

Despite that, Abelard seemed to have aged in the three days since he had last seen him. His clothes were rough, yet he had covered his shoulders with a wealthy looking cloak which all those others on the road glanced at with envy on such a frozen day. Carts were squeezing by on either side of him.

It all seemed a long way from the damp of Notre-Dame, when Hilary had stretched out on the ground by the riverbank, hidden in the long grass, after Abelard had gone. There he had been, breathing deeply and savouring his escape from the catacombs, and thinking of the strange path that had brought him to this perilous moment – from home in Nether Wallop, the years at Ste-Genevieve, teaching in Rouen, one or two quite good poems, some less successful bouts of love, most of it more romantic than requited. He never set out to wander, yet what else was he to do? He was not cut out for monastic life, quite yet at least. But what was he cut out for, especially when Master Peter had gone ahead of him?

Provins, he had repeated to himself, terrified that he would forget the rendezvous and have to track his teacher down all over again. Three days.

The front of the procession was still on the bridge, apparently delayed by some kind of blockage on the Ile-de-la-Cité side of the river. There were angry voices wafting over the distance, and people on the wharves were staring in the same direction. There seemed to be a number of soldiers on the bridge as well, in leather and chain mail.

Of course. This was some kind of systematic search. Everyone who left the Ile-de-la-Cité was being searched and questioned. What was more, it was presumably organised for himself, and organised with miraculous swiftness – such speed, in fact, that it must have been planned before he had blundered into the trap. What kind of desperation these people must feel to go to such lengths to get the papers that hung around his neck. Abelard was right: Master Hubert was a sacrifice to entrap him and his pouch. Perhaps he had been killed as they tried to force information out of him, perhaps he had been throttled just to set the trap. It seemed extraordinary that such evil could exist in the world. There must be some overwhelming reason for it, if only he could work out what it was.

The truth was, thought Hilary as he stared over the stones, that they must have heard about his visit to Master Hubert before, and known he was coming back the following day, and had conspired to set forth the gigantic hue and cry against him. Probably they overheard Master Hubert talking about him in the refectory and knew he was due to return the following day. If and when he came back, Hubert would have to be sacrificed to ensnare him. They could not rely on their own efforts alone, these shadowy forces. They wanted the whole of Paris to join in the chase to catch him.

No, not him, Hilary reassured himself. This wasn't about him. It was to ensnare the burden he carried, and all for fear of what was inside it. It was easy to fall back on supernatural fear – as if thinking too closely about the contents of the pouch would somehow make him visible to these people. That was nonsense. Hilary urged himself to think more clearly and practically.

He glanced down in the other direction. A small barge was loading empty barrels, and some boys were rolling these down the slope from the back doors to the abbey kitchens. There was a small ladder down to the river wall. Feeling a little unsteady, Hilary climbed down. He realised he was holding his breath to appear inconspicuous. Breathe, he told himself, just breathe and we will find a way out.

The barge couple at the foot of the ladder were loading empty barrels down the steps, surrounded by a number of sulky looking youths. They took almost no notice of Hilary. He would have to rely on a shared dislike of their holy customers, and probably all holy customers. Hopefully the muscular woman by the rudder was like every other bargee in France in this respect. It was going to be a risk, but a calculated one.

'Madam,' said Hilary, with great solemnity. 'I am forced to throw myself on your mercy. Please save me, for the love of Christ!'

She looked at him suspiciously, down a long pointed nose. 'Why, wretch? What have you done? You look like a proper rogue to me.'

'The monks are after me. See the bridge behind me? They are searching for me even now. You are my last hope. I can pay you for your trouble. Really...'

She appeared to lose interest and directed a flurry of swear words at one of the youths on the bank.

'They say I stole some beer,' he said, reaching imaginatively for a safe enough crime. There was a guffaw and Hilary realised her equally tough-looking husband was behind him.

'You steal away, my friend,' he said. 'The more you drink their beer, the more they will have to buy from us. In any case, any enemy of the monks is a natural ally of ours, isn't that so?' he glanced at the woman at the rudder again. She gave no sign that she had heard.

'Go aboard, my friend. We will get you away.'

A moment later, he was being hustled further into the boat and was bundled unceremoniously into an empty barrel.

Another lie, thought Hilary to himself. Another weight that Christ and his angels would one day have to lift from his soul, along with all the other sins, before he could enter heaven.

A moment later and the lid was put on. Hilary was in darkness, breathing in the odour of stale beer, lit by a few slits of light through the lid above. Was there going to be enough air to breathe? He could hear the barge woman cackling about something and hoped it wasn't him.

He was so tightly packed into the barrel that he could move neither of his arms. He could feel the sweat pouring down his face. When it reached his mouth, he realised he was bleeding from the gash on his head from the top of the window. No wonder the woman had called him a rogue. He must have looked even more of a rogue than he had realised.

The barge was now moving in the water. They must have moved away from the wharf. Yet before Hilary had time to relax, there was a sudden shout and angry voices raised. In wasn't possible inside the barrel to hear what was being said. Then there was the outraged tones of the barge woman raised in reply.

'By heaven, we are on cathedral business,' she was bawling. 'The archbishop will have you flogged if you disrupt the flow of beer. We have privileges from the chapter.'

Then there was a scream and a splash and something incoherent, followed by a bump and the sound of heavy footfalls on the deck.

'Leave my husband alone, you cunts,' screamed the barge woman. 'There are no murderers on my barge by the Immaculate Conception, may I shrivel and decompose if I lie... No – leave my boat alone!'

There was an unfamiliar vibration. His barrel was banged and jostled. Then the crash of an axe, which must have been smashed into the barrel next door. Hilary held his breath and, for the second time that day, he found himself praying to St Sebastian to spare his life.

Once more Sebastian intervened. There was more shouting at a distance, more oaths from the barge woman, more heavy footsteps, and then silence – and once more the swaying motion of a boat in transit along the Seine. Then the sound of water rippling along the hull and the occasional shout from a distance. There was silence for a few minutes, when the woman spoke suddenly right next to the barrel. 'Murder, eh?' she said in a dangerous whisper. 'It looks like you are going to have to recompense us for risking our lives along with your own.'

'I'll pay,' Hilary whispered back, fingering his silver pieces through the material of the purse.

'Shhh!' she hissed.

After as much time as it takes to say the mass, there was a rumble next to him and the blinding light flooded in. Hilary looked out at the Ile-de-Notre-Dame disappearing into the distance and realised that, against all the odds, he had escaped the clutches of those that sought him once again. It was time to take some precautions.

'I must beg your pardon, Madam,' said Hilary. 'I am quite innocent. This is a serious case of mistaken identity.'

The barge woman barely glanced in his direction. She obviously didn't believe him, but Hilary realised she didn't actually care what he had done. The husband, still sopping wet, stood next to him, ostentatiously sharpening his dagger. Hilary reached into his purse and handed the woman two silver pieces.

'We may hate the monks, but we're God-fearing folk,' she said, by way of apology. 'Murder is a serious business. Especially on the day of the Santa Lucia procession.'

This sudden sanctity lacked the ring of authenticity, but there really was no alternative but to stay with this feisty couple and the overpowering smell of stale inns in the early morning as the barge made its slow progress along the great bends of the Seine to the east of Paris, edging south at the same time. Hilary caught a nervous look exchanged between the couple and realised that he also now had the power to draw down disaster on them, for harbouring a man accused of the most heinous crimes. They sank or swam together on this barge.

Once successfully out of sight of the city, he could take no more. 'I have relatives here,' he shouted back to the stern, as soon as the first small hamlet appeared. This was the moment they would throw him over the side for his purse.

'Are we to be rid of you here, murderer?'

'If you would be so good as to set me down, I would be further in your debt.' This was the test. Hilary edged towards the left hand side, ready to jump if he saw a knife.

The barge woman snarled a little, but made no further comment. Then she put the helm over. Hilary relaxed a little and stared down into the shallow water. He was considering how deep it was, and how far up his body it was likely to go, when the woman shouted: 'Now!'

He looked back. 'Jump and let's be rid of you!'

Hilary jumped and found himself in water up to his chest, just below his purse. He struggled onto what looked like a sandy beach, and lay there on the strand, savouring his freedom in the fresh, open air, and watching the barge disappear around the next bend of the Seine.

Three days later by the gate in Provins, overjoyed to see Abelard, Hilary was just considering how grateful he was to his old teacher for being where he said he would be, when he realised he was not alone. Abelard was flanked by two heavily-armed ogres, both mounted as he was, and both wearing the same blue and white surcoats, faded from too long in the winter weather. One held a sword; the other a mace.

'Ambrose of Sarum!' announced Master Peter, with a look that seemed both to query whether he had the right false name, and which silenced any questions at the same time.

'I am he,' said Hilary loudly. 'Well met, Master Peter.'

'Welcome, Brother Ambrose. You have the protection of Count Hugh of Champagne.'

One of the armed men at his side seemed to nod their head imperceptibly, which seemed to imply confirmation. The other dismounted and Hilary's heart sank for a moment. There was his old palfrey which Abelard must have led from the gates of Paris. He heaved himself onto its back and the four of them turned towards the gates.

The two officers rode ahead. 'What's happening?' he asked, in a loud whisper. 'Are you a friend of Count Hugh? I don't understand.'

'Listen, *Ambrose*,' said Abelard with emphasis which implied that Hilary should speak carefully. 'We have to be careful. The King no less has announced a reward for the capture of a man called Hilary the Englishman. They say he has committed two murders. The whole of France is alerted. Do you understand? And yes, I had the honour to serve the Count of Champagne some years ago, and I'm glad to say he is protecting us. But he has asked very few questions – and I'm happy to make sure there are very few more.'

Hilary felt a wave of nausea. The mud and straw in the town square swam before his eyes for a moment. Everywhere seemed threatening. Everybody a potential informer or Man in Grey. He felt hollowed out, transformed into this creature of bards and poets, a caricature of an outlaw. He felt overwhelmed by hopelessness as they hobbled towards the tower, high above the rest of the town, where their mounts were taken from them and they were ushered into the hall, which was being prepared for the evening meal.

Still shaking, he chose a corner of the room and sat lost in his own thoughts and terrors, the full horror of the past two days coming home to him – the murder of Master Hubert, his escape through the catacombs and his ordeal in the barrel.

'Be of good cheer, Hilary.' Abelard was beside him, amidst the bustle of preparation. 'I must apologise for my peremptory greeting this afternoon, and for disappearing after our escape from Notre-Dame. But I assure you that, on both occasions, I was right. Our situation is now grave, but we are safe here, at least for Christmas, during which time will decide what to do.'

'But I know what I have to do. I promised to go to Anjou.'

Abelard ignored him. 'Listen, Hilary. Did you at any time reveal your name before you arrived at Notre-Dame? On the way from Orléans?'

'No ... well, I may have done.' Hilary thought back. 'I might have done to the landlady of the inn where I was staying the night I met John of Muchelney.'

'And what exactly did poor Hubert say to you before you left him? Tell me again.'

'He said I should return the following day to see if he had discovered where you were.' He struggled to remember his exact words, but they had become garbled. 'Oh yes, he said there was someone he could ask who might understand the intricate politics of it.'

'Poor Hubert. He was a genius in a small way. Did you say that there was any way you could have been overheard?'

'No, I was inside his chamber when he said it. Nobody was outside. Nobody could have heard. If anybody knew I was returning, they must have overheard him telling someone else.'

'You are right, Hilary,' said Abelard decisively. 'None of your story is explicable unless we assume that those who murdered your friends, and are presumably among those on your trail, have access to the most powerful network of informers I have ever heard of. They are clearly formidable adversaries. But who was it that Hubert talked to?'

Once more, the full horror of his predicament came home to Hilary. He felt desperately exposed.

'Still, cheer up, Hilary. I am also a formidable opponent and we will get to the roots of this evil between us. Now, show me the contents of the pouch, if you will again, and we shall begin to unravel this mystery.'

Hilary never enjoyed Christmas, wherever he was. Not even with Alys in Beaugency had he managed to escape its melancholic, nostalgic air, and somehow staying at the heart of a city of great wealth like Provins made it even worse. Thinking too much about the birth of Christ made him dwell nostalgically about his own birth. He missed his own little hamlet of Nether Wallop at Christmas as he did at no other time. The musicians in St Andrew's church, the great angels painted above the chancel steps, and the old priest intoning the familiar words, and the smell of wood smoke from the stoves to keep them warm.

Christmas 1119 seemed to be no exception, even though they were enjoying a Christmas of almost unparalleled luxury, in the castle in Provins. The sight of the gibbet in Paris had revived Hilary's faith, when he thought how he might even then have been hanging there, and would have been if it hadn't been a combination of God's hand and a lucky window in the catacombs. He knew that Abelard had begged the household to keep news of his arrival as quiet as possible, but even Provins was not nearly far enough from Paris for his comfort. He was therefore spending more time than usual on his knees. He attended the Angel's Mass at night on Christmas Eve, and rose in time for the Shepherd's Mass at dawn. He joined the household again for the service of the divine word before dinner.

'It's remarkable, Hilary,' said Abelard next to him at dinner. 'Since you became Ambrose the Carpenter, I have never seen you behave so much like a clerk in holy orders in your life before.'

Desperately trying to forget, the deaths of Hubert, John and Alys and of his own dire predicament, Hilary flung himself into the celebrations, taking part in the merry-making and music. He helped light the enormous yule log in the great hall, and fed its fire in the days that followed. Not for one moment did he forget the Man in Grey, and the king's officers scouring France for him, but he sank into Christmas with thankfulness and calm, astonished to find himself intact and within reach of excellent meals and ale.

The castle at Provins was luxurious in many ways, with its tapestries and mosaics in the style brought back by the crusaders. Hilary prevented himself from taking part in the entertainments in the evening, casting a weary and sceptical eye over the performances of two wandering poets he had never met – part irritated by their shortcomings, part sympathetic about their reception. The household tended to chat loudly through their songs, and there were raucous yells coming from the kitchen. Even the dogs slept and scratched.

In quiet moments in the daylight, he sketched out new songs about a Christmas feast.

'So golden and brown, you beautiful goose,
Give yourself to me...'

What would rhyme with 'goose'? 'Juice' perhaps. It was no good, the requisite revolutionary verve was not there. You need some kind of devil-may-care energy to write that kind of poem, a flaunting, fearless sense of creativity. It simply wasn't there. He could not honestly write a love poem, even to a dinner. Not now. Perhaps something about his current predicament.

'Jam secures, ego vivam...' he wrote. 'Now I will live in safety'...

Whoever heard of a poem about living safely. He filed it away in his memory for future use. The truth is, I am not as successful a poet as I might like to be, he admitted to himself. Then a flash of irritation. The trouble with spending time with Master Peter is that he sucks out the confidence of those around him. How can I compete with him: he is not just a great philosopher, he is a great poet too?

Some days after Christmas, Count Hugh of Champagne himself was present for the evening meal. Abelard sat talking with him late that night by the fire after the rest of the household had swayed home to the stables and outhouses. Hilary stayed in the shadows after the minstrels had outstayed their welcome.

'Caterwauling nonsense,' said the Count, and Hilary had to agree. Count Hugh was dressed in silk for the occasion. He smelled of perfume. His tastes seemed to have gone beyond what was merely oriental, but Hilary remembered he had been to Palestine. This was a sophisticated home.

'Hilary, tell me what you know of this William Rufus,' said Abelard in the firelight.

'Well,' said Hilary sleepily. 'I believe his death happened at the end of July 1100 at Castle Malwood in the New Forest. I was only ten winters old at the time. Less perhaps. Rufus was taken ill in the night and said he had suffered from bad dreams. Then, as we know, there were the warnings from the monks – not just those written about in the document, but others as well. Rufus sent them away.'

'A mistake, clearly,' said Abelard. 'Pray continue.'

'Some time after dinner, at around nones, he felt well enough recovered to discuss things with Walter Tirel, who was staying with them. Then he said something strange, or so I remember. 'Remember what you've heard, Walter, and take appropriate action.' I don't know what that meant either.'

'Neither do I.'

'Then it was a long meal and it was late afternoon by the time the King decided he would go hunting after all, despite the pleas of his closest advisors. The huntsmen were waiting below in the courtyard and it was time to go. With him went his brother Henry and other big men of the court. A few hours later, he was dead, shot in the chest by an arrow in the forest.'

For a little while at the end of the story, Hilary was aware that Count Hugh was listening.

'You are speaking of the death of William Rufus?' said the Count. 'It is a strange story. We pay lip service to those dreams as if it was some kind of accident, but I did not believe it – I do not believe it now. Who can have profited from the death? I will tell you. His brother Henry, now King of England. He was at the heart of this beastly thing, let me tell you.'

'May I ask, my lord,' said Abelard. 'Have you other reasons for thinking so?'

'No,' said Count Hugh. 'But something is happening now. I don't know what it is. A number of people have passed through here on their way to Paris in the past few weeks, as if there was some meeting. Some have stayed here and I overheard much talk of Rufus, after eighteen winters, as I overheard you talking now. The great men of France are worried, mark my word. Suger travelled the other way and I heard him mention Rufus too. One of those on their way through was Alberic of Reims. He is no friend to you, Master Peter.'

'I fear not. He has not forgiven me for the debates in Laon.'

Not Alberic of Reims again, Hilary groaned to himself. Now that he had encountered Master Peter again, his patience with tales of the great intellectual clashes was wearing thin.

Sure enough, the conversation moved on and, feeling sleepy, Hilary listened silently from the shadows, as Abelard recounted some of his great encounters in debate with the likes of Alberic and Anselm of Laon. The dogs rolled around in the heat by the fire and around the yule log, too hot to move, too cold to be anywhere else. Suddenly, he realised that Master Peter was talking about Heloise, her abilities as a philosopher, how he had come to love her, of their secret marriage and Fulbert's ferocious reaction to her departure from his house. It reminded him painfully of his own passion for Alys, but requited and without the hint of absurdity.

The Count was moved, and Abelard clearly moved himself in the telling. It was poignant to see a man Hilary revered so much, and whose intellect he so admired, brought so low by love. Poignant and shaming. If the great Abelard could be so afflicted, and yet uplifted somehow by the tragedy, what did it say about himself, whose affairs had never risen to anything approaching such grand passions? Beyond the reach of the firelight, Hilary wrapped his cloak around himself, remembering the passions of his life and wishing they had been somehow larger.

'I discovered I loved her,' said Abelard simply, and there was a silence because the listeners could hear the catch in his voice – the great Abelard, the Indomitable Rhinoceros, humbled by love for a mere girl.

'Where is she now, my friend?' Only a Count could have had the courage to touch so raw a nerve.

'She is gone,' he said. 'Gone to the convent in Argenteuil. She is lost – to me at least. Though not to God, which is some consolation.'

His voice trailed off and Hilary realised that, had Heloise not disappeared behind the sacred gates of Argenteuil, Abelard's encounter with Fulbert's thugs had guaranteed their separation as man and wife. It was a brutal kind of chastity, enforced by an intruder's knife.

All three stared at the fire, considering in their different ways the frailty of human hopes.

'I have reason to be suspicious of the ways of women,' said Count Hugh at last. 'There are things I cannot tell, but they inflame me even now. But you, Master Peter, you restore my faith in the power of love.'

Epiphany came all too soon, and each day that followed brought their departure closer. Hilary felt deeply uncomfortable at the prospect of leaving the safety of Provins, but it was going to be necessary some time. Not even the Count of Champagne's hospitality could go on forever. Yet he had also decided that he must fulfil his vow to John of Muchelney, and that – by doing so – he might find some protection against those who had been chasing him. But what to do next? Abelard was keen to begin asking questions immediately.

'It isn't just your case that needs attention, Hilary. Now the weather is lifting and we can travel, there are inquiries we need to make in my struggle with the man-eating monks of St-Denis and the fearsome Alberic of Reims.'

'I have been wondering whether the key doesn't lie in England,' said Hilary aware the he was not even convincing himself. 'The death of William Rufus clearly lies at the heart of the mystery, at least according to one of the two documents. It isn't that I am too frightened to stay in France, of course, it's just that England...'

'England? You will not find the answer there, Hilary, at least not now.'

Hilary felt a flash of irritation that his old teacher always seemed to know best, or at least spoke as if he did.

'I don't see why not. Both the letters in my pouch come from there.'

'Yes, but where would we start? They could have come from almost any monastery. All we know is that Aelfgar was using old-fashioned and rather ineffective ink. You should start with the person the letter was addressed to. This meeting of French nobles that Count of Champagne told us about interests me very much. I had hoped that he would overhear our discussion about Rufus and tell us what he knew, and so he did. As for your oath, Count Balwin of Flanders is probably too ill to know much, certainly to help us. He may already be dead, but Count Fulk of Anjou is very much alive.'

He banged the table with emphasis and looked challenging and triumphant. The earthenware pots shook. A small but fearful doubt began to creep into Hilary's mind.

'I did promise John of Muchelney that I would deliver the letter to Fulk if he could not. You are right, Master Peter. I should fulfil my pledge. But why do you say *I* should go; will you not accompany me?'

'I will do so with pleasure until you depart to see Count Fulk, and will meet you on your return to crack this mystery. But I will stay to complete my book, if you will let me, while you go to Jerusalem.'

Hilary guffawed. 'Jerusalem? This is no time to go on pilgrimage! Why should I go there?'

'But Hilary, have you not heard? Count Fulk has gone on crusade. He left for Jerusalem himself some months ago.'

Hilary found himself bereft of adequate words. They stared at each other for a moment as Hilary's face went whiter.

'Master Peter, I will never go there. I beg you... It is too dangerous...'

'Calm yourself, Hilary. I'm not telling you where to go, and I have some sympathy with you, I have to admit – though I would like to consult the libraries in Jerusalem, and perhaps Constantinople as well. That is where the secrets of St Denis undoubtedly lie.'

Hilary was staggered that, at this moment of extreme danger – possibly for them both – Abelard was still concerned about his row with the monks.

'This is really no time for St Denis. No, now I've escaped from the catacombs and from goodness knows what fate at the hands of the Man in Grey, I'm not going to fling myself into the maelstrom of the Mediterranean. I'm not going to trust my future to whatever pirates happen to board us or whatever twist the Scirocco chooses to entangle with our sails. I will not do it. I will send John of Mulchelney's letters by messenger. I will...'

'Calm down, Hilary. Nobody says you have to go to Jerusalem. That was my advice, that's all. Let us not mention it again, if you prefer. In the meantime, there is one person a little nearer at hand who could help us.'

Hilary began to feel almost overwhelmed by guilt. He had promised his friend to take the letter to Fulk. But he would not sail to Outremer and risk selling himself into slavery. He would not, and – after all – he made the oath to this man in return for supper and nine men's morris, nothing more. In the midst of this reverie, he realised Abelard had been outlining alternative plans.

'What I suggest is that we find my old acquaintance Suger, the man that Count Hugh of Champagne mentioned. He has gone to live in Maguelonne, a small port on the Mediterranean coast near Marseilles, in order to be near the Pope, who is as usual unable to live in Rome.

'Suger's the man we want,' he said, as if that was the end of the discussion. 'I heard some years ago that he was a friend of your Walter Tirel.'

'The man who shot Rufus?'

'Precisely. But that is a bonus. The point is that he understands, if nobody else does, the intricate networks of spies that operate in Paris. He has the ear of the king.'

'King Louis the Fat?'

'A copious ear, I admit, but he has it nonetheless. We need to know what is really happening under the facade, Hilary – who these people are who have been pursuing you and your friends? He will help us. He is a powerful man and, what is more important, an intelligent and well-informed one.'

'But is he not from St-Denis?' Once more, Master Peter allowed that triumphant look to creep over his face.

'He certainly is. In fact, I expect him to be the next abbot. But he's too intelligent to fall for this business about St Denis being what his monks claim him to be. He will help us. You'll see.'

'For goodness sake, Master Peter, is the question of who St Denis was really so important? This business of Rufus and the letter to Baldwin are life and death to me.'

A shadow of irritation crossed his brow. 'Hilary, I'm helping to save your life. Please have the goodness to allow me to save mine. I will not lose this debate. I do not lose debates.'

Something twitched in his upper lip and his dark eyes seemed to ignite a little. Hilary realised this was a moment for extreme grovelling. 'My apologies. I will do whatever I can to help. I can never thank you enough, as you know.'

Once Epiphany was over, Hilary and Abelard took their ponies, laden with generous gifts from Count Hugh, and hastened southwards to find Suger. They mingled with the other travellers, the Italian bankers, Moslem spice merchants, Gascon wine purveyors, cut-purses and fallen women who gathered on the road to the fair at Bar-sur-Aube.

'Now that we are on the road, let us review what we know,' said Abelard, as if he was addressing the whole class at Notre-Dame.

'We know that you have accidentally come into the possession of letters from a Saxon monastic called Abbot Aelfgar, which appear to be about the death of King William Rufus some eighteen winters ago,' said Abelard. 'The papers imply – stop me if you disagree, Hilary – that Aelfgar at least believes the death was suspicious, as indeed it was.'

'It was? It could have been a hunting accident.'

'A hunting accident that appears to have been predicted by a number of churchmen, who tried to warn Rufus in the days before.'

Two Italian clerics overtook them on the road, one carrying an obvious belt of money; the other a senior priest too important to carry anything.

'I believe the new Pope is now in Strasbourg. No doubt that is where they are hurrying,' said Abelard, as his pony negotiated a large muddy hole in the road. 'Listen, we have the opportunity to think a little on the road. Let us do so together.'

Once more, Hilary felt a surge of relief that Master Peter had remembered the nature of their quest. There had been moments over Christmas when he seemed so concerned about St Denis, and his identification with another bizarre figure from the previous centuries called Dionysius the Areopagite, that nothing else seemed to matter. Hilary also noticed an excited look in his eyes, though he attempted to hide it.

'I agree with Count Hugh. The death was suspicious and the man who profited most by it, with the motive to make it happen, was Rufus' brother Henry, now King of England and Duke of Normandy, was it not? On the face of it, then, Abbot Aelfgar's letter is an implied accusation against King Henry. He appears to be urging Count Baldwin or Count Fulk to use this accusation in their continuing struggle with the English and Normans, and offering them this Jewel in recompense – a jewel which is from the old crown of England or used in some way in the coronation. That is the offer, is it not? Help us and you can become King.'

'Then who killed John of Muchelney? Who wants these letters so much?'

'Good question. In fact, you have asked precisely the right question, Hilary. That would imply that those who murdered

John and have tried to capture you are the agents of King Henry – but that is where the whole issue becomes confused. I would not expect English spies to be able to come and go, still less murder with impunity, right inside the sacred portals of Notre-Dame. It doesn't make sense. Something else is happening, and Suger is the man to unravel it for us. Let us hope he has not gone to Strasbourg too.'

'I still wish we were somehow going straight to Fulk and finish this business. I did make a vow.'

'We will fulfil your vow, Hilary, I promise. Just leave this to me.'

7/Maguelonne

The road south from Champagne, 20 January 1120

Once out of Provins, on the gruelling journey south, Hilary and Abelard made their way through the forests and into the open grain fields towards Vezelay, through in-bred hamlets and sullen bug-infested inns, where they slept sometimes six to a bed in the guest quarters. They ventured through areas where the armies had crossed during the summer, and the crops had been burned. Starving villagers stared hungrily at them as they passed.

'I have heard of these people waylaying lonely travellers and eating their horses before their very eyes,' said Hilary, breaking a long silence which had lasted maybe fifteen miles.

'I'm sure there was an occasional wandering poet who's been consumed as well,' said Abelard, without looking around.

The roads in winter were muddy, rutted tracks at the best of times, and this winter was not the best of times. There had been floods just a few weeks before they set out. Some of the road had been washed away completely, which made their progress slow. In those periods when he had put his brooding aside, Abelard discoursed at length as they rode about the squandered Roman heritage, those magnificent roads that criss-crossed Europe, twenty-two feet across, carrying the legions, the ideas of Seneca and the poetry of Ovid, to the very corners of the empire.

'Here they still are, eight centuries since the end of that empire, unloved, unmended and yet still defiant,' he said. 'Do you not agree, Hilary?'

'Well, in theory I do...'

Relying on these defiant roads for a long journey was a depressing business of slow meanderings around vast potholes, the kind that could have swallowed a small cathedral, through fields and woods where the road had completely disappeared, of blisters under the saddle and rotten visits to the blacksmith with infected feet. And that was just the feet of the ponies.

Abelard carried on, not just about the mystery that lay before them, but about his dispute with the monks of St-Denis, and why St Denis himself was not the other man he called Dionysius the Areopagite. There were times when the attention of St Denis himself might have wandered.

'Nor was he the scholar we know as Pseudo-Dionysius. These other people were Platonists, Hilary. They believed that, behind the confusions of the world, lay reality – which all comes from God. They believed, as I have set out quite clearly, that God exists in everything. We are all sacred in some way. Hilary, are you listening to me?'

Hilary's attention had been diverted to an altercation beside the road with two young women who were obviously plying for custom. They were coming near to the gates of a small town and it was that time of day, with the dusk driving those still on the road to seek shelter for the night. Abelard followed his gaze in silence. He seemed to be considering his own lost capacity for love.

'Hold yourself with some dignity, Hilary,' he said. 'There is nothing life-enhancing about love glimpsed from across the street. It corrodes the soul. What was the name of your pupil in Orléans again?'

'Alys.'

'Love again across a room, wasn't it?' Hilary said nothing, irritated that he was being lectured in this way. It was outrageous to link Alys with these two scarlet women. As if Abelard could look into the soul of either of them.

'And was there not some business at Ste-Genevieve? Were you not asked to leave because of it?'

This was intolerable. 'That was a boy,' said Hilary, hoping to close down the conversation, 'and therefore purer.'

'Ha! Your reasoning takes on a bizarre serpentine life of its own. I absolve you.' It was true, of course, that Hilary's life in Paris had been frustrating and complicated. Alys had not been a hopeless infatuation, in fact the infatuation refused steadfastly to emerge on either side, but there would undoubtedly be others. He wasn't proud of them, though he was glad that at least he had managed to extract some poems out of the various experiences. He fumed next to Abelard, furious that – in the current state of their relations – he could hardly complain, still less make comparisons to Master Peter's own recent history. Even the subject of lust must now be a sensitive one.

In fact, the journey was beginning to get on his nerves, as they made their halting progress beyond the forests of Arden. His vigilance for anyone watching too closely was becoming exhausting, especially if they were dressed in grey. Nor could he rest much in the night, thanks to the nocturnal attentions of the fleas left behind in the beds by so many travellers. Often Hilary lost contact with his companion in the crowds for most of the day. He would look round occasionally and glance back at him, riding proudly by himself, lost in thought.

On one occasion, he felt a surge of affection for poor wounded Master Peter and wandered back to find him.

'Listen, Hilary, I've been thinking,' he said, as if he had been by his side throughout. 'I meant to ask you this before. How did your pursuers know you were returning to see Master Hubert at Notre-Dame? You are certain you could not have been overheard?'

'Quite certain. But he could have told anyone, couldn't he?'

'I think not. If you have repeated your conversation accurately – and you have, haven't you?' Hilary nodded. 'Then, as we discussed before, he had someone in mind to ask. And as we must assume, the person he asked, and the person who tipped off your enemies, were one and the same. That is what we shall ask Suger about but we need to ask more questions, do we not?'

Once more, a strange shiver ran down Hilary's spine. Somebody tipped off his pursuers, perhaps even knowing that Master Hubert would be killed as a result and that he himself would be framed with the murder. Somebody knew. Somebody he might even know himself. It was not just an accidental remark that let to Hubert's death. It was deliberate.

'But how can we make inquiries from here? I can hardly wander back to Paris with half of Europe looking for me.'

'Well,' said Abelard, addressing him directly and with a triumphant look. 'I wondered if my old patron might put some resources in that direction. I have had no contact with him since I left Paris, but he might be willing to help.'

Hilary's heart gave a sudden leap. 'Stephen de Garlande? The King's Chancellor?' Would Master Peter really allow his most powerful connections to become involved? Would they really act on his behalf?

'Exactly. I thought he could send one of his messengers, just to ask discretely around Notre-Dame.'

'Master Peter, you are right. As soon as we get to Maguelonne, perhaps you could write and ask him?'

'I'm glad you think so, because I've already written to him – and asked him to send his answer to us at Suger's house.'

'*Non credo!* You astonish me! When did you do that?'

'Before we left Provins. I hope his reply will be waiting for us. Then, according to what he says, you can decide whether to follow Fulk out to Outremer and Jerusalem.'

Hilary's heart sank again. 'Master Peter, I can't say any more clearly than I have. I would rather take my chances with the Man in Grey than with the pirates and storms and deserts and vagabonds.'

There was silence again between them.

'I realise that must seem cowardly of me, and ...'

'Not at all, Hilary. Not at all. That was just my advice for solving the mystery. Nothing more. I have a strong sense that this Jewel they speak of is important to this business, and if Hubert says that it was taken to Jerusalem, perhaps you should take yourself there also.'

Silence that followed, as their palfreys negotiated the potholes. Master Peter was at least taking their quest seriously, but whose quest was it exactly? Should he not at least have asked his companion's advice on the matter before writing? Or was that unworthy and ungrateful of him to think it?

'This Suger,' said Hilary, careful to avoid expressing any criticism. 'Are you sure he'll help us? I know he is a friend of Tirel's, and he could certainly shed light on Rufus' murder and pull strings on my behalf. But will he? I mean, whose side is he actually on?'

'Knowing Suger, he has three passions – King Louis, St Denis and himself,' said Abelard with confidence. 'Louis the Fat is currently engaged in a frustrating war with Henry of England, who has to be chief suspect if there was any plot to kill his brother Rufus. Anything that looks bad for Henry must look good for Louis. Suger will come through. You will see.'

By the time they stood outside Suger's house in Maguelonne, with its warm yellow stone neighbours clustered round the wharves, and the healing air of the Mediterranean blowing in their faces, it was as if they had walked straight into summer. There it was, chirruping in the undergrowth.

'Look at that, Hilary. The sea of Caesar, Odysseus and Hannibal. What a sight.'

It had been a long way from Provins to the country where they say *oc* for *oui* and yes, with their tapestries and songs, perfumes and wine. It was a particularly long way by pony, but Abelard's palfrey became lame outside Lyons and they had abandoned the roads, and taken a ship carrying cloth down the Rhône, past Tournon and Avignon. The great blue skies and huge horizons made Hilary feel safer, while his teacher sat on deck making notes from the great tomes he carried with him, explaining – when anyone interrupted him – that he was adding to his book for students by setting out the contradictions in thinking between the teachings of the Fathers of the Church. Quite how this would help students was beyond Hilary, but he felt inadequate for the argument. Abelard worked every day until the darkness prevented him.

It had occurred to Hilary as they progressed south that, now he seemed to be out of immediate danger, he could simply remain as Ambrose the Carpenter and live in the Oc Country with its sand-coloured stones and deep red wine, under the protection of the Count of Toulouse whose land it was. There was a matter of the carpentry of course, but nobody seemed to work down here. Yet Abelard was adamant that they must press on. Still, he had his own reasons for seeing Suger, Hilary thought. No doubt he hoped the old reptile would play referee between himself and the mad monks of St-Denis.

The truth was that Abelard seemed to believe that Suger could rise above petty disputes, and understand what he had been trying to explain. Hilary was less sure about that, and when he finally stood outside Suger's house in the small port he had gone to live in – the Pope lived there after all – he felt much less sure about everything. They had been directed to the house, right by the harbour, by a dour-looking innkeeper who looked as though he had never done a day's work in his life. 'It's the house on the end,' he said, 'but you won't find him there.'

Abelard ignored him, and led his new pony up to a palatial residence that would not have looked out of place in Paris. It was by far the wealthiest-looking building overlooking the harbour. Hilary realised it must then have overshadowed the Pope's house. Trust Suger to install himself in such luxury that it outdid the successor to St Peter himself. Unfortunately, the building looked decidedly locked.

The main door to the courtyard was also closed. There was no sound from inside, no sheets on the line, no pigs at the kitchen door, no activity, no cooking, no coming and going. Nothing. There were signs of recent occupation but grass was growing in a disconcerting way around the main door. Their sense of achievement from having made the journey was beginning to dissipate in anti-climax. Abelard marched up to the window and shouted inside. As they waited in vain for some kind of reply, the truth suddenly struck Hilary.

'Of course! The Pope is dead, isn't he. Suger came here because the Pope was here. If the new Pope is in Strasbourg, Suger will be in Strasbourg, won't he?'

Abelard gave him a withering glance. 'Of course.'

'You mean you realised that all along, and we still came here? I don't understand.' Sometimes the working of Master Peter's brain, vast as it no doubt was, left Hilary confused.

'Of course Suger was unlikely to be here. But the reply to my letter to Stephen de Garlande *will* be here, and that is what is most important. I specifically asked him to write to me here.'

Hilary's mood plummeted as he realised they had made the

journey in vain. 'Well, it's not going to help us much if the letter is inside and we are outside and there is nobody to let us in.'

Abelard ignored the note of irritation and peered in through the window. The wind was getting up and Hilary felt a cool gust on his face and dust in his eyes.

'It is strange,' he said finally. 'There are no servants about. Has Suger abandoned the house altogether? Peculiar.'

'Very peculiar,' said Hilary irritably. 'Where are we going to now?'

'We will have some dinner at the inn we passed on the way into town by the gate, and wait until it is dark. Then we will have a look inside.'

'Break in? Are you insane?'

'Hilary, you're going to need a bit more faith in me. We are going to climb into the home of the future abbot of St-Denis as efficiently as I climbed out of St-Denis itself. We are not leaving this town until I've either got that reply to my letter or I'm sure that Suger has it with him.'

Hilary could see he was right. They had travelled for getting on for three weeks. There was no way they could just turn around and go back empty-handed. So they repaired to the inn, Abelard to lay out his studies in front of him, Hilary to consume a large quantity of ale to quench the rising tension, while the wind stirred itself along the harbour wall and paraded its capacity for mischief through the windows of the inn. Hilary peered out during the anonymous stew and heard the first pattering of rain on the dust. A gust of wind blew grit from the street into his face. They were clearly in for a storm, but at least it would disguise their visit.

Some bells later that evening, echoing over the wall of the nearby convent, they walked slowly around the courtyard wall of Suger's house in the dark and now driving rain. More innocent souls were safely at compline. Hilary was trying to persuade himself that this small act of burglary in a good cause was nothing to someone who had escaped from the Notre-Dame catacombs. It wasn't as if they were going to do anything except collect a letter addressed to them. Probably Suger himself would have welcomed them in to do just that, if he was not on the trail of the latest pontiff.

By the time they reached the great dark house, they were extremely wet. Sure enough, there was a gate onto the lane at the back that was warped and rusted, and a sharp push gave them entry into Suger's courtyard.

'Close it quietly behind you, Hilary. We'll make for the kitchen and borrow some candles.'

They were in luck. The first door led to what was clearly the kitchen and there was a lamp hanging by the fireplace. There is no sadder sight than a dank, damp fire with the rain outside. Wiping the water from their eyes, they recovered for a moment. It took five minutes to light it with a tinderbox, and their long shadows flickered across the walls in a yellow glow as they tiptoed through the empty house. It was a relief to be out of the rain and the wailing wind, banging anything loose in the street against the walls. They were careful not to stray too close to windows on the side nearest the street, in case the candlelight in an empty house attracted anybody's attention, but the footsteps that went by outside sounded like people running for shelter. There was the occasional sound of drunken sailors passing on their way to the harbour wall.

Suger's home was sparsely furnished, as you would expect from an Augustinian monk. The fire in the hall had clearly not been lit for some time. A narrow flight of stone steps led to an upper storey with two rooms. The first room contained a bed and what appeared to be a whip. Abelard held it for a moment, thoughtfully. 'Suger is a great disciplinarian,' he whispered. 'He subdues his own flesh as well as those around him.'

The second room was full of books piled on the long table which ran down the middle of the room.

'*Inveni! Id est!*' said Abelard. 'I think this is it. Suger's place of study. This is where he weaves his webs of gossip. Suger is a great intriguer, in his own interest of course. You can smell it in the air.'

The only thing Hilary could smell was the damp and ink, and the briny stench of the raging sea on the wind, but he said nothing. Abelard was already deep in the books.

'Yes, I believe this is the volume that had been removed from the St-Denis library. I guessed it would be here. Hilary, I believe this will provide me with some of the evidence that I need about Dionysius the Areopagite. Now all I need....'

'What about the letter?' Hilary was increasingly nervous being inside this man's house without his permission, and was afraid their light would be visible from the harbour. As it was, their shadows now flickered in monstrous shapes on the opposite wall, visible to anybody in the street foolhardy enough to venture out in the wind and rain. He sheltered the precious candle flame behind his hand for fear the next gust through the window would extinguish it.

'The letter, yes. Suger is an organised man. It will be here somewhere.'

'You don't think he will have forwarded it to you somewhere else?'

'Yes, but where would he think of? He must know I'm not at St-Denis any more. No, it'll be here. Can you see any document trunks?'

The room was meagre in the extreme, apart from the dust on the books and the scholar's goose feathers and ink, and the stubs of countless candles that sustained him through the winter evenings, waiting for the Pope to call.

'No. You don't think it's strange, Master Peter, that the servants are absent?' The silence of the house was beginning to unnerve him.

'He probably took them with him. Ouch! Put the candle this way – ah – this could be it.'

Sure enough, in the corner by the window, was an old oak box, about two cubits long with heavy black metal edging. It looked like the Tower of London.

'Bring the lamp lower, Hilary. No, lower, over here.' He brought down the light and was distressed to see his teacher reach into his knapsack and pull out a small knife.

'You're surely not going to break the lock?'

'Honestly, Hilary, you are being squeamish today. No, I'm going to fiddle a bit....' There was a snap and the lock burst open. Abelard lifted the lid. It was full of scrolls of paper in no particular order. Hilary lifted the lamp a little higher, dripping wax down into the papers. Sure enough, on top, there was one marked along the outside 'Abelard'.

With mounting excitement, he watched while Abelard opened it onto the table, and held it down with a book. They both read it as the candle flickered above them in the wind:

> Stephen de Garlande, Chancellor to his highness King Louis VI of the Franks, to Master Peter Abelard, sometime Canon of Notre-Dame, greetings.
>
> My love in Christ and good wishes to you, and my gratitude for your letter and request. I must tell you, however, that I am unable to do as you ask. You are dabbling in matters you do not understand, Master Peter. I urge you for your own safety to desist and return to your studies. Do not burn yourself through ignorance of what

you seek. These tragic matters are not for philosophers...'

'Damn,' said Abelard simply. 'This is peculiar, Hilary. I confess, I don't understand. Come, roll up the letter and I will find this other volume and we will be on our way.'

Bitterly disappointed, and increasingly nervous, Hilary rolled up the letter as fast as he could. But shaking with nerves, he dropped it accidentally between the box and the table, and bent down to retrieve it. It was only because of this small accident that the light shone once more in Suger's document box, and he glimpsed what he thought was Abelard's name again. He looked again. Sure enough, there was another paper with his name on.

'Peace, Master Peter, stay a moment. There is another.'

Once more he reached into the box, unrolled the paper and laid it on the desk. Once more there was silence between them, except for the noise of the rain battering the stones outside and the higher notes of a tempestuous wind:

> 'Stephen de Garlande, Chancellor of France, to our much valued and trusted Suger, of the Abbey of St-Denis, now in Maguelonne, greetings.
>
> This is to let you know that Master Peter Abelard is on his way to see you, and that he remains under my protection. He has asked me to inquire into the circumstances of Master Hubert's death in Notre-Dame, a tragedy of which you have no doubt heard. I have indeed inquired, long before his request, but I have refused him the details he seeks.
>
> As you must know, our knowledge of Master Hubert's contact with the fugitive Hilary, called the Englishman, came to us through our particular friend who was visiting Notre-Dame at the time. Master Peter has requested that

we furnish him with this identity, and once again I have told him he is meddling in matters he cannot understand. If you have the opportunity of conversation with him, I hope you will reinforce this message. As you must understand, it is imperative that Master Peter's talent for mischief and interference is not directed at this matter for reasons that you know as well as I do. He also asks about the Great Jewel. Please say nothing of this to him.

He is accompanied by this Hilary, and I must ask you to detain him in the name of the King. Remove the documents that he carries with him and deliver them to me by royal messenger. Master Peter's safety must be guaranteed. The fate of this Hilary is for you to decide, but it would certainly be inconvenient if he were to return to Paris....'

They read this terrifying letter together, the candle between them. The wind screamed outside. Hilary looked at Abelard as he reached the end. He was staring out of the window.

'You know what this means,' said Hilary. 'It means they knew we were coming.'

At that moment, Hilary heard a distant crunch of breaking earthenware, which sounded as if it was in the house. They both froze.

'I think it's time we left. Let me just find this remaining book.'

'Are you mad? They'll be coming up the stairs any minute!'

Hilary glanced out of the window and kicked himself. If he had not been so engrossed in the letter, he would have seen the lights and flares in the distance along the road. Abelard was peering at the spines of ancient volumes and heaving them on top of each other to give himself space.

'Master Peter, I beg you!'

'It's no use. It isn't here. Come on. Extinguish the candle. I think we passed a smaller flight of stairs down to the courtyard.'

Hilary felt his throat tighten with fear as they made their way as quietly as they could onto the corridor. There was the noise downstairs of creaking hinges and stifled thuds which seemed to imply the presence of people who do not yet know they have been heard. As they reached the top of the stone step used by the servants, he could hear the heavy sound of footfalls and intense whispered orders from below.

'I knew this was a bad idea,' he whispered as he hurried down the stairs to the pantry. Abelard ignored him and Hilary could hear his soft padding behind on the stone.

'You have got the letters, haven't you?'

Hilary's heart went cold for a moment. He had put them down to adjust his grip on Abelard's stolen volume. 'Surely we don't need them now?'

'Of course we need them, you fool. We need to study them more closely. Give me the book. Go and get them back, quick! Give me the candle. I'll wait here.'

There was an urgent flurry while they exchanged books and the now extinguished candle. Hilary agonised about the term 'fool'. It wasn't fair. Abelard was, apparently, under the protection of the Chancellor of France. He was emphatically not. It was all very well for him to call anyone 'fool'. Abelard didn't have the possibility of a noose around his neck within the next hour. His mind racing along these lines, Hilary dashed back up the narrow stairs and into the room where Suger kept his papers.

By now he could hear heavy footsteps in the hall downstairs, and the sound of even heavier rain now sweeping through the town, with flapping canvas and banging ropes from the quay. With no light, the letters were not immediately obvious, but he found the two rolls on the end of the table and grabbed them. Splashes of water flicked into his face as he passed the small window outside the study in search of the stairs, aware that he had only a moment before his pursuers arrived. There was a clatter from the main staircase. As he reached the first step, a new glow of candlelight suddenly suffused the corridor. Without being able to stop himself, he turned around and, to his horror, there was a face emerging from below.

Hilary's heart almost stopped, but the instant he saw him – and they seemed to become aware of each other at the same moment – the wind lashed through the window behind them, put out the candle and plunged them into complete blackness. Hilary could hear the man shout and stumble. At the same time, he flung himself down the stone stairs in front of him, and plunged into Abelard at the bottom.

'Hold onto me, Hilary,' he hissed. 'I believe I've found a back way.' He pulled him down a small corridor leading to the kitchen and then an even smaller entranceway that led to a yard. Two minutes later, they were into the driving rain, across the yard and over the fence and once more in the street, brushing the water out of our faces.

'Did they see you?'

'I think so, yes. Come on, we've got no time now,' Hilary urged him.

'Hold on.' Abelard reached down into the dust, pulled out a stone the size of his fist, and taking a short run, he flung it over the house and into the courtyard. Hilary could hear the faint crunch on the other side of the house.

'They probably won't hear above the rain but, if they do, it will give us a few more minutes. Come on now. Down to the quay.'

They ran towards the harbour. Once they had made it out of the immediate vicinity of Suger's house, they walked in a more dignified way across the main street, glancing back at the small posse of soldiers at the entrance to the building, and the pinpricks of lamps now animating the windows of the house.

Abelard's ruse seemed to have worked. There were no signs of pursuit until they had reached the sea, to find the small boats there desperately hauling down their sails in the face of the rising storm.

'You're mad. I'm not going out in this. I value my life.'

In the first boat they came to, Abelard marched on ahead. Hilary could see the bearded seaman gesticulating as they argued. He was clearly refusing to set sail. It was the same with the second. Hilary could hear almost nothing above the screeching wind, but it seemed pretty clear that nothing would induce them to set sail. Who could blame them? He was doubtful of surviving the experience myself.

Hilary glanced back through the rain to see the torches streaming out of Suger's house in the distance. 'We can pay well,' he yelled at the next boat in line.

'I'll take you. It'll cost you, but I'll take you.'

They both swung round. It was a tall bearded matelot with a weather-beaten face. 'There's no northerly wind That's the only one which has beaten me yet.'

'Can you set off immediately? I mean this very moment.'

'Running away, are you?' said the man pointing towards a tiny fishing boat with the single mast and the sails furled. 'I'll ask no questions. I don't know where you're going, but I'm going to Marseilles.'

'Marseilles is good,' Hilary shouted above the wind. 'Just get under way, as quickly as you can.'

They both climbed down the quay and into his boat, heaving Abelard's new collection of books. Hilary realised they had been removed from Suger's house. Hilary's own meagre belongings had increased since his flight from the inn, but they were negligible in comparison. Even so, the boat was so small that it seemed an imposition bringing their luggage. Where would it go? Where would they sit? The two-man crew were staring at them as they hurriedly undid one small sail. In a moment, Hilary looked back and found they were already yards from the quayside.

'Hold on, heads down!' shouted their rescuer, and the boom swung round, the boat leaned over, and Hilary ducked just in time. They were away. He looked back to see a crowd of men with torches gathering on the wharf.

'They seem to be shouting at us, Hilary,' Abelard bellowed in his ear above the noise of the rain and wind. 'What do you think they're saying?'

'They're probably telling us we'll be drowned.'

'I think that is the least of it.'

They cleared the headland in the dark at high speed, with the wind behind them, driving them eastwards along the coast. The fisherman sat calmly at the tiller as if this was how he spent every night, as perhaps he did. Hilary drowsed a little after their intense evening's work, hardly aware any more of the rain on his face and the howling in his ears. But after some considerable time, a wave slapped him in the nose and he woke. For the next few hours, he clung to the sides, wiping the salt out of his eyelids and mouth, praying once more to St Ambrose. There was no moon and no stars, just the roar of the wind and the heaving sea.

There was one moment when the boat seemed about to heel over completely. He looked back to see their helmsman struggling in the dark, and next to him in the prow of the boat, wrapped in an old sheepskin, Abelard slept, his head on one of the books he had purloined from Suger.

In the darkest part of the night, Hilary could stand it no longer. He poked Abelard in the ribs, and immediately regretted the intimacy. Then he stirred and his eyes opened. 'Master Peter, wake up,' he shouted next to his face. 'How can you sleep when we're about to be drowned? Wake up and pray with me.'

Abelard looked up, a little bleary eyed, and looked at Hilary as if to ask, if he could have made himself heard, why he was so frightened. Then he rose, and Hilary stared open-mouthed as he clung to the mast, the salt wind attempting to tear his hair from his scalp, and waved his arm across the waters ahead of them. He shouted something, but Hilary could barely hear him. And then, miraculously, the wind did indeed begin to slacken its insanity. Some moments later Hilary realised that the sea and the rain were also calmer.

'Master Peter,' he breathed, astonished, as the rain lifted and he glimpsed the stars for the first time. 'What kind of man are you?'

Abelard laughed. 'Don't flatter me, Hilary. A bit of luck, that's all. Now ask our friend at the tiller how long before we reach Marseilles.'

The fisherman could hear them now, and he gestured ahead in the dark, and turning round again Hilary could see that the dawn was beginning to break ahead of them. It was barely night at all. There, in the morning light, were the distant walls of an ancient city, and the sight of masts and sails in an enormous port, like nothing he had seen before. He and Abelard stood shoulder to shoulder in the boat, holding the mast, and stared as the light grew ahead of them.

'You did bring those letters, didn't you, in all that chaos?' He nodded. 'You see, Hilary, I want to know who the Chancellor refers to in his letter – the man he says that Master Hubert spoke to before he died, and who he clearly hints was the one who betrayed to him to your pursuers. He says he was visiting Notre-Dame at the time.'

'You mean, Master Hubert wasn't betrayed by someone working for the King of England, he was betrayed by someone working for the King of France?'

'Exactly.'

'For God's sake,' said Hilary in confusion and despair. 'Didn't we assume that the papers in my pouch could only be a threat to King Henry of England, because they imply that he was involved in some kind of plot to kill his brother in the New Forest? Isn't that what you said? Didn't you say that the men who killed John of Muchelney, and who chased me across France, were agents of the English king?'

'I did, I know. To be honest, Hilary, I think we need to do some re-consideration. The basic facts are the same. The conclusions we have to draw shouldn't logically be any different. What we have to ask is this: what is it that is so important that both the kings of England and France – who are, after all, at war with each other – have to co-operate? What secret is so frightening for them that those who advise them have to put aside their differences? Whatever it is you have around your neck is very much deeper than I supposed. That is the conclusion I draw from the letter from Stephen de Garlande. I should have known I could not trust him absolutely. I apologise for that.'

Hilary's heart sank again. He had felt so hopeful once the light of dawn had seeped into the sky. 'It would be deeper. It *would* be.'

By now the harbour of Marseilles was visible, and the small white houses reaching down to the boats drawn up on the beach, and some huge ships anchored further out. The scene was one of dawn activity that goes with the early morning tide, not something he had never seen before in the life of a wandering scholar. The early sunshine was breaking through in slants through the clouds.

'No, there's no doubt about it, Hilary. Something else is going on here which I don't understand. Hold on, there's something happening at the quay?'

Hilary looked more closely. They were only some twenty cubits or so away now, and he could see that they were the object of attention from many of those on the harbour wall. Some of them were pointing. He checked and checked again. There was no doubt that some of those were also soldiers. The early morning light was flashing on an iron helmet. Then he saw him, horrible in the dawn, his own personal demon, a man in grey with the familiar blue motif. The man he had seen last by the gates of Orléans.

'Oh no, Master Peter, I believe....'

They were now just cubits away from the stone wooden harbour, and he caught the man's gaze. The Man in Grey stared knowingly back, almost friendly in his intimacy, as if he knew Hilary completely, but he imagined there was a menace behind it. Hilary stood rooted to the spot, unable to wrench his eyes away.

When he pulled himself free and turned round, Abelard had already persuaded the fisherman to turn the tiller. Both men ducked to avoid the heavy boom swinging against their skulls, and sat quickly down as the boat turned awkwardly against the wind. Hilary felt a bang on his temple and was momentarily dazed.

When he recovered some minutes later, they were alongside the nearest and most active ship. Abelard appeared to be aboard already and was giving instructions for his books and bags to be carried up. 'Here, Hilary, reach up to me. My friend, give my companion some help, will you!'

Seconds later, Hilary was sprawling on an unfamiliar deck and, as he got to his feet, he could see the crew all around him hauling ropes and the great striped sail was reaching slowly up the mast and filling with wind. Other people with many more belongings than them were leaning over the sides. In the distance, he could see the Man in Grey shouting and gesticulating in their direction, and a handful of armed men hurriedly commandeering a boat. They struggled with the oars and came inexorably towards the ship, but Hilary and his new ship-mates had begun to move. The prow reached up and the sail billowed, pulled tight at the end of the triangle by a gang of hardened seamen.

Hilary looked down and saw the sea was moving in bubbles along the side, and the soldiers in the boat – which had nearly reached below him – began to fade into the distance as they accelerated towards the open sea. He could hear the ripple of water running underneath the hull.

'You see Hilary, we are safe again, and we have Suger's books and letters too. You can relax. They can't touch you here.'

'They can't now. But they are magicians. They have powers beyond yours and mine. How could there have been soldiers in Suger's house and someone also waiting for us here? Explain it, please, for God's sake, tell me he isn't a demon of the air.'

'I don't remember any mention of demons of the air in the New Testament, Hilary. There's no need to dramatise the situation. The storm must have delayed the boat and, in any case, I believe these were different soldiers to the ones we encountered last night. They must have guessed from the start that we were on their way to Marseilles. Still, we have escaped their clutches, and for some time. We have happened upon the first pilgrim boat of the season. I fear we have spent most of your remaining silver pieces, but we are on our way.'

'Pilgrim boat? Where to? Where are we going?'

'To the holy sepulchre, of course. We are going to Jerusalem.'

The day was becoming an emotional rollercoaster, but this was a real shock. The spray splashed his face as the speed picked up. Hilary could already see Marseilles in the distance behind them.

A group of fellow passengers were gathering round the mast mainmast and were singing 'Help us, Holy Sepulchre' which added to the sense of foreboding.

'For God's sake, I never wanted to go to sea. Certainly not to Palestine.' A profound misery descended over Hilary. He did not articulate it, for fear of disappointing his teacher, as visions of pirates and tempests and pagans swum before his mind, not to mention his ever-present memory of one particular storm in the English Channel that he was lucky to survive – and England too. Perhaps he would never go home after all. He sat on the deck in despair, unable to summon up the energy to protest. Every wave on the increasing swell reminded him that he was heading for another kind of bizarre demise.

'Peace, Hilary, we will unweave this conundrum, believe me,' said Abelard, kneeling beside him. 'We will go back and unravel the mystery and restore your name and mine. We will go to Jerusalem where I have an idea that will, I believe, provide us both with the key.'

PART II

1/Jerusalem

Acre Harbour, 6 May 1120

The heat hit Hilary like a great warm breath, but it was the blinding light that really took him by surprise. The sunshine was obvious from the deck of their ship, but the sheer intensity of it when it was reflected off a hundred white walls, and back from the very dust on the ground, was like nothing he had ever experienced. 'I don't know if I will be able to see after an afternoon of this,' he said. 'It is like living in the heart of the sun.'

But Abelard had other matters on his mind, staring into the middle distance as if his gaze could pierce the city walls. The long voyage and the heat of the city after two months at sea brought on a kind of dreamlike state for both of them as they stood in the main street in the crusader city of Acre, with its dust and pigs, unsure how to proceed. Hilary, in particular wanted to eat more than he had ever felt in his life before. Somehow the relief at having set foot on dry land – and this land was seriously dry – had brought on a terrific hunger.

'Master Peter, may I suggest that we should fill our stomachs before proceeding?'

There was no reply. There they were amongst the bazaars and camels, and the huge numbers of Italian prostitutes in gaggles at every street corner, but Abelard seemed in no hurry for anything. He stared into the middle distance.

'You know, Hilary, I never realised that what marks out these Platonists, and the murderous monks of St-Denis, is that – for them – a king must be a king. It is a mystical business for them...'

The heat seemed to cut through Hilary's skin like a knife. The sweat poured freely off his face. The dust seemed to be filling his lungs. How did human beings live here? Yet it seemed clear that, not only did they live there successfully, but the detritus of Europe seemed to have been washed up there, shouting out their slogans and meandering through the dusty streets, with the rotting carcases and the flies. Everything seemed to be on sale, from bizarre and unearthly fruit and vegetables, to the strange coloured fish, to the hastily manufactured pieces of the True Cross, to the bodies of young women from here to Stockholm. And amongst all this selling, the customers fingered their wares, or slumped in the sand, or pushed their way aggressively through the crowds.

'Hilary, we must find ourselves a guide to accompany us to Jerusalem. Otherwise our journey is going to be in vain. Even so, I believe the King is in the north, which may mean that his barons are there as well.'

Hilary stared at his master through the sweat. 'How do you know all this? We have only just set foot in this pestilential country.'

'I believe Our Lord felt comfortable here. I see no reason why you should not.'

As they made their way down away from the slaughterhouses by the docks, they encountered a dark skinned boy, bronzed in the sun, wearing britches and a belt, with his hair tied back. He was looking uncertain. Something about the boy struck Hilary immediately as incongruous.

'Let me guide you,' said the boy in perfect French. 'I can guide you through the city, show you where to eat, show you the bath-houses. I'm a very good guide. Ask anyone.' Hilary saw a bracelet with a fish charm around the boy's wrist.

'Are you a Muslim?' asked Abelard, peering at him fascinated.

'No, no, no, for the love of Christ,' said the boy.

'Pity. Never mind – come with us. We can do with your services.'

'We are on our way to Jerusalem,' said Hilary. 'Can you take us that far?'

The boy looked nervous, but followed them anyway, his faded brown robe dragging in the dust. 'Maybe I do need to go back to Jerusalem,' he said. 'Shall I tell you what these buildings are? That's the Florentine gate,' he said, pointing out the defended gaps in the walls along the street. 'That's the Genoese gate. See, the banner of St Lawrence.'

'What's that one?'

'That is the accursed Venetians.'

'I see that, now the Muslims are defeated, there's a new infidel,' said Hilary. 'How much easier it always is to fight each other. As I know to my cost.'

'Come, Hilary, it's a mere twenty years since the crusade. It takes time to sort these things out. There are great hopes of the new King of Jerusalem, I believe.'

The traders were now beginning to pack up for the afternoon. The smell was an overwhelming mixture of urine and rotting meat, and of intoxicating spices and unimaginable fruits as well. It was as if the very air was thicker here in the heart of the city of Acre, surrounded by forbidding city walls even within this subdivided city. Hilary was still wearing his cloak and was now profoundly uncomfortable. He had become used to the cool sea breeze but, since being rowed ashore that morning, he had entered an oriental dream world where the atmosphere was more like molten treacle.

'What are those ungodly yellow things like bent yellow moons?' said Hilary, as they passed another market stall of ginger, cinnamon, pomegranates, figs and nutmeg. A camel nuzzled his head in a disconcerting way.

'They are apples of paradise,' said the boy.

'I believe they are considered a delicacy in Granada,' said Abelard. 'You have to peel off a thick skin like an ox-hide before you get to the fruit.'

Hilary suppressed a flash of irritation that Master Peter should know about apples of paradise when he had barely travelled outside the libraries of Paris and Brittany. But so God has ordered the world. He must accept it, he told himself. All he really needed was a huge plate of boeuf bourgignon.

'Follow me,' said the boy. 'We will join a convoy through the desert.'

Going to sea had always been an uncertain business, hugging the coast like a child clings to its mother, landing where possible at night, watching for the lamps lit for mariners in the ancient churches and temples on the land, then letting go of all control in the occasional storms – when the main task of the crew was simply to pray with all their might. For pilgrims, of course, the terrors of the voyage held their own reward. For reluctant pilgrims like Hilary, the voyage was particularly exhausting and corrosive of faith and purpose.

Yet nearly eight weeks on the deck of the *Grace of God* seemed to have suited Abelard, as he sat in the corner by the quarter deck with his books, writing away, cursing the occasional wave which blotted out his work. For Hilary, Abelard's calmness and ability to concentrate made the journey even more frustrating. It meant safety from his pursuers, but it meant other more ever-present dangers from pirates to storms. He dreamed nervously of sea monsters and ancient classical gods of the ocean, with their tridents and their sacrifices. They had barely been out of sight of land during the whole journey, except for crossing the Adriatic, or the amidst the storms among the Greek islands, but – when the wind and the waves made work impossible – Abelard had packed his books back into the box, covered them with oxhide and slept.

Night after night, as the ship's passengers gathered on the dock of some small harbour for dinner, he felt the ship was taking him further from any kind of resolution of his nightmare – or any decision about where to go or who to be. It had also been debilitatingly cold, especially on the first leg of the voyage from Marseilles to Genoa.

He was wrapped in the cloak he had been given in Provins, but even huddling next to the ship's brazier was barely enough to stop his fingers going numb in the evenings and early mornings. It was warmer to pace about the deck, getting in the way of the crew, and helping keep a look out for the next coastal temple which would be lit to guide mariners in the dusk or fog.

Sometimes, all he could do was to stretch out below, next to the green-faced pilgrims and fortune-hunters, and give way to seasickness, and listen to the hymns of his fellow pilgrims.

'What are they singing now?' Abelard asked him on the final leg of the voyage, as they swept past Tyre – still in Muslim hands – on the final leg of the voyage.

' "Help us Holy Sepulchre" again.'

'I suppose you're right. I had hoped it was something different at last.'

Hilary had liked the crew, and had come to understand their Provençal language, but he had failed to strike up much of a rapport with his fellow passengers.

'They seem to fall into two categories,' said Abelard one morning, with the spray on his face, stealing a moment away from his personal library.

'I know. Religious maniacs and thieves.'

'I was thinking more along the lines of Aristotelians and Platonists. It's the way they deal with the weather. Half of them feel safe enough wrapped in a sense of divine destiny. The other half just panic. Some of them panic so much that it would make a mermaid seasick.'

Both men had endured more than their share of seasickness, but by the time they hit the worst storm in the Adriatic, and limped into Ragusa harbour for repairs to the mast, their stomachs had begun to recover. Some of the pilgrims continued puking down below for the whole eight weeks. Some felt too ill to come ashore, even for mass and had their cold dinner carried back to them every night. For some reason, it was the religious maniacs who seemed least able to deal with the weather.

It seemed to Hilary as if a whole lifetime had passed until their ship finally slid past the Tower of Flies at the entrance to the harbour at Acre, and the great chain was lowered to let them pass. Only an hour later, he and Abelard had heaved the box of books through the Court of the Chain – the customs house – and into the city, along with the other pilgrims, from Genoa Pisa, Florence, Antwerp and Southampton, swarming down the rue de la Boucherie.

Now they followed their guide, along with the other pilgrims, to a huge cookshop on the Galilee Road and then, after a short rest, out onto the coast road in a small convoy of carts, camels and mules which headed south along the coast road. It was heavy going, village after village, as sullen and hostile looking peasants watched them pass. Hilary imagined them sharpening their knives once they were out of sight.

The pilgrims from Jaffa, when they joined forces, were even more heterogeneous than those on the ship. There were Germans, Sicilians and Catalans. There were people from the far north who ate stockfish and spoke in a language neither could decipher. There were even a few Danes. 'I heard your native tongue spoken just now,' said Master Peter, breaking his usual silence which he reserved for these journeys. Hilary looked around with excitement, but it was hard to pick out a few English speakers in this melee of European voices. Monks from a mysterious order gave out blankets and water. The crowd began to steal themselves for the sand and heat. The wagons lurched. Hilary checked round to see if the boy and the mule carrying Abelard's books were still following along behind, and saw behind them a human river streaming across the sand. The boy seemed at ease with the mule, he noticed.

Towards the end of the third day, they approached a village of sandy coloured buildings, almost rising by themselves out of an oasis. The crowd seemed to perk up at the sight and surge forward with more hopeful steps. Jerusalem was not far now. Perhaps tomorrow, perhaps the day after, said a knowledgeable fellow traveller. There even seemed to be a glint in the distance between the scrubby grey bushes that promised liquid. Hilary's mouth began to water. As they approached the village, the buildings began to take on that disintegrating appearance of abandonment. Doors had fallen off hinges. There was no human sign at all.

'You know, I think it's deserted,' said Hilary. 'Why would a place like this, next to water, have nobody living here? I don't understand.'

'Don't you understand anything, Hilary? Our Christian armies were not exactly peaceable when they arrived here twenty years ago. There are many places where there is just nobody left. Do you know how many they slaughtered when Jerusalem fell?'

'How many?'

'I don't know either, but there were said to be none left alive.' He broke off and stared into the distance.

The boy stared open-mouthed at him. 'My lord, what you say is true.'

It was at noon the next day that they finally glimpsed the David Tower in the distance, and marched triumphantly through the great gates and into Jerusalem. Hilary was taken unawares by the experience, all the more intense because of the wait, and wondered why his companion seemed not to be.

'Are you not impressed, Master Peter? To see the very city of our Lord, where Solomon reigned and Christ was crucified?' Hilary was sweating profusely, but deeply moved. The very stones seemed to be some kind of sacrament, despite the cacophony of different voices demanding custom from the market stalls and stench of camel's urine.

'It is remarkable, certainly. But I can't forget that these stones have blood soaked into them.'

'Indeed, but the blood of infidels, Master Peter.'

'The blood of everyone. It is holy, yes, but it is also a fearful place. I prefer to build my holy sites somewhere safer. Inside my own conscience.'

Hilary noticed that the boy was particularly nervous, but gave no explanation. Hilary was also confused about Abelard's attitude. Did he mean there was no difference between Christian and blood and the blood of pagans? If so, why mount a crusade at all? Why then venerate this city, he wondered? But he felt too hot to argue.

It was anyway time to divide their forces. Abelard would seek out a kinsman of the Count of Champagne, Hugues de Payens, in the hope that he might provide them with lodgings. Hilary was to find the whereabouts of Fulk of Anjou so that they could beg for an audience and finally to hand over the letters that still hung around his neck. They paid the boy handsomely and sent him on his way. He hesitated before leaving.

Hilary reminded himself that Fulk of Anjou held the key to the riddle. He would tell him his story, hand over the letter, and then

– at last, his ordeal would be at an end. He could go home and take up his uncertain life where he had left it, along with Alys, somewhere in the Loire. He breathed a sigh of relief, put his hand in the pond by the gate and used the water to cool his brow. If the past few months had taught him anything, it was that his wandering days were over. He needed to find somewhere he could belong. Maybe even find somebody to belong with.

Over the next few hours, Hilary questioned everyone he could find. He had managed to find a cookshop with something to eat. He had given thanks in the church near the gate for his safe arrival. He had identified Count Fulk's temporary residence and had been told, in halting French, that he should return the next day. He had wandered down Temple Street in the direction of the Golden Gate, among the small shops and market stalls, and found that it was easier to make himself understood in Jerusalem, compared with the bizarre mixture of European cultures which co-existed in Acre.

Some hours later, as the sun sank slowly in the west and the grain traders around the David Gate made their way haltingly out of the city, Hilary waited for Abelard back by the pond. One of the sergeants at the gate wandered over to where he was sitting, his sword banging against his leg.

'God be with you, but the evening is closing in. Have you just arrived in the city? Do you need somewhere to stay? The curfew will begin soon. There are many empty places here. I could direct you to the new Hospital, for a small consideration?'

It was true. Hilary realised that was exactly what seemed so strange about Jerusalem. It wasn't like Paris, of course, but it was so empty. There seemed hardly enough people to fill the streets. So many buildings were abandoned, and the trees were growing round the lintels or through the empty windows. He wondered who had lived there before, realising as he did so that they must have been the previous Moslem inhabitants of the city. He knew all too well what had happened to them. Their shadows seemed to hang heavy over their old homes.

Hilary looked across the city, down the narrow streets and whitewashed buildings, and saw them for a moment running with blood, Christ's blood and all the blood which followed. I should never have come here, he said to himself. I may never survive the journey home, but I am going to fulfil my vow to John of Muchelney. I am going to see this through and go home to England, and I am not going to think any more about who killed William Rufus or even who killed poor Master Hubert.

Dusk began to fall with the rattle of the last carts and the creak of the great gate as the soldiers began to heave it shut. There was an anguished shouting and a flurry of activity as those inside struggled to get out in time, and a number of those outside tried to squeeze past them to get in. It was then that Hilary saw Alys, shimmering as she seemed to him in the dusk of the departing sun.

It cannot be. You are insane, said Hilary to himself. The sun has turned your head to mush. How can Alys be here? How can she be anywhere except in her grave?

He stepped forward and stared again. There was no doubt that the vision was real. Alys stood by the gate as the sentries forced it shut, oblivious to what was around her, staring out across the desert as the view closed. Her straight hair, her thin arms and her tight, thin uncompromising lips. She was turning now in the half light, with the dying sun on her face. Now she was staring straight at him.

Hilary came to with a jolt, realising at the same time both that this was not Alys and also that the carts which had swept in last through the closing gates were in danger of running her down.

'Hey!' he shouted, dashing forward into the path of the cart and pushing this ghost out of the way. He felt the wind of the horses as they rushed by and, a second later, he and the girl were in the dust and dirt.

'What are you doing?' she screamed at him. 'Are you quite mad? Who do you think you are? Do you know who I am? Get up, get up!' Hilary rose unsteadily to his feet to see her brushing the dust off her long blue robe, her eyes flashing with rage.

'My apologies, my lady,' said Hilary, aware by her manner that this was no ordinary girl. 'I thought you were someone else.'

'Someone else? Is that how you greet them then? I don't believe it.'

'I beg your forgiveness. I could not let that cart run you down. Pray forgive my roughness, in a good cause.'

'That cart was nowhere near running me down,' she said, staring back at him, her anger melting away in the last rays of the sun. 'I am well able to look after myself. Well able. May I ask who you thought I was?'

Hilary thought for a moment. The whole series of events since the death of Alys overwhelmed him.

'My former pupil. Alys de Beaugency.'

There was a strained silence by the gate. The streets were emptying. The girl seemed to pick up his change of mood. She smiled slowly and nodded to him.

'My name is Isabella de Payens, at your service. I know who you are, because I have met your friend at my father's house. You are Hilary some call 'The Englishman', travelling with the great Master Peter Abelard, and I want you to teach me to write songs.'

By the time Hilary and Isabella had reached some understanding, it was almost dark. For Hilary, the girl's nod of recognition was a double relief. Not only was it clear that Abelard had succeeded in finding Hugues de Payens, but it was also clear that Alys had not risen from the dead to haunt him in the Holy City.

'Should you be out at this time, before the curfew?' he asked, as she led him down the narrow streets to her father's house.

'I am quite able to look after himself, thank you, Hilary. They breed us tough here, in Outremer. Is it true that Master Peter is the greatest philosopher in the world?'

'It is true, yes.'

'And you are the greatest teacher?'

Hilary laughed. 'I fear not but, if you were my pupil, I would scold you severely for hanging about the city gates at nightfall.'

'Hilary, Hilary. If I was your pupil, I should have no need to wander...'

Once again, Hilary laughed. It felt good to laugh. He had not laughed since John of Muchelney died. For all his greatness, Master Peter did not often provide the raw material for laughter.

It was now dark and Hilary became aware of the shouting in the distance, coming nearer. Soon the torches were being lit and the voices had reached them on their way through the city. The shadows from these flames were falling long and menacing on the sides of the yellow stone buildings as they approached. Two people seemed to be shouting particularly loudly and apparently at each other.

As the group came closer, Hilary realised that, in the middle of them, was the boy they had brought from Acre. There was a rope around his neck and he was being partly pulled and partly dragged behind them, but Hilary recognised him immediately. He looked exhausted and terrified. He was also gagged. Once or twice, Hilary saw one of the men-at-arms who were with them direct a sharp kick in his direction. Once the crowd was fully in the street, Hilary could hear what sounded like a bitter argument.

'You have no authority here. You get straight off the ship and come and tell us how to run the kingdom. You think you know how to deal with the infidels. You wouldn't last five minutes during a charge by the Turks.'

The next voice was more measured. 'And yet you do as I demand.' It was Abelard. 'You do so because you know there is a higher law that must be adhered to. You shall not put people to death lazily, because of who they are.'

'We will see. We will see. We will see what the Constable says about it.'

By the light of the torches in the square, Hilary could see three sullen looking men-at-arms. The voices were now fully audible, echoing a little around the empty stone street. Soon the lamps were being carried into the house behind him, and the boy was pulled inside, up the two steps and in through the great wooden doors. As they filed in through the door, the house was also now coming alive with activity. Servants were appearing in all directions. Women were standing on the archways. Children were peering out behind the arras.

Abelard looked exhausted too as he leapt the two steps, and he and Hilary squeezed next to each other through the door. Isabella was one step behind.

'Master Peter, what's happening?'

Without looking at him, Abelard snapped. 'I will not have it. Assassins in the dark hours. I will not allow it.'

The heavy boots of the soldiers rasped on the rush-strewn floor. The elegant wall-hangings fluttered in the evening breeze. The gagged boy sat before the fireplace, his eyes bright with fear.

'This is our boy,' Abelard whispered in Hilary's ear as he went by. 'They were going to hang him by the Jehosophat Gate.'

'But why?'

'They say he is a Moslem and a spy.'

'Yes, but... What does the boy say?'

'He tried but they have gagged him.' Abelard turned his attention to the man in charge, the Constable of the city. Hilary could not hear exactly what was being said because his attention was distracted by the arrival of an older man whose commanding presence seemed to subdue the room. He had long grey hair, a full grey beard and small, cruel eyes. There were prominent golden rings in his ears. There was a short sword stuffed under his leather belt and a longer sword hanging from his waist. With him were two equally sullen looking fighting men. He had none of that deep brown tan that so many of the locals seemed to have developed in Jerusalem.

'What is the meaning of this?'

'My lord of Montgomery,' said the Constable. There was obviously no love lost between them. 'I am but visiting here. Would this dispute not wait?'

The newcomer nodded in a perfunctory way. 'Tell me exactly why my men have had to drag the prisoner here and have been prevented from despatching him in the normal way?' he said. His voice was deep and dangerous. He fingered the pummel of his dagger as if itching to wield it.

The Constable looked irritated. 'This is not normally a matter you would concern yourself with, is it, my lord? Have you not more pressing matters worthy of your attention. This is not my home, though I have no doubt that you are welcome here, but this matter is below your notice.'

'My men have been prevented from the doing their duty and despatching a Moslem spy. That is hardly below my notice. Both those we serve would agree on that. But give me the boy and we will say no more about it.'

The Constable thought for a moment and turned to Abelard.

'Please tell me your name, pilgrim.' Abelard told him.

'My lord Hugues de Payens told me of your arrival. You are welcome, though your understanding of our ways may still be wanting. Master Peter, let me present you to my lord Arnulf of Montgomery.' The man with the long grey beard and cruel eyes stared implacably back. 'You will have heard of him no doubt, and his exploits in Ireland. Let me ask you on his behalf. He wants the boy. What is your response?'

'Master Peter,' whispered Hilary. 'It doesn't help to make us so conspicuous.'

Abelard addressed Arnulf directly. 'God, be with you, my lord. I am at your service.'

'Don't patronise me, whoever you are. Hand over the boy immediately, and let us retire to our beds. You are protecting a Moslem spy. That is a serious matter.'

The Constable stepped forward and interrupted. 'I am the Constable, my lord. I decide. Please continue, Master Peter.'

Four men-at-arms stepped forward between Arnulf of Montgomery and the boy. Hilary searched the faces for Isabella's but she seemed to have slipped away. He shuddered that once again he had fallen into the midst of some kind of dispute which seemed about to involve drawn swords.

'My lord Constable,' said Arnulf of Montgomery with decision. He brought out his dagger and weighed it in his hands as he spoke. 'I will not parley with you on this matter. Still less will I debate it with this newcomer. You are harbouring a Mohommedan spy and therefore endangering the city of God. Now, what do you say?'

'You made that claim some moments ago,' said Abelard quietly. 'Do you have evidence for it?'

'They are all spies. I need no evidence.' The smoke from the torches was beginning to make people choke. 'I understand that this boy came to Jerusalem with a Christian convoy. Not exactly a coincidence, is it?'

To his surprise, Hilary felt a thrill to hear the Indomitable Rhinoceros once more in debate. It emboldened him.

'I was also with the convoy,' said Hilary, astonished to hear himself speak. 'Am I therefore a spy?'

'He wanted to come to the holy city,' said Arnulf with a sneer. 'You don't need to be a master of philosophy to work out why.'

'Of course he did,' said Abelard. 'His parents no doubt lived here as well. How do you expect him to eat? How do you expect him to live? Even Moslems deserve to eat, do they not?'

Arnulf of Montgomery was now black in the face with fury.

'Be careful, Master Peter,' Hilary whispered next to him. 'Don't push him too far.'

'My lord Constable,' bellowed Arnulf. 'Do you allow me to be spoken to like this under the roof of one of the lords of Outremer? What does this clerk know of our life and dangers here?' The dagger lay in his hands. He absent-mindedly looked down and cleaned his fingernails with the point. Pieces of dirt fell silently to the floor.

But Abelard couldn't stop. 'So let us examine this logic,' he said, stepping forward and pacing up and down as he spoke. 'All Moslems are spies, therefore this boy is a spy. Tell me, when did he become one? At birth?'

'Do you, a mere clerk, doubt me? Do you dare doubt me?'

'Certainly I doubt you. I doubt everything. Because by doubting we come to inquiry and by inquiry we come to the truth. Or does the truth not matter to you, my lord?'

'My lord Constable, I will not be doubted by this renegade. I will not parley with him. I expect you to take the necessary action. I wish you all good night.'

With a flick of his cloak, he replaced the dagger in his belt and was gone, followed by his soldiers, clattering across the stones and down the steps. The hall darkened again with the departure of their torches.

The Constable laughed. 'Master Peter, I enjoyed your impertinence, but you do yourself no favours. But we are in a difficult position, you and I. We cannot take the risk of harbouring spies in this city, especially not while the King and the army are in the north. Now pray untie the boy.'

The Constable's men struggled with the ropes and the gag. Abelard walked over to him and touched his head.

'This boy is my servant,' said Abelard. 'I brought him here from Acre and a respectfully request his return to me. He is my responsibility.'

The company fell silent. The Constable considered. Hilary saw an older man standing next to him. He wore a long coloured shift, and patterned pantaloons, and a sword buckled to his side. Like the other men, Hilary had seen in Palestine since his arrival, he was clean-shaven. Now the Constable turned to him.

'My lord de Payens, this is your home and I am your guest. The decision shall be yours. Do I hand over this boy to Arnulf and his men or do I give him back to Master Peter, as a guest under your own roof?'

The old man bowed deeply to the Constable.

'He is no Moslem, my lord,' said Abelard.

'How did you know this, Master Peter?'

Abelard walked to the boy and held up his wrist. 'I noticed some time ago that he wore a charm around her wrist like a fish. A Christian symbol. I don't expect that on the wrist of a Moslem boy.'

'A disguise perhaps?'

'Perhaps, but he is also my servant. I am a visitor to this city and I demand the considerations due to a guest and his chattels.'

It was clear to Hilary that the atmosphere had lifted. The old man smiled and raised his arms. The Constable bowed. The men-at-arms began to withdraw.

The old man with the beard stepped forward. 'Master Peter, my house is your house,' he said. 'We will do as you ask. But I tell you this, the lives of suspicious Muslims caught in the city are pretty cheap. Now let us sleep. The night is past her youth and so am I.' Hugues de Payens, fat , beardless and scrubbed clean, kissed Abelard on both cheeks and ushered them deeper into his house, its sumptuous tapestries, cushions and veils all lit with smoking lamps. 'Isabella, to bed.'

Hilary was woken at dawn by a gentle tapping on the shoulder. The servants of the house were already up around him, sweeping the floors and arranging the awnings. The smell of baked bread was wafting from the kitchens. The arras was being beaten.

Hilary started up, frightened that the whole rigmarole of escape and pursuit was beginning again. 'Master Peter! What has happened?' Abelard seemed a little over-dressed in a cloak and heavy boots.

'Calm yourself, Hilary. Nothing has happened. The dawn has broken, that's all, as it so often does.'

'But why are you dressed for travel?'

'Well, Hilary. I had a conversation with our host last night. I understand that he has received a letter in the past few days agreeing to his terms for the marriage of his daughter. Do you understand what that means?'

Hilary struggled to drag himself from sleep.

'Very well, let me make it clear. If our host has received mail in the last few days, then so has everyone else. We thought we were the first ship of the season, but we were not. Those who pursued us in France know we were coming here so there is every reason to expect some kind of unwelcome reception. We need to move fast. You need to find Fulk of Anjou, and if possible make some enquiries about this famous Jewel. I need to consult the libraries.'

'The libraries? Are you mad? We are being pursued.'

'Listen, Hilary. I know this is inconvenient for you, but I must find the truth about St-Denis. I owe it to myself. If and when my great rival Alberic of Reims takes me on, I want to be ready for him. I know he is preparing to do so. I feel him dogging my footsteps, even here. You are not the only one to be pursued, Hilary. Alberic will never forgive me for my demolition of his old master in the Laon debate. I believe that the great St Denis was actually three distinct people. I now want to prove it. The clues are all here, Hilary. I feel sure of it.'

Hilary's mood had been plummeting since the moment he saw Abelard dressed for the road. Was he being abandoned? What would happen when he finally met Fulk of Anjou? A cold wave of isolation swept down his spine. What would become of him without Master Peter's protection and advice and sheer *facultas*?

'Come, Hilary. It is only for a day or so. I shall return tonight and we can resume our quest as soon as I have found what I am looking for. Or perhaps tomorrow.'

Hilary was irritated at Abelard's assumption that he was frightened, though he realised of course that he was. 'It isn't that, it's just that... I've got used to your company in the past few months. We have seen a great deal together.'

But Abelard was now busy with his shoes and belt and didn't reply.

Hilary began brushing away the insects which had taken up residence in his clothes during the night. There was certainly a more fearsome style of night creature in the bedding in the Holy Land. Yes, it was time to take some responsibility for himself again. Without his mentor, he would have to face Count Fulk of Anjou alone. He was at least temporarily out of the reach of the Man in Grey, though perhaps not from his friends, but he was within reach of some kind of answer to the mystery. He would at least be able to fulfil his promise to poor John of Muchelney, he thought. Had he not crossed the world to do so?

Hilary felt alone amidst an unfamiliar crowd. The household swarmed around him. Outside the window, the holy city was beginning to come alive for the day, as the traders began to set out their wares, their pots, their cloth, their damask and muslin, and their brightly coloured vegetables. The whores were taking up their accustomed places. The insects were beginning their incessant buzz. He was alone in a polyglot crowd of newcomers, for whom he meant less than nothing. As they said, life was cheap here.

He made use of the water butt in the yard for his refreshment and to wash his face, and he had cleaned his teeth with a brand new stick – and felt more able to face the world – and he once more became aware of a presence behind him. He swung around quickly, still nervous from months on the run. Standing there was the master of the household, Hugues de Payens.

'Master Hilary, you are welcome. I have arranged for lodgings for you at St John the Almoner tonight. You will be comfortable there.' Hilary bowed, irritated that Master Peter was to be allowed to stay in the house, but he was being treated as a servant. Was he being relegated to the level of the boy who had guided them across the desert? Why was he always having to wander?

Hugues rubbed his carefully washed hands together in a gesture of finality. Perhaps he believes he is being generous, thought Hilary. He told himself to smile.

'Now, I must travel north shortly to join the King outside Antioch, once I have despatched my daughter to her new husband, but I must say something to you first. I understand I have you to thank for the return of my daughter last night. Isabella has taken to wandering the city, despite my instructions. She is unhappy at the prospects of marriage. I do not wish her to leave either, but she is promised and the dowry has now been partly paid. It is the way of the world.'

Hilary realised he was still swaying a little from eight weeks at sea.

'She has always been headstrong and boyish. I have just heard from her betrothed husband.'

Hilary bowed. 'May I ask, my lord? Does this mean you have received a letter?'

'Two days ago, yes. Why, is anything the matter?'

'My friend and I had believed we were on the first ship from Marseilles. If you have had a letter, it means that we were overtaken at sea.'

'So, you were not the first pilgrims of the year – well never mind. I am sure that God will forgive such a failure,' said Hugues de Payens with great bonhomie. 'Now, please, be my guest, sleep in comfort here tonight, and from tomorrow the greater comfort of St John the Almoner awaits. I am grateful to you for bringing Isabella home unscathed. My home is your home. Now I have something to ask you.'

Hilary began to sweat more profoundly than usual in the morning heat. Why this close questioning?

'Ask me what you like, my lord. I will answer as best I can.'

'Master Peter. He is well known to you?'

'As well as any man, I believe.' Where was this conversation leading?

'I have heard from Paris about his, how shall I say, little tragedy. The loss of his lady and ... well, other things.'

'You know of it even here?' Hilary was astonished. 'You knew about Master Peter even before we came?'

'Who hasn't heard of the Indomitable Rhinoceros? Of course I know. The whole world knows. What I want to know is how he has managed to survive the ordeal.'

'I don't know, my lord. I dared not ask him.'

Hugues looked grave and nodded sagely, as if Hilary had stumbled upon the right answer. He stared out of the window as if engaged with deep thoughts. 'You see, I had intended to question Master Peter about some theories of my own regarding the number of angels in the world...'

'I fear I know nothing of these matters, my lord.'

Hugues became suddenly animated. 'I believe the scriptures imply that we each of us have angels, yet does that mean that a man and a woman create an angel when they create a life? Surely it is God's prerogative to create an angel. You see, Master Hilary, I am in deep waters here.'

Hilary groaned inwardly. He had no idea that Hugues de Payens was some kind of theological crank. 'You will have to ask Master Peter. I have little experience of angels.'

'I shall indeed. Certainly, Master Peter's – how shall I say? – injuries, have made him no less ferocious in his disputations, as I heard he was last night in defence of his servant. He was right, of course, and yet there are dangers from the desert. Many were killed among the pilgrims last year. These outrages happen too often, I fear. It is a dangerous journey, but then our armies are in the north. It is most unfortunate.'

Hilary thought back to their week-long trek through the sand, past the abandoned villages and under the heat of the implacable sun. They could have done with more protection.

'I am grateful to you, my lord. It was true that that the monks who accompany the pilgrims ought to have been more like soldiers, and perhaps the few soldiers we had could have been a little less like monks.'

It was a moment of levity, and Hilary regretted it immediately. He glanced at his host to see what his reaction was and he looked even graver than before. He paced up and down a little faster, and then over to the window that looked out at the courtyard. Hilary wondered whether he should tiptoe away, when his host looked as though he had been slapped. Then a beaming smile appeared on his face.

'Master Hilary, you are more right than you know. I believe you have stumbled upon my own plan. I have set this very idea before the King myself. Preparations are under way as we speak. You shall hear more of this. Now,' said Hugues with enthusiasm, looking disconcertingly at him, 'My daughter is very precious to me. There is little I can give in the way of wealth, but I can offer you a bath.'

Hilary was not familiar with the term, except from his classical studies in Paris, and he was pretty convinced that his host possessed nothing equivalent to the Roman baths he had pictured in his mind.

'It is an ancient custom of Outremer,' said Hugues de Payens. 'Something we inherited from the previous inhabitants of this city, but none the worse for that. I promise you, this is something you will never forget.'

These words echoed in Hilary's head as he was led down the long stone passageway to the back of the house. The two servant girls looked at him and giggled. There was a cool breeze coming from somewhere. It could hardly be the street, which felt like an oven. The drapings moved gently in the air. On either side of the corridor, doorways were filled with hay, beer or wine. Finally, he was led into a small room with a white cloth on the floor and, in the middle of the cloth, a large circular basin like a huge half barrel. There were rose petals on the floor.

Hilary watched fascinated, horribly aware of the sweat embedded in his clothes, as more servants entered one by one with huge pitchers of what appeared to be hot water. Steam began to fill the room, together with something else. He sniffed and wondered.

'It's roses and lavender. I'm here to help you undress.' Hilary stared at the servant boy and submitted to having his dirty and sweat-encrusted coverings removed over his head, watching the lice fall on the white cloth as his old clothing – so generously provided in Provins – was pulled over his head. Finally, he stood beside the bath naked, except for the two pouches around his neck. The young man stood expectantly. What harm could there be now? With relief, Hilary removed them over his head as if divesting himself of the lead weight and handed them over. Then he stepped carefully into the warm, perfumed water.

As he relaxed into the heat, his first sensation was desire. The young man who watched him, the dark-skinned girl who helped him climb in and poured warm water over his back, were too evocative for a moment to think of anything else. He tried to control his body, but then was aware of a huge sense of relaxation, and dizziness. He could not see clearly through the steam, but something else was affecting his awareness – some cool, balmy sense of contentment, almost alcoholic. He could see the young man place his clothes and belongings carefully on a table covered with a colourful carpet, then he leant back and closed his eyes.

He lay in the water as it slowly cooled for what felt like an hour and may have been more. As he relaxed, he dared to shift his body down further and to lie back into the spiced liquid, feeling the warmth and the potent scents in his hair. Then he put his whole head underneath for a moment, coming up a second later with the petals on his eyes.

The servant servants clustered round when he tried to get out, feeling a little unsteady and barely able to talk. They helped him over to a bench and dried him and led him to the table with his clothes. His host had thoughtfully provided a new tunic, linen under-tunic, hose and leggings. He slipped the tunics on over his head. They felt light and airy.

It was only when he reached for his other possessions, and put the pouch of silver back around his neck and looked for its companion, that he realised anything was wrong. The pouch with the documents had gone.

2/Isabella

Jerusalem, 15 May 1120

'What are you looking for?'

Hilary was confronted by Isabella, sitting across the narrow stone corridor at the back of the house. Now it was absolutely obvious that she was not Alys. Alys would never have dressed in this way, like a young man, in leathers, hose and britches, though despite her dress, Isabella's femininity was obvious. She may have carried a small whip, but her dark hair and eyes now had a bewitching quality which they lacked when she was standing by the great gates of the city. The image of Alys had now faded from Hilary's mind; he found it hard to summon her up. Why had he suddenly imagined he had caught a glimpse of her? Perhaps it was the heat, thought Hilary, where every brick acts like an oven.

The sun outside was slanting steeply through the windows in intense brightness, indicating that noon was approaching, but Hilary barely acknowledged the fact. For some hours now, he had been searching desperately for his letter pouch, but he still had nothing to show for it. It was all frustrating and worrying. Most of all, it was embarrassing, and he could not stop kicking himself for his intense stupidity. The moment Abelard had left his side, Hilary felt he had managed to confuse everything and made the most ridiculous error. Of course he should have bathed with the papers still round his neck, he told himself. It was an elementary mistake.

His host was absent, but Hugues de Payens's bailiff had professed ignorance. He asked no questions at all about the papers. It was almost as if he knew instinctively that they were important. The house had been turned upside down. New straw had been swept off the floor. Ancient hangings had been beaten and peered behind. Boxes had been opened. The household had even been paraded in the hall. There was no doubt about it; the boy was gone – or perhaps he had never been there in the first place. In fact, Hilary was beginning to doubt his own sanity. Perhaps the heat had led him to imagine that the boy was there. Perhaps the debilitating worry of the past few months had affected his ability to see clearly. Perhaps the servant had been a bewitching enchantment sent to delude him.

Hilary stared uncertainly at Isabella, unsure how to engage her, fascinated by her ambiguously boyish chin and long dark hair which had confused him when he first saw her across the cart track.

'Go on, you can tell me what you seek,' she said. 'You never know, I might have seen it somewhere. You'd be amazed at what I see.'

Her long legs tapered into pointed leather shoes. They barred the way.

Hilary checked himself. Since Abelard's warning, he had begun to wonder whether he could even trust this household. 'I'm looking for a boy who is a servant here. I don't know what he is called. He was here last night. He helped me into the bath...'

Her expression changed. She brought her legs forward and paid more attention.

'Ah, you had a bath. Well, you deserved one, Hilary. First for rescuing me from that cart, and then for not telling my father. For those things alone, I bless you.'

She made the sign of the cross at Hilary and looked at him challengingly, as if he was about to tick her off for blasphemy. Then she laughed uproariously. She did not seem in the least the worse for her encounter with the traffic at the David Gate, or their encounter with Arnulf of Montgomery and his thugs.

'Ah, Isabella...' said Hilary, then he tailed off, unsure how to answer her. 'If you could help me look, then I will bless you in return.'

'I will help you, but tell me about your bath. I heard that you hadn't washed for two seasons. Is that true? You must have smelled.'

What an extraordinary girl this was. She dressed like a boy and teased like a boy. Despite himself, and despite his panic about the papers, Hilary warmed to her.

'Perhaps one season and a half. I hadn't realised how clean everyone was in Outremer until I got here. We're a bit less fastidious where I come from. In any case, you walked back across the city with me last night, so you know perfectly well that I smelled. Now, please, do you know the servant I mean? I believe he has something of mine and it is intensely important that I find it, and quickly.'

'Yes, Master Peter was tremendous last night, was he not?'

'He was indeed,' said Hilary. He had also been thrilled by Abelard's performance, but also irritated by it. There had indeed been something of a performance about it, a public statement, to demonstrate his arrival in a new city, and Hilary was nervous about Arnulf of Montgomery. His feeling of safety when they had first arrived had become to seep away.

'Tell me why you want this boy, Hilary. I so want to know.'

'Listen,' said Hilary, very deliberately, trying to change the tone of the conversation with the girl. 'He's a little older than you. Or maybe this high, a little taller than me, with rather a distinctive smile. Or maybe you've seen the leather pouch that I've lost. It really is a matter of whether I live or die. When I've found it I will be asking you why you ran away from home yesterday.' Isabella looked mysteriously into the middle distance. For the first time she looked a little embarrassed.

'Because I am soon to be Isabella of Montgomery.'

Hilary was aghast at the horrific combination. It seemed monstrous, disastrous. 'You're not marrying that monster from last night, are you?' A strange intimacy had emerged suddenly between them which made him drop his guard a little, but he stopped himself. It would hardly do to insult the girl's fiancé, even if she was about to marry the grey-bearded, piggy-eyed Arnulf of Montgomery. Luckily she was laughing.

'No, thanks be to Christ. His nephew. He will inherit land in Ponthieu. Arnulf hates him. You know I was betrothed when I was five, by letter. Now I'm going on the ship to get married. I had hoped something would happen to avoid this fate, and now I am to leave in only a week. Everything is ready.'

'Why are you unhappy about it?'

'Who would be happy? To leave my father and the holy city and go to – well, Normandy? They say there are many sheep there, but I don't understand why that should excite me. They say worse than that actually...'

Hilary felt awkward. What could he say? He could hardly agree and yet he could hardly disagree either. The tragedy of young women consumed by bearded monsters in draughty northern castle overwhelmed him.

'I'm praying for a miracle,' she said. 'Only weeks days to go, but I'm sure St Monica is listening. So, Hilary the Englishman....' The conversation was taking another careering turn. 'I haven't seen your pouch and I don't believe this boy even exists, though he sounds lovely. But you can help me.' She swum aimlessly on the candle niche, jutting out from the stone wall.

'If you find me my pouch, I really will consider anything,' said Hilary hopefully.

'Poor Hilary. I'm afraid it's gone. Now, will you teach me to write songs before I have to leave?'

But it couldn't have just gone. The whole affair made Hilary's head spin. Someone helped him into the bath last night. That pouch had hung from his neck like a noose for nearly half a year and now it had disappeared. The pouch containing what remained of his silver pieces was still there. It couldn't have been a simple theft. Yet somebody had taken it. It occurred to him that the whole household – even maybe this glorious tomboy before him – were in on the plot. No, it was too complicated a solution.

'I can't tell you how important it is. If you'll help me look, I will teach you. Just a little. How about that?'

'Hilary. Saint Hilary. I agree. We'll start in the solar room. Why is that man staring at us?'

Hilary leapt round and peered out of the tiny stone window onto the street. There was indeed a man there, with a dagger in his belt. Now he was looking, the man had shifted his attention elsewhere. The terrible sense of pursuit, that he believed he had escaped, took one more step back into his head.

It was late afternoon before Hilary found himself once more alone and on the street outside Hugues of Payen's palace. He shook his head, remembering the luxuries he had experienced there, the silks and damasks, the coloured wall hangings and cushions, the soft carpets and the slippers. Could such living be justified in the City of God? If these had been his student days, he would have sung about it. Never would satire have been better designed, but this was not the moment now. Now, he must keep his head down and clear. The spiced wine he had been offered had made him spin a little, and there was still a sense of swaying that had not left him since the ship. He shook himself as he searched for St John the Almoner where he was to spend the night. There had been no sign of Abelard or his pouch and papers.

The man he had seen from the window had disturbed him too. It might have been imagination. It might have been just a passer-by staring through the window. It might be many things, but he could not be too careful. He picked his way through the detritus of the street, the rotting smells and pools of dried blood. How was going to end his ordeal without the papers? He could only hope that his audience with Fulk of Anjou was going to be so open-minded and generous that he didn't need to produce the crucial letter. If only Master Peter was there. Hilary reminded himself that, if he had been, there would have been Abelard's corrosive tongue to deal with, renowned across the schools of northern Europe.

When he found St Stephen's Street, it seemed to be deserted and Hilary breathed a sigh of relief. He reassured himself that once he had managed to see Count Fulk of Anjou, the whole nightmare would be over and the problem of papers would be out of his hand. But it was worrying that, even there, in the celestial City of God, someone had managed to steal the mysterious pouch which had even eluded the Man in Grey.

He could see the church of the Holy Sepulchre in the distance. The streets of Jerusalem were even more empty than they had been the day before. There were said to be only 300 knights left in the whole of Palestine to defend the new borders of the new kingdom; in this echoing city of ruins and ghosts, Hilary could well believe it.

The occasional mule and vegetable cart passed him in the other direction, but as he walked towards the walls, he began to be aware of a new excitement in the air. Children were running ahead of him. There was shouting and some people in leather and chain mail began to hurry past him with the air of being a little late, carrying lances and banners. Even the occasional stallholder seemed transfixed on the road ahead.

As Hilary came closer to the St Stephen Gate, he was aware of music and shouting. Then he could hear cheering, bagpipes, drum beats and chanting prayers. Then finally, with just a few hundred yards to go, he realised: it was a detachment of soldiers leaving for the north. There was Hugues de Paynes on his horse in the distance, wearing a big red cross on his white shift. Surely he was not leaving yet. There was the Constable giving the small detachment of soldiers a good send-off. There were the streamers and pennants fluttering from lances and the soldiers in chain mail or boiled leather, with crosses on their surcoats – red for the French, green for the Flemish and black for the Germans.

There were the mules and baggage carts loaded with equipment and supplies, the great leather firkins of water and the sheep and cattle tagging along behind for slaughter along the way. There were the war horses led by page boys, and the knights with the sun flashing on their helmets. There were the musicians and the priests, raising their fluttering banners and crosses high above the dust, clouds of which were now obscuring the gate. Another detachment of horsemen galloped past him and Hilary had to leap out of the way. The choir was mustering itself for a final carol and then, as he began to approach within hailing distance of the gate, there was a great cheer, and the huge wooden fence moved slowly open and the whole raggle-headed procession moved slowly out into the blinding sunlight of the desert.

Suddenly he saw, disappearing through the gate, surrounded by men-at-arms wearing black and white surcoats, something that looked at first like an old stick. But he noticed the people watching next to it were falling to their knees. Was this the piece of true cross which followed the army on campaign, or some other battered relic? Hilary stared in wonder and awe as the last soldiers disappeared through the gate, the dust began to settle and the quiet returned to the street. It had been a magnificent sight but a nervous one too. If the army had now left Jerusalem, who would defend the holy city from the rage of the defeated locals? He stood contemplating the swirling dust and watching the sense of emptiness descend as the great gates shut again, watching the pigs rootling among the rubbish – the proof that this was no longer a Moslem city. It was then that he caught sight of another man watching him.

It was a different man from the one he had seen through the window. But the stare was bold and unambiguous. The man made a sudden sign, the finger across the throat and a hideous leer. Hilary's heart skipped a beat. It was time to leave the heat of St Stephen's Street. He walked swiftly away and dashed down a side street. It was completely deserted.

Trying not to look too conspicuous by indecent haste, Hilary hurried as fast as he could. Ahead of him now were two men. They were moving inexorably towards him. Cursing his luck, he turned down an alleyway to his left. There was more offal and detritus under foot but, with a sinking feeling, he realised he had chosen a dead end. He glanced backwards. The two men were still there. This time there was no escape. Abelard was relaxing in the Patriarch's library; he could rely on nobody else but himself. A large lump of wood lay in the gutter. Hilary hurried over and grabbed it, thinking quickly how he might defend himself against two men – who he now saw had long knives drawn and were advancing on him.

This is disastrous, thought Hilary. I am going to have to be very determined and very aggressive. How does a clerk in holy orders fight, when they have not fought anyone since boyhood?

In almost no time, they were before him. He brandished the wood. As they fell upon him, on an instinct, he swung the wood as hard as he could. It hit one of his assailants on the ear. Blood gushed out of the side of his head and he dropped his knife. Hilary tried to grab it, but was not quick enough. The other man was stooping down himself and edging towards him.

At that moment there was a shout from the end of the alley and a tall soldier was running towards them, sword in hand. Hilary despaired, but his assailant glanced round, saw him too, turned and ran. His comrade, clutching the side of his head to staunch the bleeding hobbled after him. The two men met near the end of the alley and clambered over a low wall. The soldier reached it too late. Hilary's assailants had gone. He sat down heavily, mopping his brow. He could not believe that had been *him* fighting for his life, let alone landing such a heavy blow. It seemed so unlike him. He stared faintly into the distance.

'You have had a lucky escape, my friend,' the soldier bawled at Hilary. 'You are Hilary the Englishman, I believe? You are welcome in Jerusalem. I am one of the Constable's men. I too am English.'

Hilary was staggered. 'How do you know my name?'

'Your friend told me when she warned me of the attack. The young lady.'

'What young lady?'

At that moment, the now familiar boyish figure of Isabella de Payens emerged from the corner of the alley. The soldier jerked a finger in her direction.

'She saw you were in trouble and fetched me.'

Hilary stared at her with a mixture of irritation and intense gratitude. 'Isabella, I owe you my life,' he shouted. 'But you must not follow me. I am in danger and you could be too.'

'Please Hilary, don't prattle on. It's a good thing for you I did follow you. I didn't want to lose you so soon after meeting you.'

Hilary looked down into her eyes and was surprised to find

real sincerity there. He realised how fond of Isabella he had already become. There was something compelling about her mixture of innocence and worldliness. He stared at her.

'Isabella, I forgive you. But I don't want you to come to any more harm. Don't tell me you are wandering again?' He turned to the Saxon who had saved him. 'My friend, you have my gratitude. God bless you. May I ask how you came to be here in Jerusalem?'

The soldier laughed hollowly. Hilary realised, from the lines on his face, that he was not exactly in the first flush of youth. 'I walked all the way here. Never got home. I am old now. I have not the strength even to join the army outside Antioch. But I work for the Constable while the army is away, and for my lord de Payens. It's a good enough place. If it was good enough for King David, it's certainly good enough for me. Are you really English, with a name like Hilary?'

'My father was Norman, but my mother was English.' Hilary caught himself using the past tense about his mother. He had no idea whether she was alive or not. He realised he had slipped into Anglo-Saxon.

'Well, you speak the language. Thank goodness for small mercies.'

'Do you live in the Saxon monastery?' asked Hilary, reverting to French to include Isabella. 'There must be thousands of men in your position?'

'What? Take those vows? Live with those busy-bodies? You know, there are people who say I'm Godless for not living with the Carmelites or the Augustinians. But no, I take my oaths seriously. I took my crusader oath seriously, didn't I? I'm not going to vow something I can't keep. Poverty, well, I have to keep that one. I've never been very obedient, and as for chastity, well... They can take those vows and then break them every time they have a meat for their dinner, but I can't. So I live in the hostel for soldiers. I used to live at the hostel of St Edward the Confessor, the Saxon convent, but I moved on. Not a bad life. Isn't that right, young lady?'

They walked down St Stephen's Street, Hilary glancing about him looking for more watchers and potential assailants, while he talked gently about England, the cold misty mornings and the drizzle comparing it to the brutal sunshine in Palestine. Hilary glanced about him again as the soldier prepared to leave. 'I have forgotten to ask the name of my rescuer.'

'Aldwyn. I come from Farnham. Let me advise you to stay on the main streets. There are lawless corners of this city, despite its name.'

'Tell me, Aldwyn of Farnham, there is something that has been worrying me, and you might be able to help. I heard a phrase recently that reminded me of home. '*Hit waes geara iu.*' Do you know what it means? I don't mean what the words mean, of course I know that, but why would somebody say it?'

Aldwyn looked dreamily into the distance at the bustle of the market ahead. 'Ah well, those were the old days. All gone now. There was a time when people would greet each other with that those words, to remember King Alfred and say that the old ways would not die. But they have died, haven't they. King Henry and King Rufus have seen to that.'

Silence fell between them for a moment. There was a murmur of voices in the distance. The sun was now noticeably lower in the sky. It was searingly hot. Isabella was listening intently.

'It's all gone, you know. Those ancient freedoms that I was born to in old England. My birthright. The laws of King Alfred. Those laws that made us as sturdy as oaks. Those were the days when a man could not be taken away from his village and tortured, while the church looked on and blessed it. That's what happens now, or so I've heard. We keep in close touch with each other, we crusaders of England. We know what's happening under the rule of that bloodthirsty tyrant Henry Beauclerk.' The old man spat out the name of King Henry of England like a piece of poisoned meat. 'Henry the first – the first in torture and bloodshed and tyranny.'

'Bloodshed?'

'Well, he killed his brother, didn't he?'

'Rufus?'

'Of course Rufus. They say he did so with the Saxons, but they have not profited by it, have they?'

'How do you know he killed his brother?'

Aldwyn checked himself. 'How do I know? Well, good question, young man. Because I was a soldier in the King's pay in Winchester the day they brought in Rufus' body on a farm cart. I never forgot that day. I took the oath afterwards and sailed here. I did not dare stay.'

'Why? Who were you afraid of?' Hilary felt a quickening of his pulse. This seemed suddenly to be relevant to his quest.

'Why? I was afraid of those friends of the King who wanted to remake history a little. I saw Rufus' body like a great heap of rotting meat, smelling after the long journey in the heat through the forest. Stripped naked. By then Henry had already been into the city, the very day of the accident – that very evening – and seized the Treasury. Three days later he was crowned in Westminster before either of the archbishops could arrive. But, listen to this. When Henry arrived in Winchester, he brought with him a proclamation declaring himself King. Tell me this. How could he have had that written already? How could he have known what was going to happen?'

Hilary shifted around. He had been so hanging on these words that, for a moment, he had forgotten that he needed to stay vigilant.

'Is that why you had to leave?' asked Isabella.

'That's right, my lady. Because of what happened at the door of the Treasury. William of Breteuil was there and refused to let Henry pass.'

'Sorry, you are going too fast,' said Hilary. 'Who was William of Breteuil?'

The old soldier looked distracted. 'William of Breteuil? The last honest man in England, he was. He was with the King in the New Forest, in another part of the wood like Henry was. When he saw Rufus die, he must have known what was going to happen and he took his horse and raced to Winchester, you see. Henry's older brother Robert of Normandy was the rightful King, he said. The two men had galloped back from the New Forest after the accident, and Breteuil got there first. There was I outside the Tresaury, and I stood beside him, along with a handful of other soldiers. But Henry drew his sword, and a great crowd gathered around him and there was no choice. Breteuil backed down, Henry took the money and he was King. That's all there is to it. He stole the crown, and not just the crown either. But, listen to me, *he was prepared*. He was all ready for the accident. He murdered God's anointed, that's what he did....' The old soldier broke off, clearly moved.

People were beginning to look at them, a small group stuck on the corner of St Stephen's Street.

Hilary felt overwhelmed with pity for this old, brave man. 'Why don't you go home?'

'Home to England? I have no money to go by sea. I'm too old to make that journey back by foot. And in any case, where is England now? Gone. Stolen once by the Conqueror and stolen all over again by his youngest son Henry. Nothing for me there. And King Henry has a long memory for those who stood next to Breteuil before the Treasury.'

'What did that mean?' asked Isabella.

Hilary ignored her. It was interfering with his thoughts having the girl with him. 'Why did I not ask him about the hostel of St Edward? That might have been a clue to the whereabouts of Saewulf.'

'You're talking in riddles, Hilary.'

'Yes, I am. For your own good, Isabella, I speak in riddles. But what that old soldier has told me confirms what I suspected – that King Henry of England was ready when his older brother was killed. My friend John of Muchelney was right. At least his documents were. The murder was known about before it happened.'

'Murder? King Henry? Tell me, Hilary. If you tell me, I will show you the old Saxon convent.'

Hilary looked at her properly. 'Isabella, I am grateful to you for saving my life just now. I don't want to get you into any more trouble. I will tell you a little, but you must not ask any more. I will tell you on the way to this convent. Then, perhaps you will show me the way to Count Fulk of Anjou. If you do all that, and I manage to survive the day by God's good grace, then tomorrow I will teach you to write songs. Though I warn you: I am not nearly as proficient at writing songs as I sometimes claim to be.'

Isabella looked at him with delight. 'Then I shall seal our bargain with a kiss,' she said, and pressed her lips firmly on Hilary's unshaven cheeks. Again, those who passed them, with their leather satchels of meal and milk, stared with disapproval. Hilary reddened and searched the horizon for more dangerous watchers.

'Now follow me,' she said. 'It's just through the Cloth Market.'

The sun was lower in the sky and the stones giving back the day's heat, and Hilary was confused. Was that attack by those two men in St Stephen's Street just one of those things that happen to newcomers in Outremer, or were his pursuers back on his trail? And if the latter, why were they still after him when presumably they now had his pouch and letters? It was disturbing. On the ship, he had grown used to the idea that he had shaken them off, and now – well, was he going to be chased for the rest of his days?

But despite all that, he was aware of a welling up of pleasure. He wondered what it was, aware once again of his peculiar shifts in mood. Calm yourself, Hilary, he told himself. There is nothing to be thrilled about here, except perhaps treading in the very footsteps of Christ. No, that wasn't it. No, it was the presence next to him of this girl, perhaps a little more than half his own age, about to be married to some Norman brute, half walking, half running, like a sprite, with a spring of joy – or was that *his* joy? It was no doubt improper for him to be alone in the company of an eligible daughter of one of Jerusalem's foremost aristocrats – but he was, and he smiled to himself, looking at her bare legs below her shift and her sandals skipping through the dust.

No, there was something else. The blow he had struck his assailant kept coming back to him, and with satisfaction. It could not be right to take pleasure in drawing blood in the holy city – but Hilary felt that, at long last, he had hit back. He had not waited for Master peter to defend him. He had not hidden in a ditch. He had been, just for a moment, the master of his destiny.

'This is it,' she said, standing back.

Hilary glanced up the street to make sure. It was a wooden door in the sandstone wall. Once more, the street was deserted. Hilary pushed it. It rattled irritably. 'It's locked, God curse the place,' he said.

Isabella beckoned him on. A few yards further there was a tiny door deep in the wall, hardly big enough to walk through in a crouching position. 'This must be the one,' she said. 'Now push!'

With a grinding noise, the door opened slowly. They found themselves in a great bare sandstone space, with paintings on the walls of angels and a skeletal Adam and Eve with a huge snake. Some tiny windows let in the light high above them. It seemed not to have been used for some time. There was a musty smell about it.

'What are we looking for?' asked Isabella, staring at the walls.

'Well, the monk Saewulf was supposed to have brought a significant Saxon jewel to Jerusalem some years ago. I suppose we are looking for signs of him.'

'Like that, you mean?' Isabella indicated the inscription above the locked door. Hilary peered upwards. It read: 'SAEWULFUS AEDIFICIT'.

'*Di immortales!* You are right. How extraordinary. He came here. He built this chapel!' So Saewulf the Saxon had been here. Hilary's eyes swept the bar yellow building with new interest.

'Perhaps this jewel is here, Hilary.'

'Perhaps it is. But where?' The Saxon chapel certainly looked empty. There was not a stick of furniture anywhere to be seen, let alone an obvious hiding place.'

'Is it a sacred jewel?

Hilary considered for a moment. 'I suppose it is, in a way. Why?'

'Well, would it not be kept with the other relics?'

'You mean in the altar?' Hilary leapt onto the dais at the eastern end of the church and, sure enough, there was clearly a stone compartment inside the top of the altar. It was not locked, but it was closed with a stone lid that fitted exactly in place. It would not be easy.

'Aren't you going to force it open?'

'Well, I...' Hilary considered the ethics of breaking into a reliquary. Isabella stood next to him and looked him full in the face.

'Hilary, ask yourself – what would Master Peter do? Here,' she said, reaching under her shift and pulling out a short dagger. 'Take this.'

'Good lord, Isabella. I hope you won't go about armed after you are married,' said Hilary. He took the dagger and forced it into the crack in the top of the altar. Only its point fitted inside. He twisted it about. Nothing gave. Then he noticed that the corner of the stone lid was slightly chipped. This time, the point of the dagger went in a little further. He twisted it again. There was a satisfactory grinding sound. He levered it up. It moved a little, enough to push the dagger further in.

At long last, the stone lid edged upwards and he heaved it out with the tips of his fingers. His heart in his mouth, he peered into the hole, but Isabella got there first.

'There's nothing there,' she said, deflated.

'Ah well. It was always going to be unlikely.... Hold on!' Hilary reached inside and withdrew a small piece of metal. There were letters on it.

'Keep still, Hilary. I'm trying to read it.... Mother of God!'
'It's a message. A clue. It might even be intended for me, or others like me. A picture of a bull, and two numbers:

XXIV   VI

'I don't know. It could mean anything.'
Hilary stared hard at the metal. 'Tell me, Isabella, what does a

bull mean to you?'

'Something fierce.'

'Was there not some Roman cult involving a bull? And the two dates. The twenty-sixth day of the sixth month perhaps. The sixth month was when the angel visited Mary...'

There was an unmistakable scuffling from somewhere in the vicinity of the chapel. Hilary and Isabella stared towards the door. The next sound was a heavy thump on the wooden door. They froze but it wasn't repeated.

'Maybe it was a camel in the street or something.'

'Maybe,' whispered Hilary. 'Either way, I think it is time to go. In case somebody saw us come in here. I am responsible for your safety as well as my own, and I don't want your father thinking you have wandered off again.'

'I will not run away. I accept my fate. What else can I do?'

Hilary peered carefully both ways down the street. It was empty. He pulled Isabella after him into the late afternoon heat.

With a whiff of irritation, Hilary remembered that Abelard had disappeared deep into the archives and libraries of the Patriarch. 'I wish we could lay this mystery before Master Peter. He would know what it means. But unfortunately, he has disappeared, seeking out the real St Denis.'

Isabella was a good pupil. She sat at his feet the next morning in the courtyard, while he told her about rhetoric and Latin verse and the music of the ages. Very quietly, so that the household would not hear them, he sang her one of his own songs. Then he sang her one of Master Peter's. 'The merry face of spring,' he sang from memory...

'It returns to the world,

The bite of winter
Escapes, vanquished.
In their coat of colours,
The flowers begin to rein,
And the sound of the woods
Sings in celebration...'

Isabella applauded happily. Why had teaching Alys not been more like this? Why is it my fate to let the best pupils slip through my fingers, thought Hilary.

'It is now time for you to tell me your story, and tell me about love,' said Isabella firmly.

'I cannot. It might put you in danger.'

'I am in no danger here. My father guards me ruthlessly and within a few days I will be gone. Go on, tell me. Tell me what was so special about that purse? It is time I was told. I have a reason for asking.'

So Hilary told her, leaving out the chase through the catacombs and his own indecision. 'The truth is that I have been mistaken for someone else and am in great danger,' he said. 'Master Peter helped me to escape. That is how we came to be here in Jerusalem. You rescued me from two of them yourself. As for the reasons for this, I can tell you little. I feel like Job in the face of such a complexity of reasons that I will never understand. As for love, I find that is not so different. Such a complexity of reasons, so much you do not understand, so much fear and excitement...'

He told her about his oath to John of Muchelney. He told her of his confusion and the fears he had about the future, and he looked up as he spoke to see her staring up at him with tears in her eyes.

'Isabella, what is the matter. Have I told you too much?'

'No, Hilary. No, I must confess to you. I had no understanding of what it meant, but I took your purse.'

'You?' said Hilary, the relief rushing in. Thank goodness; he would not have to confess the loss to Master Peter – he could give the letter intact to Count Fulk. 'But the boy..?'

'The boy was me. You did not recognise me through the steam. I should not have been there, but I could not resist the joke. I made a good boy, did I not?'

'You did indeed.' Hilary smiled. How extraordinary this girl was. 'But Isabella, you must give it back as soon as you can. Can you fetch it now?'

To his surprise, Isabella burst into tears. He caressed her hand and told her not to worry, that he forgave her the joke and how relieved he was.

'That is the problem, Hilary. The pouch has gone. It was taken from me.'

'Gone?' His heart sank again.

'I put it safely in my box, which I keep in my parent's chamber, behind the screen. I keep all my most precious belongings there. This morning, I went there to give it you back and it had gone. I asked the servants and they said they had chased a man out of the upper storey yesterday and that he carried something with him. Hilary, I am so sorry. My stupidity has threatened you.'

Hilary stared hopelessly ahead of him. So they had the letters. Perhaps now they would leave him alone.

'Do you offer me your forgiveness?'

What was she saying? His forgiveness? He could barely think clearly. What was he to do? 'Oh yes, of course. Of course. I fear Master Peter may not forgive me, on the other hand.'

Isabella rose to her feet and took his hand. She spoke directly into his face.

'Listen, Hilary. You are every bit as good as Master Peter. He is not your lord. He argues well; he disputes with great skill, I grant you, but he lacks something – I don't mean that. He lacks humanity. He talks about humanity, but he lacks it himself. He does.'

Hilary laughed at her efforts. 'Isabella, you are kind, but...'

'I will show you. Take out that message we found in St Edward's convent yesterday. Saewulf's message. Take it out. That's right. Now, you can tell me what it means.'

In a moment, she had extracted the mysterious piece of metal and put it in his hands. He stared at it stupidly, gesticulating hopelessly.

'Come on, Hilary. You are a clever man too. What does it mean? What does the bull mean?'

Hilary held the metal. It glinted in the sunlight. It must mean something, but it was beyond him. 'Really... Really, Isabella...'

'Come on, Hilary. What do bulls mean? You know, don't you? Are they in the stars? Are they gods?'

'No, it means ... It means St Luke, of course it does. St Luke's gospel. St Luke the evangelist.'

Isabella smiled at him. He felt great pride. He could do it.

' I think this is a biblical quotation. But which one? Sometime around the resurrection, I believe... Luke 24 verse six... I can't remember. Yes, I can: '*He is not here, but is risen: remember how he spake unto you when he was yet in Galilee.*'

'Well done, Hilary. Risen? What does it mean? That the Great Jewel of Alfred has risen? Does it mean it has been hidden somewhere more important – in the Holy Sepulchre or the Temple perhaps.'

'No, I believe this is a dead end.'

Hilary sat down after the intellectual effort. He felt proud and grateful. He took Isabella's hand for a moment. What a tragedy that he was to be sent to Normandy. How he could have loved her if she had been in Paris with him. How strange life should turn out, and how frustrating. Then he realised what she had said.

'The Temple? Is that still standing?'

'Solomon's temple was destroyed, but it was rebuilt and is now the palace of the King of Jerusalem. Or it was. It has been abandoned now, though my father goes there sometimes. I will show you before I leave. There is nothing there, Hilary. Just rubble.'

Sleeping on the straw at St John the Almoner that night, Hilary woke in the middle of the night and became aware of a dark figure praying over him in the shadows.

'Your name is Hilary,' said the old man in the dark. 'I am right, am I not?'

Hilary nodded. 'It is one of my names,' he said. He felt too tired to be careful. 'May I ask who you are?'

'My name does not matter. I have been many years. Since before the crusaders came. Tell me, Hilary or whatever name you care to chose. Shall we pray for your soul?'

'Yes, father. If you will.'

'Come then, let us pray together.' The old words flowed out. He had felt estranged from them, perhaps since his outrageous behaviour in Paris, ridiculing the bishops and priests. Now it felt different, almost a relief.

'Come Hilary, let us send a blessing in the night. It is more powerful that way. Who would you pray for, my son?'

'Isabella de Payens. May she reach Normandy safely and find happiness there.'

'Yes, and...'

'Peter Abelard.'

'God send his blessings on them. Amen. Is there anyone else?'

'Yes, father. John of Muchelney. May he rest in peace.'

'*Requiem aeternam dona eis, Domine, et lux perpetua luceat eis.*'

3/Fulk

'Here it is at last. I found a copy. I had to bribe a merchant from Pisa.'

Isabella was holding out a book. It was a valuable specimen and Hilary opened it at random, pleased that his pupil was progressing in this way, even if these were quietly informal lessons in the courtyard of his hostel. The writing was beautifully executed. He read the familiar words and then shut it again quickly.

'I'm sorry, Isabella. I can't possibly read you this. It is Ovid. It isn't the kind of thing you are supposed to read to pupils, and especially not young women. Where did you say you got this?'

Isabella pouted. 'Hilary, I'm about to be married. I'm a grown woman and there is a great deal which I need to know. Now, don't let me down.'

'How can I, Isabella? I'm a clerk in holy orders...'

'Really, Hilary, I thought you were more fun. Now, give it here...' She lunged at Hilary and snatched the book from his grasp.

'Now listen,' she said, dancing around out of his reach.

'Behold Corinna comes, her clothes unbuttoned,
Her hair hangs loose along her snowy neck.'

'This is good poetry, Hilary!'
'Isabella, I beg you. Somebody will hear.'

'Listen to this!'

> *'In such a guise did fair Semiramis give*
> *herself to loving. Yes, and thus did Lais*
> *give welcome to her many lovers, one and all.*
> *I raised her shift. The cloth was soft and fine*
> *and but a flimsy obstacle. Except Corinna*
> *was not willing to quite lose her clothing yet.*
> *She strove, but yet not wanting quite to win.*
> *Soon she let herself succumb to conquering...'*

Hilary marched over while Isabella struggled with the Latin for 'plump thighs' and snatched it back.

'Hey! Don't do that, Hilary – I need to learn!'

Hilary felt safe inside St John the Almoner's hostel, though he paid daily visits to the home of Hugues de Payens, in the hope of finding Abelard. Nor had he seen the master of the house since his arrival. He could imagine the hired men outside in the city searching for him, and for Abelard who spent his days in the Patriarch's library or lecturing in the convent. On the day following his adventure in the street, a message arrived from Isabella, delivered by one of the monks at St John the Almoner, asking to meet him in the garden next door. For the next six days, he fulfilled his promise to her and taught her how to write songs. They were increasingly poignant meetings because he knew she was bound for Normandy, marriage and the unknown.

The day she arrived with Ovid, she wore her habitual leather boots and a dagger hung from her belt. Her hair was hidden inside her hood. She could easily have been a boy, and Hilary realised that was how she had managed to get into the

Hospitallers' grounds. They stared irritated at each other, while Hilary smoothed down the creased pages of the book.

'Hilary, tell me. Have you ever loved?'

He coloured for a moment, thinking back. 'I don't know what you mean. You mean like that? Like Corinna? Not quite like that, no.'

Could he really confess the unsatisfactory arc of his life to this girl?

'Well, why am I asking you to help me write songs then? You've never loved. You're a priest.'

'Not quite a priest, actually.

'Then tell me, Hilary! Tell me before I have to leave. Tell me about you and tell me how to love. I can ask nobody else but you. How can I face a husband when I don't know what I'm supposed to feel? Tell me. Tell me.'

Tears had appeared in her eyes. Hilary took her hand and looked at her. He realised he had never really looked at her properly before: her boyish shoulders, the way her long hair curled up at the ends. Her cheeky nose.

'Isabella. I can tell you about me, but I have to trust you. You must swear to say nothing of this. Nothing. Do you understand?'

'Who would I tell?' Isabella made the sign of the cross over her heart and put her finger to her lips.

'I don't know.' Why was he telling his most intimate secrets to her? Why did this seem the most intimate confession of all? Why were some men born for action and some men born to aspire to poetry like Ovid's? He looked Isabella, fascinated by the way she swayed a little in front of him. No, he would tell.

Isabella seemed to be hanging onto his very lips. 'Tell me who you loved, Hilary. I beg you.'

'Well, I probably loved too often, if the truth was told. But I thought I loved a lady called Alys, not much older than you. She died. St Anthony's Fire.'

'Did you love her like... like Corinna?'

'I never struggled with her clothes, if that's what you mean. I never so much as touched her. But I wanted to love her. I liked the way her legs moved. It wasn't exactly a Godly love, and yet I can't believe that God who loved the world would look unkindly on my loves, which are simple at least. Maybe you will love like that too. Maybe I will again, but I no longer welcome these overwhelming, lonely loves. We must hope for something shared.'

'Hilary. I hope so. I hope you do too. We are like each other, you and I. Now show me how to write a song about it.'

The multiple crowing of cockerels all over the city had heralded the dawn, and Hilary was up early. He felt rested and ready. There had been no sign of Abelard for days. He would have to act without him.

The crowd was already in St Stephen's Street, and there again was the whole gamut of crusader life: soldiers without limbs, resigned looking women, burned to a crisp by the sun, a couple of dishevelled priests, a whole family of German artisans, a threadbare Benedictine on hard times, each one – no doubt – with their story of misery and their unique and cajoling plea for help which they aimed to set before one of the great magnates. All around them, the horsemen and carts were gathering, as well as the merchants and fruit-sellers and their wagons setting up for the day.

Hilary retraced his steps past Covered Street back towards Temple Street, past a foul-smelling cess-pit and into furriers district, in search of the Temple itself. Abelard had promised to investigate the Church of the Holy Sepulchre to see if there any clues about the whereabouts of Saewulf's Great Jewel of Alfred. If the Temple was now crumbling and empty, he would find a way in and see for himself. Perhaps that was what the inscription meant when it used the word 'risen'. Where would you 'rise' from if not the very place where Christ himself rose?

Thinking about how to manage this, his eye was caught by a flash of what could have been rags disappearing behind a pony in the distance, but then nothing. Scanning the horizon in the market behind him, Hilary suddenly made out instead a figure in a blue hood. He could see no face in the shadow cast by the clothing. He seemed just to be waiting, turned away and pretending to be looking closely at one of the market stalls. The watchers must have realised he was back in the streets already.

It was when he turned into the side streets, near where he believed the Temple was to be found, that he began to get seriously concerned. He looked behind himself, almost alone in the alleyway, and there in the distance was the man in the blue cloak busying himself with his shoes. He was still there two corners later. Hilary dodged into another alleyway and hid in a doorway waiting for him to pass. After five minutes he gave up and looked back in the street. It was empty. Then he doubled back towards the market.

There was still no sign of his pursuer by the time he reached the Street of the Furriers. Doubling his speed, he half walked and half ran through the small crowd of shoppers – as much of a crowd he seen so far in Jerusalem – once more doubling back into Temple Street and retracing his steps again to the Temple. Feeling pathetic, he glanced through some broken brickwork and then he stood and stared. Before him was a wide expanse of terrace, much of it overgrown. Some of it was in the process of being colonised by a small forest of live bushes which had managed to force their roots through the ancient paving slabs. Behind them was a wide flight of stairs, wider than anything

Hilary had ever seen, even in Paris, and then a whole series of arches, and in the distance, sagging and dilapidated, a huge wooden dome.

'This is it,' said Hilary aloud. Unwilling to risk announcing himself at the gate, even if there was a gate any more, he climbed over the broken wall, and started towards the crumbling arches, picking his way through the rubble and fallen stonework. It was like discovering ancient Rome after the arrival of the barbarians. There was a melancholic air.

Across the courtyard was an even more dilapidated building. He avoided the crumbling steps, leading up to another series of arches, each one becoming a little more overgrown. Nobody seemed to be around. There was a gaping hole in the wall, filled with masonry and cobwebs, but there were shafts of sunlight penetrating the roof, and marble on the floor. Hilary climbed in. He had no idea what he was looking for. It was not at all clear to him what significance this jewel had or why it mattered if it was lodged in Jerusalem, but he needed to have a look. He would know what he was searching for when he saw it.

Once inside the building, reaching the first pillar, it first struck Hilary that the interior seemed very different to what it had seemed on the outside. There was no rubble and no holes in the roof. In the distance, and to his great surprise, he could see carpets. Then there was the noise of the clank of metal against metal and he turned to find himself looking down a drawn sword. On the other end was a soldier wearing a black and white surcoat.

'And you are?' said the soldier, his beard sweating above his chain mail.

'My name is Hilary the Englishman and I am an associate of Master Peter Abelard.'

As he said this, Hilary felt himself grabbed from behind, could feel the chain mail biting into his hand, and realised that he had been arrested. The two soldiers searched him for hidden weapons, and felt his bag that contained the remainder of his silver pieces.

'What's this? A donation?' they guffawed but, to Hilary's surprise, handed back the purse untouched.

'What are you doing here?' said the second soldier. 'Do you know where you are?'

'I told you...'

'Don't answer back, there's a good boy. We don't like intruders here, do you understand? We have to be very careful.'

Hilary realised he had been seriously mistaken that the Temple had been abandoned. There was a brisk efficiency about the place; a gleaming array of weaponry was fixed to the walls. There were black and white shields along the corridors. The pillars had been draped with damask that separated parts of the great space from each other. There was a functioning altar, and carpets. There were military-looking men resting and drinking. There were white hoods walking purposefully around. How could he have imagined that he could sneak in here?

'Come along then. We'll lock you up until the under-master is ready to see you.'

'Really, all I was doing was...'

'Quiet. Things will be much easier if you just shut the fuck up. Nobody messes with the Templars. Nobody wanders around our house without good reason.'

'Wait!' said Hilary, falling back on the only defence he knew. 'I'm a clerk in holy orders.'

'Where do you think you are? Hades? We're all in holy orders here. Come with us if you know what's good for you.'

Some hours later, Hilary sat with his back against the wall, sitting on the flagstones, a small pile of straw beside him which had obviously nurtured the last poor wretch to be incarcerated here, and considered his plight. Something nagged away at him. Didn't he know something about this transformation of the Temple? The word 'Templars' was unfamiliar too him, but still there was something...

Once he had calmed down, desperately trying to persuade himself that this crypt was a temporary residence, he began – as prisoners who are unfamiliar with the situation tend to do – to contemplate his own life. Was he just one of those people who life acted upon, to whom things happened, he asked himself? Was there no part of himself capable, like Master Peter, of making things happen on his own account? Must he always wait upon events, and have them thrust upon him so disastrously? A wave of self-pity overwhelmed Hilary. He bowed his head in despair. Then he remembered Isabella, and the blow he had struck his assailant in the street, and felt a little better.

The temperature was at least cool down in the cell. A small shaft of sunlight pierced through the crack above him, shifting slowly with the passage of the sun. He must have slept because, the next thing he knew, he was being woken roughly and pulled to his feet.

'You're in luck. The under-master wants to see you.'

'I can walk, thank you,' said Hilary loudly, as one of his captors began to drag him. They looked at him, thought better of the effort, and let him walk along behind. Shaking with apprehension, Hilary followed. This could be the end of the whole story, thanks to Isabella's mistake about the Temple being unoccupied. What was going to happen now? Hanged as a spy, despite having innocently stumbled into something he had no reason to expect. His feet echoed on the flagstones towards his fate.

A bored looking potentate, half obscured by his grey beard, was dismissing a man with a missing arm. He had gold ear-rings and an air of quiet menace. It was only when he could see his small eyes, standing under his full gaze, that Hilary recognised – with a sinking feeling – who he was. It was Arnulf of Montgomery. The man who had wanted to execute Abelard's boy as a spy.

'Your name?' said Arnulf in his familiar rasping voice. This time his favourite dagger lay across the table in front of him, no doubt so that he could admire it. 'Speak quickly. I don't have very long.'

Hilary collected his thoughts. The Temple had been decked out as some kind of headquarters, or was it a convent for soldiers? There was a huge crucifix on the wall and carpets on the floor. It was hard to categorise what kind of organisation this was. It looked monastic and yet Arnulf wore a sword.

'No, wait. I've seen you before, my friend, and I know exactly where. You were with that insufferable philosopher who argued with the Constable, were you not? I should fling you in the cellar and forget about you.'

'Master Peter is not with me, my lord.'

'That is all the better for him, by God. The fewer philosophers we have in Jerusalem the better, with their luxurious baths and their logical nonsense. You can start by telling me what you are doing here, uninvited. If the reason is not excellent, we will deal with you as we should have dealt with that spy last week. Don't waste my time, I warn you.'

'I believed the Temple was empty, my lord.'

'I'll be honest with you,' said Arnulf, staring into space. 'We have found people snooping around here before. I know there are innocent explanations. We're not stupid, but we prefer to take no chances. We are a new order and we are the defensive shield of

Christendom. We are the very front line of its defence. Christ himself expects us to take no chances. So I will ask you one more time. What were you doing in the Temple?'

Hilary felt himself stiffen at this outrageous blasphemy. If Master Peter were there, this man would be tied into intellectual knots. Though it was true that his presence might not encourage leniency, so perhaps it was just as well he was not there. But what was he to say? Any mention of Saewulf or the jewel would probably be a mistake. 'I seek Count Fulk of Anjou, my lord.'

Arnulf was clearly surprised. 'Is that so? And what is your business with Count Fulk?'

Hilary was extremely reluctant to tell Arnulf anything.

'It is a complicated story, my lord.'

'Don't patronise me. I'm as capable as your philosopher friend of understanding complicated tales. Just tell me the truth.'

Hilary thought quickly. 'I was asked to deliver a letter to him. I came to Outremer to find Count Fulk with no other intention than handing over the letter...'

'And earn a fat fee no doubt. Very well, hand over the letter and be gone.'

There was the noise of banging and shouting in the background, and a warm rush of heat from the outside. The builders were demolishing a wall. The conversation was not going at all well.

'I fear I do not have it with me.'

Arnulf erupted. 'God's truth! Why must I waste my time in this way? The Grand Master will have to decide. Bring him!' He motioned to the soldiers, eased himself up from his seat in a flurry of gowns, and adjusted his belt. Hilary was manhandled after him. His back hurt from sitting on the flagstones in the cellar crypt and he was beginning to be seriously frightened.

'I can walk, thank you,' he snapped again at the most

enthusiastic soldier. He followed Arnulf up some steps towards what had once been the altar of the ancient Temple. Before him was a long table laden with fruit and goblets of wine. Behind it, a beautiful tapestry hung and sitting there were three men, one old, one middle-aged and one younger, resplendent in the most colourful cloaks of red, purple and green. As he approached them, they collapsed into laughter about some joke. The joker was a rotund elderly man at the end with a beard and sparkling eyes. He slapped his thigh and banged the table.

Arnulf bowed slightly and without deference. 'My lords, this wretch was found...'

Suddenly, and huge relief, Hilary realised that the middle-aged man in the middle was his former host Hugues de Payens, still apparently not with the army.

'My lord of Payens,' said Hilary without thinking.

Hearing his name spoken had roused Hugues de Payens, and he leaned over to get a better look.

'You are talking to the founder of our order,' snapped Arnulf. 'Do not dare to question him.'

The light of recognition seemed to dawn finally in Hugues eyes. 'Hilary the Englishman, by the testicles of St Peter.'

Hilary started. The wine was clearly having its effect at this party.

'Well met, Hilary. Welcome to our humble headquarters. Welcome to the Order of the Poor Fellow Soldiers of Christ and of Solomon's Temple.' He banged the table with decision. The glasses wobbled and clinked. Arnulf stood awkwardly looking at them both.

'Arnulf, I can vouch for this man. He is a colleague of Master Peter Abelard. Thank you for delivering him.'

Hilary stood before the trio of lords, wondering what he had stumbled into. He had heard of this new order, of course, but had not yet understood that they had been recruiting, let alone settled on a headquarters. Hugues turned to the large giggling man next to him.

'My lord Duke, Hilary and I were speaking some days ago about the need for a military order of monks to protect the pilgrims on their way to Jerusalem. Well, look around you, Hilary. That is what we are. We still have some way to go, but as you can see, our holy task has begun. Hilary, I present you to my distinguished and celebrated guest, Duke William IX of Aquitaine.'

Hilary stared. Duke William? Did he say Duke William?

'An honour to meet you, sir.' Hilary bowed. What was the most famous aristocratic performer in France doing here, he wondered? The man guffawed again and waggled an arm at him.

'May I ask, my lord,' said Hilary. 'Are you in Jerusalem to perform?'

Duke William stared at him with amusement. 'I fear not, young man. I am in Jerusalem to honour God and entertain the ladies. I must shortly return home to confront my dear wife, who has accused me of the most heinous theft. She is currently lodging at the home of my friend the Count here, in Anjou, where she is turning into the most magnificent pain in my backside.' He burst out laughing again, drank deep from his goblet and slumped down.

His two companions laughed hilariously. But Hilary was thinking. Count? Anjou? Could this red-faced younger man possibly be Fulk? Did he dare ask? No wonder Arnulf of Montgomery had looked surprised. Fulk of Anjou was actually here in the Temple. But Hugues was looking at him as if expecting him to withdraw politely. It was now or never.

'My lord Count,' said Hilary with decision, turning to the third man. He had uncontrollable black hair and bright red cheeks, which may have been the wine but must have been pretty red to begin with.

Hilary took his chance. 'I came to Jerusalem that I might deliver a message to Count Fulk of Anjou, given me by a dead man, one John of Muchelney. I do not understand the message. May I now discharge this debt of honour?'

'Speak. I am listening. You have travelled a long way.' Fulk sat bolt upright and waited.

Hilary looked at him properly for the first time. He was watchful and serious, but the look of slightly alcoholic amusement was still on his face.

'I was given a letter for you which has been stolen from me in Jerusalem.'

'I am sorry for it,' said Count Fulk, looking watchful and careful now. 'Did you read the letter?'

'I did not.'

'I have to say, letters very rarely give me pleasure,' said Duke William. 'If they are not from my wife, they are from my irritatingly po-faced son.' Count Fulk stared at Hilary, as if summing him up.

'I confess, I do not understand why you are here if you have nothing to deliver. Are you sure you read nothing in the letter?'

'I did not, my lord,' said Hilary, trying not to let his own face go red in this bare-faced lie, and wondering what he could say instead. 'But I did have a message. Simply this: *Hit waes geara iu.*'

Fulk stared at him. The half smile had now disappeared from his face. For a second, there was a flash of fear in his eyes. He considered Hilary slowly.

'You have no understanding of the message? Is that right?'

'That is correct, my lord. The message was given to me but not explained.'

'Then I must warn you, you are dabbling in dangerous territory. I don't know which meddler or spy or cloistered philosopher has been misleading you, but I do not believe that this message has any meaning at all.'

'Then I am to forget it.'

'Aye, forget it. Forget it. It will do you no good, and it has done me no good. Yes, there was a time in my youth when I might have been tempted to trace the source of the message you have given me. There was a time, certainly. Have I not seen action at Bures-en-Brai? Believe me,' he said, his hand sweeping around to include Hugues and Duke William. 'I hold no affection for the King of England, and I choose my words carefully. I hold no affection for him even now. I would not entrust my life to him. Certainly not. Or dine in his great hall in Westminster. But I will not fight him. I will not. Christendom requires a new spirit from us. The very boundaries of Christ's kingdom must be defended, and I put my youthful squabbles behind me. You can witness this, my lord Hugues.'

Count Fulk stared suspiciously at Hilary.

'One hears rumours,' said Hugues de Payens, absent-mindedly. The atmosphere was now electric. Fulk sat on the edge of his chair as if about to rise. He appeared to have forgotten Hilary altogether.

'You should not listen to rumours, but I will not join this Saxon alliance they propose. I will not seek to overthrow God's anointed in England. They must look to themselves.'

Duke William sniggered and Count Fulk looked back at Hilary.

'I forget your name, my friend, but listen carefully to my advice,' he said. 'I don't know what your mission is, and it interests me not at all. But let me tell you about King Henry of England. He is lethal to those who pose any kind of challenge to him. Do you see these eyes? He takes a special interest in people's eyes. He plucks them out if they have seen too much. And if he finds these Saxon plotters, then he will take out more than their eyes. Take care, that is all I say. Now, go on your way, and let us amuse ourselves.'

It was only as Hilary was ushered out down the steps of the Temple, past the new stable building on the courtyard and a detritus of a barracks, horses, weapons and arrows – with the roar of the stoves in the smithies – that he saw the Temple complex clearly in its new guise. If he had not tried to slip in unnoticed at the back, it would have been obvious that Solomon's Temple now had a new role. Only back in Temple Street did he breathe a long sigh of relief.

No, Count Fulk did not seem to welcome the message at all. In fact, if the others had not been present, Hilary felt unsure whether he would have been allowed to leave. His suspicious stare remained with Hilary as he made his way carefully down the path out of the Templar compound. John of Muchelney's promise had now been discharged, and much good it had done him.

As he walked down the steps to the Temple, looking afresh at the trees bursting through the broken slabs, a servant ran out of the building. 'Your friend asked me to tell you that he will meet you in the road that leads to the gardens between Beaucayre Gate and Zion Gate,' he said breathlessly.

'What friend?' said Hilary, suddenly confused. 'Master Peter?' But the servant had gone. How had he known? It made no sense. He made his way quickly into the street.

The sun was now high in the sky. It was blindingly bright and the heat in the narrow streets was now intense. Hilary glanced round and froze. Behind him in the market, now with fewer people in the full heat of the day, was the blue cloak again. He was still being followed.

The man was too far again to recognise. Hilary dodged into a side street to make sure. Sure enough, some hundred yards back, the blue cloak had turned as well, and was now busying himself with his shoes. For the second or third time that day, a chill went down Hilary's spine. Could the whole rigmarole be beginning again? He had discharged his message. The letters were gone. Why was he still being pursued? Then he remembered Count Fulk's words: there is a Saxon plot. No wonder the Normans were exercised by the letter he had carried. John of Muchelney was indeed playing a dangerous game.

He dodged through the leather market and then asked directions. 'There is a man at the turning with a goat, and at the end of it there is a fountain there. It is hard to miss.'

As he approached the gardens, with St James Cathedral in the distance, he could see the alley. There was the man with the goat he had been warned about. Not long after, he saw the fountain. Extraordinary that the goat should have been so predictable. With one more glance around him to make sure he was not being watched, Hilary turned down the alleyway. He could see the fountain at the end of the road. There appeared to be baggage beneath it. There was no sign of anyone, let alone Master Peter. He stood indecisively in the road.

Suddenly he felt himself grabbed from behind, he wheeled around, and there was his old teacher, smiling and confident.

'Hah, Hilary, I surprised you, did I not!' He had not seen Abelard looking so confident since their recent reunion.

'Master Peter? What are you doing here?'

'Well, I thought you needed a little help,' said Abelard in a cheerful way. A sword that hung in a unclerical way from his belt. 'I have news for you. Three pieces of news. I guessed you would visit the Temple and took the precaution of directing you here afterwards. I have reason to believe you are being followed.'

'I am only too aware of that, Master Peter.'

Abelard's arrival seemed to have disarmed him. He was, once more, the stammering pupil.

'My first news is that I believe the Patriarch's library has solved my problem. There was not one St Denis, a miserable apologist for the King of France. There were three of them! The real Dionysius the Areopagite was the Bishop of Athens, I believe, but then you get the writer whose wisdom has been attributed wrongly to St Denis, and this is the important part. Listen, Hilary...'

'Master Peter, I have to confess – I have lost the papers.'

'What? How?'

'It really was most incompetent of me. My Lord Hugues offered me a bath on our second day in the city and I took the pouch off from around my neck. When I came to dress, they were gone. I cannot apologise enough.'

'Hilary, Hilary, please do not criticise yourself. I myself have realised only today that we are being watched. All I can say is that, at least they did not kill you for them. Perhaps now they have those cursed papers, they might perhaps leave us alone. But you must forgive me for speaking only of myself when you arrived. There clearly are more urgent matters. I must ask you to tell me exactly what has happened from the beginning, and to leave out no details. What of your meeting with the Templars? I understand Count Fulk was there.'

'Since when have you known? You might have told me.' Abelard was insufferable when he was in a good mood. To think that he might have prevented his incarceration in the Temple and failed to mention it.

'Hilary, you never asked. Now, pray continue, what did he say?'

Hilary related the story of his days since their arrival – the loss of the papers, the search, the attack in the alley and his rescue, the conversation with Aldwyn the Saxon soldier, and finally the discovery of Saewulf's church and inscription in metal which said that was a dead end. He explained what Fulk had said: that John of Muchelney's letter had been inviting Count Fulk to share in the spoils once the Saxons had overthrown King Henry and installed a Saxon princeling in his place.

'Fascinating, Hilary. You have done well. It is as I suspected, but I remain in the dark on some questions. I do not yet understand why poor Hubert died. I do not yet understand why William Rufus died and by whose hand, and I do not enjoy the dark. And in any case I fear this tale is not over for us. We are going to have to lie low for a while. It is clear that there are spies even in my lord of Payens' house.'

Was there to be no safe haven in Jerusalem, after all? Hilary's mind reeled. How long was this ordeal going to continue?

'Master Peter, I do not need to know the answer to these questions. I just want an end to this.'

Abelard flicked his wrist in irritation.

'Listen, Hilary. There are things happening and we have very little time. You and I are both in danger now and we must somehow extricate ourselves from this city. I overheard in the Holy Sepulchre. Count Fulk's daughter is to marry William the Aetheling, the son of King Henry of England. You realise what that means?'

Hilary racked his brains.

'It is simple, Hilary. Count Fulk has changed sides. He may have flirted with this Saxon plot, and these letters from Abbot Aelfgar offering him the throne or perhaps offering him Normandy. But now he has buried the hatchet with Henry. It means his grandchildren will sit on the throne of England. The last thing he wants to happen is for news of his involvement with the Saxons to reach Henry and threaten the wedding. Now, you have told him these letters were being re-directed to him. Now he knows that *we know* he was involved. As I feared, you were followed. He will try to make sure we do not leave Jerusalem alive.'

A fury at the perfidy of the rulers of the world filled Hilary for a moment. How could he have been so stupid? He went all the way into the Temple and spoke to Fulk.

'God damn them all, Master Peter. Will this nightmare never end? Wait!' Hilary caught sight of a flurry in the crowd ahead of them. The man with the blue hood was there again. They moved quickly towards the main street again, watching carefully.

'Master Peter, I fear we will have to retrace our steps to France.' Hilary felt sick at the prospect of that voyage again and, as the words came out, he realised how sad he would be to leave his new pupil.

'I fear so, Hilary. I have omitted to give you the third piece of news. My lord Hugues de Payens has asked me to accompany his daughter to Europe. She will have an armed guard, but he wanted a priest to watch over her spiritual welfare. I told him I was no longer a priest, but – if he would overlook that – I would go. You will come with us, Hilary?'

The news that he was to spend the journey back to Europe in the company of Isabella gave Hilary and inexplicable surge of joy. He took a deep breath, his eyes shining.

'I will come with you, Master Peter. But first, I would like you to come with me'.

'This stone is slightly chipped,' said Abelard, peering down at the altar in the deserted English convent of St Edward the Confessor.

'I confess, I do not yet understand why you have brought me here.'

'I think that was me, Master Peter. I chipped it with Isabella's knife.'

'Her knife, you say? She carries a knife?'

Abelard peered some more, with an air of disapproval. 'I wonder if that inscription simply meant 'He is not here', and referred to the Great Jewel. Perhaps that was all we were intended to glean. Hilary, I am not sure we have been sensible coming in here. If they know where we are, we are likely to be trapped.'

Hilary looked around. He would look peculiarly stupid if his idea led nowhere, and it did mean somehow finding the steps up to the roof. There were small wooden doors in the nave. The whole place smelled of dust and decay. He pulled the first door open. It was a cupboard containing bottles. The next one led to a narrow spiral stone staircase going up. They pulled the door closed behind them, and listened to make sure there was nobody above them.

'It is like Notre Dame all over again,' said Abelard.

'Except this time, we are going upwards.'

There was a trap door which opened out onto the roof. It was searingly hot and it was hard to walk on the slanted roof and the semi-circular pottery roofing tiles. Hilary stared around him. The view was extraordinary, north to the St Stephen Gate and the Holy Sepulchre, east to the Temple and the Valley of Kidron beyond the walls, and all around them the empty streets and dilapidated yellow stone of the ancient, half-deserted city. It felt like a kind of cloud: the whole city was spread out before them, with the markets and the ruins side by side. There was a flock of sheep, there was a sleeping soldier, there the road out through the David Gate to the desert.

Hilary's foot slipped. A roof tile fell off the edge of the roof and smashed noisily down in the street. The two men froze and waited. Nothing moved.

'You see, Master Peter, I wondered whether we were supposed to take the inscription literally, and just simply go upwards. Now, it is as I imagined – there are crenellations along the roof, and if we just count twenty-four this way and six that way, we might perhaps find what we are looking for.'

Hilary waited for Abelard to pour scorn on his idea. There was silence. He could hear the noise of the people below in the street.

'Why would it be so simple, Hilary?'

'Perhaps because Saewulf would not know who would come, or when they would come, to collect this coronation jewel – whatever it is.'

His heart sank. There was no obvious hiding place in that spot.

'Perhaps it is paces, not crenellations.' It was clear from the first glance that both sides of the roof were too short for twenty-four paces.

'Perhaps you have simply chosen the wrong side,' said Abelard. 'Here, look at this...'

Hilary made the calculation himself. Twenty-four crenellations along, and six across. And there was indeed a stone which looked a little loose.

'Hilary, I believe we have it! What a pity we don't have Isabella's knife.'

'But we do,' said Hilary in triumph, bringing out Isabella's dagger and working it around the edge of the stone, in the thin crack.

It was hard work, as the sun beat down. A stream of instructions issued from Abelard until Hilary handed him the knife.

'You might do it better than me, Master Peter. You do it.'

'Well, Hilary. I merely suggest that I should pull up this side of the stone with the knife, and it may be possible for you to hold it with your fingers, while I then turn my attention to the other end.'

Slowly, ever so slowly, the stone worked its way up, until Hilary lifted it away, revealing a small chamber a foot down. He reached down with his hand and pulled out what looked like a small bundle of black cloth.

'My congratulations, Hilary. You appear to have found a small rag.'

Hilary said nothing. He unwrapped the cloth and there before him, resting in his palm, was a peculiar object, quite heavy but no longer than his finger. It was clearly a jewel of great price.

'What is it?' asked Abelard. 'What do those words say?'

'AELFRED MEC HEHT GEWYRCAN,' read Hilary. 'It means: "Alfred ordered that I be made". I believe it is a pointer for those reading a holy book, for use in some kind of ceremonial. This has to be it. This has to be the Alfred Jewel.'

Abelard stared hungrily at the object. It was dirty and unloved, but made with care and craftsmanship. It was a thing of beauty and ceremony.

'You know what this means, Hilary. It means that England and Normandy are on the verge of the most terrible civil war. We could right an old wrong, and take this back to Abbot Aelfgar and the rightful king of England. We could reunite it with its makers. We could give it to King Henry. Or we could use it to bring peace. We stand between England and slaughter now.'

'Master Peter, I doubt your sanity. I want to live out my days in peace and security. If I can clear my name, there will be no meddling in the affairs of kings and princes for me. I want to keep my eyes in their sockets. I don't want King Henry's torturers to put them out. I don't understand why you want to.'

To his surprise, Abelard was now red in the face with passion or rage. It was hardly clear which. 'No!' he said, with great emotion. 'No, Hilary. I will do it because it is the truth, and what else is there before me but pursuit of the truth? What else? That is what I offer the world, and if they put me on the rack, for my part, it is a price worth paying. Now, take that jewel, and put it somewhere safe. We will need it, I am telling you. So keep it safe.'

Three days later, with the jewel in a new purse around Hilary' neck, they swung out of the David Gate into the cacophony of carts, people and animals, with the squawk of hens and cockerels, the curses of the ostlers and the creaking of wheels, and headed out into the desert. Alongside them were three armed associates of Hugues de Payens and Abelard's box of books and papers, and Isabella's nurse and her women servants and their baggage and boxes, and the dowry.

In front of them, on a small brown pony, flicking the flies with its tail, sat Isabella herself. She was white faced and erect, evidently holding herself together by willpower alone. Her hair was pinned up on her head like a grown woman. She wore a long gown that shimmered in the bright sunlight. Beside her rode her father, looking proud and capable, with his long flat sword hanging down. He was to travel with them as far as Beit Nuba.

She sat rigid and brittle and moved no muscle in her face. As Hilary watched her kick her horse into the slow pace of the convoy, he saw a tear run down her cheek.

4/Winchester

Winchester, 6 September 1120

It was market day in Winchester as Hilary and Abelard walked up through the South Gate, with the castle towering above the city to their left. The cattle and carts were all around them as they ambled down Silver Street, and it was immediately clear where the cathedral was. They could see it ahead of them, its new square tower gleaming in the sunlight, visible over the wall around the abbey precincts.

'This time, we will go in the front door,' said Abelard. 'No more climbing through windows of monastic establishments for me.'

The warm autumn sunlight shone on them with an air of harvests and meadows, and the cool interior of the cathedral beckoned to them. Through the door they walked, marvelling at the new stained glass and the colours which danced under the great arches. They stared in wonder as they walked silently down the nave, ignoring the throng of people around them doing business, negotiating and jostling in the arches.

'You know whose tomb that is?' said Hilary, indicating the squat black tomb before them.

'No. Whose?'

'I believe it belongs to Rufus himself.'

The two men stared down at it, wondering what secrets it concealed. Abelard touched the edge of it and, a moment later, two monks were at their side.

'We would like to see the Prior,' he said.

The decision to come to Winchester had been made for them, since their ship had docked some days before in Southampton. It had been a long voyage back to Marseilles, and a journey along the Pyrenees to take a second ship, carrying wine to England, to hug the coast of France northwards, putting into small ports and bays overnight. Abelard had continued with his writing, oblivious to wind and waves, occasionally joining in the singing at night and during the occasional storms.

It was a journey of extremes, and of long periods of debilitating boredom too. From the moment their ship had felt the swell of the Mediterranean, and the huge striped sail had been hauled up and filled with a breeze from the Khamsin, straight from the North African desert, Abelard had settled down with his studies. On the long journey from island by island along the Mediterranean, he stayed deep in his books, oblivious to the waves. The men-at-arms had slept for whole weeks at a time, or so it had seemed to Hilary.

For Hilary, it had also been transformative. His friendship with Isabella had blossomed. Day in, day out, wind or rain, he had taught her, sung to her, listened to her and written songs on scraps of vellum along with her, performing them in the tiny ports along the coast of Italy and France. They made each other laugh. Isabella told him about her life in Jerusalem, the spices, the wine like honey and the beggars at the Jehosophat Gate. Hilary told her about his home in the tiny Hampshire village of Nether Wallop, of his life in Paris and the debauchery of the wandering scholars. When the conversation lagged, he taught her about Boethius and Proclus.

'I am sad to think that I will never hear you sing again, Hilary,' she said as the ship entered the Bay of Biscay.

'We will pray for each other, you and I. You will have to stay still in your castle; I am fated to be pursued around Christendom.'

When they were tired of poetry, they played checkers with Isabella's nurse.

'Come on, Hilary, you old lecher, throw the dice!'

'Isabella, I would ask you not to use that description of me. I am a man of God.' But he laughed nonetheless; there was something pure about her energy.

'No, Hilary. I know about wandering scholars, and you are a wandering scholar.'

'You know nothing about wandering scholars. I am the first one to wander anywhere near you.'

'Their reputation wandered here first.'

But despite the games, for both of them, the future loomed heavy. The prospects of marriage to a Norman lord like Richard of Montgomery were unknowable but they made Isabella shiver. Hilary's prospects seemed unchanged. He dwelt long on them, still pursued by those who killed John of Muchelney and those who believe he was the murderer, and now perhaps also pursued by Fulk of Anjou and his men. The prospects for clearing his name.

'I feel as if I am just a pawn in the titanic struggle that I don't understand,' he told Abelard one night.

'That is exactly what we both are, Hilary,' said Abelard, staring at the waves lapping against the side of the ship. 'We are just the pawns of a greater game, you and I. God has involved us in a bigger game and we don't know the rules. But you are wrong that you are pursued by many different factions. The truth is, they are all one. All on the same side. For some reason, the Normans, the French and the Angevins have sunk their many differences, put aside even the differences between them, and are acting together. For some reason, they all take these letters by Abbot Aelfgar seriously, with all this talk of the Great Coronation Jewel of Alfred. They are in league with each other, even though they are supposed to be at war. And, as you say, now that Count Fulk as arranged the final details of his daughter's betrothal to William the Aetheling, we have to assume he is on the same side.'

'As you say, the heir to the English throne.'

'Quite. The prospect of the Saxons on the throne of England once more, and controlling Normandy too, seems to appall the French and English so much that they are prepared to work together to make sure it never happens. But why do they think it will happen? That is what I don't understand. What has changed to make them feel insecure?'

John of Muchelney, Hubert, and who next? Hilary stared dreamily into the rising waves with the white tops. The wind blew onto his face as he thought about the implications, how his mere existence had brought disaster onto Master Hubert. He must take care that happened to nobody else, and Master Peter seemed so definite about everything. Perhaps he had been wrong to involve him at all, especially as he disappeared into libraries for weeks at a time, just when you needed him.

'We must take nothing for granted, Hilary. That is the basis of my method.'

'Quite so, Master Peter.' He was aware his voice was dry.

'Learn to doubt. But forgive me, Hilary, your tone is a little on edge.'

Hilary drew a deep breath. For the first time his irritation with his old teacher was beginning to get seriously out of hand. 'Master Peter, I apologise. I suppose I did not understand why, while I was in such peril, you were in the library in Jerusalem...'

'Hilary, Hilary, listen to me.' Abelard was now giving him his full attention. 'I realise I have had other things on my mind. But, on the day you went to the Temple, I was due to meet someone at the Patriarch's palace and I was loathe to abandon the meeting.'

'Oh yes,' said Hilary, a little jaded and sounding sceptical.

'The Patriarch recommended his physician to me.'

'Are you ill, Master Peter? I had no idea?'

But the look on Abelard's face, a mixture of embarrassment and human grief, pulled Hilary up short. Of course he knew why the poor man had been reading about medicine. He would have done in the same situation. He felt himself blushing.

'Of course. Did you find him helpful?'

'Not very,' said Abelard, and turned back to stare at the sea.

Nearly two months later, they finally reached Marseilles. Then, through August, there was the long mountainous, back-breaking journey by pony from Marseilles, along the foothills of the Pyrenees to the coast of Aquitaine. There was the strain of peering through the incessant rain and gales in the Bay of Biscay. Through all of these, Hilary endured. He accepted the discomfort and exhaustion because finally, after all the running, he was going home, and because each new day brought a new lesson with Isabella, a chance to see her away from her nurse and servants. God willing, he would also see his mother again, if only he could endure the fear, thirst, hunger and sheer dullness just a little longer. Meanwhile, each day, he slowly smelled a little more, his clothes became more ragged, his face a little more drawn, a little more despairing about the rutted state of the roads. His apparently inexhaustible supply of silver coins also finally began to run short.

The final leg of the journey required them to board another ship to hug the coast of France, and there were more immediate dangers. There were corsairs well-known to be hidden away on the coast of Aquitaine. There were rock shoals and inconvenient islands all the way, but worst of all was the weather in the Bay of Biscay. Hilary kept up a lonely vigil in the bows, whenever he was not with Isabella and her entourage, muttering under his breath at every new cloud and breeze, until they were almost within sight of end of the long journey.

'Barfleur ahead!' shouted the man in the crow's nest.

'I believe I can see the port,' said Abelard, with a huge sigh of relief. 'God be praised.' Hilary's stomach rumbled expectantly, but he was not viewing the port with any sense of relief. There were instructions from Hugues de Payens to deliver Isabella and her entourage to the Constable at Barfleur. Her new husband would arrive from England some time in the early autumn.

'I am to be collected like a pig,' said Isabella with disgust as the ship rocked at the entrance to the harbour. There were sails in port of every colour, and in the distance the white walls and buildings of the town. It looked like home but Hilary's heart was aching.

Why am I feeling such things, he asked himself? Am I not delighted to be home? What is Isabella to me? She is a young girl, too young for love – too young for marriage – and too high for me. I refuse to feel abandoned...

Yet he did feel abandoned. Isabella had grown inside him during the months at sea. There was no doubt he would miss her remarks, her teasing, even their games of chequers. The Lord takes away, he murmured to himself. He takes away forever, over and over again.

'Hilary, I have decided. I will continue the journey with you. This mystery must be solved, for both of our sakes. I will not leave the ship here at Barfleur after all,' said Abelard. 'I will come with you to Southampton. I will help you deliver that jewel.'

The jewel. It still lay in Hilary's breast, but he had all but forgotten it. The whole incident with John of Muchelney, Hubert and the chase across France, seemed decades ago, from another life. If he had to say goodbye to Isabella – and he did – then

Hilary wanted to go home. To start again, maybe with a small farm, maybe to help his father, perhaps teach a little at the abbey in Winchester. It was time to be quiet.

But the proximity of his home reminded Hilary again of the old Saxon soldier, Aldwyn, and his story about the day Rufus was killed, and the furious encounter outside the Treasury in Winchester. 'I will come to Winchester myself,' said Abelard with finality. 'We can take our inquiry into the heart of the mystery.'

The final days in Barfleur were too busy to think too closely about the future. The ship was repaired, the casks of stockfish and bales of cotton in the hold replaced by casks of wine, and Isabella and her entourage deposited into the care of the Constable to await her future. She stood apart from them on the dockside, tears running down her cheeks, her hands by her side, her brown hair and her blue robe blowing in the wind, as the ship moved out again into the harbour with Hilary and Abelard still aboard. She had hidden away so that there should be no goodbyes, but at the last minute she had emerged, to stand there sadly, looking out to sea. Hilary stared back across the broadening gulf of ocean, watching her until they had rounded the headland, still standing lonely and proud, until she was out of sight.

'Master Peter Abelard, you are welcome. Your fame goes before you. We are honoured to receive you here.'

They stood in the cloister in Winchester, the new stone tower rising behind them. A tall, rather suspicious monk in black robes advanced, his hands hidden inside the sleeves of his habit. Gingerly, he extended his ring towards them. Abelard kneeled dutifully. A small entourage of nervous monks had gathered behind him. Abelard's reputation, either for theological dispute or for seducing young women, seemed to be attracting fascinated admirers already. There was a nervous expectancy.

The Prior bowed. 'I pray you, please, I would be honoured if you would dine with me in the refectory tonight. What can I do to make you comfortable? Perhaps I might persuade you to teach some of our brothers about St Augustine. It seems a pity to waste a visit by the great Peter Abelard.'

Hilary noticed the tiny glint in the Prior's eye as he mentioned the great woman-hater, Augustine. Clearly the news about Heloise had reached Winchester. This man is not to be trusted, he told himself. He requires careful stroking and careful handling. He is a man who has risen far in Henry's England, with its damp cells and torturers.

'Alas, my companion and I are only visiting briefly, delivering Isabella de Payens to her new husband,' said Abelard. 'We bless you for your hospitality, my lord Prior. I have long hoped to visit to Winchester, both to see the new cathedral and to consult your famous library.'

He is being unusually self-deprecating for Master Peter, thought Hilary. The Prior did seem a little more at ease.

'So there is one favour I might ask you.'

'Ask away, Master Peter.'

'Books. I mentioned the library. We have a small matter of history we would like to resolve, a small dispute between us. May we see it?'

The Prior seemed relieved.

'Indeed. It would be an honour. Brother Simeon, would you show our visitors to the library and introduce them to our librarian. In the meantime, we dine before vespers and perhaps we might have the pleasure of your company at that service afterwards?'

He bowed once more and withdrew.

'Hilary,' whispered Abelard, as they followed the monk along long, stone corridors and through the cloister, into a much older building. 'Ask the librarian about recent books of history and engage him in conversation while I look around. Do you understand?'

'Yes, we do have some books of history,' said the librarian, his hand shaking a little. He had a wispy white beard and a permanent stoop from decades of peering over bound vellum by candlelight. He looked up at Hilary as if unused to conversation.

'We have a small library here, but we are proud of it. You must be from round here, sir?' he said to Hilary. 'I'm afraid your friend's accent has defeated me.'

Hilary felt warm towards the old librarian for recognising his status. Master Peter might be famous throughout Christendom, but he was unable to hide his Breton-accented Latin when he was here.

The books were not quite as plentiful as he had expected. This was not a library on the same scale as Notre-Dame or Ste-Genevieve, nor the Patriarch's library in Jerusalem, but there were still shelves of great volumes, stacked spine inwards, with obscure numbering systems on their visible pages. Other larger volumes were very obviously chained to the reading desks. A small number of monks were looking up from their work, their fingers covered with paint.

'Could you show me? I am interested in accounts of the death of the late King William Rufus.'

'Ah well, God's will, I fear. King William was contemptuous of the privileges of God's church. I confess I was not surprised...'

Abelard raised his voice from the other side of the chamber, already staggering under the weight of two books. 'Do you remember the events yourself, my friend?'

Two of the monks sat up and glared.

'I confess,' said librarian quietly, 'I find it hard to understand what your friend says.'

'He was asking if you remembered the events around the King's death. Were you here in Winchester?'

'I was. I remember the lights in the sky in the days before. We knew something momentous was about to happen. I remember the new King Henry arriving here. My assistant – sadly no longer with us – urged me to come down and we saw the confrontation in front of the Treasury, the pushing and shouting and the drawn swords. I saw with my own eyes the King's body, all bloated and bloody, drawn in by the charcoal burners. I remember King Henry breaking through the Treasury guards.'

'So you knew Rufus was going to die?'

'Well, I would not claim that. But there were those that did claim it.'

'Would you show me the accounts? I would be very interested.'

'The Prior has asked me to look after you, so yes, if you would follow me.' The old man stumbled a little as he led Hilary between the two shelves and into a side room. It was hard to see in there.

'Orderic Vitalis. A small part of what I believe will be a much larger work, still in progress. Here it is.'

He struggled a little under the weight of a new volume, and almost straightened up to heave it onto the desk.

'Now, my brothers in Christ, I believe you were looking for the account of the death of the old King, which I understand is... if you will be patient a moment....' The librarian flicked quickly through the pages. 'Ah, here we are, yes... Oh! How very peculiar. I really ... absolute blasphemy and destruction. The page is missing.'

Sure enough, one page had been torn from the tome before them. Who would do such a thing?

'Really?' said Hilary, suddenly paying close attention. 'May I see?'

'I fear there is nothing to see, sir. The critical page is missing.'
Hilary glanced over his shoulder. He recognised the writing immediately. It must have been the page from his missing pouch, which was clearly missing here. This must have been where it had been taken from. This very copy. It was too much of a coincidence to believe the same page could possibly have been missing from two copies, and – yes – it ended at precisely the same point.

Abelard was behind them in a moment.

'Brother Librarian,' he said, speaking carefully. 'Would you mind if I asked you some questions?'

'This really is most distressing. Most distressing,' the librarian was saying to himself, as he heaved Orderic Vitalis back onto the shelf. 'Yes, pray ask me, if I can help you. The Prior has asked me to help. Dear me. Dear me.'

'I wondered if you had a copy of the Anglo-Saxon Genealogy?'

He spoke as distinctly as he could, and rather louder than was necessary. Hilary saw one of the monks jerk his head up and listen. A moment later, he had put down his pen, pushed back his chair with a screeching noise on the flagstones and was gone.

'We have, we have. Let me show you. Is it history that interests you brothers?'

The librarian hobbled down the shelves, heaving down another volume and set up a chair for Abelard to read it. A moment later he was flicking through it hungrily. A few minutes later, he was beckoning Hilary over.

Without speaking, he indicated the page of the Anglo-Saxon Chronicle. It was the entry for the year 1066:

> '... and there was a great slaughter made on either side.
> There was slain King Harold, and Leofwin his brother,
> and Earl Girth his brother, with many good men.'

The name of King Harold had been crossed out by somebody. Hilary peered at the scrawled pen. Had that been the work of his friend John of Muchelney? Why would he bother to do that? Abelard flicked forward and showed him the descriptions of the death of William Rufus, and how blood had apparently sprung from wells beforehand.

'Other convenient stories for anyone who wanted to explain how they knew in advance,' whispered Abelard.

'Wait!' said Hilary before he turned the page, keeping a close eye on the librarian pottering around elsewhere in the room.

There in a scribbled marginal note. It said: 'This was the year that Saewulf went to Jerusalem with the jewel.'

'Extraordinary,' said Abelard under his breath.

There was something else scribbled underneath. What was it? With growing excitement, Hilary realised it was a picture of a bull, with the familiar numbers 24, 6. Yes, the trail was becoming a little clearer, and underneath there was a message:

'This was the year when Guthwine, the son of Leofwin, gave birth to a son.'

Then he shut the book with a snap as the old librarian approached. Hilary just had time to read the Latin inscription below: 'REX FUTURUS', it said.

'Yes, it was a sad day for Winchester when they brought Rufus' body in,' said the librarian. The two visitors stared at him patiently.

'It was sad, you mean, because of the fight outside the Treasury?' said Hilary.

'Oh well, I mean that as well. I meant the collapse of the new tower. When was it? Some twelve or thirteen years ago, I believe. It never would have fallen down if Rufus had not been buried beneath it.'

'I see.' Hilary thought for a moment. 'Have you by any chance known a colleague of mine called John of Muchelney?'

'Patience, patience, please, brothers. One question at a time.' The librarian was looking increasingly flustered. 'No, I fear not. Was he a monk here?'

'He may have been here under another name,' shouted Abelard, shutting the genealogical book with a thump.

'What did he say?' said the librarian, increasingly querulous.

'He said he might have been called something else when he was here. Did you have any unusual visitors in the last few years, maybe recently, who left very suddenly?'

The librarian thought, but he was shaking his head.

'Have you finished with that book, sir?'

'Thank you, Brother Librarian. You have been extremely helpful. I am very grateful. The peace of the Lord Jesus Christ be with you.' Hilary bowed, and nodded to Abelard.

'Well, there was Brother Wulfstan, of course. He just disappeared one day. We never saw him again. I don't know what became of him. But he seemed too impatient to be a scholar. More a man of action. I don't think the contemplative life suited him. I believe he came from Glastonbury.'

'Glastonbury? That is Somerset is it not, near the Levels?' Abelard stood transfixed.

'Glastonbury Abbey, of course. He was a righteous man, but angry sometimes, and I believe he came close to heresy. Perhaps that is why the Lord took him.'

'Did he have dark hair? A beard?'

'He did. Did you know him? It sounds as if you did. The reason I wondered is that he also spent many hours studying the Anglo-Saxon Genealogy that your friend was just looking at.'

'He did?'

'Yes, but one morning he was gone. Some soldiers came looking for him afterwards and I feared for him. It was just like that time we were speaking of some moments ago, after the death of the old King. Soldiers everywhere.'

'That must have been a difficult time for you, when the old King died. Having soldiers searching a monastery is a kind of blasphemy, is it not?'

'Oh, it was indeed, Brother. But they weren't all searching. Oh no. Some of them were hiding. They were in the cathedral as well. Those soldiers who had prevented Henry from seizing the Treasury. Those who were with my lord of Breteuil. They came and claimed asylum. We managed to save most of them. They eventually went on crusade.'

'That is most interesting. I am extremely grateful to you,' said Abelard, bowing to the librarian.

'Well, I hope you found what you were looking for.' Out of the corner of his eye, Hilary saw another of the monks from the Scriptorium hastening downstairs.

They had reached the corridor, their feet echoing on the ancient stones. Hilary's mind raced. If Leofwin was the brother of King Harold, then this Aelfred must be his grandson, thought Hilary. No wonder the Normans were worried. If Aelfred had been born in 1095, as the note had said, he would now be of age. It was only five winters after the year he had been born himself. No wonder the Normans were worried. No wonder John of Muchelney had been working so urgently. No wonder this collusion by the crowned heads of western Europe to prevent change. It was hard to drag his thoughts back to the present, but the old librarian was waiting to leave them.

'Why did you not give sanctuary to your friend from Glastonbury when the soldiers came?' Hilary asked.

'He had already gone, Brother. I fear he was involved in some kind of heresy, which would have made things more difficult for him here. He was a Platonist, Brother Wulfstan was. He was interested in St Denis and the Areopagite. He believed in real things beyond – as we all do, of course – but he went further. He believed that this world must reflect the inner truth.'

Abelard stopped and turned.

'Did he say St Denis?'

'He did.'

'I thought so.' Abelard swept his new cloak, bought in Southampton closely around him, and headed off. 'Come, Hilary.'

'Before we go, Brother Librarian,' said Hilary, left behind on the threshold of the library. 'Could you possibly direct us to the Treasury?'

'It is extraordinary, Hilary, and I've noticed it before. When you search diligently, the Almighty seems to send some signal that you are on the right track,' said Abelard, extremely animated as they strode in the direction that the librarian had given them, via the gatehouse of the royal palace. 'It is almost as if these flashes of coincidence are signs that you are favoured in your search. If you believe such things. But extraordinary that your librarian should mention St Denis.'

'Even more extraordinary that John of Muchelney – I assume it must have been him, given the missing page – extraordinary that he was interested in St Denis too. What is the connection? There must *be* one.'

'I don't know, Hilary. Perhaps there is none, except for the pleasure of coincidence. Ah, this must be the place.'

It was irritatingly typical of Master Peter that, when he did not know the answer to a question, he arrogantly assumed there was no answer.

Where was Isabella now? In the royal palace with her entourage, perhaps meeting the man she was betrothed to marry. Dear God, make him gentle.

They had reached the gatehouse of William the Conqueror's old palace, within which lay the royal treasury. It seemed to have been recently rebuilt, like much of Winchester. Hilary stared at the gate, wrenching his thoughts away from Isabella, trying to imagine the feelings of the participants in the drama two decades before. The courage of William of Breteuil and his soldiers, unsure which way to jump – yet willing to stand up to Henry for what they believed was the rightful succession. Summing up the man before them as a king, and as a potential enemy. Knowing that if he was frustrated, or even mildly threatened, then he would never forget this moment and hunt them down. Unless of course, the crowd backed the defenders and Henry turned away. He could almost hear the shouts from the crowd on either side, and the clash of weapons.

Was it sensible to venture through this gate, Hilary asked himself? It seemed to be tempting fate, but he had suggested it in a weak moment, and now there seemed to be nothing to stop them. Their pursuers should have no idea they were even in England.

'So your friend John of Muchelney was a Platonist. A man who believed a king was not just someone who happened to seize a treasury, or who was in the right place at the right time. He believed someone had to BE a king. An inconvenient thing to believe, is it not? But then, I believe that is the way these Saxons think when they are of Abbot Aelfgar's persuasion, clinging to the old ways. They are Platonists, and followers of Pseudo-Dionysius the Areopagite – who is not, as I have proved, St Denis.'

'John of Muchelney seemed more of a warrior to me,' said Hilary. 'But he certainly stirred things up. How many were chasing him? The King of France, the King of England maybe. I do hope that word of his death and my escape has not reached these shores, Master Peter. Perhaps we should have been more careful.'

'Nonsense. We are quite safe here. Perhaps it would make sense to question the Prior a little about Wulfstan of Glastonbury.'

Hilary felt overwhelmed for a moment by irritation with his former teacher. He was so definite about everything, and there was he, with a great hole shaped like Isabella in his heart. His feet were sore and he was still swaying from months on board ship. All he wanted to do was to go home to his village and sink into obscurity, quietly and tidily. Before the sleeping pursuers were roused.

As if his very thoughts had woken them from sleep, there was a clatter of hooves behind them on the cobblestones and the two men swung round the corner on horseback and leapt from their saddles in front of Hilary.

'Why is this always happening?' he said as they approached. The feeling of being approached aggressively by soldiers was becoming ridiculously familiar.

'You will come with us,' said the senior of the armed men. 'Follow me, gentlemen. You will find it easier for all concerned if you follow silently.'

Abelard and Hilary exchanged glances and fell obediently behind. The jewel around his neck seemed to hang heavy. Was this the last sight of the open air that he was vouchsafed? There was no option but to obey. The two soldiers in chain mail went before them; two more joined them from behind – through the gate and into the courtyard of the royal palace, some of its walls obviously blackened by fire. They marched around the edge of the courtyard, clattering on the stones and through a stone archway.

Very well, thought Hilary. We wanted to get to the heart of the mystery and here they were. They very heart of power in the heart of King Henry's capital city, inside the Treasury itself. Be careful what you ask for. Be careful, he told himself. Be silent as a tomb – to avoid the tomb. He willed his companion to silence as the tramp of the soldiers' feet echoed on the cobblestones. The officer hammered on a huge wooden door with metal studs. It swung open heavily to reveal a heavy red curtain.

Inside the large room was a powerful looking, clean-shaven man, with his hair cropped so close against his head that he looked bald. He was as neat as a crusader aristocrat but pale white like an Englishman. He was sitting at a large table, a golden chain around his neck, and a fine red padded robe. The table was weighed down by papers and books. Hilary glanced around the room. There was no fire in the grate and, compared to the rooms he had seen in Jerusalem, this one was stark and bleak, with rushes on the floor and a sharp smell of damp. The man finished writing and fixed them with an irritable look, beckoning them to come forward. To Hilary, he seemed to stare deep into his eyes, as if it was his eyes that particularly interested this important personage.

'You are?' he said venomously. 'Speak, and quickly. I am an impatient man.'

'My name is Peter Abelard and this is my colleague and friend Hilary, the famous poet. We have returned from the Holy Land and are here in Winchester seeking answers to some pressing questions. In fact, we would be very grateful if...'

'And those are? I gather you have been in the library of the cathedral asking about the death of the late King.' Once more, the man's eyes bored deep into Hilary's.

Abelard adopted a light, detached tone of infinite reassurance. 'I am also studying....'

One of the soldiers was whispering in the ear of the man. He waved his hand and dismissed him. 'Very well. I also understand you have been asking about a man here called Wulfstan of Glastonbury. You will tell me precisely what your interest in him is.'

'Well...,' said Hilary, but Abelard cut in.

'Our primary interest is in St Denis, the patron saint of my own monastery in France, and whose origins I am studying. I believe Wulfstan was working on similar ideas. Perhaps if I explained in detail the significance of St Denis and Pseudo-Dionysius the Areopagite for the Platonic world view...'

Hilary looked at his teacher with renewed respect. He certainly knew how to bore deliberately.

The man, slammed his palms down loudly on the table. The books bounced and shook. His face took on some of the colour of his red robes.

'Who in heaven do you think you are? You sail in here asking impertinent questions in the King's palace, as if you have to right to march from one end of the King's dominions to the other just asking what you like. Yes, I know who you are, Abelard. I know you are a under the protection of the Chancellor of France. He has told me so himself in no uncertain terms. Well, let me tell you this...'

He rose and walked unsteadily towards them. He had a slight limp. Hilary wondered if he was going to strike them. A breeze swept through the empty windows above them and swing the metal chandelier to and fro. There was a frightening silence.

'Let me tell you who *I* am. I am Ralph Basset, the King's Justice. This is the King's city of Winchester. I am the law here. The King of France's chancellor is of no interest to me. Nor is your reputation for dispute, though I will have no truck with heresy either. We will have no heresy here. Nor will we have treachery. Nor will we have meddling by clever people who don't know what they are dabbling in. I'm not interested in peasant's tittle-tattle. They knew about the Rufus' death in Gloucester before it happened, yes I know. They knew about it in Devonshire, did they? I don't care if they did, but I *do* care if you start reviving those old women's tales.'

'Perhaps...' said Abelard hopefully, but the diatribe wasn't finished.

'Listen. Make sure you're listening now. Because if I ever catch you wandering around here again, within half a mile of the King, asking treacherous questions, then I will show you exactly where you will go. Did you see that black building as you came in? That's the Balk-house. That's where Earl Waltheof and other enemies of the King spent their final hours. I don't want any trouble now. I can't be bothered to imprison you or set the King's torturers to work to find out what you're really after. I'm too busy. But if I ever see you again, we will be asking a great deal more. Now get out of here. Soldier, escort them to the gate, and show them the King's prison on their way out. And then kick them up the arse.'

'What an extraordinarily rude man,' said Hilary under their breath as they retraced their steps under guard.

'It was a little undignified,' said Abelard. 'But they evidently don't really know what we are looking for, do they? Otherwise I'm afraid we might have ended up in that prison after all. We must be more careful in future. You were quite right, Hilary. Incidentally, who was Earl Waltheof?'

'He was one of those who rebelled against the Conqueror. I don't know what happened to him. There was rather a frightening story about his death, I seem to remember. He asked if he could just say the Lord's Prayer, and got to 'Forgive us our trespasses' before the axe fell. Then guess what. His head carried on saying the rest.'

'For goodness sake, Hilary. I really don't think that is relevant to our inquiries.' Hilary looked a little crestfallen. 'What is relevant is what we have discovered. Remind me, would you...'

Hilary wracked his brains. It was extraordinary how Abelard managed, time after time, to return them to the relationship of master and pupil. 'Well, we now know that John of Muchelney was really Wulfstan of Glastonbury,' said Hilary obediently, 'a Platonist 'heretic' according to the monks here as well as an Anglo-Saxon revolutionary. We know that Saewulf took the jewel to Jerusalem for safekeeping. We know there is a Saxon heir to the legacy of King Harold who has emerged in the full flush of manhood, and needs to be crowned. In fact, we know almost everything.'

'Quite so, Hilary. But Ralph Basset just told us something else which I find extremely surprising. He said that the Chancellor of France told him personally that I was under his protection. The two kings are supposed to be at war. When did they meet, that is what I would like to know?'

They had followed Basset's men now to the gate to the royal palace, where William of Breteuil and King Henry had faced each other that critical day in the summer of 1100. One of the soldiers walked back to them.

'Take my advice and leave the city,' he said. 'The London road leads through the North Gate, through the market and to the right. He's not a gentle man, my master. You don't want to see him again.'

5/The New Forest

Nether Wallop, 7 September 1120

'But where are my books?'

Hilary looked down as if he was somehow searching for them, though of course he knew perfectly well where they were. The scent of harvest wafted across the fields and the smell of late summer after rain. Every chirrup, every waft of sunshine reminded Hilary of home.

'They are back in my home village. I couldn't bring them. Some soldiers passed me on the way there and I couldn't be certain they were not searching for us. The box would just have weighed me down.' Was that entirely true, he asked himself, or was he just too irritated to heave them onto his pony's back?

Abelard stared in astonishment, checking himself as if – by some slim chance – Hilary had brought them by mistake.

'*Stultus fatuus!* Those books represent years of work. Some of them come from Jerusalem. They are invaluable. I don't believe it. Have I taught you nothing, Hilary?'

'Master Peter, ...

'No, don't say any more. Let's just turn around and go on into the Forest.'

Hilary stared in astonishment. 'Turn around? You mean you don't want to go back and fetch them.'

'Of course not. Not now. I want you to follow me closely.'

'Now wait a moment.' Hilary got down from his pony. He could not remember ever being so angry before. 'Wait a moment, Master Peter. Against my advice, you barged in to see the Prior of

Winchester and made him suspicious, and may have brought the whole pursuit back to life again. And while you continue to have the protection of the Chancellor of France if you put a foot wrong, I – on the other hand – am likely to be hanged for a double murder which I did not commit. Now, I may have given the Prior's men the slip again, and not without worry and nervousness, and you won't even tell me what you are intending to do or why.'

Abelard stared for a moment, turning round in his saddle. Then suddenly he dismounted. What was he going to do? Hilary had never shouted at his master before. This was uncharted territory. His hair shuddered in the summer breeze.

'Hilary, my friend, you are quite right to admonish me. I've been high handed. Of course it was impossible for you to bring the books. We will collect them when we have completed our task. But listen. Do you think for one moment that they will ever let us escape? The only way out of this is to find out the truth. We must go on, Hilary, you and I. We have come so far – we need to *know*. And when we do know, then we can use that knowledge to prevent a great evil.'

What is the man talking about? What great evil can he see? Hilary thought carefully about what to say.

'Master Peter, you know I revere you as a teacher and I owe you my life, many times over just since this affair began. But we are not in St Genevieve now. There is no great love of the truth here. This is *England*. If someone killed William Rufus, then the chances are that he is now on the throne. Nobody with any power is going to thank us for opening up that tankard of poison. Can you imagine it? It really is astonishingly naïve for someone of your intelligence to think that we can sail over here, just find out the truth and proclaim it – and escape with our necks. Yes, maybe the Church might possibly protect us, but at what cost to us...'

As this speech progressed, Abelard stood staring at him, increasingly impatient.

'Hilary, Hilary, don't you see? There is only one way forward now. We can't go back. Not just on our own account. God wants us to know. God loves the truth. What is truth, asked Pilate? Well, I can tell you, there is one truth. Do you think our lives are significant in all this?'

'God? Don't bring God into this. I just wanted to live a little longer, that's all. Is that so much to ask? Don't you think God is interested in my prayers too? In my life?'

Abelard swung round and slapped his saddle. 'Yes, Hilary. But what is your life *for*, that's the question?'

'Of course the truth is important,' Hilary interrupted irritably. 'But not if it gets in the way of the main objective. Not if it means I have to run for the rest of my very short life. What if we go to the New Forest, and we look at the place where Rufus died and – by some staggering stroke of luck – we confirm that his brother King Henry killed him, or at least paid Walter Tirel to do it. What do I do then? Go and tell him to his face? What kind of peace is that going to bring me?'

A small crowd of people had gathered by the Winchester gates city gates and were pointing at them. The sight of two men in dusty clothes and such impassioned debate seemed to be amusing them. Someone threw an ancient carrot. It landed at their feet. Abelard came a little closer and patted him encouragingly on the arm.

'Listen, Hilary,' he whispered, afraid that the people watching them might hear. 'Do you not understand what is at stake? Who do you think suffers when the great men of Europe challenge each other for their thrones? The peaceable tillers of the soil in their huts, that's who. Do you not see what pressure is building and what will happen when it releases? John of Muchelney and

Master Hubert are just the beginning. What can we do? I know –
that is the question – what can ordinary mortals like ourselves do
before it is too late? Well, we can find out the truth, and then use
it. Somebody has to act to prevent the next great conflagration.'

Hilary stood undecided, speechless. Was this vanity on behalf
of the Indomitable Rhinoceros, or was this something that they
could really achieve? Was this folly and death, or...

'In any case, Hilary, I have done it. I've found a man who can
take us into the forest and introduce us to Purkiss.'

'Purkiss?'

Abelard struck his brow in frustration. 'For goodness sake, pay
some attention, Hilary. Purkiss was the charcoal burner who took
William Rufus's body in a cart from the forest where he was shot,
all the way into Winchester. He's the one we need. I've agreed
that we will meet by the West Gate at nones.'

Hilary was silent. He climbed on his pony and stared into the
middle distance. If he turned around and headed down the old
road to the ports, the way his forefathers had all travelled, down
the rutted ancient track that led to London and the South Downs,
he might – with luck and some more money – put this whole
business behind him. If he headed north, back along the chalk
causeway and the river, he would eventually come back to the
Wallop brook, the familiar stream, the church of St Andrew and
his own relatives, where he had spent the night, perhaps then his
pursuers might forget him and he might even in time forget them.
On the other hand, if he headed back into Winchester with
Abelard, deliberately set out to find Purkiss and to investigate the
death of the former King of England, there was really no going
back.

It would be a race for the truth against the forces of anyone
who owed their position to the new King – and that was nearly
everyone in any authority. He had discharged his oath to John of

Muchelney, but there was something else to be done – if he had the courage. If Abelard was right, it was to prevent a new conflagration in England. Somehow.

'Hilary, what's the matter? It is time to move,' said Abelard impatiently.

Maybe it was anyway now too late for him to extract himself and the race for survival had already begun, for him and the Saxons. Maybe it began the night that John of Muchelney was killed. The chances were that was the case, thought Hilary. That was the real message of those soldiers in chain mail. The only way out was to go on.

Hilary breathed a huge sigh of determination. 'I accept, Master Peter. We go on. But this time, we make the decisions together, you and I. No more surprises and mysteries. Do we agree?'

Abelard reached up and shook his hand. 'Agreed, my friend.' He shook the reins and headed back towards the gate of the city. 'In fact, very well put, if I may say so.'

Hilary warmed to his old teacher again. Perhaps Master Peter was human, whatever Isabella had said. Perhaps that streak of charm he retained made him so. Either way, he was proud to travel the English countryside next to such a man, even if his conversation still reeked of Dionysius the Areopagite.

They had divided their forces the day before this conversation, after a night in an inn outside Winchester, in the village of Alresford. Abelard had gone back to Winchester to seek out a guide to help them find their way to the New Forest, and Hilary had stolen a moment to go home.

The late summer had bloomed around him across the downs that morning, and the carts and occasional oxen ambled along the old road in front of him, carrying Abelard's books on huge saddlebags on either side of him and the Alfred Jewel around his neck. He had only two of his silver coins left from John of Muchelney. He had managed to hoard them safely through those sweaty weeks in Jerusalem, aware that he would need them to get home and, now that he was so close to home, he longed for it.

It was a slow journey those ten miles northwards, with the faint English sunshine on his face, and a large white cloud drifting slowly towards the sun, and he remembered the familiar angels above the chancel steps in St Andrew's at home. He remembered his mother's face and on their small strip of land and the old abandoned Danebury fort beyond. Would any of it still exist? What about his brothers, who must now be fully grown, if they lived? Hilary felt a sinking sensation that they might well not be after all. He had not been in England for more than fourteen winters, not quite back to that fateful moment when William Rufus had met his own untimely end, but long enough.

It was the afternoon by the time he reached the familiar brook and his first impression was that nothing had changed at all. He had hidden in the ditch twice to avoid passing men-at-arms, and one pair of horsemen, who could perhaps have been looking for him, and now he had arrived at his village. Would anyone be there? Would his parents still be alive? Would their old farm still stand? The water rippled as it always had. The trees were larger and more luxuriant, but perhaps that was just the late summer. He got down from the pony and hurried across the ford, down the familiar rutted track, and there was the farmhouse. There was smoke coming from the chimney. Hilary stood and stared, too terrified to walk further. Then he tied the pony to a tree and ran on.

The courtyard was empty, except for the hens and ducks. There were animals in the barn. He slipped on the muck before he reached the steps. He leapt through the door, and in the dark corner he could see an elderly woman hunched over her sewing by the window.

'I'm looking for my mother,' he said. 'Is she here?'

They stared at each other for a moment. Then the sewing was flung down and the woman was on her feet, hobbling awkwardly towards him, her arms outstretched.

'By all the saints in heaven. Is it my Hilary? Is it? Can it possibly be? My Hilary who I thought was dead? Hilary who I thought I would never see again? Is it you? Tell me now gently – is it you?'

'*Moðor*,' said Hilary, and burst into tears.

How had she become so small and wizened, that powerful woman who had run the house? Hilary marvelled that time had passed in Nether Wallop so much faster than it had in Paris and Orléans, and yet so little had changed, except the faces of the children and servants around the farm.

He heard quickly that his father had died some nine winters past, his brother Harry was the shire reeve and absent from the farm, though his children ran with the ducks and hens in the courtyard. His brothers Edgar, Will and Robert worked in Sarum or Gloucester, or some such place, and returned home regularly. His sister Eadgifu was in the next village, married with children of her own. Only Hilary had never returned.

He felt he had little to say to his mother. Tales of faraway places seemed to interest her little. He could see her eyes narrow in disbelief, though she held his hand as he talked. He poked the familiar fire after she had retired for the night, and lay down to rest beside it, sleeping deeply and with comfort for the first time since Alys was alive. But his dreams were all of Isabella now, and her songs and her smile. Why should I go back, Hilary asked himself? Why should I keep my appointment with Master Peter, when I can sink into my old world and disappear? He fingered the shape of the Great Jewel in his breast. Why should he right any of these wrongs? Why should he care that a tyrant king had stolen England from his forebears?

But when he awoke, he knew he must. If he abandoned Abelard, then he would never forgive himself. He would live out his days on the farm and always wonder.

'At the very least, you must tell me where you have been, Hilary. Then I can imagine you going back there. If you must go, at least I will know where you are.' His mother had wept that he was to leave so soon, and by the time the cocks crowed across the village and the dawn seeped into the sky he was ready to leave.

'Tell me, Hilary. Where did you come from yesterday? Have you come far?' his mother asked as he packed his few belongings and arranged his threadbare clothes. 'How did you get so weather-beaten? Tell me, to reassure me that you will be safe.'

'Really, I have come further than you can imagine,' he said. He toyed again with telling her the whole truth – from the Holy City, through storms and mountains, chased through the halls of the dead – but he stopped himself. It would not help. 'Just from Paris. With Master Peter. The philosopher,' he added.

'Tell me the truth, Hilary. I always know when you're not telling me the truth. I asked you many times last night.'

What was the point of hiding it? 'You are right, of course, Mother. I have come many miles, hundreds of miles from the furthest east, and – when I return again – I will tell you the strangest tale and...'

Now it came to parting, Hilary could hardly bear to leave. He might never see his mother again. Time seemed to pass here faster than elsewhere in the world. He held her hand. It seemed aged and bony and so small. He never remembered it like that.

'I will come home again. Soon,' he said. 'If I possibly can, I will. In the meantime, I would like to leave my books and saddlebags. Just stay here if you can, and stay the same.'

'I will always be the same, *deore*. I will always be here for you.'

Hilary walked in the pale light down to the church, feeling empty and excited. The grey building nestled in the side of the hill, and you could see the old hillfort across the way, where his ancestors had lived out their lives. The old wooden door opened smoothly and he was inside. It was cold and a little damp. The picture of angels across the chancel arch held his attention and took him back to days when he ran around in here with sticks, and was beaten for it.

He walked up the side of the nave. Yes, sure enough, there was the hole he remembered, no broader than a penny piece, but enough to ease the stone out. Yes, inside, there was a piece of parchment. It all came back to him. He glanced at the lines, his own hidden poem from a long forgotten summer. Still there. He read the first line, and screwed it up. No, that was too much.

He reached inside the purse around his neck and pulled out the Great Jewel, still wrapped in black cloth, and pushed it deep in the cleft, and replaced the stone. You could not see the hole now. He looked at it from above. No, nobody would know.

It was evening the next day by the time he had met Abelard again, outside the city walls of Winchester, within sight of Hyde Abbey, and admitted that he had left his books behind. And it was nightfall by the time they reached the abbey guesthouse in Romsey, together with their guide, who they had encountered without difficulty at the west gate of Winchester's city walls. By the time he rolled over and went to sleep, Hilary had become so irritated by the guide – a cattle merchant – that he could cheerfully have strangled him. The way he talked and scratched himself almost continuously might easily have driven him insane. Abelard was oblivious to it but, by the time he had described his flatulence for the tenth time, Hilary began to recite the Credo quietly to himself just to prevent himself saying anything rude.

'Do you carry any weapons?' said their guide as they trees of the New Forest hove into sight the next morning.

'I'm a clerk in holy orders. He's a priest,' said Hilary dismissively.

'Only I have to ask,' said the guide. 'You know what the penalty for hunting is in the royal forest? Lose your bow hand. Chop chop. And don't think the sheriff's men ask any questions about whether you're a clerk in holy orders or anything else. It's best not to take the risk. That's all I'm saying.'

Hilary ignored him, but realized he was sweating more than he should be. Then, some hours later, hungry and thirsty from the heat and the dust of the forest trails, they arrived outside a small, dingy hovel, smelling of the sweet smoke of charcoal. Great mounds of smoking earth lay around them like huge anthills. It was as if they were burning under ground. In front of the hovel worked a large surly peasant, covered in charcoal dust.

'You are Purkiss? I'm delighted to meet you,' said Abelard dismounting from his pony. 'The peace of the Lord be with you.'

Purkiss scowled.

'Forgive me,' said Hilary, but aren't you a little young?

'Young? What do you mean young?'

'To have carried Rufus' body all those years ago. I just wanted to know that's all, because we've come a long way to see you.'

Purkiss looked impassive.

'That's my father you'll be wanting.'

'Is this is house?'

'Yup, this is his house alright.' He seemed a little defensive.

'That's the man we want to talk to then,' said Abelard jauntily, tying his pony up to a tree.

'You'll have trouble. He died these eight years back.'

Abelard stared at him. The man stared back, apparently without a sense of humour. Abelard and Hilary exchanged glances. It was at least some connection with the events of August 1100.

'Did your father tell you about what happened when he found the body of the King?' said Hilary, while Abelard recovered himself. 'You know he dragged the King's body by cart all the way to Winchester?'

'I might do. I might have helped him too.'

'Excellent. Might you also tell us about it, if we make it worth your while? A silver penny for example?'

'And take us to where it happened?' said Abelard.

Purkiss considered for a moment. 'For two silver pennies, I'll take you there and tell you the story. You won't believe me though.'

Hilary reached into his purse.

It was a serious ride, Purkiss way ahead and Abelard trailing behind, through the forest that was sometimes thick with leaves and undergrowth and sometimes miserably sparse. There were also new trees growing abundantly around the sad ruins of villages, a reminder that this was now a forbidden place.

Only once, Purkiss stopped and led them deeper into the wood and they heard – in the far distance – the sound of the yelping of hounds and the crash of horses hunting. There were none of those cheery groups of women washing clothes in the stream or the waving peasants gathering in an early harvest. In fact, there was nobody to be seen apart from the occasional crone carrying sticks. It was as if the Norman rulers had swept the place clear of people and let nature take over.

'You see that hill? Through the trees?' said Purkiss, ambling back towards Hilary. 'Castle Malwood.'

It seemed hardly a castle at all, a small wooden keep on the top of a mound of earth, with a series of huts inside the outer palisade. It rose above the trees, like a deserted village itself, more a hunting lodge than a defensive position, hardly dignified enough to be the place where William Rufus slept his final night on earth. There were crows above it and no signs of life. A shiver went down Hilary's spine. It seemed to him that, the deeper they travelled into the forest, the more they trod on forbidden territory, and the deeper into danger they rode. It was as if they were defiling some evil power, and the appearance of Castle Malwood in the distance simply heightened the sense of evil enchantment. This was the castle where those monks had come to warn him in the night, at least according to the papers which had been hung around Hilary's neck.

The heart of the mystery which had dominated his recent life seemed to be edging closer. An overwhelming sense of danger made Hilary feel dizzy. The sun was slanting through the trees as they followed a well-worn track into a boggy clearing. Every step seemed to disturb the slumber of secrets.

'Tell me, Purkiss,' said Hilary. 'Why were you here in the forest when the King died?'

'We were beaters, weren't we.'

'Driving the stag towards the king?'

'That's right.' There was a silence as Hilary waited for him to say something else, but Purkiss stayed taciturn.

'So you came through the trees and there he was – under a rich cloak, lying on the broken arrow.' Purkiss remained silent like a great stubborn cart horse.

'And someone asked you to carry the body to Winchester?'

'Nobody here. We had a cart and we were told to take the body. I didn't want to, but we didn't get the choice.'

'And then what?'

'What do you mean? We put him in the cart. Got the pony. Pulled him into Romsey by nightfall. Then up at sunrise and into Winchester.'

'Did anyone join you on the journey?'

'Oh well, people began to get the news as we got near to Winchester. They came out and stared.'

'Did they say anything? Did they shout? Were they angry?'

'Some of them wept. Some of them just stared. One of them nicked the silk cloth on the body. We could hardly get through the city gates. Then we got to the cathedral and they were all there.'

'Who was there?'

'You know. Barons. Princes. Bishops. Funeral straight there and then, some time before terce.'

'And you went home. Nobody said anything more.'

Purkiss looked even more stubborn. 'More questions, more money.'

'Well...' said Hilary. Abelard had been listening from a distance and now he bounded over and looked closely at Purkiss.

'Wait, wait. So just tell me again. When you got to the cathedral, which was before terce?'

'Maybe,' said Purkiss, looking nervous.

'When you got there, everyone was there already waiting for the body, and the funeral went ahead there and then? No waiting, no muddle, no confusion?'

'That's right.'

'And what you said before about when you found the body – you must have arrived there only a few Hail Marys after the shot

252

had been fired and the King had died. That is correct, is it not? You were a beater, only a few hundred poles away through the woods?'

'I said you wouldn't believe me.'

'I believe you, I believe you. Now listen. When you got there, just moments after the death of the King, you were almost alone – I mean, the prince, the barons, his friends – they had all gone. That's correct, isn't it?

'Yup, it was.'

'No panic, no wringing of hands, no argument about what should happen. They had gone.'

Purkiss nodded. They trudged on through the undergrowth, pulling their ponies behind them as the grey, forgotten outline of Castle Malwood disappeared behind them into the forest and the sun drooped lower in the sky.

'You realise what this means, Hilary?' Abelard spoke under his breath so that their guide could not hear.

'It does seem strange.'

'Strange? It is more than strange. It confirms everything. People panic when kings die unexpectedly. Of course they do. Their futures depend on how they act. One word out of place and they lose everything. But in this case, they were completely organised. Within a few beats of the heart they have organised themselves and set off for Winchester, leaving Rufus behind. A sad story, Hilary.'

'Could it not have been sheer panic?'

'It could, but look what happened next. The King's brother Henry and his friends dashed to Winchester overnight. Early the next morning, they seized the Treasury from William of Breteuil, as we know. Then they sent letters to all the bishops, and one to

Anselm – the exiled Archbishop of Canterbury.'

'How do you know all this?' asked Hilary. 'I didn't know all this and I come from here.'

'While you were entertaining the deaf librarian, I was looking through the various archives. But listen, Hilary, that isn't all. They also issued a proclamation explaining that Henry would succeed his brother, even though the eldest son Robert was still very much alive, because he was born of a king *when he was king*. Henry was born in 1068, after the Conquest.'

'That is ingenious. Wasn't there a Roman emperor who claimed his position on that basis?'

'You are quite right, Hilary. Well done. It was Constantine. And having done all that, there was still time to get down to the cathedral to meet Purkiss and the cart to have the funeral – still very early mind you – and then go straight to London for the coronation. Now, what does that suggest to you?'

'That they were very well organised indeed, I suppose. That they had planned it.'

'Exactly. This was no panic after an unexpected death. They had thought it all through, including that ingenious justification, so that all that could be done – all the preparations made – in the time it took Purkiss to pull his cart from Romsey to Winchester, maybe the time it might take for us to walk ten miles or so. It's possible, but not without planning. No, they knew Rufus was going to die – or some of them did.'

'Hush, Master Peter,' said Hilary. Young Purkiss was walking towards them.

'This is it,' he said. 'This is where my father found him. Just there.'

'By that wooden cross?'

'That's right. The monks put that up to mark the spot a few years back. This was the place.'

'Let's get this over with quickly,' said Hilary. 'I feel nervous here. I get the sense that people are watching us.'

'Aye, there are ghosts here,' said Purkiss. 'Some dead ghosts and some live ones also.'

They tied their ponies to the same tree, and Abelard marched ahead towards the rough wooden marker in the middle of the clearing.

'Were you here? I mean when the King was killed?' Hilary asked.

'Nope,' said Purkiss, as if it somehow didn't matter. 'But I saw the body, with the arrow snapped off.'

'So you can't tell us how it happened?'

Purkiss shook his head defiantly. 'Why are you so interested anyway?' There was a note of fear in his voice. The implications of being mixed up in this inquiry after the truth were beginning to sink in.

Abelard stared at the clearing from the point where the King's body lay. There was a slope uphill away from the spot, with solid phalanxes of trees on either side. It was getting towards evening and the sun was coming from straight ahead and low in the sky. He seemed to sniff the air and came back.

'Purkiss says he wasn't here,' said Hilary in a whisper.

'Of course not. He must have come with his father later. I'm not sure how much we are going to learn here. We know who was here that day, but that's all.'

'The King, Walter Tirel and that was about it. All the other aristocrats were in another part of the forest. Was there anyone else?' Purkiss was looking increasingly uncomfortable.

'But there was someone else here, was there not?' said Abelard

'I told you. I don't know.'

'The chief huntsman was here. I am right, am I not?'

For the first time since the star they had met him, Purkiss

became suddenly animated. He leapt forward as if to prevent Abelard from opening his mouth.

'No, hush, I beg you, sir. Say nothing.' He glanced nervously around over his shoulder and into the thicket. 'I told you. There are ghosts here.'

Abelard and Hilary exchanged glances. Hilary could imagine the three of them waiting for the beaters to drive some hapless deer in their direction. A silent moment before the horror of the accident, if it was an accident. A moment of quiet before the storm.

Abelard walked once more across the clearing to where the path disappeared once more in the woods and then came back. The sun was sinking in the sky.

'You see, Hilary. We are at a similar time of day to when the accident occurred and in a similar season. You see how the sun slants down ahead of us, as it would have done that evening. This is the scene the King would have seen if he looked that way. The breeze is also in our faces. I believe that is the prevailing wind here? You can tell by the shape of the trees. See the way they seem to strain away from the West. I think we can safely assume that the wind blew at them as it does today, and you know what that means.'

Purkiss eyed them suspiciously.

'Mr Purkiss, which way did the beaters come that day?'

He shrugged his shoulders angrily.

'Well, which way did they usually come from?' Purkiss stared for a minute and then jerked his thumb in the direction of the sun.

'Which means the beaters came from that direction, and so did the stag,' said Hilary.

'Right. Very good Hilary. But I confess that is as far as my thinking has progressed. We are in the dark about exactly where the deer emerged.' Purkiss was now standing bolt upright. Hilary wondered what he was listening to, and then he heard it himself. In the far distance again, the noise of dogs.

'Time we went,' said Purkiss nervously. 'I don't want to be found here, even if you do. They'll come right down this path, they always do.'

Hilary looked at the path in the direction of the sound. It had gone quiet again and he could hear the breeze in the leaves. Perhaps Rufus had heard this very same sound before he died. Then he looked down. The marks of deer in the mud were everywhere. He walked a couple of yards in either direction. There were no hoof prints at the sides of the track or in the edge of the thickets on either side, and inside the thickets were too thick and overgrown.

'Master Peter, I think I know where the deer went. They kept to the path. This is the route they use through the forest just as it is ours. Look at the prints.'

Abelard looked down with excitement.

'*O di immortales*! Hilary, I believe you are right. So we know where the deer came. It came straight down this path away from the wind and the scent of the beaters, and – if Rufus was standing there – it would have dashed up the hill, just as the chronicle I read said it did.'

'There is no time. We must go. Don't you hear?' The sound of the hunt was getting nearer. Purkiss was increasingly impatient. Tugging at his pony and pulling at the halter's of the other ones.

Abelard took no notice. He strode up the incline between the two lines of trees, picking his path carefully as the ground got wetter and marshier. There were two tongues of trees reaching out into the hillside clearing. Abelard headed up hill towards them. He paced the ground carefully as if he was measuring with his strides, glancing every now and then to the direction from where the deer must have come. The sun sank lower in the sky. Purkiss became frantic.

'What's he doing, your master?'

'He isn't,' said Hilary, but Purkiss wasn't listening.

'Look, I don't know what you both want. I'm going. And don't blame me if they chop your hands off.'

'Master Peter, it's time to go,' said Hilary loudly. The yelping in the forest seemed now to be quite close. He could hear the crash of broken twigs and lashing leaves.

'Hilary!' shouted Abelard from up the incline. 'Stand by the cross and shout to me when you are there.'

He marched to the spot where the King had died. It was the same time of day. This was Rufus' last sight of the world.

'I'm here'. There was no sign of Abelard. 'Master Peter?'

Then suddenly he reappeared, hurrying down the slope. 'Bring the ponies, Hilary. It's time we left.' As Hilary untied them, munching a final green shoot, he could see Purkiss heading deep into the bush, pulling his reluctant pony after him. He ran up the hill with the ponies running behind. As he reached the second tongue of trees, Abelard grabbed him.

'You couldn't see me, could you?'

'No, but shhh!'

At least fifty hounds, in a white slithering mass of barking and yelping, burst into the clearing and headed towards the sun. Behind them, with a deerskin jerkin and a quiver of arrows on his back, an aristocrat on a fine horse, with attendants and hunters carrying spears. Hilary held his breath, peering through the leaves, wondering what it was that Abelard had discovered on the slope, too nervous about the hunt to ask him.

When they reached the cross, the hounds stopped for a moment and sniffed the air. For a moment, their fate hung in the balance. Then there was renewed yelping and the white hounds headed off along the track towards the place from where – on that August day two decades before – the beaters had driven the stag towards the King.

6/St Paul's

The Thames, 12 September 1120

'Something is happening, Master Peter. Is the English Channel shrinking? I can see the shore on both sides of the ship.' The heavy canvas crashed and flapped in the wind, which seemed equally confused now by the confluence of geography.

'No, I believe we are finally approaching our destination, Hilary. This is your famous river Thames, as important and wealthy as the Seine in its own way.'

They were certainly not alone. All along the south coast, there had been companionable coasters and cogs of all shapes and sizes squeezing past them in and out of harbours, but now it was even more pronounced. Wherever they looked, there were barges and sails, beating against an uncertain wind, or hauling on oars heading in the same direction or the opposite one to themselves. They passed little ports on either side, and the occasional church tower recognisable on the shores against the sky.

The oars were out now and the crew strained against the current, until finally, round a sharp bend in the river, the city came into sight. First, the great white castle on the north bank and the city walls beyond it, then the accumulations of and huts and hovels and busy wharfs on either side, with ships drawn up beside each other in line after line on the beaches of sand and mud.

'We are nearly there,' said the captain, as he passed them. 'Have you been to London before?'

Hilary ignored him. He had not but, as an Englishman, he

preferred not to admit it, certainly not in front of his old teacher.

'It isn't quite Paris, is it,' said Abelard half to himself.

But for Hilary, this was a moment of pride. It was everything Paris was, it seemed to him, perhaps a little easier to take in because of the gentle slope up past the great tower of the cathedral and into the distance. There seemed, moreover, to be a sense of business and mercantile bustle that even Paris lacked. This was a city that had not dignified itself by attracting the court, though clearly King Henry was frequently up river in Westminster, but it was all the more devoted to the business of growing rich. There was a terrifying singleness of mind about it. Both horrifying and thrilling at the same time, and that was obvious just peering through the gaps in the houses to the intensity within, the frenetic selling and travelling in all directions at once.

Their ship passed under the lifting bridge, an ancient rickety structure across the river beyond the Tower, and they headed into the northern shore and a spare wharf below the cathedral. Shouts went up from the docks as they moved slowly towards them, and it was soon possible to *hear* this wealth that before they had only seen, the cacophony of dockers, boys, apprentices, women, prostitutes, sales people of all kinds, mingling with the boxes of dried fish, the barrels of beer and wine, the bundles of fine cloth, the precious boxes eastern spice, the smell of pepper, tar, excrement and beer all rolled together in one almighty force of nature – the prevailing smell of London.

The dock itself had seen better days. It was rotting and broken in places and the rope holding it together was frayed, knotted and failing. Not many more ships and this piece of wooden detritus would be sailing off down the Thames itself, headed for the sea, Hilary thought as they came closer to the tender administrations of the ragged dockers.

'Is that mist?' asked Abelard looking beyond the dock and up into the city. A hazy curtain of something that morning gave the city a dreamlike appearance.

'No, it's smoke,' said Hilary. 'London is a dirty place in some weather.'

Their crew leapt over the side to prevent the locals taking control of the ropes. There was a slight altercation.

'London,' said Abelard, partly to himself, as he leapt across the gap while the crew and dockers were still arguing. 'The King is here; this is where the answers will be.'

The smoky haze began to clear as they made their way through the docks, the ropes and masts and rudders and piles of forgotten cargoes, sheepskins, turnips and mounds of rotted meat. Even before they cleared the docks and moved into the street they began to be accosted. A young man with a painted face and accommodating expression plucked at Hilary's coat.

'It appears your reputation has proceeded you,' said Abelard laughing.

Hilary glowered to himself and was delighted to see a huge woman open her gown as Master Peter walked by. He caught a glimpse of breasts and the look of shock on his face.

'Too late, madam,' he said. Then they looked up through the gap in the buildings towards the huge tower they had seen as the ship made its way up river, the scaffolding hugging it closely, looking out across the huddled wooden houses below. Hilary stared upwards at the burgeoning cathedral, and the tiny men along its walls, and envied them – their creativity, their permanence, their companionship, and above all their security. Even high on the scaffolding, they were safer than he was.

'That's where we are going,' said Abelard. 'The cathedral.'

Abelard and Hilary had ridden south out of the forest to the port of Swanage, just as Walter Tirel had done that fateful day in 1100. With the salty breeze on their faces, they had stood by the stern of the coaster, leaning against the bales of wool that had been squeezed into the little ship as if it was being stuffed. The sunlight glittered on the flat ocean and, far into the distance, they could see hundreds of similar square, off-white sails, dotted along the coast ahead of them, hoping for a breath of wind. The sound of heaving effort wafted up from below as the oars of the ship were wrenched through the ocean current by a complaining crew. The boat seemed unobtrusive enough to be safe.

From the stern of the ship, Hilary looked about him furtively to make sure none of the crew was listening. 'So King Henry killed his older brother and seized the throne. That seems pretty clear.' As he spoke, the wind suddenly rushed across the sea towards them, ruffling the waves and filling the huge canvas sail above him, and the dragon figurehead of their ship rose towards its journey. Beside them, off the bow, he could see a small row of sharp rocks sticking out of the water at the end of a narrow promontory.

'That cannot be France, can it?' said Abelard, momentarily confused.

'They call it Wight. A strange place, still stuck in Roman times, I've heard.'

'Interesting,' said Abelard, grabbing the side as the ship hit the new swell. 'I agree with you, but we must not omit our duty to doubt, Hilary. We must doubt. There was certainly a conspiracy, but then we knew that already. Purkiss confirms what your Saxon soldier told you in Jerusalem. Henry or those around him were prepared for Rufus to die. They were all ready.'

A huge ship passed them, its prow rising into the wind, its colourful banners streaming from its mast, the glint of sunlight on weapons on the deck. Some Norman magnate was making for his continental estates.

These monstrous families, thought Hilary. Those semi-divine figures, Baldwin of Flanders, Fulk of Anjou, and the great aristocrats who were with Rufus when he died – Gilbert Clare, Robert de Meulan, Robert FitzHamon and all the rest. Great men, giants whose ambition could lay waste counties, or countries or generations, in the pursuit of their merest whims. Why did God tolerate them?

'Master Peter, why do powerful, cynical people like that care about the Great Jewel of Alfred?'

Abelard was suddenly playing close attention. 'Good question, Hilary. The answer lies in those books about St Denis I have been reading. Because this Abbot Aelfgar and his friends, John of Muchelney and all the rest, are extreme Platonists. They believe there are eternal truths in this world.'

'Do not we all, Master Peter?'

'Yes, but they believe everything is a pale reflection of the one, true, archetypal model. They believe that only a real king can be king. They believe that kingship relies on a coronation, with the right words and right paraphernalia. They believe a king must be crowned at Kingston, with the Great Jewel of Alfred to read the holy texts, and the magical words of coronation, or they will not be a king.'

'But why does anyone care what they believe? Why is this important to a man like Ralph Basset?'

'I do not know. All I can say is that King Henry was not crowned at Kingston like his Saxon predecessors. He was crowned at Westminster. Nor was he crowned using the Great Jewel. And if someone persuades the common people of England that he is therefore not a king, that their oaths to him are invalid, then perhaps that is a problem. But there is another possibility too, is there not?'

Hilary wracked his brains. Why was Master Peter always putting him on the spot like this?

'I do not know. What is that?'

'That there is another possible king, the great-nephew, who *wants* the Alfred Jewel to be crowned with it. That is what Basset fears. That is what keeps him awake in the long winter nights and, because it keeps him awake. He will destroy the West as he searches for his Saxon rival. That is where we come in. Our task is urgent, Hilary. We are doing God's work.'

Hilary pursed his lips and was silent.

They jostled through the crowds climbing Ludgate Hill, the gate itself in the distance proving a magnet for carts and horses, then through the dirt and mud on the streets, bawled at by stall holders, pushed by boys and pigs, tripping over abandoned cauliflowers and old rib-cages, as slowly the great tower of the cathedral came nearer, with its vast buttresses and its builders and masons bustling across the still unfinished roof.

'You have a plan?' Hilary said at last, bellowing in Abelard's ear above the noise of the street. It irked him increasingly that it was his teacher's plans that seemed to dominate their every move.

Abelard turned with a smile. 'My dear Hilary, what do you take me for? Of course I have a plan. We are here to see my old friend Stephen of Boxley, who is a canon of St Paul's. I believe he can be prevailed upon to help us.'

'Help us how? What is he going to do? Ask King Henry if he killed his brother?'

'Come come, Hilary. This is no time for sarcasm. No, what we need is an intermediary and we can trust Stephen. What we will do is send a message to the bishop, and ask him to intercede with the archbishop. We will tell him what we know and ask him to intercede with the King. We will explain that we know Fulk is now committed to him – he told you so himself. We will explain there is no threat from the West. Then, with God's good grace, we will bring peace – and also, at the same time, clear your name. We will explain what was in the message of those letters, and why they no longer matter. The letters given you by John of Muchelney...'

'Who is dead. Who can't speak for us.'

'John of Muchelney who, as you quite rightly say, has passed to glory or wherever such people pass to. My friend will, I hope, explain this and suggest that perhaps we can swap information. We know the contents of his message and, in return, we want to know about John. Were King Henry's men having him followed across France? If so, do they know who killed him? Can they clear your name, in other words, Hilary? If they can do so, and my friend can persuade them to – then I believe I can do the same over poor Master Hubert in Paris. And we might get a clearer idea of who these shadowy forces are who can kill apparently so carelessly. Then, well, we will have to see what we can do – there are many lives at stake here, not just yours.'

Hilary had been thinking of Isabella, imagining her meeting her new husband on the quay at Barfleur, but Abelard's words penetrated. He felt suddenly guilty about being so curmudgeonly.

'Master Peter, you have given me a moment of hope, for which I thank you. I apologise for my mood. I am tired and hungry.'

'We both are, Hilary. Let us hope for the best. It is at least a plan.'

Outside St Paul's, the crowds were even thicker than before, and it was clear that some kind of event was taking place. There beside the south transept, there was a wooden cross and some kind of wooden pulpit on which a preacher was setting forth, waving his arms at the crowd. He was a ragged looking priest, dressed in black, but black which might perhaps have had some relation with the colour some decades before. It was a sun-bleached apology for black, and the words likewise seemed to have been drained of content. It was clear that the crowd were mixed in their reaction to him. Some were listening with close attention. Some were throwing the occasional vegetable, which the preacher dodged with practiced inattention.

'Yet my friends, listen to the exemplary lesson of this story,' he was shouting. 'For God there was still a debt to pay. Yes, the sin was done, the gold had been stolen from the abbey of Our Lady, but God does not forget. His immutable laws will turn in their own way, like the wheels of a mill. They must turn, my friends. At length, the knight died and he left the gold behind in his own crypt where it was found and returned to the church. But the chain mail that he wore, passed down to his son, did not forget either. And when the son first put it on, in imitation of his father, the blood began to flow from the holes. 'Take it off, take it off!' shouted his friends. But it was too late. He had put on the armour of sin.'

'The exemplar of the lavatorium,' said Abelard. 'Why do people listen to this kind of rubbish?'

There was a flurry of people crossing themselves and a broadside of vegetables from the back of the crowd.

'I don't believe it,' said a voice next to them. 'Can this be true? Not the Indomitable Rhinoceros himself? In London?'

A hefty priest stepped out of the crowd next to them and grasped Abelard's hand. He had food stains on his robes and carried a half-eaten chicken leg.

'Stephen of Boxley, by the gods,' he said. 'Of all the people to run into. You are the very man we are seeking.'

'Master Peter, I can hardly believe it,' said Stephen, taking another large bite. Then he seemed to remember himself, put the chicken leg inside the folds of his garments and became suddenly confidential.. 'I had heard you had left Paris. Bad business, bad business. Nobody knows where you are? Some say you are in Jerusalem, some Byzantium. Some just say you are back in Nantes, and all the time you were actually in London.'

'Actually, we have only just arrived. This is my colleague, Hilary the Englishman.'

'The poet? God be with you. You are most welcome, but listen – you must preach! And quickly otherwise because otherwise this faded fish will carry on with another tale. This is the Cross of St Paul's. This is where the services were held when the cathedral was being rebuilt and it continues as a place of public preaching and exhortation. Listen, I must get you up there. Master Peter Abelard preaching in London. What a sensation.'

'Wait, Master Stephen. Should I not be licensed? I don't really...' Hilary's heart sank. He wondered if there was any pulpit that would not somehow draw his teacher into speaking his mind.

'Nonsense, not here. Anyone can preach. Every Christian is licensed by the dean to preach here.' Stephen took Abelard's arm and pushed breathlessly through the crowd, with Hilary following meekly behind.

Hilary could hear that the whisper had caught on, at least with those clerical members of the audience. Peter Abelard. The Indomitable Rhinoceros. He is going to preach. Yes, now...

'My friends,' shouted Master Stephen from the platform, pushing off the reluctant priest in the faded garb. 'We welcome from Paris, the most brilliant, the most learned man in the world, the fiercest intellect for Christ. The man whose teaching shook Paris and caused the ungodly to shiver in their shoes, and not a few churchmen as well. Let me tell you this. A thousand years from now, your children's children's children will know his name and marvel that you heard him now in London, at the St Paul's Cross...'

'I don't think this is a very good idea,' Hilary whispered.

'Neither do I, but what can I do?'

A great cheer went up as Abelard was pulled up onto the platform. He looked less reluctant that he had claimed, Hilary thought. Perhaps he had not spoken in public now for at least two years. He must miss it. It was, after all, what he did best.

Abelard surveyed the crowd nervously, and then – filling with confidence – he spoke.

'My friends,' he said haltingly, surveying the expectant faces. A turnip whizzed past his ear. 'My old friend, and man of God, Stephen of Boxley has kindly asked me to say a few words. I am a priest, but I am not a preacher...

There was a shout of derision. Had he lost it? What was wrong with him?

'No, certainly not a preacher. But a teacher, yes. And as a teacher, I will tell you what I know. Other teachers you will have heard undoubtedly, and every one of them will tell you how unworthy you are – how unworthy we all are. They are right of course. But they will not tell you this. So listen carefully my friends.'

Then suddenly he seemed to find his stride. 'Take note of my words and I will tell you how all of us – from the very least of us, the very merest lepers and beggars in this crowd, even those propelling the fruit of the earth in this direction as I speak – all of us, all of us, share a little piece of Almighty God in our own breasts. A little piece of our saviour too. Listen and I will tell you.'

As Hilary watched, the old Abelard seemed to be returning. There was an acceleration of confidence and tone, and the bearing of the man was transformed in just a few short sentences, and the crowd quietened as they saw it too.

'How did God save the world? Let me ask you this. I know, you know, it was because he sent his son to die upon the cross and defeat the forces of evil. Yes, but *how* did he defeat them? He made a sacrifice, yes. He laid himself on the altar, yes, but *how* did he defeat evil and how does that act carry on its echoes through into today? Let me tell you, my friends. Because even as we contemplate the cross and that sacrifice, and that pain and suffering, we are changed by it. Our conscience cries out in response. Let me tell you this. *That* is the exemplar of our lives, not all this tittle-tattle about bleeding armour. And which part of us responds? Our conscience. Our God-given conscience says, this means something – and it means something for the way I act in my life hitherto. We can hide from our own consciences – God knows, I have done so myself. We can flee from them. We can run for a thousand miles. But it is still there, speaking to us in a small voice. Because it is God's voice. It is the part of the divine we carry in our own breasts as surely as we carry our staffs and our clothes we wear...'

It was working. There was a rapt silence in the crowd. They were not used to this kind of preaching.

'Therefore let me say this you. You have been told you are dust. You are unworthy sinners. You are spawn of the devil in a fallen world. All that is true, my friends. But now I tell you also that you carry the divine within you. You are pieces of God. You are made by God in his image and take his voice and his love wherever you go...'

'Rubbish. This is heresy,' said a gruff authoritative voice in the front. 'St Augustine said...' There was a commotion from those around him, with everyone shouting at once.

'Wait, sir, you make take your turn in this debate,' said

Stephen of Boxley. 'You may have a turn next when Master Peter has finished.'

Heavens, thought Hilary, his stomach rumbling again. This is going to take a long time. He waved at Abelard in mid-flow and motioned that he was going to find them some food. They had not eaten since the open sea, after all, and that had been the previous evening. Abelard nodded and went on.

The sight of Master Peter speaking with such animation and the attentive faces of the people listening – and the peroration that was clearly coming about the message of Christ's atonement – all brought Paris flooding back to Hilary so painfully that he needed to get away. He realised how much Abelard could still be moved by his adopted city. That had not been clear to him before. Perhaps he had avoided the pain of it, and the indignity and the injustice of his ferocious ejection from it, just two short years before. The realisation hit him with a sense of loss.

It wasn't just his stomach. He needed to escape and be by himself for a moment. He stood still at the great front of the new cathedral, looming above him, with its buttresses and arched windows. He was astonished at its size, and found himself comparing it favourably with the crumbling pile on the Seine dedicated to Notre Dame. He had never seen a cathedral on this scale before, except perhaps the old temple in Jerusalem, but that was ancient – this was brand new, with stone-masons and carpenters swarming around the outside and artists in evidence inside in the gloomy interior.

He could still hear Master Peter and the crowd in the background, so – despite his desperate stomach – he ventured inside through the doors to find a huge vaulted Romanesque ceiling and a nave longer than anything he had seen before. He stared up into the ribs, dimly visible in the pale light. Jonah must have felt like this in the belly of the whale, but without the candles presumably.

He wandered slowly down the aisle, accosted first by a prostitute, and then by two money-lenders, and found himself ushered towards the back of a queue which snaked away down a hole in the stone floor going into the crypt. 'What's this?'

'St Erkenwald. Stay here please.' The queue was moving quickly, and was being policed to do so by a whole phalanx of monks, taking the gifts of coins and food and blessing the donors with a perfunctory wave. In only a few minutes, he was inside the dingy crypt, which was obviously very ancient indeed. Down there, in the smoke from a thousand candles, with the heaving mass of pilgrims, he lost his nerve and dropped out of the rapidly moving line before he reached the rail where the pilgrims knelt with their personal supplications.

He did not want to be checked quite so closely as the pilgrims who had reached the tomb. No doubt there were fears that Erkenwald's bones might disappear to a rival institution unless the monks were too careful. He knew the story of one devoted worshipper who stole a relic by biting off two fingers under the guise of a reverent kiss. No, none of that. He stepped back in the darkness and fell headlong onto the flagstones.

'Sorry, friend,' said a voice in the blackness. For a moment it looked like a heap of dirty blankets. '*Hit waes geara iu.*'

'Never mind,' said Hilary. 'I'm not hurt.' Then it struck him what had been said. 'What did you say?'

The heap of blankets seemed to shrink before him.

'Nothing, sir, I assure you. Just a rhyme from where I come from in the West. No more. A children's rhyme.'

Hilary stood up and came closer. He knelt before the pile of clothes and realised it was a man with only one leg.

'Don't be afraid. I mean you no harm. I come from the West myself.'

'Alms then for the love of God. Help an old soldier for the pity of Christ.'

'I will help you if you tell me what you said and why.'

'I told you, an old wives' tale.'

'I am interested in old wives. Speak and I will pay you,' said Hilary, aware that he had very little money himself now. 'Who are you?'

'I am a soldier. I fought at Tinchbrai. I fought at Brémule. Now I just wait for the Almighty, and any gifts that fall from the table of St Erkenwald.'

He laughed, not bitterly but as if he was in some privileged position. Hilary inched closer to him. He stank of urine.

'Listen, tell me why you said that phrase to me. Do you know what it means?'

'Of course I know. It was just in fun. We used to say it when we were younger, where I come from, to say that the days of King Alfred were returning. We could not fight King William, could we? But we could speak, *quietly*. Not now. Nobody speaks now. So just a game. Take no notice of an old man.'

'And where were you from?'

'From Wessex, of course.'

'Yes, but where? Wessex stretched from here to the western sea where the sun goes down.'

Hilary was used to the dim candlelight now and could see the old man look away. He saw his dirt-encrusted his eyelids as he looked down.

'I came from Glastonbury, hard by the great abbey, surrounded by water for most of the year. I was born there, not so far from Athelney.'

'Athelney. Of course'

'Athelney, where the great king Alfred escaped to when the Danes were on the march. Athelney where he burned the cakes. It is a strange place. I have been there, you know. In my youth.'

'Listen, here is my payment. It is all I can afford.' Hilary handed over one of his last small coins. Then man looked hungrily at it and hid it among his dirty robes. 'But tell me one other thing. Do you know of a place called Muchelney?'

'Aye, Muchelney. Of course I do. It is a daughter house of Glastonbury, in the levels, in the very marshes. In the lakes and ancient marshes where only the stout-hearted may go. Only those who know the safe ways or who travel by boat.'

Hilary stood up, staring into space, and mulling over what he had been told. Muchelney, Glastonbury and Athelney were the keys to this mystery. That is where John had come from and it was probably where the letters came from too. For the first time, he felt ahead of his old teacher. The thing to do now, if he could, was to stay ahead.

Back out in the open air, Hilary made for a bakery he could see down the hill towards Ludgate, but then he realised something was not quite as he had left it. Abelard's voice was no longer audible. In fact, there seemed to be no speaker's voice emanating from St Paul's Cross at all. There were rather alarming shouts and protests, which came in waves, but he could not make out the words. Once more, Hilary abandoned the allure of bread and ham and hurried back towards the cross.

The crowd had gathered around something. There were helmets glinting in the morning sun. For a moment he missed Abelard, but there he was in the midst of them in heated discussion with a soldier. Stephen of Boxley was with him.

Hilary edged closer and could see that there were six soldiers in chain mail standing there with spears. They had evidently not come for the preaching. He also began to be able to hear snatches of conversation.

'I tell you, this is sanctified land,' Stephen of Boxley was saying. 'This is consecrated part of the cathedral. You can make no arrests here.'

'And I tell you, I'm making no arrests. Who is making an arrest? Not me. I am simply conducting these gentlemen to see the King's Justice.'

It was clearly time to go. Master Peter would have to look after himself on this occasion, thought Hilary. His own presence would do neither of them any good at all. As he turned, he caught sight of someone else in the melee pointing at him. He dodged behind the cross and back towards the cathedral. With a rueful smile, he realised he was running away again. When would this stop?

A second later, he found himself clasped closely in the arms of another soldier. His chain mail hurt his skin. The man smelled of goats. Finally, after nearly a year of running, he appeared to be under arrest.

Chapter 7/The Aetheling

London, 7 October 1120

'I said this was not a good idea,' said Hilary bitterly, as they sat on the wooden seat in the middle of a small boat rowed speedily up river by their captors. Red and green streamers from the rear of the boat announced whatever regiment these soldiers belonged to, or whichever lord they owed allegiance to. The bits of offal thrown into the water flick occasionally into the boat as the oars move rhythmically forward.

'You were right, as you so often are,' said Abelard staring back towards the disappearing tower of St Paul's. 'But at the very least, getting arrested is an excellent way of contacting the authorities directly.'

'You don't think it might start the relationship on the wrong basis. Were we not supposed to be talking via an intermediary?'

Abelard ignored him, and the flotillas of boats on that passed by on either side, and going in every direction, announced to them that they were just a small and insignificant sideshow in the huge energy of this sleepless city. Who will catch sight of this small boat, ploughing its way against the tide, and understand that the Indomitable Rhinoceros is on board, heading for the deepest dungeon the city can provide.

Hilary's stomach made an almighty rumble. 'You don't think they might have at least offered us something to eat.'

'*No possumus!* Hilary, I must have heard more about your stomach since we met in St Denis than the average sinner has heard about the Trinity. You tend it well.'

'The trouble is, I have barely been tending it at all.'

In a remarkably short time, the boat approached the beach below the white castle they had seen from the ship. The streamers of red and green flew in the breeze from the topmost tower, like blood and grass. One of the soldiers leapt out and pulled the boat up onto the sand. The others motioned Hilary and Abelard to follow. It was strangely comforting having soft sand below the feet, but the huge gate by the river in the castle walls, and the imposing white edifice of the Tower of London – with its four distinctive towers at each corner – was less comforting. The soldiers had turned noticeably more brusque and irritable as they had progressed down the river. There is an atmosphere of damp and menace.

'This is the Conqueror's tower,' said the officer. 'This is where you will be staying in London.' He guffawed. 'And those that stay here tend not to stay anywhere else again.'

Hilary imagined the inside of the great tower before him, and the dungeons and chains that hung there awaiting him. Then his mind wandered to Isabella and the chains that bound her, figuratively speaking, to her new husband. Was she married? Was she happy? He felt around his neck for his mother's charm, closed his mind against despair and followed Abelard and the soldiers down some stone steps inside the building and into a small arch in the outside wall, then down a damp spiral staircase.

They marched down a long unhealthy passageway, with water dripping from the ceiling. It must be below the water level, thought Hilary. Light filtered down from skylights above them. The prospect seemed ominous, to say the least. Hilary dared not even exchange glances with his friend. Abelard strode on confidently, apparently oblivious to danger.

Finally, they stopped outside a large wooden door with a grill. A man they had not seen before stepped forward with a bundle of huge keys. The studded door creaked open, as if it had warped in the damp and, a moment later, they were inside. The door was shut behind them and, as they grew used to the darkness, they stood listening to the strange sounds all around them of the human detritus of London, writhing, moaning, staring in the ragged corners of the cell. There was the occasional clank of a chain. A few hiccoughs and little snatches of brutish conversation.

When his eyes could see through the murk, Hilary noticed they were the centre of attention for about ten pairs of eyes, peering at him in the semi-darkness. An air of fetid mist seemed to prevent him from focusing.

'They're coming in pairs now,' said a gruff voice. 'Come and join the party. Join the church of the resurrection. We dream of rising up one floor.' He guffawed again. 'Make yourself comfortable. You'll be here for some time. That corner is free since Robert of Sittingbourne died last week. Too much sitting, he did.'

'Well,' said Abelard when they settled in Robert's old place in the corner. 'This is something that has never happened to me before. I shall use this in my lecture on hell.'

'Let's hope you live to give it and me to hear it,' said Hilary weakly. His stomach was now hurting profoundly.

'Hilary, do not despair. They will come, I promise that...'

As he spoke, as if by magic, there was a jangle of keys, a crashing of feet, the great door opened and the soldier stood there again.

'Peter and Hilary,' he shouted with a glint of amusement. 'The King's Justice wants to talk to you.'

'I move fast, do I not?' said Ralph Basset, his red-padded robe hitched up into bunches at his shoulders and his gold chain round his neck, glinting in the firelight. He sipped a goblet of wine. 'I expect you thought that, once you had said farewell to me in Winchester, it would be the last you would see of me. Well, let me tell you, Abelard: when I told you not to meddle, I meant it. You do not know what you are meddling in and I am a man of my word. I did not expect to see you in London, and now I have seen you, there are consequences.'

'In fact, we have come especially to see you, my lord,' said Abelard. 'Now, I would be grateful if you could let us sit down. My friend and I have not eaten since yesterday.'

Ralph Basset stared at them menacingly from behind his desk.

'Leave us please,' he said to the guards. 'Do you know what this place is?'

'It is the Conqueror's tower,' said Hilary. 'So I understand.' A cockroach walked across his foot, and he flicked it away.

'It is indeed, and do you know what happens here to the Conqueror's enemies, and now what happens to his son's enemies? Do you?'

An ominous silence descended on the room. Hilary prayed quietly to himself. The tales of King Henry's cruelty had long since wafted over to France. He was well aware of the tales of eyes put out, ears cut off, and horrible deformities before brutal deaths.

'Well, I have a proposal for you,' said Basset. 'You may sit down, and eat. Indeed, you may go free from here, if you will just fill in a few gaps in my knowledge for me. If you do that, and you are completely honest. Completely honest to my satisfaction, and we can put this matter behind us, then you may go. If not, however, you may have to call the Conqueror's tower 'home'. Many have done before you, I can tell you.'

Another silence descended. Basset looked from one to the other, deep into their eyes, as if he was about to gouge them out. Abelard and Hilary looked at each other.

'My lord, that is a hopeful speech for us,' said Abelard.

A flash of irritation crossed the Justice's face. 'And don't tell me you are under the protection of the Chancellor of France, because I care nothing for that. The Chancellor of France can kiss my arse, if he dares come over here and do it. You are in England now and we do what we like in England without continental interference, either from the Pope or the Emperor or the King of France.'

'I quite understand, my lord. What I was about to say was that we were coming to London expressly to share our understanding of the events which you speak of, mainly in order to clear the name of my friend here, who remains accused of the murder of two men.'

'So you will help me? Splendid. You may sit on that bench, and when I judge that you have told me everything I want to know, I will send for some food.'

Hilary sat down with relief. Events were taking a more positive direction after all.

'Now,' said Basset, taking a deep breath. 'You met a man calling himself John of Muchelney just before Christmas the year before last. Am I right?'

'That is correct, my lord,' said Hilary, realising he must now take the lead. It seemed possible, just possible now, that this conversation was going to go the right way and he would see the sky again.

'The next morning, he was dead. You see, I have been doing a little investigating of my own in the days since we last met. Now, John carried something around his neck, did he not, and when his body was discovered – an unpleasant sight, I believe – that item was missing. I am right again, am I not?'

'Yes my lord.'

'You took it?'

'I did, my lord.'

'Why in the name of St Anthony did you do that?'

'He asked me to. In fact, he put it round my neck when I was asleep. In fact, the night before, he asked me to take it to Count Fulk of Anjou. I knew nothing of these matters. I *still* know nothing of these matters.'

'I am glad to hear it. So then, you took it. Did you read what was inside?'

'I did, my lord. It seemed sensible to do so. Inside was a letter to my lord of Flanders which appeared to be... which said...'

Abelard interrupted. 'What my friend is trying to tell you is that the letter appeared to be offering Count Baldwin the throne of England. It was extremely hard to understand. There had clearly been a previous letter which might have made it more comprehensible. There was also a page from torn from a history book, from Winchester I believe, which described the events that preceded the death of the King's late brother.'

As he spoke, Basset began to look a little discomfited. He got up and paced around the room.

'Yes, yes, yes. I am not interested in the King's late brother, do you understand? You don't tell me anything I didn't know. But now we come to the crux of the matter. I don't like the idea of those papers falling into the wrong hands. That would be serious. So I would be grateful if you would hand them over to me.'

He stretched an open palm forwards. Abelard and Hilary stared at him.

'I assure you I will put them to good use. I am grateful to you – I'm sure the King will be grateful to you when he knows – that you have had them in your safekeeping for so long. But it is imperative that I take them now.'

'But we don't have them any more,' said Hilary in a small voice.

Basset looked impatient. 'You are testing me, sir. I know you did not deliver them. So please hand them over and we will say no more about it.'

'I am telling the truth. The letters were stolen from me in Jerusalem.'

'In Jerusalem?' Basset sounded incredulous.

'Yes – my friend and I travelled there after we left France.' Hilary's heart sank. Could he imagine a way out of this before it was too late?

'You told me before you had lately returned from the Holy Land and I assumed it was a figure of speech. What are you trying to tell me? You left these vital papers lying around in the Holy City. You might as well tell me you took them to hy-Brasil or the moon, except that they are not full of spies like Jerusalem. I don't believe you.'

Basset had worked himself up into a rage of frustration. He paced faster around the room and looked red in the face.

'But what can I say?' said Hilary pathetically. 'They were taken.'

'Perhaps I can assist?' said Abelard. 'I have a complete recall of everything in the letters. I can probably reproduce them for...'

With a flick of his sumptuous cloak, the King's Justice exploded. 'No, you try me too far. I am not negotiating with you. If you will not do as I ask, or tell me where you have hidden them, then I can do no more for you. You can live and die here for all I care. Guards!' There was a clatter as two soldiers in chain mail burst into the room. 'Return these two to the cell. We are not speaking the same language. Get them out of my sight before I remove their eyes myself.'

Abelard stood before he was manhandled and risked the crucial question. 'My lord, you said you had heard from the French Chancellor himself about me. May I ask when...?'

'Get out!' roared Basset as they were dragged from the room.

It was a bad night. A raw turnip and a few sips of water had appeared sometime around nightfall. Abelard snored beside him, apparently unconcerned that this might be their final resting place. Hilary could not sleep. The events of the past year turned over and over in his head. Why was it that he had run into John of Muchelney? Was he led somehow into doing so? Was it somehow his luck and his fate? Why had God so forsaken him to allow these things to happen? He wondered if maybe he had told the *whole* truth, and promised to hand over the Great Jewel, perhaps he might now be free.

His companions in the dark cell moaned and raved as they slept. The chains rattled. Scuffling sounds all around him in the dark suggested to Hilary unpleasantly of river rats. The very night seemed to be alive with evil. There were tramping military boots along the dank passageways above him and around him. Some hours after dark, there were screams from somewhere else in the building. It seemed invidious to interpret them as such, but it was hard to avoid the conclusion that this was Ralph Basset's torturers at work, even at night. Perhaps torturers can only work at night, he wondered to himself, when even the angels sleep.

Hilary realised he must have dozed off, because the cell suddenly seemed a little lighter. A dim damp glow seemed to be creeping in from above. He could almost make out Abelard still sleeping peacefully beside him on the straw.

What is the day going to bring, wondered Hilary? This could be a bad day indeed. He stared at the stones in front of him, noticing how they came slowly into focus with the dawn. Then there was a crash outside which shattered the calm. Boots banged along the stones. The familiar key jangled, the door opened and two men came in, one carrying a blazing torch.

'Two men, and I want them,' said one of them, apparently unconcerned that he might wake his prisoners. 'They are here somewhere. Peter and Hilary.'

A cold fear clutched at Hilary's heart. The second man brandished the torches in the faces of the sleeping prisoners.

'No, not him. Not him. Over here.'

A torch was thrust in Hilary's face. 'Are you Hilary the Englishman? Come with me please. Wake your friend. I will wait for your outside. This place makes my flesh creep.'

Hilary reached out to the sleeping form of Master Peter and shook him. 'Master Peter, we are fetched. Wake up please. This is the hour.'

'Ah, Hilary... What do you want?'

'They have come to fetch us. They are waiting outside. Come quickly.'

Abelard heaved himself up, shook the pieces of straw from his back and stretched until his arms banged into the stone roof of the cell.

'I'm coming. I will follow you. Lead the way.'

Outside in the passage, next to the soldier with the flaming torch, Hilary found a young man in simple but wealthy clothes, golden in the flush of youth. He was dressed in a short tunic, and wore a jewelled dagger on his belt. He had time to notice the golden rings the man wore and then looked into his face. He was young, barely more than 20 and clearly, judging by the way he stood, supremely confident.

'Do I have the honour of addressing Hilary the Englishman and Master Peter of Notre-Dame?'

'Yes,' said Hilary nervously.

'Then follow me. I will explain everything upstairs.'

A sleepy Abelard followed a few feet behind. Hilary felt he had never been so awake, though his stomach gnawed away at him and his head felt like a heavy ball of lard. They turned into a spiral staircase and their feet echoed on the stone steps. Two floors up, they were still going on. When would it end?

'Can you manage?' shouted their captor. 'I know a night in the cell can make it seem giddy up here.'

Hilary remained silent. Abelard still seemed to be asleep.

Two more floors and he was beginning to flag. Could he manage another? Finally there was a blast of cool air and they were out in the light on the battlements, staring down at the busy river from between the grey crenellations. One way the rickety bridge; the other way the route to the sea.

The man led them a little further and then stopped, staring out over the river himself. Then he dismissed the guards, gave the pair his full attention and a confident smile. 'My apologies for this journey, and for your night at my father's pleasure. Basset is not an easy landlord. I have brought you up here so that we will not be overheard.'

Staring at his smile and unusually bright teeth, Hilary reluctantly admitted to himself that their new captor was not just charming, he was also good-looking. Attractive even. His tunic was embroidered with gold, and an extraordinary Saxon silver broach held his red cloak together at his neck.

'Let me introduce myself. They call me William the Aetheling. You will have heard of me no doubt. This is not my habitual residence, but my informants told me last night that you were here and I wanted to talk to you, confidentially, if you don't mind.'

Hilary bowed his head in submission, and reminded himself silently that this was King Henry's son and heir, and the man who was now betrothed to the daughter of Fulk of Anjou. He might sound friendly, but it was time to be particularly careful.

'My lord, I am at your service.' Abelard just stared. He seemed to be slowly waking up. Not even the heir to the English throne could quite prize him from his walking slumber.

The Prince nodded in acknowledgement and stared out across the shipping below them. 'Now follow my gaze if you will. You know this river? The Thames. Do you know how long this city has been here?'

'I believe Caesar came here,' said Abelard. 'I hope he had a better welcome than we have.'

Hilary was aghast. 'What my colleague means...'

'Do not concern yourself, my friend. I understand him very well. This was not a proper welcome for a man who is famous throughout Christendom. The point I was making, if you will, is that this city has been a place of trade for a thousand years. I do not want to ruin that. I want no civil war in England. I want nothing that can undermine the life of this place and the wealth of England that comes from it.'

'But...' said Hilary, afraid he was about to be accused of fermenting a war.

'Listen,' said the Prince. 'I am going to take you into my confidence. I don't want to inherit a divided kingdom. I don't want to inherit a kingdom impoverished by conflict. I know there remain doubts – how could there not – about the death of my uncle, the man they called William Rufus or William the Red. He died just before I was born, but I know all about it. I experienced the shock in my mother's womb, and I have heard the whisperings in the years since then. It is only a matter of time before some foreign Prince uses these doubts to foster war over here. I want to inherit without dispute, unlike any of my family since the Conquest by my grandfather, and then I want to *reign* without dispute. But to do that I must know what happened. Do you understand? I must know.'

Abelard finally seemed to jerk awake. 'My lord, I believe we can help you.'

'I believe so too. When I heard about your presence and the questions you had been asking, I knew that you had some chance to reach the truth. I am grateful that the greatest mind in Europe is available to me. Listen, I believe that Rufus' death was an accident. I know about the stories and the warnings, so you don't have to tell me. I believe Walter Tirel made a fatal error. Perhaps it was somebody else's error, but the evidence certainly points to him. But I need to know for certain. If it was deliberate, I need to know who paid him, or – if not – why he shot that fatal arrow. So if you will undertake this task for me, I think we can dispense with my lord Basset's justice. Will you do it?'

Abelard stared again. This time he seemed to be thinking. 'What if we find out the truth, but it suggests that you were wrong about Tirel?'

'Then I need to know that too. I need to be prepared. Either way, I need to know.'

Hilary could wait no longer. 'I apologise. I may be obtuse, but what is it that you actually want us to do? Have you not had investigators with access to better information than us? What can we do? I am certainly grateful to be out of that cell, but can we actually help you? How do we find out what Tirel did?'

'Well, you can ask him.'

Hilary stared in astonishment. '*Ask* him?'

'But how will we know he is telling the truth?'

'Ah, the great Abelard will know, I am sure. What do they call you in Paris? The Indomitable Rhinoceros? And in any case, I hardly need tell you that there are ways of making sure people are telling the truth.'

'I'm not sure Ralph Basset's methods will work here,' said Hilary, still doubtful. 'We're just priests. Just wandering scholars.'

'I am a priest no longer, I fear,' said Abelard.

'Ah well, I leave that to your imagination which I am sure is more powerful than mine,' said the Prince confidently. 'The question is: do we agree? Will you undertake this task and report back to me honestly what you have found?'

Abelard stared again. What was the matter with him, Hilary wondered? 'Yes,' he said finally. 'I think that is a task we are uniquely suited to do, am I not right, Hilary? But I would like to ask one thing if we succeed?'

A slight cloud gathered in the forehead of William the Aetheling. 'Ask, Master Peter.'

'My friend here can speak for himself,' said Abelard, looking at Hilary in a meaningful way, as if urging him to speak. Hilary searched his brain. Was this something they had rehearsed? What was he supposed to say? He opened his mouth to speak, and light dawned.

'I am a fugitive, my lord, in France. I am accused of the murder of John of Muchelney and later of Master Hubert of Notre Dame. I am absolutely innocent of both of these. I don't know who killed them, because their deaths involved the hidden matters and intricacies of kings and princes which I do not pretend to understand. I don't need to know who killed them either. But if there is any knowledge in your own court, using your own sources of information, and you satisfy yourself that I am not guilty, could I ask you to provide me with a letter to the Chancellor of France which sets out your findings and clears my name? Like you, I ask no more than the truth.'

William the Aetheling stared out across the ships sailing into London. 'These are deep waters, Hilary. I do not know the answers. But it is a reasonable bargain you ask – the truth in return for the truth, and I make that pledge willingly.'

Hilary sank to his knees on the flagstones. There are moments for abjection, and this seemed to him to be one of them. 'I am grateful, my Lord. Fervently grateful. I will do what I can to fulfil my side of the bargain.' The glimmer of hope that Hilary had glimpsed talking to Abelard only the day before now seemed to be stronger.

'No, come, come,' said the Prince. 'We work together, you and I. Come, you will sail with me to Normandy. I have much to do to make ready. My own soldiers will look after you. You must be hungry,' said William striding down the battlements, calling for his guards. 'Come, we leave at terce. I will see you then, fully clothed and equipped.'

It was one of those meals, in the great hall of the Tower, which Hilary believed he would never forget. Fruit, followed by lettuce, followed by roast kid, goose and ham, followed by quince tart, a slice of pie with live starlings inside which collapsed stunned on the table as they emerged. The aromas stayed on his fingers to colour the remaining hours of the day. Abelard picked at his food moodily. Hilary glanced at him every so often, aware that there was something about this miraculous bargain with the heir to the throne that worried his former teacher. It was strange to be in league with King Henry's heir when Abelard had been considering delivering the Great Jewel to his Saxon rival, but there were more important considerations – his own freedom.

In fact, for Hilary, it seemed almost too good to be true. Only that night he had believed it was his fate to die of starvation underground in the dark, with the clanking of chains and the screams of forgotten prisoners around him. Now he was being decked out with a warm cloak, a horse, food for the journey and a bag of silver. Travelling in the prince's train had major compensations as well. Feasts at night, warm lodgings, clean straw, not comfort exactly on the road but something approaching it.

There followed a luxurious journey by barge down the River Darent before joining the old road to the sea. There was the thrill of riding behind a party of soldiers with streaming banners and colourful cloaks, and the red cloak that Prince William habitually wore. It was also fascinating to watch the Prince at a distance. He was relaxed and confident, and obviously loved by the men who worked for him. There was a great deal of laughter from the front of the column, his habitual place. Even in the early autumn, with the leaves falling from the trees, and the pale sunshine a constant reminder of the disappearing summer, it was a privilege to be among them.

It was an easy crossing of the English Channel too, the spray in their faces and the wind behind them as the great warship hurtled across the narrow strip of sea and then clung to the Norman coast for the rest of the day, seeking out the port of Barfleur. The next morning, bleary-eyed from lack of sleep, Hilary watched the Prince gather his closest companions and ride off in the direction of Caen.

'Wait,' he shouted, raising his hand, the banners fluttering behind him. 'Wait, where are my emissaries?'

He trotted back in high good humour to where Hilary and Abelard were struggling with their own horses and saddlebags by the dock.

'Master Peter, Master Hilary, I wish you good luck and good hunting. I will return here to Barfleur on St Edmund Martyr's Day. I will meet you then and we can sail together. You can tell me then what you have found. God go with you.'

'Yes,' said Hilary, as they watched him and his companions gallop away. 'But how are we going to do it? Why should Tirel tell us anything?'

'I have been waiting three days for you to ask that question,' said Abelard. 'It is no simple one either. But, as I said, I suggest we just *ask* him.'

'But Tirel is Lord of Poix – why should he tell us? Why should we believe him if he does?'

'Now think, Hilary. There are times when people always tell the truth, are there not.'

'Are there?'

'On their death bed?'

Hilary was horrified. '*Non credo,* Master Peter, you don't mean to kill him?'

Abelard laughed. 'Of course not. What do you take me for? I am just saying that somehow we need to engineer a situation whereby he makes his final confession, or what he *thinks* is his final confession.'

'How?' Hilary felt increasingly confused.

'How? I have no idea. That is what we have to work on as we ride together. I believe Poix is near a week's ride.'

'For heaven's sake, why would he ask you to hear his confession? It's tough is it not?' There was an edge of panic in Hilary's voice.

'I am not going to,' said Abelard firmly. '*You* are. Listen Hilary, I am no longer a priest. I cannot, have not... But you are a clerk in holy orders. You will hear his confession.'

'*Me?*'

'Yes. I have been thinking about our adventure together. Being in a prison cell makes you look at things differently, don't you agree. And I have come to the conclusion that I am still your teacher and must act accordingly. This is *your* tale, not mine. I am not going to be the hero of it; *you* are. That is the way out of this conundrum. I will seek out the truth as fervently as ever. But you – you who it affects so closely – will rescue yourself and fulfil our promise to the Aetheling. And when we have done that, we will ask him to intercede and prevent bloodshed in the West.'

Hilary opened his mouth to protest but then fell silent. Deep down, he knew Abelard was right. It was his own story, and his predicament, and he must now take charge of it. There would be no more waiting for Abelard to decide, no more assumption that Abelard would know. He would have to do the deed, whatever it was that unravelled this web of lies and peril in which he found himself, and he must start to do that in Poix and whatever he found there.

PART III

1/Tirel

Poix-de-Picardie, 8 November 1120

Poix was a prosperous place on the road to Amiens, but it was hardly a town. There was an inn outside it, a large gate surrounded by agricultural carts, and a handful of houses and a castle inside. There were sullen haymakers lining the fields, peasants toiling in the fields with the dregs of the turnips, sweating despite the late autumn chill. The village idiots drooled at them as they passed by. This was a town that might easily be overlooked if you were in haste.

It was also getting chilly, and Hilary congratulated himself for his choice of a thick cloak at the Tower. He and Abelard and ridden in silence. It was hardly clear which philosophical issue his companion was wrestling with – what theological dispute or historical confusion he was unravelling – but, for Hilary, one thing dominated every step. How on earth were they to get Walter Tirel, the Lord of Poix, to speak to them and how they were to get him to tell the truth when they did so?

They would arrive as wandering scholars and minstrels. Abelard would pass as a minstrel; Hilary would be a travelling priest. That much they knew. Beyond that, it was simply not clear. But Abelard's silence seemed impenetrable and Hilary did not intrude on it as their horses picked their way between ruts and potholes on the road from Rouen. It had been a difficult few weeks and both men needed silence to compose themselves and recover from the shock. Whenever the prospect of extracting information from the Lord of Poix slipped his mind, Hilary thought of Isabella, starting her married life and the draughty castle that would be her keep.

The clue to Hilary's dilemma emerged in an unexpected place – the inn outside Poix – and in a very unexpected shape.

He and Abelard slept on straw batons in the dormitory at the inn. It was full of farmers and minor merchants on their way home from the autumn fairs in Champagne and smelled of body fluids even more than usual. The straw was also alive with insects. It was hard, in those circumstances, to get to sleep. Hilary was just drifting off when a background noise began to intrude. He turned over on the other side to sleep, but it was no good.

'What is that noise? It sounds like some kind of tournament.'

There was no answer from next to him, except the deep breathing of a philosopher fast asleep. The outside noise was almost like cheering, and maybe even music, but that seemed scarcely possible so late at night. Hilary dragged himself upright, gathered his bedclothes about him – a cloak is as useful at night as it is in the day – and headed out across the courtyard to investigate. The moonlight shone on the horse trough. What was Isabella doing now in her cold, dank castle, facing the cold, dank hands of her husband?

The moment he pushed open the wooden door to the inn, he was hit by a wall of sound and the overwhelming smell of beer and hops. The main room of the inn was full. A roaring fire lit and warmed the room almost as if it was cooking the people inside. As well as being roasted slowly, they were reaching a point of hysteria, shouting and laughing and banging their plates and the handles of their knives on the wooden tables. Many of them seemed well-dressed, a cut above the farmers and traders who he had been sharing the straw with a few minutes before. There were red tunics among them and some swords. Their hair was worn in the curly style long fashionable in Paris. A huge cheer erupted as

Hilary shut the door behind him, but it was a few minutes before he could see where it was directed.

Then he saw him. A rubicund figure, thoroughly overweight, dressed in a pair of huge boots and in a green jerkin with a large leather belt. He had a red face and a forked grey beard and he was laughing harder than any of them. It took a few moments for Hilary to realise why he was familiar. It appeared to be the very man whose acquaintance he had made as a fellow guest of the Templars in Jerusalem. Then he had been introduced as the Duke of Aquitaine, but could this possibly be a duke?

'No, no, no more!' he was shouting. 'The Duke must have his sleep if he wants to stay beautiful and attractive to the ladies. No more.'

There were more cheers and the figure shook his head and his hand with great good humour but finality.

'Yes, well, since you insist, my lords, let me give you one more...' There was another huge cheer.

Hilary's first thought was astonishment at this collection of people. His second thought was to wonder whether it was legal. Singing? In an inn deep in the night? He had seen singing in inns before across Europe, but those were dull amateur affairs. This was something different, more like a wandering scholar – but a very great deal more amusing.

A man on cross-legs in front of the singer started up on the lute. The 'Duke' stepped forward, took a deep breath, and a large gulp of beer, and began:

> *' 'Infallible master', they call me – they do!*
> *I've never had a woman one whole night through*
> *Who sees the day dawn in the sunshine or rain,*
> *And doesn't demand me all over again –*
> *Yes, this is trade where I am the master*

So come on and take me, come on now – faster!'

It was an amazing performance. There was more cheering at the end, and more banging of metal on wood. But this time the 'Duke' collapsed on a bench next to table, waving exhaustedly and began to consume a large plate of chicken and ham which had been placed before him.

Hilary was astonished. He had heard singing, of course, in cathedrals and castles and great houses, from here to Jerusalem. He had heard the performances of jongleurs, scholars and clowns. But he had never heard anything quite like this. It was both funny and sad, but it was also intelligent, in a bawdy kind of way. The songs he sang himself, and the other wandering scholars, had occasional flashes of humour, but mostly they were very serious. It was shocking enough to be singing about lust, and using spiritual metre and rhythm to sing about the world, but *this* – this was practically pagan.

It was shocking, but it was also exciting. The audience began to drift away into the night, slapping each other on the back in a tired way, and Hilary edged towards the table and sat next to the man who had been such a centre of attention. Tin coins were dropping into a pitcher, presumably for the performance. The final admirers were congratulating him and banging their tankards down on the great oak tables.

'That was an extraordinary performance,' he said.

The 'Duke' did not look up but filled his mouth over full with ham. 'You enjoyed it? Good. Glad to hear it, my lad. Good of you to say so.' He stared across the table with his mouth still full. 'Hold on, I remember every face and I have seen you before. Remind me...'

'My name is Hilary. They call me 'the Englishman'. We met in Jerusalem, I believe.'

'Hilary the poet? I am very glad to meet you, Sir,' said the 'Duke,' looking at him, with streaks of meat jelly in his beard, and grasping his Hilary's hand with both of his. 'We are fellow performers in this cruel world. My name is William, the ninth of that name, Duke of Aquitaine, at your service.'

Hilary laughed nervously. He remembered the giggling presence with the leaders of the Templars on Temple Mount, but could this really be a duke? The idea of a duke sitting in this particular inn, let along singing ribald songs, was almost the best joke of all. He had no idea that Duke William of Aquitaine entertained in quite such style. His new friend's face fell.

'You laugh? That bit was no joke. I am indeed the Duke, sadly fallen from my position in life, it is true. A sad embarrassment to my family it is true, a pox on them. But there certainly are compensations for the wandering life...' He gave an obscene leer.

As he spoke, a distant memory about the Duke of Aquitaine began to filter slowly into Hilary's mind. Did he not take an army to Jerusalem and see every one of them slaughtered? Did he not set out for a life on the road as a wandering scholar?

'My lord, forgive me. For a moment I...' They had indeed met in Jerusalem, but this did not seem to be one of the most powerful magnates in France.

'No, no, no, my friend,' said Duke William, reading his mind. We are not lords and commons here. We are fellow wanderers. I am the Duke, it is true, but my duchy is in the competent hands of my rather dull son William and his advisors, and now I wander – as you do – from house to house, seeking alms where I will, entertaining where I can, and tasting the food and – well, of course tasting the women.' There was another raucous outburst of laughter. 'I have nothing now except perhaps a talent to amuse people. Now, tell me about yourself. You are going to Poix, you say? I used to know one of your poems, called 'Beautiful youth'.'

'Yes,' said Hilary, squirming a little. 'I am with my companion. I am travelling to the castle. I hope to go there tomorrow to sing.'

'To sing before Walter Tirel, the lord of this place? Well, met my friend. My very intentions as well. We will go together and sing. Of course you wandering scholars have a higher calling than mine. You are a clerk in holy orders, no doubt? Your songs will thrill and inspire. Mine will tell the truth about life. We will be a match made, as they say, in heaven. A potent combination for the Lord of Poix. Come now, some food for my friend here...'

'Your colleague is very silent. What is he? A philosopher or something?' The Duke guffawed again.

The three men were on the road in the bright autumn sunlight heading towards the walls of Poix. Abelard rode behind, deep in his own thoughts. It was clear to Hilary that he did not very much approve of their new acquaintance. The Duke himself was fresh as the dawn wind. Hilary had expected his new friend to be sullen, yellow and exhausted, the inevitable result of his carousing the night before. Not a bit of it. He was actually in an ebullient mood, boasting about the night before and looking forward to an evening under Tirel's roof with keen anticipation.

'So, my friend, will we eat tonight? Will we feast? My Lord of Poix is careful with what he eats and drinks. Only the very best, and I am well-known there. There is a certain lady in the kitchens who is most accommodating. In fact, I'm not sure which is the thing that draws me most, the food or the pleasure.'

'Do you know him well? Walter Tirel? '

'Difficult man to know. Reserved. Serious-minded. He is a friend of Suger, from St-Denis you know, and you can't get more serious than that. But I like his family and his home and yes – I love his table. I certainly do.' 'What of Aquitaine, my lord?'

asked Abelard from behind. 'Do you not pine for it a little? I confess I pine for Brittany.'

'You are from Brittany, are you, my lad? A lovely nation. The smell of fish and sheep. Well, Aquitaine is God's little corner of the empire, but I'll tell you this about it. The climate is sublime. The civilisation and the poetry is intense. But the people, they are like ferrets. They fight like ferrets. They can have it, as far as I'm concerned. My gloomy son and his gloomy wife are in charge and they are welcome. I get to see the world in a way they never have.'

'You are a frequent visitor to Jerusalem, my lord?'

'I have been there recently, as you know, but let us not speak of that,' said the Duke, suddenly subdued. 'Let us talk of what I have seen on my travelling. I have seen the Alps soaring away up to the snow. I have seen the Pyrenees in all their grandeur. I have seen the holy city.'

'You have been to Rome?'

'Not Rome, idiot. *Paris*. I have seen Notre Dame and St Denis and the Chastelet. I have sailed on the Seine and the Rhone and the Rhine. And the people I have met, noble and savage, holy and profane. The stories I could tell. The men. The women – especially the women. Though most of my conversations with women end with my hands under their cloak. Yes, I have planted my seed in the four corners of France and I am proud of it.'

Hilary was aware that Abelard was now riding next to him and asking him to lean over. He whispered as close to his ear as he could get.

'Ask the old goat how he does it,' whispered Abelard. 'I have an idea.'

'My lord, may I ask how you manage to keep so young?'

Duke William guffawed do much that he nearly fell off his horse. The walls of the castle were now just ahead.

'Well, we all need a little help, my friend. A little help, that's all. A wise man in Paris came to my rescue with some potions which help me sometimes. Shall I show you?' He patted a small pouch on his waist.

'Two little potions. One to help with the performance – and I don't mean the songs,' he said, spluttering with mirth. 'The other is to help with the husbands. It sends them so fast asleep that the Second Coming would not wake them. I could trample through their rooms with my horse in my chain mail and they would not wake.'

'It sends them to sleep?'

The Duke giggled mischievously. 'I admit it has some unfortunate side-effects beforehand. They sweat and shake and many believe they are going to die, but only for the length of a mass, and then *bang* – asleep like babies. Many are the last rights that have been administered before I give their wives the first rights, if you see what I mean. I am sorry for that.'

They had reached the great gate of the castle in Poix. A bedraggled looking man-at-arms was approaching them to find out what they wanted.

'Minstrels and scholars, my man,' shouted the Duke, flinging his arms wide in generosity. 'Tell the house they will be entertained tonight!' There was a perceptible lightening of the features of the gate-keeper, and the great doors were swung further open. Hilary could hear the sound of their horseshoes echoing on the cobblestones in the courtyard.

'You see,' whispered the Duke to him as they were helped down from their horses. 'The way I see it. If I can reconcile a few husbands to their creator before their death, it is perhaps a small recompense for what I have taken from them.'

'You did say it made them think they were on their deathbed?'

'That's right young man. Unfortunate, but what can you do?'

The solution lies before me, Hilary said to himself, girding up his courage. The Duke carried on his person some potion which, as well as rendering people asleep, gave them briefly the illusion that they were on their deathbed. It was cruel, especially to afflict their host with such an ordeal, and when he was feeding them and providing them with shelter. But there was a task to undertake and – as Abelard would have it – the truth to uncover.

The autumn sun shone through the afternoon while the Duke lay snoring on the straw in the stables, sleeping off the effects of the previous night. The occasional woman from the kitchens looked in, stared at his sleeping bulk for a moment, giggled and went away again. There was nobody else there. It was now or never.

Hilary remembered that the hiding place for this particular potion, at least as indicated by the Duke, was round his copious waist. There was the waist, and there was the small satchel attached to it. This was the moment.

Shivering with suppressed nerves, Hilary knelt before the huge aristocrat. The buckle of the little satchel undid easily, but the Duke moved in his sleep with a groan and flung an arm across Hilary as he bent over him. 'My beauty,' mumbled the Duke, with a deep sigh, but his eyes stayed closed and his breath stayed deep and regular. Hilary extricated himself slowly and jumped out of the way, but the satchel was now covered.

Gingerly, he uncoiled the Duke's arm and put it over the other side. Obediently, the Duke shifted again. This time, the satchel was clear. His heart racing, he lifted the lid. Inside was a handkerchief, a small comb and a quill and yes, two small glass bottles. But which one? Hilary kicked himself. This was going to be more difficult than he thought.

Then he noticed that one of the bottles was battered and almost empty while the other had an old cloth tied to the stopper.

One of them was clearly used all the time while the other was almost full. Judging by his age, Hilary guessed that the Duke might have recourse to the potion which replenished his libido more often than the one which put his love rivals to sleep. It seemed logical. Hilary grasped the full bottle. The liquid looked green and fearsome. He pulled out a small bottle of his own he had purloined from the kitchen for the occasion, and it was the work of a moment tipping a tiny amount of the green liquid in and replacing the cork. It smelled like drains. Then the bottle went back into the satchel in its old place and the buckle was re-fastened. He breathed a sigh of relief. The deed was done.

'You did hear what he said,' said Hilary to Abelard. Both had been welcomed by the household and given fresh clothes and some food. The Duke's snores were now audible through the wooden wall in the courtyard.

'I did. A solution, perhaps.'

'Is such a thing possible?'

'I don't know, Hilary. They say that Livia used something of the kind in ancient Rome. It is probably some distilled version of valerian root.'

'You don't think it is a little immoral?'

'I confess that I do, but since *you* are doing it – not me – I am trying not to let that concern me unduly.'

'You won't help?

'Yes, of course I will help. Just don't ask me to take the confession, that's all. We are in search of the truth here. A little stratagem or two is forgivable.'

Hilary breathed another small sigh. He had been afraid Master Peter would balk at the idea. It seemed too bold somehow. 'Good, because I have managed to extract some drops of the potion from one of the bottles around the Duke's waist. It is almost as if he took some himself. He is still fast asleep. My only worry is that I borrowed from the wrong bottle. There were two of them in there.'

Abelard laughed bitterly. 'Well, we will soon know. If Walter Tirel falls asleep, we will know you chose right. If he disappears upstairs with his wife, or seems awkward behind the table, we will know you chose wrong. Tell me, did it smell like our cell in the Tower of London?'

'It smelled foul.'

'Valerian. I told you. Be careful of it, Hilary.

They were interrupted by Tirel's steward, marching briskly through the courtyard. The sun had finally disappeared. The evening meal was wafting its aroma from the kitchen. There was the unmistakable smell of bacon and roasting meat, and the sound of barrels being rolled across the courtyard.

'Come on, come on,' said the steward. 'We are gathering in the hall for supper, and I hope you are ready. It is months since any minstrels came here. You are anticipated with hunger and excitement, I can tell you.'

Hilary kept checking nervously that the pouch containing the bottle was attached to his belt, where the terrifying green liquid waited. He was particularly worried about how he would put drops into Tirel's food or beer, but almost equally nervous about his own performance that night. He would do 'The Boy of Angers'. He had not performed himself since last Christmas, the Christmas they spent on the run, sheltering with Count Hugh of Champagne.

The great hall was now packed with the household and their families, waiting excitedly for the entertainment. At a signal from the steward, the noble family filed in and took their places at the great table at one end of the hall. In front of them were a series of goblets and huge platters filled with every kind of cooked meat, beef, hams, racks and thighs of lamb, with a whole pike, a casserole pie, on great wooden treachers. As they sat down, the steward and his assistants arrived with the first flagons of ale. Hilary was able to get his first glimpse of Tirel himself. He was thin and rather frail, and looked older than he had expected. He hoped he survived trauma that the potion would evidently cause him. He could really do without a real murder on his conscience.

Tirel wore a sumptuous fur-edged cloak and tunic. His wife was beautiful, with a fur-lined mantle over her kirtle and her hair hidden in a white coif. His daughter looked unexpectedly like Alys, and for a moment Hilary allowed his imagination to take him back to the happy days teaching her at Beaugency, and then to Isabella in her castle and the tender ministrations of her husband, and the songs they had tried to sing together as the ship rocked on the Mediterranean swell. Whoever would have guessed in those carefree days that he would now be trying to slip a hereditary lord a sleeping draught.

He still had no clear plan how to do it either but he would wait for an opportunity. In the meantime, he had to make sure he remembered all the lines of his song. As he ate his plate of pike and lettuce, he repeated the lines over and over:

> 'More than a brother to me,
> Jonathan.
> One soul we will always be,
> Jonathan.
> How gladly I'd die to be buried with you.
> Even death will unite the both of us two...'

As the meal progressed, the servants and townspeople began to get restless. There was loud raucous laughter, which the steward stilled with a fearsome look. There was occasional larking about by the boys and some dropped implements. So it was with some relief that Tirel rose in his seat after the meat course and clapped his hands for quiet.

'As you know, we are privileged tonight,' he said. His voice was reedy and unsuited to public debate. 'A party of minstrels and jongleurs has arrived here in Poix to entertain us.' He seemed to struggle with something else to say. For a moment it hovered on the tip of his tongue but it stayed firmly unarticulated. Desperately, he sought out Abelard in the crowd and nodded to him. 'Pray begin, sir.'

Abelard stepped forth, rather to Hilary's surprise. He had assumed he would be first to perform himself. He was greeted by tumultuous cheers from the servants and tenants. Without any introduction, he began to sing:

> *'Love is not wrong because,*
> *If it were a crime,*
> *God would never have used love*
> *To bind even the divine...'*

Hilary was lost in admiration. For the first time, he felt seriously jealous of his teacher's performance. Really, it was infuriating. But by the time the second verse of Abelard's song wafted out across the great hall, with its soaring high notes, Hilary was still wondering how he might get anywhere near Tirel, let alone insert something into his cup without being seen. But there was one clue. He looked down at their dining implements, along the rustic knives and wooden platters, and saw that, alone among his family and senior servants, Tirel drank wine. All the rest were knocking back copious quantities of ale or mead.

That might be a way forward, he thought to himself, then his attention found itself shifting – almost against its will – to listen to the song. Not only was it beautiful, but Abelard was performing it brilliantly. There was a hush around the great room. One of the women was in tears. Even Tirel seemed to be wiping his eyes on his sleeve. It was a triumph. No doubt about it.

Despite himself, Hilary found he was resenting this success. Not only was he could to have to perform next and was bound to suffer by comparison, but also – for goodness sake – why could Abelard not just stay with his chosen profession of philosopher? It was all very well being the most triumphant and skilful theologian in the known world, why did Abelard have to trespass into everyone else's area? Was there going to be no space for anybody else compared to Master Peter's overwhelming skills? Why did his old teacher have to transform himself suddenly into a wandering scholar, and beat him so soundly? Was there to be no area where he was not going to be overshadowed?

The song ended. Abelard hung his head. There was tumultuous applause and banging of wood on wood. Abelard bowed low and was beckoned over to the high table. Tirel clapped his hand on his back, engaged him in conversation and shook his hand warmly. Abelard could have put the drops in then, thought Hilary. Unfortunately, he had no bottle with him.

Now, his moment was coming. Tirel banged on the table and the chatter died away. Hilary took two deep breaths and prepared to walk to the centre of the room. He took one step forward to show Tirel where he was, then he felt a restraining arm on his shoulder.

'Not you,' said Abelard.

'What? Why not?'

'How would you like to make your deathbed confession to a wandering scholar? Save yourself for the main challenge,' he whispered urgently. 'You can't put yourself forward as a serious father confessor if you perform tonight, can you?'

Reluctantly, Hilary stepped back. Abelard nodded to the Duke and he bounded forward to great acclaim, knocking over a small dog as he leapt into action.

'You're right, of course,' said Hilary. He felt hugely deflated. 'Your performance was wonderful, Master Peter,' he said sadly.

'Thank you, Hilary. There will be other times. We just need the truth that's all.'

'I am interested, my Lord. How in fact do you usually administer your potion to the unsuspecting husbands?'

Hilary was relaxing the next morning with the Duke, who was boasting of his exploits in Rheims some years before. The Duke slapped his thighs.

'I do believe you are considering the same tactics yourself, young man. Who do you want? The wife. She is something of a rounded apple, is she not. Not the daughter. Hah! You just say the word and I'll lend you my little bottle.'

'I just wondered how you did it, that is all.'

'Usually I just blunder into them, spill their goblet and then give them mine instead. It is true, I don't usually try such tactics on the gentry. Too well protected. Too risky.'

'I agree.' Hilary reflected that he lacked the courage to run into the lord of the manor, even a delicate type like Tirel.

'Yes, but worth it – I can tell you. Nothing like the illicit roll. Better the feeling that you are enjoying something you should not.'

Well, thought Hilary afterwards. For want of another plan, this was therefore the task before them. Abelard would be invited up onto the table to converse with Tirel, as he had the previous night. He would carry with him a goblet of wine, with the potion added. While he was there, he would either swap them or he would accidently spill Tirel's goblet and offer him his own. It was risky way forward, and Abelard would not be keen on it, but he would agree because he could think of nothing else.

'Stay flexible Hilary,' he said. 'Something else will show itself. It is in the nature of things that opportunities arise that no-one may predict.'

By the evening, the hall was once more full of the household staff, together with Tirel's family and favoured tenants. The smell of the fields and wet straw, and the dogs unravelling next to the fire, mingled with the smell from the kitchens. Once more, the lord of Poix trooped in with his fur-lined cloak and presided over the proceedings. Once more, Abelard sang a succession of songs. Once more he was invited onto the table and sat next to Tirel conversing and reminiscing about Paris in days gone by.

But where was the Duke? There was a moment of panic as the steward searched the hall. 'Where is your big friend?' he demanded.

The answer was pretty obvious. Hilary dashed across the courtyard to the kitchen. If he knew the Duke – and he was beginning to – he was availing himself of the opportunity of further acquaintance with his friend the cook. The temptation of ample food and women in such close proximity would be too much for him to resist.

'*No*, my lord. Leave me alone, I beg you,' shrieked the cook as Hilary entered the room. It was hot and steamy and there she was fending off the Duke with a pair of black, sooty tongs. 'I must take the pie into the hall. You must sing your songs. Go on with you. No, be careful of that table. That is my lord's wine just opened. I will talk to you later, just not now.'

'Maud, Maud, just one kiss and I will go on my way.' There was a crash as a large dish hit the flagstones.

'My lord Duke,' shouted Hilary above the racket. 'You are wanted on stage. Please! Your moment has arrived!'

'I thought it had arrived just here,' said the Duke. 'Maud!' he shouted. 'You have escaped me for now. I must do my duty. My gratitude, young man. I go to spread a little light and generosity in this thankless and frustrating house.'

And there was the wine, standing open by the door. The cook was busy clearing up the broken dish. Her assistants were serving food or cleaning the spit. It was the work of a moment to get out the small glass bottle. One, two, three drops. Pray to God it doesn't taste like it smells. Now the die really was cast. He would have to dash back to make sure Abelard did not, after all, take the risky step of upsetting Tirel's wine.

Back in the great hall, the Duke was working himself up into his first song – his famous 'A song about nothing'. The great tapestries which hung from the gallery seemed to shimmer in the alcoholic and festive air. A mood of expectation rippled around the building, just as it had done the night before.

From the back of the hall, Hilary made frantic signs at Abelard, deep in conversation with Tirel. It was well into the second verse that he finally looked up. Hilary waved his hand and mouthed a desperate 'no'. Abelard responded with a little nod. This was no time for upsetting a goblet all over the table.

As soon as he had done so, Hilary saw the steward carry in a bottle with Tirel's wine. This was it. It was poured out into his goblet. A few minutes later, his heart in his mouth, Hilary watched Tirel take his first sip. Abelard watched with distaste and went on talking. What on earth did they have to discuss, Hilary wondered? Abelard the Indomitable Rhinoceros conversing with a man known mainly for his prowess with bow and arrow? Tirel wiped his mouth and replied.

The tension was now overwhelming. What was going to

happen? Would he keel over or break out into a sweat? Would there be a distressing scene before their very eyes? The Duke acknowledged the cheers of the crowd and embarked on another song, then he too was welcomed up to talk to Tirel. Still nothing. The household broke up. Tirel talked by the fire to his steward, the only source of light now in the dark autumn evening. The women withdrew, the rush lamps which had been lighted in the fading light were doused. The workers of the estate wended their way happily back into the courtyard to sleep. Soon Abelard and Hilary were in the straw themselves in the guest stables.

'I wouldn't stay awake, Hilary, if I were you,' said Abelard, lying next to him. 'It may never happen. It may just have been an erotic fantasy of Duke William's.'

It seemed only moments later, but Hilary realised he had been dreaming. There had been banging and shouting in his dream, when he was back in his student days at Ste-Genevieve. He hauled himself out of his sleep. Abelard was already awake.

'Prepare yourself, Hilary. I believe something is happening after all.'

They gathered their cloaks about them and made their way into the courtyard. Lamps were lit in the house and the servants were running to and fro. Lady Tirel appeared at the foot of the stairs in an advanced state of agitation. 'Get some water, in the name of St Agnes. Where is the steward? Why is nobody listening to me? I wanted sheets, I told you. Not those.'

Hilary's conscience stirred. He had almost certainly caused all this pain himself. 'What is happening?' he asked a passing maid. She was white as a sheet.

'My lord has been taken ill. Please don't detain me.'

'What do we do?' Hilary asked Abelard.

'We offer our assistance. *Mox nox in rem,*' he said, hailing the steward, who marched in through the great doors.

'Mother of God, what is happening?' he asked. The lady of the house was down in a moment.

'I fear it is the ague,' she said. 'I have blankets. The physician is too far. My husband fears he is about to die. We must have a priest. It will at least allay his fears of dying unshriven.'

The steward nodded towards Hilary and Abelard.

'My colleague here is a clerk in holy orders,' said Abelard. 'May he assist?'

'Heaven be praised. Listen, my husband has been taken ill. It may be a passing squall, but he believes he has only a short time left. Men are sometimes disposed to think that way unnecessarily, but perhaps he is right. Will you hear his confession? I would be most grateful.'

Hilary nodded. 'I will need some wine,' he said, making a mental note not to drink it, and drawing himself up to walk like a priest. 'It will be a privilege to help, my lady. Please lead the way.'

'Thank you. My gratitude to you. Now, please hurry.'

As he passed through the door to the rest of the house, a terrible thought struck him and he doubled back. He had never conducted the last rites before, or anything like them.

'Master Peter,' he whispered desperately. 'I don't know the words. What are the words?'

'My dear Hilary,' said Abelard looking round furtively. 'I have anticipated you. Take this piece of parchment. I took the trouble to write out the words against just such an eventuality. There, have you got it? You will also need some cotton, lemon and salt.'

'Heavens,' said Hilary, dashing back to the kitchen, and then – armed with his crib – he hurried after the mistress of the house through the dark passageway, in search of the answer to the riddle.

Tirel's bedchamber was bare and lit by a tallow candle guttering in the breeze. A pile of blankets and embroidered cloth and a bath of water were beside the bed and a young servant stood there helplessly mopping his brow. Tirel did indeed look like death.

'Hurry, hurry, please,' said the wife. 'Out, come on now,' she urged the servants. 'Leave them together.'

The door shut and Hilary felt very alone and inadequate to the role he was about to play. There was a groan from the bed and he walked sheepishly towards it. 'No, I am ordained. I am a clerk in holy orders,' said Hilary to himself.

'You are a priest?' said Tirel in a rasping voice. Sweat was pouring down his face.

Hilary nodded. He felt unable to speak.

'Please shrive me. Please hear my confession while I still live.'

He knelt down by the bed and took Tirel's hands in his own. He put the bottle of wine next to the bread on the floor beside him.

'*Per istam sanctan unctionem et suam piissimam misericordiam,*' said Hilary carefully, trying to read the scratched notes from Abelard's pen.

There was a long silence. Should he repeat it, or was Tirel just collecting his thoughts? Hilaty repeated the crucial words in French: 'Have you anything to confess, my lord?'

More silence. Hilary was wondering what to do next when the patient spoke.

'I was not a dutiful son,' said Tirel in a quiet voice. 'Many times I disobeyed my father to practice archery. I was guilty of lust many times. I betrayed my vows of marriage with women...'

'How often, my lord?' asked Hilary.

'Many, many times in my youth, but only in other countries, I swear. I have not loved my own son as I should have done.'

Slowly, Hilary began to panic. This unwelcome intimacy was

not why he had come. Not only was it embarrassing, it was wasting time. More minor sins came out. He nodded and made priestly noises. Above the great bed was a bow, bent and discoloured with use. Perhaps it was the very bow which had shot Rufus.

'*Indulgeat tibi Dominus quidquid per visum, audtiotum, odorátum, gustum et locutiónem, tactum, gressum deliquisti....*'

'There,' said Tirel in an exhausted voice, ignoring this. 'Please give me absolution.'

'Is that all, my lord?'

'Yes, that is all.'

There was an embarrassed silence. He had to do something.

'Was there not something else? It is time to confess everything, my lord.'

Tirel gripped his hand and stared at him. The sweat poured down Hilary's arm. There was an intensity about him that was terrifying.

Still he said nothing. Tirel seemed to be choosing his words carefully. His mouth opened and closed unnervingly. He seemed all but delirious.

'It was not me. It was the Saxon, I tell you. I will not die with that on my conscience. It was not me...'

Then he suddenly gripped Hilary's arm, pulling him closer onto the bed. Hilary extracted himself and peered closely at Tirel when the end of the sentence did not come. The man was flat on his back, unconscious. For a terrifying moment, Hilary was afraid his host had actually died. Then a huge snore echoed through the chamber. By the time he had gathered his belongings, he could see that the sweating had stopped and Tirel was once more a healthy colour. He tiptoed from the room, listening to the rhythmic breathing of his host, and cursing his own stupidity.

Abelard was dressed at first light. 'The Duke is preparing to leave and I think we should go with him, Hilary. Please wake up. The fewer questions they ask about last night, the better.'

Hilary groaned at the memory of his stupendous failure. 'But we still do not know the answer. We have to ask Tirel outright – you have to ask him.'

'But why should he confide in me, and in any case – I know the answer.'

'You *know*? What is it then?'

Before Abelard could answer, there was a clattering outside in the courtyard and a cacophony of female voices. It was clear that one of them was calling to him.

Abelard went outside. Hilary flung on his cloak and followed.

In the pale autumn sunshine, there was Tirel's wife.

'Ah, I am glad to see you. As I was saying to your colleague, I was extremely grateful for your help last night. Of course my husband is fully recovered, but I feel sure you helped him recover by hearing his confession.'

'It was of no consequence, my lady,' said Abelard. Hilary caught his eye. It certainly was – no consequence at all.

'I want you to accept these sheepskins as a small token – steward? Where are they? Ah, here they are. Just between you and me, my husband suffers so on these occasions. He has never forgiven himself for failing to prevent the death of the English king William Rufus. I expect you know the tale. He has been quite unforgiveably saddled with the story that his was the fatal arrow. It is a lie, of course. He shot no arrow. He did not kill the King. Of course he should not have run, but who can blame him for that. History has maligned him.'

Abelard stayed still as the lady became more excited. 'My husband has been blamed for a conspiracy. It was the King's brother and the Saxons who planned it. The Saxon huntsman who did it. My husband was simply a pawn in their chess game, and now look – he has worn himself out with guilt that he did not prevent it...' She remembered herself suddenly, took a breath and looked around her, as if seeking out those who were responsible.

'But – these are ancient tales and I delay you with my chatter. God be with you, my friends, and my deepest gratitude.'

Hilary and Abelard bowed deeply, mounted their horses, swept their cloaks around their shoulders and were gone.

2/Heloise

The road west, 10 November 1120

'Prince William is not going to like what we have found, is he?' said Hilary in the saddle of his royal horse and heading in the vague direction of Rouen. 'Tirel never fired the arrow. Not only that, but his uncle's death was indeed the result of a plot. Just as we thought, it was a plot between King Henry and the Saxons, maybe our Saxons. The chief huntsman fired the shot and allowed Tirel to take the blame.'

'You are right, Hilary. That explains the implied threat in the bundle of papers you were given. Abbot Aelfgar, whoever he is, wanted to tell Baldwin or Fulk that they had killed a king before and could do again. I wonder why the plot went wrong for Aelfgar before. I believe Henry married a Saxon princess. Perhaps he believed he had therefore discharged his obligations.'

They had been riding in silence for more than half a day, down the broken and dilapidated roads that led from Poix north of Paris. Both had their own worries to brood upon. Only the Duke, who rode along behind, whistling and making a running commentary on the women they passed, seemed oblivious to the mood.

'I believe I know the identity of your friend,' he confided that morning as Hilary packed his saddlebag. 'There is only one person who sings that song like that and it is the man who wrote it. Master Peter of Notre Dame.'

'I say nothing, my lord.'

'Only I'm surprised he does not now sing some octaves higher,' said the Duke, spluttering with mirth.

Hilary thought of this as the miles passed by, and the strange scene at Tirel's bedside, and the gnawing guilt he was increasingly feeling to have put any man through that. Still, against all the odds, they had fulfilled their promise to William the Aetheling. They had asked Walter Tirel the crucial question, and his wife had answered. It may have raised more questions, but they had at least carried out their end of the bargain.

'Do we know anything about the chief huntsman?' asked Hilary, when the Duke was out of earshot.

'According to the books I read in Winchester, he was called Ranulf de Aquis. In fact, it cannot have been Tirel who fired the arrow. I confess I had already reached that conclusion myself. I allowed us to go ahead with the deal with William the Aetheling because he was offering to clear your name.'

'You mean you guessed?'

'I never guess. It is really very simple. You will remember that, in the New Forest, we were able to deduce where Tirel was likely to have stood – on the tip of the narrow spit of forest that stuck out into the marsh. You remember that I asked you to stand where the cross marked the spot where Rufus died? I realised when you did so that I could not see you. You could not see the King from where Tirel stood. He could not have fired the shot.'

Hilary was silent trying to take in this new information. 'Master Peter, why did you not tell me this before? It is weeks now since we were in the New Forest.'

'So it follows from that,' said Abelard, ignoring him, 'that the killer was Ranulf de Aquis. Nobody else was with them. Almost certainly not then an accident. The chief huntsman would have had no business shooting before either the King or his guest.'

'But why did you not take me into your confidence before?' Hilary was now overcome with irritation.

'If I had done, would you have accepted the Aetheling's offer with such alacrity?'

'That is not the point I am making,' said Hilary with rising anger. Why did his old teacher continually treat him like an idiot?

'No, Hilary, but it is now clear what we must do. William the Aetheling is a lover of truth. He is the one man in England who can prevent disaster, if Henry marches west to root out the Saxons, as I fear he will if he believes himself under threat from them. You had a Harrying of the North, I believe. Henry will harry the West, unless we can intercede with his son. Somehow we must use the Great Jewel to prevent much bloodshed. William is the key. Mark my words.'

Hilary pursed his lips and said nothing. The last swallows swooped above them, lining the fences as they passed by. An ancient milestone hove into view. 'LUTECE', it said, but the numerals were unreadable.

'Now,' said Abelard, with the air of a man drawing the conversation to a close. 'We must set this aside for the time being because we now come to a place where we must take some care. This is the road to St Denis.'

Here indeed was the road south to St Denis and Paris beyond. It looked more than usually damp and rutted. The road from Poix in Picardy to Normandy took them north of Paris. It made sense not to go too close to the group of churchmen Abelard called the 'murderous monks' of St Denis.

'We must bid you good day,' said Hilary to the Duke, who was himself making for Paris. 'May God be with you, my friend.'

'Alas, my friends. Change your minds and accompany me after all.' The Duke looked hurt that he was going to be expected to go on by himself.

'I fear we cannot,' said Hilary. 'We have an appointment in Barfleur we must not miss.'

They looked both ways along the road. The sky above them was dark and the puddles were wetter and deeper than last time they had travelled this way. The only other travellers on the road were a couple of carts laid down with root vegetables and making slow progress in either direction.

'No Parisians here. No monks either. This looks like as good a moment as any,' said Hilary, and their horses moved forward onto the rutted track. The Duke raised his hand in salute.

'Farewell. I go to visit a fair maid in a convent because of the love I bear her father. I go to Argenteuil. The nuns await me – farewell!'

Hilary glanced at Abelard. He was absolutely still. The word 'Argenteuil' had shaken him. He looked thunderstruck, staring at Duke William as if his mind had been wiped clean.

'You go to Argenteuil?'

'I do. The daughter of my lord Hugues of Payens is there, awaiting her marriage. Because of the love I bear him, I will venture inside that nest of holy hyenas.'

Now it was Hilary's turn to look thunderstruck.

'Isabella? She is not married?' A flicker of hope twitched in his chest. Nor married? *Why* was she not married?

'Indeed she is not. I saw her some weeks ago, and her husband-to-be had sent her to Argenteuil while he finished some matters with King Henry. He is planning an expedition, I believe. She is to be kept pure by the nuns of Argenteuil. I bear a little comfort for her while she waits. I have known her father many years. If you are who I believe you to be, then you have accompanied her yourself across the ocean. He could have entrusted her to me, but – well, you can see why he did not.'

Abelard ignored him. He stared ahead, rising slightly on his saddle as if in two minds where to go. 'He is planning an expedition, you say. Did you hear that, Hilary? King Henry will destroy the West to seek out his rival. With William the Aetheling's help, we can prevent it.'

'We have ten days or more before St Edmund Martyr's day, when we must be in Barfleur,' said Hilary. 'Argenteuil is no more than half a day's ride away. I say we go there on the way and break our journey at Argenteuil. What do you say...?' For a moment he had forgotten Master Peter's *nom de plume,* but Abelard just stared ahead, as if struggling to grasp the situation afresh.

'You can, perhaps. Only I am a little nervous of this place, I confess. I approach it with some trepidation.'

'Why, Master Peter? It's only a convent.'

Abelard paused again and then looked away. 'Because my wife is there.'

It was getting dark before they reached the Seine, glittering in the last rays of the sun when the skies suddenly cleared. They had come closer to St-Denis than Hilary thought was wise, but he could see that – once the idea of visiting Heloise had come into Abelard's head – he was determined to go through with it. The light was disappearing as they stood finally by the great wooden doors of Argenteuil convent, and as they reached there the wind gathered up its energy again, ruffling their hair and getting inside the gaps in their clothes. The Duke hammered on the door.

The door opened a few inches. 'We desire admittance,' he intoned. 'Preferably before the rain begins.'

The door opened further, revealing a small bent man who motioned them inside until all four were standing shivering on the great stone flags inside the lobby. A nun in black arrived and bowed to them. She looked up at the Duke and then Hilary. When she looked into Abelard's face, Hilary could see the glance of mingled recognition and excitement. To her would fall the great privilege of imparting some important gossip.

'We wish to see Isabella of Payens,' he said, but the nun had already rushed off to announce their presence. Hilary stared at the floor, unsure where he should look, unwilling to witness the coming encounter. Abelard stood rigid and alert.

'I wouldn't have missed this for anything,' muttered the Duke. 'I knew who he was when I heard him sing.'

'We are here to see Isabella,' said Hilary firmly.

'Quite. For the last time before she disappears into the tender embrace of the Montgomery family. I encountered Arnulf in Jerusalem, I remember. Not a man who appreciates a good song, I can tell you. They are relatives of Robert le Diable and other brutes, I believe. Dreadful family here in Normandy too. I never sing there. I was lucky to get out alive the only time I did.'

'And the castle,' said the Duke, getting into his stride. 'Undecorated. No perfumes, no baths, no tapestries. Not a home for someone like Isabella from Outremer. Windows which let in the cold and the wind. I mean, you might as well just live outside.'

She is so young, thought Hilary. So young, and yet she can be the wife of a relative of *Le Diable*. It is not right. It is not the fate she deserves. He imagined her again in that dank castle. All he could do was to see her one more time.

Hilary mulled these things over in his mind, when there was a clatter in the corridor. Abelard fell to his knees.

'Up, up, Master Peter. You do not kneel for the sub-prioress. Now follow me please.'

Abelard followed obediently and, a few moments later, there was the sound of raised voices in the distance. 'What is this, Peter Abelard? How many of your women will you be lodging with us now?'

'Madam,' he said. 'It is not I who comes to visit Isabella de Payens, it is my friend who was her teacher...'

'Well, she is not here. She is gone to Barfleur to meet her betrothed. They sail for England. She is gone from here.'

For Hilary, the disappointment was almost physical. He leant against the wall, drained of energy. For a moment he thought he would see Isabella again. He should not feel these things so strongly. She was betrothed to be married. Now he would never see her again.

There were more footsteps on the stones, and in came a middle-aged lady in a strange hat, with a cross around her neck. She seemed small yet filled the corridor with a commanding personality. Hilary rose and then knelt and kissed her ring. Abelard did the same.

'Now you, Duke William?' she asked. Sheepishly, the Duke knelt and kissed. The prioress turned to Abelard and held out her hand.

'You are welcome, my son. This is God's house and he shelters those who can shelter nowhere else.' Hilary breathed deeply against the wall, realising clearly what he had lost and what he felt, struggling with his conscience. This was not erotic love, he told himself. There had been no furtive planning to inviegle poor Isabella into his bed somehow, no excruciating songs in praise of her. He had just loved her, and now – above all else – he wanted to comfort her. But he could imagine no way in which it might be possible.

Silence descended. 'You did right to come, Master Peter,' said the prioress. 'Now, do you want to see her?'

Abelard flushed. 'You mean...?'

'Of course. I will ask them to send her. I fear I must ask you to remain here for the time being.'

Hilary felt embarrassed. 'Master Peter, let the Duke and I leave you alone. You would prefer to do this alone, I am sure.'

'No matter, Hilary,' he said, staring down the passageway. 'This is a convent. Wandering is not allowed for us men. In any case, they are only allowing me to meet her because you are here as well.'

There was the sound of quick footsteps down the stones and there she was, in a black habit and coif, petite and beautiful in an unconventional way. She moved gracefully, with a lithe athleticism which belied her brown habit. Each step had energy and determination. Hilary noticed immediately how intelligent her eyes were, but they were uncertain eyes. She was trying hard to control herself. He recognised her from the cloister of Notre Dame, a decade before, when she was no more than a girl. Now she did not even glance in his direction.

Abelard stood rigid as she approached. Both stopped some ten feet apart and stared at each other. The flames from the torches flickered in her face, giving the scene an eerie unreality. It was nearly nightfall and the lamps would soon be extinguished. The very stones of the convent, bathed in the flashing light from the flames, seemed to wait breathlessly to hear what would be said. It was not clear which of the two would unbend first.

'Is there to be no embrace for your wife?' said Heloise. There was a hint of nervousness in her voice as if she was unsure whether there would be an embrace after all. 'Why come all this way otherwise?'

'Go on!' said the Duke. Hilary hushed him and stepped back further into the shadows. The couple would know he was there but that was no reason to get in their way.

Abelard made a defensive gesture, half loving, half intended apparently to keep his wife at bay. He seemed unready to be touched, desperate not to behave as before. They stood awkwardly opposite each other as if a chasm lay between them.

'Peter, I thank almighty God that he has sent you to me. You know – you have no idea...' Heloise looked up, perhaps for inspiration, perhaps to stop the tears overflowing. 'I have longed to see you, do you understand. I have prayed for this moment.'

Abelard nodded and opened his mouth. He seemed too moved to say anything. He made a foreshortened gesture towards her with his hand as if to acknowledge that he felt the same.

Silence fell again.

'What are they waiting for?' muttered the Duke.

At last Abelard spoke. 'Heloise. My Heloise,' he said, as if clearing his mind for an announcement. 'I have been wondering, praying, struggling... To work out how best I can help you and support you now, as your teacher... No stay there. For a moment. Please!' Heloise stayed obediently.

'It occurs to me that, perhaps, I can write you letters that can help in your new life....'

'Oh, Peter,' she said despairingly. 'I don't want your letters. I don't need your letters. Do you think I care about my new life in comparison? Do you think this habit, this brown robe, is now all that I am? I am your *wife*...'

'Heloise, how can I be your husband now?' said Abelard. The words seemed to have been torn out of him. 'I can be no-one's husband, not even yours. And you have taken your vows.'

She stared at him. 'My vows?' she said dismissively. 'Who wanted me to take my vows? Not me. I did it for you. Listen, Peter. I may now be a nun, but I will always be your wife. Whatever the prioress says. Whatever the pope says. Whatever the emperor says. There is not a member of this community who does not know that I would prefer to be your concubine. I would prefer to be your whore than the greatest abbess, the most sublime empress, that ever lived. I am God's – of course I am God's – but I am yours before all things.'

Hilary looked away in embarrassment. He had a powerful sense that this was private. He should not have been witnessing this scene. 'Come, the past is behind us now,' said Heloise, suddenly moving towards him. Abelard started and backed away.

'No, don't touch me. Don't touch me. I am not a man now. I could not bear it.'

'No power in earth or heaven can prevent me from touching my husband.'

He sank to his knees, muttering 'I'm sorry, I'm sorry.' Heloise ran to him and held his hands. Great sobs racked his body as he put his head on the stones.

Hilary edged back to the great door, unfixed the great wooden latch and motioned the Duke to follow. They both slipped away. As he did so, he could hear Heloise's soothing voice behind him.

'Hush now Peter, I am happy here at least. I have much to do.'

Then the door crashed behind them, and Hilary and the Duke were alone in the wind.

The first drops of rain splashed in their faces and they looked at each other. The Duke shook his head. 'There, that is passion. That is passion beyond any of my songs – or his songs come to that. That is worth the meeting. I can use it. I *will* use it!'

'You are surely not going to sing about them?' said Hilary, a little shocked. The rain spat in his eyes.

'Not about them, but about that passion I will. Oh yes,' said the Duke. 'Listen, young man, I am not staying the night in a convent. Nuns are not for me. They remind me of my wife. No, I will ride on into Paris tonight.'

'In this weather? Are you sure?'

'Certainly. In this weather I can write my song as I ride. That is what I do, young man. I am no scholar like you and Master Peter.

I find what I sing about in little scraps, little threads of life, and I stitch it all together into songs. That is why I call myself a Finder, a *trouvadour* – the only one of my kind. You should be proud to have met me!' He roared with laughter as he headed off towards the stable.

'I *am* proud, my lord,' Hilary shouted after him. 'Go well, you one and only trouvadour. May God help you multiply.'

The rain poured down. Hilary took shelter in the orchard. The storm swirled above him for a time, and then he heard the convent bell trolling for vespers and he made his way back.

'Where have you been?' said the nun who opened the door. 'We have been looking for you. Your friend has been taken ill. He is in the infirmary. Sister Lucia will take you.'

'Ill? What's happened to him? What sort of illness?'

'I do not know, sir. Please follow me and Sister will tell you when we get there.'

Hilary thought immediately of the appointment with William the Aetheling, only ten days away now in Barfleur. Then he dismissed the fear. The most important thing was Master Peter. He must recover no matter what. Should he carry on by himself? What kind of illness could overtake someone quite so quickly?

The smell of potions and sweat hit him as he door to the infirmary opened off the cloisters. A small dumpy woman approached him smiling.

'I am looking after your friend, who fainted this afternoon. He fears he has a fever.'

Behind her, laid out on the pallet, was Abelard. He was wide awake.

'Hilary, please do not concern yourself. I just was overcome for a moment. I will be perfectly well soon enough and we will continue our adventure. Prince William will not be disappointed, I assure you.'

'The most important thing is that you rest to get well, Master Peter. I can go on alone to Barfleur to catch the prince's ship.'

'Under no circumstances. This is *our* adventure now and I want to see it through. Now sit by me a moment while I rest a little.'

So Hilary sat and Abelard slept, and the events of the past two years unwound themselves in his mind into different shapes and possibilities. He thought of Isabella, perhaps already in England, getting ready for the night, taking off her clothes and shyly looking at her husband. He thought of the Duke, battling the wind and rain on the final miles into Paris. He thought of Abelard and what he owed him.

He realised he was still angry with his old teacher for not sharing the information about Walter Tirel before. Tirel could not have fired the shot. But then, he still had not shared his own suspicions about Muchelney and what it meant. They had travelled thousands of miles together, but they still did not seem to tell each other some of the crucial things they needed to. Still, it would all be different now. Somehow his witnessing of the scene between Heloise and Abelard had changed their relationship. He would no longer be so subservient. He and Abelard had both suffered for love. They were more equal than he had realised.

It seemed like hours later, when he was suddenly shaken awake and found himself lying in a darkened room in what he realised must be a guest dormitory. He had no memory of going to bed and struggled to remember where he was. 'Please come with me,' said the nun. 'Your friend needs you.'

The storm seemed to have worsened. There was a wild hissing

from outside the walls as the building creaked and moved in the wind. Back in the infirmary, he could see a small lamp burning on the floor where Master Peter had been recovering. He was still there, but panting and now seriously sweating, shaking his head from side to side. Two nuns were bending over him and mopping his brow.

'Master Peter has the fever,' said one of them, getting up. 'I fear the passion of his love for his wife has overcome him. He is not well. Not well at all.'

Appalled, Hilary sat beside him. He looked up into the face of the nun opposite and saw it was Heloise.

'You have been here all night?'

'I have. You are Hilary the Englishman, is that right? Peter has talked of you many times.' She smiled at him.

It was a compliment that demanded to be returned, but the truth was Abelard had never spoken of Heloise at all. The subject had seemed too painful to bring up.

'Forgive me, sister, if I speak too brutally,' said Hilary. 'But are you not angry with him?'

She laughed a little. 'Angry? Of course I am angry,' she whispered across the bed. 'If I were not a nun I could never forgive him. Maybe I will never forgive him anyway and break my vows. But I also love him and it is a small gift from God that he has returned to me, even for a day so that I can watch beside his bed. This will give me comfort in the years to come. He ill-used me, it is true. I believe him too great a man to bring down by insisting on my marriage rights, even if that had been possible. But I accepted the penalty, as Pompey's wife says. Then I changed my clothes for a habit which does not suit me. But Peter made me what I am and I adore him, as God alone knows.'

She smiled at Hilary as if to recognise the sin she had spoken. 'I believe God will always forgive love,' she said.

'You are a quite astonishing woman, Heloise. You are the stuff of legends.'

Heloise brushed the remark aside. 'He has also told me something of your quest. This fever is perhaps divine justice for the fever you inflicted on poor Walter Tirel, the Lord of Poix – yes, he has told me about it. I told him he must do penance for such a trick, and it looks as though he is doing it.' She grinned mischievously at Hilary.

'You are right, of course.'

The wind outside flung itself against the wall of the convent. The leafless trees clattered in the wind. A little rain dripped through the windows and the lamp guttered.

Abelard's eyes flickered. She mopped his brow and lifted him up. 'Help me please, Hilary. See if you can lift him and I will see if he will drink.'

There was a struggle as Hilary lifted Abelard's shoulders. But there was no sign of consciousness. Abelard's head lolled disconcertingly, and he put him gently down.

'So you are left with Ranulf de Aquis, the chief huntsman' said Heloise. 'It is a solution to the riddle of who killed Rufus that means nothing, is that not right? That is what Peter told me before the fever came on so powerfully.'

'I fear so, Sister. But we know why he was killed. What we don't know is what to do about it.'

'A strange name, is it not, Ranulf de Aquis? Part Saxon, part Roman. What does it mean? Is it real?'

Hilary considered for a minute. It did sound an invented name.

'I believe there is a place called Aquis in Greece,' said Heloise, with a face that implied she was not quite serious. 'Was he perhaps Greek?'

'You are right, thank you Heloise. The real question is why did he kill the king? Who was he working for? We know now that it was Henry and the Saxons together who plotted the murder, his closest friends, those who were in another part of the forest at the time. Waiting, perhaps, to hear whether their plot had succeeded, but not so close that they might be implicated in it.'

'Maybe,' said Heloise. 'Listen Hilary, tomorrow I have something to show you which might shed some light on this. I don't know, but it might help stir your thoughts. Tonight, we must tend to Master Peter.'

'You have sat here long enough. You go to sleep and I will take over until dawn.'

'No, Hilary. I have waited long enough to tend my husband. If he is still like this tomorrow night, I will let you take my place. If he lives, or if he dies tonight, I would like to be here.'

Abelard slept through the night and through the next day. Hilary visited the infirmary as often as he could, and joined the nuns for their services through the day, from lauds at dawn to compline at dusk. He was painfully aware that there were now only eight days to reach Barfleur to meet William before he sailed.

He struggled with what he should do. He had promised Master Peter to stay with him and owed him that much, yet it was imperative that he find the Prince to let him know that the bargain still held. That was the way he might find this shadow lifted from his life. And yet and yet, if Abelard woke and he had gone – or worse, if he died, he would never forgive himself.

Heloise gestured to him after terce the following day. 'I am allowed to show you my novices,' she said. 'I teach them Latin and a little Greek. They also learn to write and to sew. I have asked the prioress for permission and she said I may. Come now.'

He followed her out into the orchard to what looked like a

small chapel, detached from the rest of the convent. He could see the river in the distance snaking away towards Paris. The wind had calmed down and the rain had reduced to a fine spray. There was mist on the next field. Inside the building, six girls in black sat patiently with slates and chalk in the hand. Perhaps this was where Isabella had sat, he wondered for a moment..

'This is Hilary the Englishman,' announced Heloise. 'He is a famous poet.' They peered shyly up at him in excitement. 'I have brought him to see our tapestry. Now please, if you will, while I show him, I want you to construe the words into Latin and then into Greek. I want you to do so alone, without help from each other. Off you go.'

The moment they were through the next door, Hilary could hear the chatter of excitement from behind it. In the new room there were three nuns bent over what looked like embroidery. In front of them was a long piece of tapestry, on rolls at either end. They seemed to be copying it.

'They are mainly the younger daughters of wealthy aristocrats. Argenteuil depends on them for revenue,' she said. 'Now, this is Sister Marguerite. This is her project which the novices work on, but so do many of the other members of the community here. Do you know what it is?'

Sister Marguerite bowed a little and stood up and back. It was a evidently a huge undertaking. The tapestry rolled on either side was enormous. It was obvious that one of them was complete and the other was a copy in the process of being made.

'It is magnificent,' he said. 'How long will it take?'

'Oh, many hands make it fast work,' said Sister Marguerite. 'We manage about a foot in one week, sometimes a little less. It depends on the weather. In the sunshine, the sisters are working in the fields.'

'Do you know what it is?' asked Heloise. 'Look more closely.'

Hilary read the words in Latin across the top of the part they were looking at. 'ISTI MIRANT STELLA', it said, with a picture of a comet. Hilary slowly recognised he story. 'I don't believe it. It is a tapestry chronicle of the invasion of England. Am I right?'

'Ah, you have heard of the great tapestry at Bayeux? It celebrates the invasion by William who they call The Conqueror. This is a copy of it and we have been commissioned to make another copy. We have been encouraged to do it by our masters in Paris, because they believe – well, I don't know about this, but they say there are hidden messages designed to undermine the Normans. I am not sure if they are right. The main point is that we are twinned with the abbey at Bayeux and, in return, they will make us a copy of the Bible. We are very short of books here. The world does not consider that women read, for some reason – or they disapprove of it when they do.'

'I had heard of this tapestry. I have never seen it. I have never been to Bayeux.'

'Now, may I show him more closely, Sister?' said Heloise. She leant over the finished copy and turned the handle. Hilary could see a stray wisp of black hair escaped from her coif. Then he looked down at the tapestry again. There were spindly figures walking across it, with a commentary at the top. There was Harold's oath to give William the throne. There was the death of Edward the Confessor. There were William's ships landing at Pevensey in 1066. The story was so familiar.

Heloise wound the other end so that it did not become loose. 'Now, Hilary, wind on a little more. You would like to see the battle of Hastings, would you not?'

There were the embroidered soldiers and the arrows flying, the strange shields, tapering to a point like petals. 'Now, this is what I wanted you to see. What does it say there?

'It says *Haroldus interfecit est...* Harold is killed.'

'And do you notice anything strange about it?

'No,' said Hilary, looking carefully. 'It's just a battle. There is a soldier getting an arrow in his eye. There is another one being cut down by a horseman.'

'Come, Hilary. What would Master Peter say? Sometimes you have to look not just at what is there, but what is not.'

Then suddenly Hilary did see. 'I understand. There is no picture of the English king. There is no picture of Harold being killed, is there? These soldiers are not kings. Yet the words clearly say that he died. What does it mean?'

'And look above. What do those birds mean?'

'They are mythical, are they not? I do not know. Is one of them a phoenix?'

'I do not know either,' said Heloise, winding back the cloth. 'I do not know any more than you know. But when I heard your story from Peter, I thought of this and was determined to show you. You never know when it might make sense. Whoever designed this section seems to have known something secret.'

As the darkness fell on their third night in Argenteuil, Hilary took his place in the infirmary with a book he had borrowed from the guest mistress. It was St Augustine's *Confessions*. Abelard tossed and turned next to him, white-faced and sweating. It was hard to believe his body could take much more.

Every hour, the infirmary nuns came and mopped his brow, looked closely at his face and listened to his breathing.

'It must break soon,' said one of them, 'or it is he that will break.'

In the early hours of the morning, Hilary dozed off himself. He was woken at dawn by the light streaming in the windows and by a rough shaking. 'Hilary, Hilary, wake up. We must go. How long have I been here? We must reach Barfleur before William the Aetheling sails. It is our only opportunity to prevent disaster in England.'

Hilary struggled to understand the situation. Through his bleary, sleep-encrusted eyes, he began to discern a revitalised Abelard. The colour was back in his cheeks and the deadness gone from his blue eyes. 'Master Peter, you have not been well. You must wait and recover.'

'Nonsense, I feel well now. I feel released, in fact.' He flung aside the bedding and his cloak, heaved himself upright and marched to the window. 'It is still raining I see. Very well, let us have a good meal after terce and then we shall leave.'

'How many days do we have until St Edmund the Martyr's day? Nine?'

'We have seven, Master Peter. Can we possibly make it to Barfleur in seven days? When you are not well?'

'Listen, Hilary. I am now perfectly well. My apologies for keeping us here. But we owe this to the truth and to those who will otherwise die. We must keep that appointment.'

'The truth is important, I know, Master Peter. But it is not more important than your life. It is not more important than God.'

'God is the truth, Hilary. Please can you help me pack my bags.'

Even the Prioress begged Abelard to stay. A tearful Heloise bade him stay two more days and then blessed him. Hilary could hear her determined footsteps echoing away on the stone flags. Abelard stared after her for a moment and then determinedly set his face to his bags.

Outside with their horses, it was clear that this would be a gruelling journey. The drizzle got into every crevice of their clothes even before they made it onto the road. The wind had dropped and the clouds dashed across the sky indicating that the weather might not be over.

'We head for Mantes and then Rouen,' said Abelard. 'One day to Mantes and then two more days to Rouen. It will be tough going. I only hope we are not too late.'

3/Barfleur

The road to Rouen, 13 November 1120

As soon as they had left the convent at Argenteuil and felt the force of the wind, the roads became increasingly difficult. The potholes were deeper and the mud more profuse. The obstacles, the cracked trees across the roads, the landslides, were that much tougher. The weather had improved but the wind was still high and the dark clouds dashed across the sky before them like armies on the march.

The two men rode in silence, their horses picking out a way through the mud, Abelard preoccupied and staring straight ahead. Hilary did not know how his final parting with Heloise had progressed. The prioress had taken pity on them and allowed them a few moments alone. He himself was equally silent, not wanting to intrude on Abelard's thoughts, and exhausted from the night's vigil by his bed.

Both men urged their horses on wherever they could on the brief passages of straight roads. Hilary was constantly adding up the distances in his head. There must be at least two hundred miles to Barfleur. If they could make forty miles a day, which would be perfectly possible in normal weather, given that they were unencumbered by baggage carts or companions, they might make the journey in seven days and reach their assignment with William the Aetheling before he sailed. But with the mud and the filth and the uncertain weather, it hardly seemed possible.

Abelard was displaying an iron constitution. How could he have tossed and turned in fever for the previous three nights, and now be able to ride at speed through the mud and rain? Apart from his mood, he was looking in rude health, but it might not be enough even so.

Once they had joined the old Roman road from Paris to Rouen, the pace improved. 'Come on Hilary,' shouted Abelard from some way in front. 'On this part, we might even be able to canter.'

Hilary had never been forced to handle horses on quite such project before. Cantering was difficult in the rutted tracks, especially on the lanes of northern France. The old Roman roads were no better with their great gorges of missing flagstones where a horse could easily stumble and break a leg.

'I will do as you do, Master Peter,' said Hilary bravely. He wondered what he would say to William the Aetheling, and how to present the truth to him. Abelard clearly had some plan which would prevent bloodshed in England – and of course he wanted to prevent bloodshed in England too – but he also wanted William's help to clear his name. The Prince had promised to be his champion. The truth for the truth, he had said.

The truth was that Hilary was also preoccupied about something else. Finding Isabella de Payens was not yet married had sent his pulses racing and he was trying to control his imagination. She was not yet married, but she would be. It was ridiculous to cling to this chink of hope, he told himself, and yet he did so – this tiny possibility that they would meet once more. She had been a small gift from God, a ray of light in a dark and vicious world, and so was this moment's grace. God willing, if they could meet the Aetheling, tell him what they had discovered and – if he kept his side of the bargain – Hilary would be free, not to see her again, but to find someone like her and maybe keep his memory of her alive.

But then what? It was hard to see. Even if he saw Isabella

again, he could hardly marry her – she would soon be married, to yet another Norman magnate. God willing, she was still singing their songs even now. Perhaps even her own songs, which showed signs of being better than his.

They pressed on through the wind, and the occasional shower, wrapping their cloaks around them, urging their horses over each snare and quagmire. Outside Poissy, they were confronted by a serious mudslide. 'There is no way through, Master Peter,' said Hilary. 'Nobody could ride through that, and there will be rocks in there as well.'

'Patience, Hilary,' he shouted through the weather. 'Follow me to the right, through that field and we will be able to rejoin the road further on. That is how our roads change, in moments such as these. Our descendents, those of us who have them, will follow this same path, I expect.'

As it was, they were not the first to forge a path through the field and the forest to rejoin the old road a quarter mile further on. Hilary felt elated as if they had cheated the weather. He shook his fist at fate. There was still time. Still time.

Or was there? Hilary made the calculation again. They were not even at Mantes. They could barely reach it by nightfall. How far was Mantes from Barfleur? He could not remember. Each time he worked it out again, with the November the Twentieth staring at him from what was now less than a week away, there was the sight of the Seine snaking away to the west, glinting in the remaining light, speeding on towards to the sea at a rate faster than they could imagine. Swelled by the rain, the river was bearing the barges heading north at prodigious rates. But then, they did not want to go north. Once they reached Rouen they would turn West. Unless...

'Master Peter, I have a proposal. Wait for a moment.'

Abelard did not look. 'Hilary, we must go. Tell me as we ride.'

'No, Master Peter. Please do as I say. This is important.' Abelard wheeled his horse round and looked expectantly.

'We have six days before St Edmund's Day and at least a hundred and eighty miles to go. We might make that in good weather and on good roads and when you were well.'

'I am perfectly well, I assure you.'

'Be that as it may, we might make it in good conditions, but these are certainly not good conditions and, judging by the clouds above us, it may get worse. On the other hand, if we stabled the horses in the next town, whatever it is...'

'I believe it is La Roche.'

'If we left the horses there and went instead on one of those barges that are speeding up the Seine,' Hilary continued, 'we might reach the sea in maybe three days. We would then find a ship to take us across the bay to Barfleur. We would then be there in just over five days and we could catch the Prince before he sails.'

Abelard stared. 'Hilary, you are a master. That is one of the best ideas I have ever heard. Let us do exactly that. We can buy some food in La Roche as well. I feel hungry.'

The Seine in full flood was a terrifying experience, as their barge – filled with root vegetables – careered northwards along with parts of the riverbank, whole trees, driftwood, the occasional dead cow and sheep. The powerful current swept them along at a speed that Hilary had never experienced before. He kept looking at the ship's crew, who stood at the stern steering occasionally, apparently unconcerned, keeping the barge in the middle of the stream. There were hardly any vessels trying to beat the other way.

It had been the work of a moment to stable the horses, and to hand over a considerable sum for their safekeeping – it seemed ungrateful to actually sell the Prince's horses – and to find some food. Finding the barge had been more difficult. Most of the crews had deserted the quays or sat under shelter looking disconsolate, hoping to resume voyages south. But a few barges were preparing to go north, and Hilary negotiated a passage as far as Honfleur in a barge called, ironically, *St Denis*. 'Even the barges are getting it wrong,' said Abelard, whose mood was improving the further they reached away from Argenteuil.

As darkness began to fall, they seemed to accelerate towards a great city, with a huge Romanesque cathedral rising above them.

'We are approaching Rouen, gentlemen,' said the owner. 'We will berth here for the night.'

'Can't we go on?'

'Go on, in the dark, when the river is behaving like a ravening beast? You must be mad,' said the bargee good-naturedly. 'No, we stay here. You may sleep with us in the barge or find an inn, as you wish. We leave again at first light.'

Abelard seemed to have recovered his spirits as well as his health as they wandered through Rouen in search of sustenance. In the Abbaye-aux-Hommes, Hilary stood at the great tomb of William the Conqueror which towered above him. What does it say about a father, he asked himself, when his sons conspire to kill each other. But then even Rufus had stolen the throne from under the nose of his crusading elder brother Robert. What a family, he said to himself. What a dynasty to inflict on the English.

It was nearly sunset on November the Eighteenth when the air began to change. Hilary could smell the sea. Seagulls swooped over the barge as the Seine widened out into the estuary. The church towers of Honfleur were in sight, with its masts and sails and ships drawn up onto the beach to avoid the weather. There was storm damage too. Small trees had been uprooted, and roofs had been dislodged. Rubbish had been strewn around the docks.

They paid the bargee and went in search of a likely looking coaster somewhere along the dockside. Nobody seemed to be sailing. 'Have you looked at the sky?' said one captain. 'I will be in port until the sky is the colour of your eyes again.'

'I sail on Monday. Not before.'

'My regrets, Good Sir. I am not due to sail – and certainly not in this weather.'

It was now just two days before St Edmund Martyr's day, when William the Aetheling was due to sail. Even now, if they found boat in time, they might just make it across the bay.

'This is getting desperate,' said Abelard as they settled down for the night. 'Somebody must need to sail. We have already wasted four hours here. We must set sail tomorrow morning or we will miss the Aetheling.'

The inn was crowded with people delayed by the weather. The dormitory was full and Hilary and Abelard were forced to sleep on the floor in the inn itself, among a number of other travellers, with its filthy straw and rushes and lice from the sailors.

'Perhaps we could pay them to sail,' said Hilary. 'We still have money left from what we were given.'

'I sail tomorrow,' said a voice from a straw pallet invisible at the end of the room. 'I sail tomorrow no matter what the weather. I am contracted to deliver a cargo of stockfish and vegetables to Barfleur. If you gentlemen would like to accompany me any of that way, then I am open to offers.'

'We will make you a suggested price in the morning,' said Hilary. 'Please wake us at dawn if you are preparing to sail.'

Sure enough, in the dark in the early hours of the morning, Hilary felt a hand on his shoulder.

'Are you awake, *mon ami*? We leave now and I will intervene with the captain. Please wake your friend.'

Hilary and Abelard scrambled to gather their belongings and dashed out into the first light of dawn. The walk to the docks was only a matter of minutes. The wind was still clattering on the roof tops. The clouds were still forging a frantic path across the sky. The dark outline of the small ship could be seen ahead of them at the wharf with the sailors loading the last of the cargo of dried fish. The final arrangement was made quickly and, within the time it takes to say a couple of paternosters, and they were installed in the stern and heading out to sea.

'Master Peter, the Prince will leave some time tomorrow,' said Hilary as Honfleur disappeared behind them in a swirl of gulls. 'But we could still make it. In fact, I believe we *are* going to make it, after all.' The first hint of sunlight flashed on their square sail. They had already stopped at Cabourg and the wind was behind them. Hilary congratulated himself on the decision to go by sea.

'Don't commit yourself yet, Hilary. That cloud seems to suggest to me that we may yet be delayed.'

Hilary turned around. Sure enough, a black cloud had appeared menacingly in the far distance ahead of them. Even as he turned, he felt a fresher breeze on his face, and his lengthening hair began to blow in his eyes. He shivered in apprehension.

When the weather struck them, not long afterwards, it was one of those unearthly storms, the mere rumour of which was enough to dissuade the keep the vast majority of Europe's population to keep away from the sea. Even the crew were soon reduced to a terrified heap, muttering prayers as the rain and waves began to lash the bulwarks and deck. Hilary clung to a post in the relative shelter under the stern while the sailors around him sang hymns and mumbled terrified snatches of the scriptures. As the wind rose in ferocity, the captain clung to the mast and waved a crucifix in a desperate attempt to exorcise the thunder and waves.

Hilary watched him latch on to the figure of Abelard, sleeping under a huge leather oxhide, as he always did in bad weather. Dripping wet, sea water pouring from his beard, the captain struggled towards him across the heaving deck and knelt at his side. Abelard woke, listened and nodded. A moment later, bread and wine was fetched across the deck.

'They want me to say mass, Hilary,' he bellowed in Hilary's ear against the screaming wind. 'Will you assist? I've agreed to do it, if only for the sake of the others.'

Hilary nodded. Slowly, the terrified crew began to crawl towards them through the waves crashing over the deck, and gathered round. Kneeling down and trying desperately to keep himself steady under the quarter deck, Abelard began.

It was a short version of the mass, and he intoned the familiar words. Hilary could barely hear them, but he could see progress was being made through the ritual. Abelard broke the bread and grasped the cup.

'*Simili modo postquam coenatum est,*' he said. Those around him held onto anything that could keep them steady, hanging on his word and crossing themselves.

He knelt forward, but Hilary watched in horror as he leaned further forward – and further, until his forehead lay on the deck in front of him and stayed there.

Nobody spoke. The waves crashed against the side of the boat. The wind screamed in the rigging. 'Master Peter?' said Hilary as close to him as he could get.

There was no reply. Hilary put an arm across his back and shouted in his ear. 'Master Peter? Are you ill again?'

'Put it all away, Hilary,' he mumbled. 'I am not a priest. I am not a priest any more.'

Hilary looked up at the expectant faces around them. He looked back to Abelard, unsure whether the wet soaking his face was the sea or tears of despair. This was no time for niceties of canon law, he told himself, moving the bread and wine in front of him, and taking up the cup himself.

'*Hic est enim calix sanguinis mei, novi et aeterni testamenti: mysterium fidei,*' he said. The crew crossed themselves again. Was it his imagination, or was the wind less intense than it was?

When the mass was over and the sailors dispersed again to their clefts in the deck, Hilary saw his old teacher holding tight to the bulwark and staring out to sea. 'This is a strange a prehistoric sight,' he shouted in Hilary's ear.

'Are you not terrified too, Master Peter?'

He seemed about to ignore the question, staring out to sea at the mountainous waves.

'I'm not sure it matters what happens to me now,' he said.

By now the coast, which had disappeared in the ferocity of the storm, was visible again and Hilary realised they were running for the safety of a small harbour. There was a final struggle with the sail and tiller, with the crew heaving on the oars, until they rounded the point and into a neat fishing village.

'I regret, my friends, that we must stay here until the storm abates,' said the captain, as they edged into the harbour. 'I could not turn before for fear that the whole boat would go over, but we are safe now.'

'But we need to be in Barfleur tomorrow morning' said Abelard. 'We are committed. We promised the King's son.'

Two of the crew looked at them both, sitting bedraggled and caked in salt amidst the ropes and detritus from the storm which was still scattered around the stern, and waggled their fingers to their temples, raising their eyes skywards.

'My apologies, Father. That is not possible. If we set out in these waves, we would not reach Barfleur. Do not lay the blame on me; blame the storm. Blame the devil.'

Abelard shrugged his shoulders in despair. 'I fear we have been defeated, Hilary, unless this storm blows itself out in an hour or so. And it shows no signs of doing that.'

'We can hope perhaps that Prince William is also delayed. He will not put to sea in this weather either.'

This was the hope that inspired Hilary and Abelard as they waited patiently on the quay, under cover from the driving rain, sometimes in the tiny, thatched mariner's church, packed with other sailors and their passengers, and sometimes in the mariner's society, with its lists of members and shrines to the various maritime saints. There was no sun to set that evening but, when the darkness finally fell, they bedded down in the church with the other passengers, so as to be near the quayside if the weather changed.

Sure enough, just after dawn on St Edmund Martyr's day, they were shaken awake by the captain. 'The wind has lifted a little, my friends. The waves are less intense. We have decided to go on.'

Feeling hopeful again in the pale morning light, Hilary packed his few belongings once more. The wind was still rattling the flimsy roofs and making the leather covering the cargos flap insanely and desperately in the wind. The spray still leaped over the quay and into their faces. Only a few minutes later, they were on board and pushing off from the jetty. The crew looked mutinous. It was evident that Abelard's mention of the King had influenced the decision to go to sea. He was also Duke of Normandy, after all.

It was a gruelling voyage, battling the waves around the coast for much of the day. Hilary, whose seasickness had returned, was painfully aware that – with every ghastly churning of his stomach and every hideous evacuation over the stern – their chance of keeping the tryst with the heir to the throne was slipping away, and with it Hilary's hope of resolution and Abelard's chances of preventing the Harrying of the West..

'Courage, Hilary. He may still be in harbour waiting for good weather,' said Abelard, ever the optimist.

They called into the harbour at St Laurent and turned north towards Barfleur, and the weather began to improve. Hilary's heart sank once more. What if the Prince believed they had simply departed with his horses and his silver? Would there be any redemption then? Would he ever be able to return to England, still less achieve any kind of agreement?

The church towers and masts of Barfleur came into sight as the evening began to gather. The sea was calmer now, with great green hills and valleys, as if seeking for some kind of respite after the violence of the previous night. Hilary strained to see into the harbour. There were the familiar huge striped sails and dragon prows of the Channel ships. It was just possible that the prince would still be there.

At the quayside, Hilary paid the captain as quickly as he could and climbed the rope ladder onto the stone quay. It was rough and slimy to the touch. At the top, the quay was empty. Those people who still remained were tidying the dock for the night. The dark was falling. The sails that they had seen were being taken down and stowed away.

'We seek Prince William the Aetheling,' said Hilary desperately, as he accosting a sailor carrying a broken oar. 'Have you seen him?'

'Gone, my friend,' said the man, pointing out to sea and there

– caught in the last rays of the sun – was a sail, in the far distance, and the faint outline of a huge ship. They had missed him by less than the time it took to say mass. William had sailed. Hilary watched the sail, striped in red and white until it reached the horizon and turned broadside on to catch the wind. As it did so, the darkness made it impossible to see any more. He stared until he could see it no more, watching the disappearance of his hopes into the unpredictable English Channel.

'The King was here. What a to-do. They have all gone now. Left now.'

'The King?'

'King Henry was here. He sailed while it was sill light. One of the admirals offered Prince William the use of his own ship, brand new. There must have been three hundred passengers on board. They sailed just now. With his half brother and sister with him, and the Bishop of Hereford too. Quite a party they were having. The beer was flowing, I can tell you.'

'Why did they leave so late in the evening?' asked Abelard, staring out into the darkness of the sea, fearful that it might have had something to do with waiting for him.

'I believe there was some wager involved. They wanted to catch the King's ship.'

More sailors were mobbing quietly along the quay, caught in that alcoholic haze after a raucous party. Barfleur was unwinding for the night.

'If you want to go to England, there is still one ship leaving tonight. Not a big one. If you go past the mariner's club, on the small quay. Say that I sent you. He may have a place on board if you can pay well.'

'All we can do is follow,' said Hilary.

The quay was almost deserted as they headed to the place that had been indicated. There were a few late visitors hanging about, stowing ropes or staring at the night sky, which was now clear and starry as if the storm had blown every mist and cloud over to England. Negotiations completed and Hilary was preparing to tackle the ladder down to the level of the ship, its prow a sea monster of uncertain provenance, when a group of people by the dock buildings caught his eye. One of them seemed familiar.

He looked twice, hardly able to believe it. His pulse raced. That figure looking out to sea, silhouetted against the dying light. He had seen it before.

He climbed back onto the cold, wet stone of the quay and hurried over. It was only when he was right next to her that he dared say the word. 'Isabella?'

She turned and stared. Her companion was in the garb of a convent. What an extraordinary coincidence. When you think about people enough, they can suddenly appear, and here she was – but was she real?

'Hilary, Hilary. You have arrived like an angel to answer my prayers. I never believed I would see you again.'

They fell into each other's arms. The nun next to her turned away.

'Where is he? Where is my lord of Montgomery? Has he not arrived?' Hilary could not work out what circumstances could possibly have left her alone on the dock, with no companions and no entourage. Had she run away? Had she been somehow rejected by her lord? Or forgotten? It hardly seemed possible.

'He was here. I saw him. So tall and powerful, Hilary. He was on the ship with the prince. It was crowded and hurried and they were so impatient to leave. The bishops and lords were all there. They wanted to catch the King's ship. The admiral welcomed them on board and I went on board myself. So did my nurse and Robert, my father's servant. But I missed my bags and I came back up the gangway to seek them and, Hilary – when I came back, they had sailed…'

'They left you behind?'

Isabella broke down. 'He will be so angry. Oh, Hilary, what am I to do? What am I to do?'

The nun next door stood implacably between them.

'My lady is betrothed to be married. She will return to Argentueil with me. She is under my protection.'

Hilary recognised the sub-prioress. Abelard was approaching too. He must think fast.

'Isabella, we sail tonight for England. I seek Prince William, who has vowed to clear my name and I believe will prevent a great evil in England, if we can reach him. We sail tonight, if we can find a ship. Come with us. Come with us, I beg you.'

The sub-prioress drew herself up to her full height. 'That is out of the question. I will not release my lady into the custody of two men, unknown to her husband-to-be – and especially if one of those men is Peter Abelard. I know you, Master Peter. She will stay with me.'

'Stay with me, Hilary. I cannot leave now. Not with you, but you can stay with me.' The tears ran down her cheeks in the cold, salty air.

Hilary breathed deeply. What could he do? He loved her, he knew that now, but it was another doomed love and it would do no good. Both of them would suffer, and he must keep his tryst with Prince William if he possibly could.

'Master Peter, what should I do?'

'You know what you must do, Hilary. God asks us to sacrifice love sometimes, for his purposes. You must keep your word and prevent a great wrong. You must sail with me.'

Hilary closed his eyes. When he opened them, he could see Isabella's chin wobbling as the sub-prioress led her firmly away. She did not turn back.

The small ship was indeed leaving for England that night. There was space aboard and the captain charged them two pennies each, the same as the fare on the big ships. 'We leave at vespers,' said the captain. 'But I must call into Cherbourg to pick up a cargo of wine casks. We will overnight in that harbour and then set out at daybreak tomorrow. That is the fastest route for you to England right now. There are no more ships from Barfleur tonight. If it suits you, you are welcome.'

Once more, Hilary and Abelard sheltered in the stern as the ship moved slowly out into the darkness. The sea looked like ink and smelled of dead fish. Hilary listened as the great oars splashed into the water for the first time, and the power of human muscles began to drive them through the water and he would have breathed a very tentative sigh of relief, had it not been that he was repeating and repeating his snatched conversation with Isabella in his mind. He was repeating and repeating the decision to follow after the Prince. It had been the right decision, had it not? How could he have stayed, with everything unresolved, and with the Harrying of the West about to begin?.

'Where do you make for after Cherbourg?' he asked the captain.

'It depends on the tide and the weather. I aim for Folkestone.'

'And the King and the Prince?'

'They always aim for Dover. They may not make it this time because the incoming tide is against them.'

In the final minutes before they sailed, Hilary climbed the plank again onto the wharf, in the hope of catching one more glimpse of Isabella. Again, he was not prepared for what he saw. For the second time, he was brought up short by recognition on the quayside. Could it possibly be? Something about the shape of the way the man held his head, although it was hard to see in the deepening evening light. He was staring across the stone wharf directly at Hilary.

A cold ice gripped at Hilary's heart. 'Master Peter, look over there,' he said urgently. 'That is the Man in Grey, is it not? I feel sure it is. How can he have found my trail? How can he have tracked me here?'

'Come Hilary, it is dark. How can you know?'

'I know because I can sense him. I can sense his malevolence. Let us get under way as soon as we can, before he identifies us.'

Hilary descended the ladder as fast as he could. Abelard heaved down his saddlebags. He sheltered in the stern, and an involuntary shudder ran down his spine. How was it possible that his nemesis should have returned? It was as if the story had come full circle. He had evaded the man at Maguellonne only to find him again in Barfleur. He must somehow reach the Prince before the Man in Grey caught up.

After an impatient sleep in the stern of the ship at Cherbourg, Hilary greeted the fresh dawn the following morning with an expectant thrill and rushed onto the dockside to find the cargo already stowed and the last ropes being coiled away. Once more the ship pulled away from the tiny harbour, the small crew straining at the oars and then heaving up the huge square sail until the wind filled the canvas. The monstrous figurehead rose to meet the waves, spray washed over the deck, and they were away again. This time for England.

'I believe that is Barfleur again,' said Abelard pointing into the distance on their right. It was frustrating to be covering water they should have crossed yesterday.

'Wreckage off the starboard bow!' shouted the lookout from above.

The captain stood on tiptoes and steered carefully round it.

The crew looked nervously as they passed a large piece of driftwood. In fact, there seemed to be wood floating everywhere. Some of it was distinctively painted white.

'Some poor bastard,' said the captain. 'The storm filled its belly yesterday, by God's truth.'

The next morning, England was in sight, the sunlight sparkling on the waves as the ship stormed through the water, great bow waves splashing over the side and into the faces of the crew. They crawled into Pagham harbour, their first stop, with Hilary champing with impatience, willing the sailors to pull harder on their pulleys to haul the wine casks onto the dock.

'We will not make Folkestone,' the captain told Hilary. 'The tide is against us now and I cannot turn. I am making for Dover.'

And so it was that, some hours later, they could see the white cliffs above them as the ship rolled in the uncertain waters of the Dover Strait. The sailors hauled down the great sail and bent over the oars to turn the ship's accelerating passage into Dover harbour. There was the great castle dominating the cliff tops, its royal standard flying proudly in the wind. The King must have arrived. They were not far behind.

But on the dockside, it was immediately apparent that everything was not as it should be. The people seemed to walk carefully, as if in some kind of trance. They tiptoed. They did not acknowledge each other. Hilary could get no attention as he asked where the royal party were.

'This is strange, Hilary. What is the matter with everyone?'

Alone and bemused, they sought some more horses and looked for signs of where the Prince might be lodged. A detachment of soldiers in the distance seemed the most likely place to start and Hilary and Abelard set off on path towards the town.

The found the soldiers at the dock gates. They also looked nervous but their banners still fluttered joyfully in the breeze. The soldiers seemed to avoid their gaze.

'Where is their captain, Hilary? I hope we do not have to make the journey all the way up to the castle.'

It was then, too late, that they recognised a fierce bald figure with a red padded robe, seated on a large black horse by the gate. He stared at them in a mixture of rage and surprise.

'Ah,' he shouted loudly in their direction. 'The mysterious and elusive gentlemen of Paris, I presume. Good of you to arrive so promptly.' Ralph Basset gestured towards his soldiers. 'Please be so good as to place these men under arrest. They will come with me to London.'

Hilary froze again. This was not at all expected. 'My lord, you do not understand. We have been on a mission for Prince William the Aetheling. We were supposed to meet him in Barfleur, but he left before us.'

Basset raised his eyebrows further. 'So let me see, you were expected to sail with him on the same ship, but you managed not to. Is that correct?'

'That is true, my lord.'

'Perhaps you have yet to hear the grave news in that case. Prince William is dead. He sailed on the White Ship last night and was drowned, we assume, when it sank. As far as I know there has been only one survivor.'

It was one of those moments of astonishment that froze the words and emotions from Hilary altogether. He stood open-mouthed with horror and loss. Tears pricked behind his eyeballs, not just for the loss of their protector but at the loss of such a young man, so confident and full of life – in battles these things can happen, but so suddenly, so completely, so devastatingly? It hardly seemed possible.

'King Henry has no other legitimate son, is that right?' said Abelard.

'That is none of your concern,' said Basset. 'What is your concern is what will happen now. You will go before me to London where I will question you properly. My place now is with the King, but we will meet in a week's time at the Tower. Then I have some questions to ask you and, this time, you will answer them.'

4/The Tower

London again, 25 November 1120

It was not until after he had walked back up the damp and mournful path from the Thames to the Tower of London, and after he had tasted again the indignities of a prison cell, that the full peril that hung over him came home to Hilary. The glimpse of the Man in Grey was, he believed, an omen of disaster. His fate must have been sealed. It seemed unlikely that he would ever see the sky again. He imagined his body rotting away under the level of the Thames, alone this time and forgotten; Isabella alone too in Argenteuil, getting the news of her *fiancé*'s death, submitting finally to the veil and cowl. He should have stayed with her after all.

This time, his tiny stone cell was shared with nobody but a couple of rats who popped out after the darkness fell every evening. They come in case I have died and there is feasting to be had, said Hilary to himself. He resigned himself to futility. There was nothing to look at except the stone, the straw and the chains. There was a skylight, but too high to see through. Hilary could only guess at the churning water of the Thames and the ships outside coming and going with the tide, with cargoes of skins from Russia, spices from the Alexandria or dyes from across the Orient. He stared miserably at his hands and paced methodically across the cell, recognising patterns obsessively in the stone. I am abandoned here, as dead as Alys, he thought to himself. As dead as Hubert.

He seemed to have been incarcerated below the level of the

river, and water dripped on him at all hours of the day and night, making him wheeze. After a few days, light and dark merged together and he lost all track of time, aware only that he was supposed to wait for a week before Basset's return, and punctuated by the arrival of the occasional drink of greasy water or bite of a stale loaf.

There was certainly time to think, but so little now to think about. It was hard to see any way out of his predicament now. His protector was dead, the fish and the seaweed dragging his body down to the bottom of the ocean. Prince William the Aetheling never would inherit a kingdom, divided or not, and without his restraint the Harrying of the West would now go ahead. He could not defend himself against the questions he was bound to be asked about the two mysterious deaths in France. Nor could he explain away his fatal interest in the death of William Rufus, and it was clear that Abelard's pursuit of the truth would cut little ice with a man like Ralph Basset. Instead, he thought about Isabella, her disappointed, grief-stricken face, and her laugh which he would never hear again.

Abelard himself, who had remained optimistic and relaxed all the way to London, was not there to ask. He was, presumably, also in a cell on his own, perhaps shared with the very same rats. Perhaps with the same mood of hopelessness and despair was also creeping over him like the night. Hilary reflected bitterly that he had ensnared Abelard in this web of intrigue and now it would bring him down too. History would condemn him for the destruction of the Indomitable Rhinoceros, and remember him for nothing else, and certainly not his songs. The Great Abelard, brought down by his involvement with a minor poet and wandering scholar.

Unable to sleep, the same desperate and unearthly screams echoing through the walls that he had heard on his previous visit,

he recited what poetry he could remember, Ovid's *Art of Love,*
Roland and Oliver and even some of his own. He tried to cheer
himself up by humming his own poem from his student days, 'To
an English boy':

> Hail to you, the handsome boy, who'll never ask
> For anything, no gift, no gain, no task,
> In whom integrity and beauty bask,
> Who captures all who see behind your mask.

Those were the days. The verse made him smile and took him
back to summer nights by the Seine, but the feeling didn't last.
Again and again, he came back to Isabella, her trusting eyes, her
laughter in the sunshine in Jerusalem, her youth – yes, he told
himself, her *youth*. It would hardly do to think so longingly of
someone quite so young. Was that not the sin that had brought
down the Rhinoceros himself? And yet, and yet, it was Isabella's
continued existence, in safety with the nuns, the bright
intelligence of Heloise, the reliability of the Prioress, that gave
him what hope there was left in the world.

It was under the level of the Thames, wrapped in his thoughts,
that Hilary realised the central truth which he had missed before.
The White Ship had sunk with Isabella's betrothed on board, and
he had almost certainly drowned along with everyone else. She
would remain at Argenteuil for life. She never would marry, after
all.

Even so, it was not until his first meeting with his captors
some days later that Hilary fully understood his peril. There was
Basset before him, his face blank and bored, sitting at a rough
table in the stone chamber where they both stood on the same
filthy blood-encrusted straw. Once again there was almost no
light but, in the dim recess, he could see a burly man in a leather

apron, checking the tools of what was presumably his trade, great branding irons, chains, hooks and knives of all sizes, and a great brazier that gave a flickering light to the room. There was blood on the walls, some of it ancient, some of it disturbingly fresh. Don't let it be Master Peter's, said Hilary to himself. As Basset spoke, Hilary looked around himself nervously to confirm his worst fears.

'So, it will save us time and trouble if you simply told us,' said Basset. He sounded so tired that he hardly cared one way or the other. He was rolling something around the table, between his hands, fiddling with it like a large marble.

'What can I say?' said Hilary desperately. 'I am the victim of a serious of unfortunate encounters. It was not me who killed John of Muchelney. It was not me who killed Master Hubert. It was I who involved Master Peter, and for that, please forgive him, and let him go. He has nothing to....'

Basset had been showing signs of boredom of an even greater intensity. 'Please, please, young man, no more of this prattle. I could not care less about these things. John of Muchelney? The man is dead and good riddance to him. I know that, but I am not interested. Do you not realise, the heir to the throne is dead? Drowned in a ship that he was not intended to sail in. Do you know who died in that White Ship? Not just the prince, but the Bishop of Hereford, Matilda Fitzroy, the King's daughter, Richard of Lincoln, Richard of Mongomery and his wife-to-be – he who was planning our punitive expedition to the West. And you, who were supposed to sail with them, managed to evade the same fate.'

Hilary stared. He was not, surely, going to be accused of sabotaging the White Ship as well as everything else? What could he say? His eyes bulged and again he looked around in growing terror and helplessness.

'You were arrested with money that I believe was given you by the Prince. But the horses leant to you by him are gone, presumably sold. It is clear to me what happened, but I need to hear it from you. I am not interested in details, and heaven knows I do not want to spend the morning talking to you. But this matter needs a solution and therefore you must help us. Do you understand?'

'You mean you need someone to blame.'

A look of irritation crossed Basset's brow. 'Don't play with me. I am not interested in whether you live or die. I need to tell the King why his son is dead. You clearly have had a role in it and I want to know how and why. The sooner I get that information, the sooner this can be resolved.'

Hilary suddenly felt weak, and it was this crucial moment that he realise what it was that Basset was playing with. It was a human eyeball.

His legs gave way and he collapsed in the straw. The full horror of what was coming was now clear. He wondered if he could resist the intense pain.

'Well,' said Basset briskly, pocketing the eyeball. 'I am too busy for this. I have much to do this morning. Let me introduce you to Master Rudolph. He will explain things more clearly than perhaps I have been able to. I give you good day.'

Hilary lay there silently, juggling his impossible options and, as he did so, the man in leather stepped forward from the back of the room. Master Rudolph spoke like an educated man.

'Hilary, I believe your name is? Yes? There is no need to get up. Let me explain to you the reality of your situation. I often find it helps to do this before questioning. It concentrates the mind.'

He stepped back like a salesman at a fairground. There was another man in leather behind him. Master Rudolph stood by his tools ready to display them.

'Now, Hilary. These forceps we usually use for pulling out teeth.'

Despite himself, Hilary could not resist swinging his body round to see. The man lifted up a pair of great black scissors.

'This fire, of course, as you will see from the branding iron – could you demonstrate, Roger? – is for later on in the process. For the eyes...'

The gruesome tour continued. Hilary could only watch in horror, his mind too full to take decisions, aware only that he would not be able to resist whatever they wanted him to say.

'So, my friend. What would you like to tell me? Anything?'

Hilary shook his head, got to his knees and vomited on the dirty straw in front of him.

'Dear me,' said Rudolph. 'Well, you know the score now. Perhaps if I return you to your comfortable cell today then, by tomorrow, you will have had a chance to think about it and then we can get down to business. Either way, we can get down to business.'

Hilary managed a little sleep before dawn. Otherwise his mind raced around his remaining options. Deny everything and lose his tongue, eyes, ears and finally his life, after which he would undoubtedly have said whatever they asked him to. Alternatively, he could avoid immediate pain, face a painful execution and undoubtedly drag Abelard into the plot as well. What kind of choices were those? He prayed passionately to St Genevieve and to St Leonard, the patron saint of prisoners and pain. What kind of place was this which, uniquely in the world, had opted out of God's pastoral care? This was where the angels slept, perhaps because they could not bear to watch.

The hours passed. Light began to seep into the dank space that was his cell. He still had no idea what to do. No strategy had occurred to him. He had still made no clear decisions when the door to his cell opened and he was motioned out. He got painfully to his feet, shaking so hard he could barely put one foot in front of each other. He felt like a physical wreck and that was before King Henry's torturers had begun their work.

Miserable and despairing, he followed the soldiers down the long passageway, wondering which of these great wooden doors concealed the Indomitable Rhinoceros, slowly becoming clearer in the morning light. But for some reason, he realised, they were not going the same way as yesterday. A moment later, having gone up two spiral staircases and down one, he stood at the threshold of the tower and was marched outside. The pale London sky seemed wintry, but he had feared he would never see it again. He must be on his way direct to execution. Perhaps they had decided to dispense with the investigation and just put him to death. Once more he prayed to St Leonard and to Our Lady who had presided over the cathedral from whose bowels he had escaped in Paris.

The great gate to the fortress approached. It swung open. One of the soldiers jerked his head towards the city outside.

'Out,' he said. 'Go on. Get going.'

It took a few moments of rising hope before Hilary realised he was really being released. What was it about the Tower which made his journeys from the cells so unpredictable? He looked from one soldier to the other to make sure, but they turned away. He walked forwards. The gates crashed shut behind him. He sank to his knees in the dust and thanked God for his mercy. Then he broke down and wept.

Alone in London, Hilary walked in a daze through the unfamiliar streets, knowing only that he must go west. This must mean heading in the general direction of the cathedral tower which he could see between other churches and wooden thoroughfares in the distance, down the curve of the river. There was only one person he knew in the city, and he had only met him briefly before Abelard spoke at St Paul's Cross. He would go and see Canon Stephen of Boxley. If Abelard had been released as well, he would know where to find him.

The streets were strangely quiet after his last visit and he realised that it must be Sunday. As he did so, the church bells began to toll. He could hear them echoing around the wooden buildings which stretched half way across the streets, and over to the hills in the north. At the corner of Tower Hill, he realised he had attracted the attention of a group of young men who stared at his strange dishevelled appearance. One of them pointed at him and laughed. He braced himself for some kind of attack. The apprentices of London were well-known. But only once he had passed did a turnip wing its way towards him. It rolled in the gutter at his feet. He did not look back.

There were ships unloading on the Thames, but God did not determine the days the winds blow and ships must arrive on the Sabbath, or any other day, he supposed. He was approaching another river, surrounded by marshes, and a damp crossroads with painted women hanging around. Two of them approached him before he realised where he was. This must be the place they know as 'Gropecunt Street', he thought to himself and hurried on. Past Broad Street and the poultry market, he realised that the neighbourhood was familiar. He must be getting closer. The people were out with their hair and clothing carefully arranged for Sunday and were heading in little groups towards the churches. 'Do I walk this way to the cathedral?' he asked them. 'Am I going the right way for St Paul's?'

'Straight on, Sir, down Westcheap and blessings on you for the Sabbath.'

So this was Westcheap, he realised. He had heard about it many times, with the bankers at their little benches and the silversmiths weighing their coins from all corners of Europe. There were no benches out now. The Jews had their own Sabbath but they knew better than to defy the Christian one by opening for business.

Finally, there before him was the majestic scale of the cathedral, its tower rising up above the wooden roofs around it, its great buttresses soaring up into the sky, packed closely around with scaffolding. Stephen of Boxley would be inside, he realised, and he joined the crowd which hurried into the nave, chattering with anticipation and expectation.

Exhausted, demoralised and hungry, Hilary found it hard to stand throughout the long service. In the distance, over the heads of the populace, he could see the fine tailoring and plumage on the hats of the London gentry in their seats further up the nave, and behind them the fine gold and gold-encrusted vestments of the clergy. He propped himself up against a pillar and waited.

He found Stephen in the melee outside the great cross at the end of the service and was pleased to see his round florid face light up when he was recognised. 'By God's grace, it is Master Peter's friend! Your name – is ... Hilary, of course, how could I have forgotten? You are most welcome.' He had a different set of food stains down his ecclesiastical robes.

They embraced. 'You must come with me to my house, Master Hilary. There are things we must not discuss here. But we must save Master Peter. I have been working all night, as soon as I heard.'

'Heard? Heard what?' Another wave of foreboding overcame him/

Stephen stared at him surprise. Then he put his finger to his lips and motioned him to follow. They escaped the crowd and went down one of the small passageways by the north transept. Stephen pushed ahead and opened the door to a fine house, painted as red as its occupier's face.

'Come in, come in, Master Hilary. God has sent you to me. You are welcome in my house. But you have not heard the news? Master Peter is in the Tower.'

'I know that. I have come from there myself.'

'Then you know he is to be tried for heresy?'

The look on Hilary's face betrayed how little he knew. Of all the unpleasant surprises of the past few days, this in was probably the most extraordinary. The consequences were profound as well. If Abelard was found guilty by the church court, then really anything could happen. He might be told to burn his own books in penance. He might equally well be burned himself. And all because Hilary had involved him in this stupid escapade after the death of John of Muchelney.

'You have not seen him then?'

'Not for a week at least, Master Stephen. *Di immortales!* We must help him. What can I do?'

'All in good time. First, I must understand what has happened since we first met. You have been to Normandy? I have heard the news about the Prince. Such a terrible tragedy. No, first tell me what has happened to you both.' He began to look around the room in search of something to eat.

Hilary recounted the story, and found he needed to take the tale further back to Jerusalem, and then backwards again to Paris, Beaugency and Orléans. By the time he had finished, leaving out the visit to Tirel and the story of Isabella, Stephen was staring at him with a look he could not quite interpret.

'What a tale! Master Hilary, I must think, and while I am

thinking I will order us something to eat. You look as though you need it.'

'Thank you. I am most grateful, for this and everything else. What I don't understand is why I have been released from the Tower.' It is extraordinary, thought Hilary to himself, that I understand less and less as the weeks go by. I will soon be overwhelmed by what I don't understand. I will be buried under it.

'Well, that is easy enough to understand,' said Stephen, pausing to shout down into the corridor that it was time to break his fast. 'You are unimportant, if you forgive the expression. I believe the King's Chancellor has already blamed the Jews for the White Ship's sinking. The apprentices were on the march last night breaking heads, demanding revenge. He will be thinking of the compensation he can claim, no doubt. If the Jews did it, it makes no sense – in fact it is positively unhelpful – to be at the same time accusing a mere wandering scholar of sabotage. No, they needed you out of the way. Luckily, they got rid of you the humane way – through the main gates. You are lucky to be alive, my friend.'

'Then why not release Master Peter?'

'Ah well, that is easier to answer. Last week there arrived, from Reims, a combative character called Alberic. He had heard a story about Master Peter preaching in London – I fear that was at my instigation, you will remember – and he has come with a letter from two cardinals demanding that the Archbishop should prevent him. He has been to see the King's Chancellor – an old fool I know – and he now unfortunately sees it the same way. There are two of the foremost theologians and scholars in Europe now both demanding action; not just Alberic but also others. And now he will get it... Ah, now here is something to feed us.'

Stephen's expression changed quickly from worry to delight as he witnessed the arrival of dinner. A servant entered the room carrying a huge platter of roast perch and turnips. Hilary's mouth watered. He felt guilty to be so generously fed when his teacher and friend was in such peril. What must Master Peter be eating now? Stale bread, if he is lucky.

'I have been doing what I can to help. I have written a letter by urgent messenger to a scholar I know in Oxenford and I hope we may get some support from there. I only hope he will come and that he arrives in time. I believe the trial will be immediately after Christmas. What can you tell me about Alberic of Reims?'

Hilary was only too aware of how little he knew. 'I only know that Master Peter speaks of him all the time because he knew Alberic was planning to challenge him. He had hoped to be ready for the challenge. Alberic has not forgiven him for the Laon debates some years ago. It was Alberic's own teacher that Master Peter challenged and defeated. If only he had more time to prepare.'

And in the midst of all these concerns, as Hilary recounted his tale again for Stephen and his visitors, he repeatedly found his mind drifting to Isabella, locked into Argenteuil. It was only then that he realised how truly isolated she was. He suddenly remembered that, during their distressing interview, Ralph Basset had declared her dead – Richard of Montgomery *and his wife-to-be*, he had said. The world believed that Isabella was under the waves with William the Atheling and flower of his aristocratic friends. Who would know, apart from himself and Master Peter – and the nuns of course – that Isabella was still alive?

5/The trial
St Paul's Cathedral, 8 January 1121

The day of the trial dawned bright and hopeful and weighed down a little by the detritus of Christmas: abandoned Yule logs, empty bottles and barrels, the bones of cooked fowl and carcasses of animals in the streets. It had been a comfortable and nervous Christmas in Stephen of Boxley's house, and Hilary had written a letter to the priest of his home village, asking him to visit his mother. He even wrote a letter to Isabella, trying to explain himself, but gave up unable to say anything conclusive or to offer any real support. Anyway, he told himself as he destroyed the draft: who would have delivered it?

Their attempts to see Abelard in the Tower in the previous weeks had all failed, but he and Stephen had discussed Abelard's potential defence before retiring every night, only too aware that they had no power to execute it. At long last, the morning of the trial, the Oxenford scholar had arrived. He was called Gerald, a gaunt and threadbare figure who began furtively seeking out food from the moment he arrived. Hilary thought he looked strangely familiar. He had already heard of him in Paris as one of the cleverest scholars and most brilliant of the teachers at Notre-Dame. He was gave Hilary a dismissive look as he surveyed the room with some distaste.

'I am most grateful to you for coming,' said Hilary. 'You are welcome.'

Gerald of Oxenford looked irritated to be addressed in this way. 'I assure you, I am here to represent the interests of scholars across Christendom. I don't believe I am here for you.'

'Quite so,' said Hilary. 'Even so, I am sure Master Peter will be grateful for your help.'

'The trial begins tomorrow, am I right?' Hilary tried to indicate that this was not quite accurate, but Gerald brushed his gesticulation aside. 'Then I must have a light room in which to study. I have brought some books that I need and I may need others. Master Stephen, is there a library at St Paul's?'

'A small one, I fear,' said Stephen. 'But I am sure we can let you use it. I will make arrangements. Hilary will conduct you there this evening – but, Master Gerald, I am afraid you are mistaken. The trial starts today. It starts immediately. Perhaps, Hilary, you could manage to help Master Gerald with his preparations a little later. But there is really no time now, my friend, because the trial is starting now. You have arrived not a moment too soon. We are summoned to appear at the Chapter House after matins. I believe the Archbishop himself is presiding.'

'I assure you, I require no help – unless you have someone who is, shall I say, better qualified.' He eyed Hilary again.

'Master Gerald, I must tell you that Hilary is a scholar of Ste-Genevieve and a long-standing friend of Master Peter. You can have no better assistant.'

'Be that as it may,' said Master Gerald, fiddling with his papers and giving Hilary a sour look. 'That is most inconvenient. Perhaps I might prevail on you for that office later.'

'By all means,' said Stephen, preparing to lead the small party down into the street.

The chapter house of St Paul's was not far and it was only a short walk. Hilary began to wonder, as they made their way past the now familiar stallholders, that he might perhaps, if he was to put his own interests first, simply disappear. As far as he knew, he was not now being pursued. He could live in France as Ambrose the Carpenter. Perhaps he could even extract Isabella from the convent. To stay in London was to risk being associated with a convicted heretic with all the risks that went with that.

It was a selfish thought, Hilary told himself. How could he leave, since Master Peter had stood by him so irritatingly and yet so magnificently? He imagined Abelard in his cell, pacing up and down as he prepared himself for this ordeal. He pictured his face, drawn and worried and, of course, how could Abelard be otherwise than frightened? But as they walked into the court room, with the great stone ribs of the chapter house rising above them, and its busy atmosphere of expectation, he realised he had misjudged the man. There was Abelard on the other side of the room, looking buoyant and confident. A little thinner perhaps, but there was nothing downcast about him. He waved over at Stephen's small party as they filed in.

Behind them, there were crowds of scholars and other junior churchmen, and they were already restless. They had been queuing, Hilary realised, perhaps even since dawn. The excitement in the room was practically tangible. Ecclesiastical lawyers, a class of human being which Hilary had hitherto held in contempt, seemed to be everywhere, carrying scrolls and books and other papers backwards and forwards. One young clerk dropped them by Hilary's feet and he bent down and loaded them back into his arms. He could see the nervousness in the young man's eyes, and something else. Was it blood lust, Hilary wondered? Perhaps it was the presence of the Archbishop. Perhaps it was because everyone knew how heresy trails ended.

There were huge carpets set over the tables in the central bay of the chapter, weighed down by books, and the seats of the main protagonists along them were also now filling fast. Everyone's eyes seemed to be fixed on a confident Abelard and on a tall, gaunt, watchful figure at the main table opposite him.

'That is Alberic of Reims, I believe,' Hilary whispered to Stephen. 'He has hated Master Peter for years. You would think the unfortunate business at Notre Dame would have been revenge enough. With Heloise, I mean.'

As if he knew he was the object of discussion, Alberic peered over towards them and glared. Then he looked quickly up. There was a ritual bang, the hubbub of voices died suddenly down and an altar boy in white, carrying a cross, followed by another carrying a mitre, entered the room. The court was now completely silent. One of two people cleared their throat nervously. Then the whole crowd rose as the Archbishop processed into the room, helped by two young monks dressed in black.

It was a slow business. The Archbishop made confident strides with one half of his body and then seemed unable to shift the other half. It was painful to watch. Underneath a mop of white hair, his face seemed similarly divided. One half looked confident, with a grin and an amused glint in the eye. The other half looked dead. One eye ranged sightless around the chapter house and the right hand side of his mouth was locked in a downcast grimace.

'What is wrong with him?' hissed Hilary.

'Archbishop Ralph had some kind of seizure some years ago. He is perfectly able to carry on. Well, half of him is. I understand he was most reluctant to preside.'

The Archbishop hobbled in front of a kind of throne, put his hands together and bowed his head, calling for blessings on the court and God's guidance in their striving towards the truth. Many of the audience went on their knees. Some crossed themselves. Hilary prayed.

The effort of speaking seemed to contort the good side of the Archbishop's face. 'Welcome to the court, my masters,' he said in a thin voice. 'We have been asked to preside over this court over most serious charges of heresy against Master Peter of Notre

Dame. It is our task in these days that follow to discover the truth and to exact a remedy. We will not tolerate heresy in this city, but our wrath will exact its measure only if heresy can be proven. We start this process with an open mind. Now, let us waste no more time.' He turned to the suspicious looking cleric to his right and stared at him for a moment as if trying to place him. A monk ran up to him and whispered in his good ear. He nodded with irritation.

'Yes, yes, Master Alberic,' he said, as if he had known all along. 'We welcome you to London. Please set out your case.'

Alberic of Reims rose slowly in his place and looked around the court, his hooked nose giving him every appearance of a bird of prey. He seemed to search everywhere except towards Abelard. There was a buzz of excited voices in the audience. Have I seen him before, Hilary asked himself, perhaps in Ste-Genevieve? Or is he just the type of embittered academic that you used to see around the cloisters in Paris?

'Silence!' said the Archbishop, who was already looking a little jaded.

Alberic nodded to him politely. 'I thank you, my Lord Archbishop. I am grateful to you. Let me say straight away that serious and damnable heresies have been preached here in this very city, and preached within a stone's throw of where we are now, by the master scholar who they call Peter Abelard.'

There was absolute silence in the room. Hilary realised he was holding his breath. Abelard leaned forward in his seat to listen.

'There are three charges which this Abelard has been guilty of, as I shall explain and demonstrate to you. They are, first, that his book *Yes and No* has encouraged people to pick and choose from the scriptures and the writings if the holy fathers.'

'Familiar stuff,' Hilary whispered to Stephen. 'They will have to do better than that.'

'Second, that he has besmirched the doctrine of the Holy Trinity by wrongly suggesting that one part is more important than another.'

'That one's new,' said Hilary. 'I don't know about that one.'

'Finally, that he has claimed that men may make their own laws, regardless of God's laws.'

Hilary and Stephen exchanged glances. Both knew this referred to Abelard's lecture at St Paul's Cross. This was the most dangerous, especially if Alberic's lawyers could find people to swear that they heard him say all manner of things – and it was not difficult in a place like London to get people to swear to almost anything.

Alberic finished his introduction with a peroration of his own, explaining times and places, adding in some ridicule about St Denis, and finished with some overblown rhetoric about the dangers of heresy. He was about to go on, when Abelard rose in his seat.

'My lord, may I question Master Alberic on his statement?'

'You may,' said the Archbishop irritably, clearly wishing that he would not. 'Only be mindful of what you say.'

The crowd of scholars shuffled in their cramped places. This was the moment they had been waiting for.

'So Master Alberic,' said Abelard, stepping out from behind his table. 'You and I are well known to each other, are we not?'

'We are.'

'We met in Laon many years ago when I won the argument against your teacher. The result was that you are still angry about that.'

'That was years ago, as you say. There are more important issues to deal with here.'

'Very well, I will deal with my book later, but let me ask you this about the Trinity. To whom did Jesus pray to in the Garden of Gethsamene?'

'To his father, of course.'

'And what did he say at the end of his prayer?' There was a short silence. Everyone knew the answer. ' 'Not as I will but as you will.' Am I not correct?'

The crowd got restless. They could see which way this encounter was going. Alberic made no answer.

'Very well then,' said Abelard, ignoring the silence. 'And if your son said that to you, who do you think was the greater at that moment – the father or the son?'

'I have no son, Master Peter. I am a priest and therefore celibate.'

There was a suppressed cheer from the back of the hall. The clerks knew that Alberic had scored a point by a subtle reminder that Abelard had been very far from celibate. They also knew that their own Bishop of London had fathered two sons in a period less exacting of clerical standards and they craned their necks to see if he was among the ecclesiastical nobility present. The Archbishop stared furiously back at the crowd.

'Nevertheless,' Abelard went on, 'I would be right in saying that the son was at that moment subservient to the father, would I not?' Alberic said nothing. 'Would I not, Master Alberic?'

'You would, but...'

'Because fathers are greater than sons, are they not?'

Alberic looked triumphant. 'Not so, Master Peter. Was not Constantine greater than his father? Was not Augustus greater than his father? What about St Paul and his father? Are we to weigh in the balance the greatness of King Henry with the greatness of his father King William, who conquered this island?'

This time the cheer was uproarious. The Archbishop banged his table fretfully.

'This is no time for cheering,' he shouted. 'You will listen in silence or not at all.'

There were other witnesses as the day wore on. A student from Paris explained that he had been misled by Abelard's book *Yes and No* with all those contradictions between holy texts. An impoverished London priest swore that Abelard had said that people must follow the dictates of their own heart. 'That is what he told us at St Paul's Cross,' he said, looking wild-eyed. 'I stake my living on it. He told us to ignore Moses and ignore his sacred law. Those were his exact words.'

'I tell you, Master Hilary. This does not look good,' said Stephen as the court closed and the participants filed out. 'I fear for Master Peter, I really do.'

'For goodness sake, let us ask again if we can see him,' said Hilary desperately.

'I have and we may not. The problem is that this prosecution is all about politics and nothing about theology at all. It is because Master Peter dared interfere in the sensitive question of who killed William Rufus. Ralph Basset wants him out of the way, but dares not accuse him of anything himself – for fear of the French Chancellor. Even if we win this case, I don't give much for Master Peter's chances.'

In the chapter house the next morning, sitting behind his desk, which – unlike the others – was free of scrolls and parchments, Abelard looked more confident than ever. He shone with excitement. Two soldiers stood next to him to prevent his escape, but he seemed oblivious, as if this was the cloisters at Ste-Genevieve again and he was about to see off his most notorious opponents. Escape seemed to be the last thing on his mind.

'Master Hilary,' said Stephen sadly. 'I fear our friend, who is so worldly in some things, is somewhat naive in others. I do not believe he realises the peril he is in.'

The first item on the agenda that day was the evidence by Gerald of Oxenford, who explained that Abelard's book of contradictions had been invaluable in his own studies and those of his most promising scholars, and had deepened his understanding of the scriptures.

'Your name is Gerald of Oxenford, is it not?' said the Archbishop, making notes.

'I prefer to call myself Gerald the Founder, my lord.'

'I have no doubt you do,' said the Archbishop. Gerald looked uncomfortable.

'I gather he was actually known as Gerald of Kidlington, a small village outside Oxenford,' whispered Stephen of Boxley by Hilary's side again. Hilary grinned. He never liked Master Gerald. By now, Alberic had risen behind his table and was ready to reply.

'I suggest that you are deluding yourself in this,' said Alberic from the other side of the court. Gerald looked outraged. 'I believe the book may have helped a few scholars of your disposition, but the rest – I believe it has led them into questioning – *dangerous* questioning. Perhaps even questing after delusions. It has led them into *doubt*. So, let me ask you this. Does the book carry any warning that it is to be read only by those of sufficient experience?'

'I believe not.'

'Does it warn of the consequences of it falling into the wrong hands, the spread of wrong-headed heresy across Christendom?'

'Well, not … in so many words.'

'Very well then, Master Gerald. You may go.'

Gerald stayed for a moment, astonished that this was all he was being asked to say. There were some muted jeers from the scholars in the audience. Oxenford was not popular in London.

Abelard looked absurdly triumphant, despite the line of

questioning. 'Oh dear,' whispered Stephen. 'He must realise that he can't win. Even if he wins they are bound to find him guilty. This is politics not philosophy.'

'Nevertheless,' said Hilary. 'Look at the Archbishop. He seems to look more uncomfortable than ever.'

'Precisely my point. Wait, something is happening...'

A silence fell on the gathering again. Abelard gathered himself together and stepped forward into the middle of the floor as if he was about to perform.

'My Lord Archbishop, gentlemen, scholars,' he said, and he bowed to some of the senior clerics. 'Those who are new to philosophical debate...' A fat canon opposite Hilary muttered to his neighbour. 'Let me dwell for a few moments on the first two accusations against me. First, that I wrote a book which, by pointing out some of the potential contradictions between statements in scriptures and in the patristic writings, that I had perverted the young and misled the unwary. I think that my good friend Master Gerald of Oxenford made it clear that, actually, his colleagues have been enlightened by the book and assisted in their faith.'

There was a shuffling in the court as people craned to look at him, walking up and down.

'I also put this to you. How to you help a young scholar who comes across such a contradiction unassisted, and suffers agonies as a result? Unless of course you are claiming that all study is somehow heretical. As if we should stand before these writings dumbly, and set aside the faculties of analysis that God gave us to use. No. My book *Yes and No* is a book of faith. These are difficult questions and even the greatest scholars need help.'

'This is good stuff,' said Stephen, impressed.

'As for the issue about the Trinity, I deny it. I am no Orthodox heretic. I hold all three persons of the Trinity to be equal in weight and standing. But I am not saying that they are all the *same*. We call them different names. Of course, they are different, and play different roles. If Master Alberic says otherwise, then he is claiming there is no difference between the Father, the Son and the Holy Spirit – as if they were one interchangeable, amorphous lump. Then I challenge him – why give them different names?'

The Archbishop was now looking so uncomfortable that he appeared to be holding his head in his hands. Perhaps he is just praying, Hilary wondered.

'Now, I come to the issue of conscience,' said Abelard, now in full flight. 'When Jesus denied that a loving father would give his son a stone if he asked for bread, living bread, he was referring of course to the tablets of stone which embodied the law in the Old Testament.'

'I don't like the sound of this,' said Hilary. A couple of scholars shouted 'No!'

'And did Christ not also replace the dead stones of the Moses Law with living bread of the new law, which is himself? And now that Christ is in the world, in his church – which is us – are we to deny that we should use our consciences, created within us by God, to help us distinguish what is good from what is evil? Tell me, Master Alberic, does God prefer us to do the wrong thing for the right reasons or the right thing for the wrong reasons?'

Abelard was now pacing up and down theatrically, and challenged Alberic from the centre of the room.

Alberic coughed slightly. 'I believe he wants us to do the right things for the right reasons. Nothing else counts.'

'Yet we live in a fallen world, where St Paul says we see through a glass darkly. We have God's word to rely on, but are we to shut off our consciences as if we were cutting off a part of the body?'

Some of the scholars who knew Abelard's history collapsed in giggles. The Archbishop, red-faced, got laboriously to his feet and banged the table.

'That is enough. Any more and I will clear this room.'

'Wait!' shouted Alberic, leaping up in his place. 'If Master Peter places his conscience above that of God's holy law then I say not just heresy but blasphemy.'

Another uproar. 'Silence!' shouted the Archbishop. 'I am going to have to clear this building. These are serious matters. Pray continue.'

'Listen, my friend,' said Abelard quietly. 'The law says we should not work on the Sabbath. Does that include everybody?'

'Of course.'

'Even when our conscience finds some case which is not covered by the law. Some child to rescue, some peasant to cure?'

'I don't believe the law is insufficient. The church is clear on the details and can be clearer still.'

There was now absolute silence from the crowd. Hilary was on the edge of the seat.

'Do you remember the passage in St Mark's Gospel where Christ is criticised by the Pharisees for healing on the Sabbath?' said Abelard, staring at Alberic. 'What does he say in return?'

Alberic stared back silently. 'Well...,' he said.

'Tell me please, Master Alberic.'

'He says it is better to save life than to kill.'

'Then,' said Abelard, rising to a crescendo. 'Was he not using his conscience, informed of course by his father?'

'No, but...'

Once more, there was uproar. A couple of vegetables were thrown. One item looked like the innards of some farm animal.

"No, that is enough,' shouted the Archbishop, struggling to make himself heard. 'I clear this court. We shall have no audience. Out, out you go! I will not have this unseemly behaviour in a sanctified building.'

There were noisy complaints from the audience, who began to file out making hooting noises. The Archbishop stared at them like thunder as they withdrew. The ecclesiastical dignitaries remained but the acoustics were different without a room full of people. Stephen took Hilary by the arm and drew him to a seat by the door. 'I am a canon here,' said Stephen. 'They cannot exclude us.'

For the first time, Hilary could see, behind the table of lawyers, the bald head and red robes of Ralph Basset. He looked extremely bored. The noise of excitement echoed into the room from outside.

'Master Peter, you may continue,' said the Archbishop.

'I believe I have made my point, which is simply this. My accuser has not fully understood these doctrines himself. Perhaps we should adjourn this trial until he has availed himself of a proper education, perhaps at Notre Dame de Paris.'

'Ouch,' said Stephen. 'Master Peter should not goad him like that.'

'I decide when we adjourn. Do you understand?' said the Archbishop. 'You decide nothing.'

'My apologies, my lord.'

But Alberic was by now on his feet. 'My Lord Archbishop, I protest at these slurs on my knowledge and skills. What makes the University of Paris the measure of all wisdom? I will not be dismissed as an ignoramus. What Master Peter does not know, because of his absence, is that I have spent some months at Notre Dame myself preparing for this case. Yes, his very own beloved institution, though he can no longer teach there himself.'

'Oh really,' said Abelard, genuinely angry now at these reminders of his brutal exit from Notre Dame. 'You were there as a student, were you? What evidence do we have that you were there as anything else?'

'Don't you dare doubt me, Abelard.' Alberic gestured wildly towards the table of dignitaries. 'Why, your King's Justice, Ralph Basset himself, can vouch for me. He and I met there, in Notre Dame, a year ago.'

Basset stood up, red faced with rage and pushed past the canons and personages around him, storming noisily out of the room. His boots echoed on the flagstones. Abelard stared after him.

Hilary gasped. A year ago? That was when he had been there himself, or thereabouts. Basset had let slip when they first met him that he had encountered the French Chancellor, even though their masters were at war; was this the moment that they met? Was this the secret given away so unwittingly?

Abelard stood silently. You could almost see his mind working. He turned back towards Alberic.

'You were in Notre Dame a year ago, is that right? Before Christmas or after?'

'My lord, I do not see how this is relevant.'

The Archbishop waved a languid hand. 'Oh, just get on with it, will you please.'

'It was before,' said Alberic.

'Was it by any chance at St Lucia? When you saw the King's Justice?'

Alberic considered. 'It was, in fact. But please can we return to the subject.'

'Yes, for goodness sake, Master Peter,' said the Archbishop with exhaustion. 'Do you want us to remain here all night comparing diaries?'

Abelard turned to seek out Hilary and gave him a look of triumph. As he did so, a soldier with a piece of parchment was striding into the room. He handed it to the Archbishop, who folded it with a look of relief on his good side.

'We adjourn for the day,' he announced. 'The King himself instructs it. We meet again tomorrow to resolve this matter once and for all.' He motioned wildly to the ushers and the court officials filed out. Abelard was accompanied out looking pleased with himself. As he disappeared through the door, he winked at Hilary.

'Well, at least he is enjoying himself,' said Stephen. 'I do hope this is not pride before a fall.'

Hilary was in the courtyard of Stephen's home near the cathedral some hours later, getting some air and thinking back over the events of the past two days. Despite the high stakes, it had been exhilarating. It had taken him back to the great debates in Paris. It seemed unlikely that his teacher could possibly be exonerated at such a trial, though his performance had impressed at least some of the crowd. There was a sound in the distance and Hilary turned. The steward of Stephen's household was looking for him.

'Listen, my friend. Something has happened,' said Stephen when he tracked him down in the main room of the house. 'The Archbishop has sent me a message asking us to call on him early tomorrow morning at Westminster Palace. I must say, that is quite a surprise. Will you come with me? I have a feeling this may be a glimmer of hope.'

6/Westminster

Westminster, 10 January 1121

Hilary could not help letting his spirits rise the next morning as he walked with his new friend Stephen of Boxley and his servant, as quickly as the crowds would allow, through Ludgate, past the beggars at the gate and Baynards Castle, and over the River Fleet. If the Archbishop himself wanted a quiet word it could really only mean a problem of some kind with the trial. At the same time, he felt deeply nervous. He had never met anything approaching an archbishop before and Stephen had lent him a more appropriate mode of dress. But what should he do? Was he supposed to kiss his ring? How should he address him? Was there perhaps something he could say, even now, to avert the coming destruction in the West?

His mind was also full of the possible implications of Alberic's admission yesterday in court that he had been there in Notre Dame, and so had Ralph Basset and the French Chancellor, on the day that poor Master Hubert had been killed.

'My dear Hilary,' said Stephen, who was biting his finger nails as they passed the ships of the Danes pulled up on the Strand below them. 'I suggest that we don't anticipate what they are about to say to us. Only perhaps nod when they express doubts about the trial and express willingness to help in any way. We will not be able to persuade them about anything. They can only persuade themselves.'

Hilary made no reply, fascinated by carts and aristocratic horsemen on the road, and unable to speak with the weight of anticipation. Muddled and worried, he watched the soldiers on the road alongside them, their coloured streamers waving from the end of spears and pikestaffs indicating strange and unknown regiments. Where were they heading, Hilary asked himself? Along with him to see the officials in Westminster or further – much further – to wreak havoc in the villages of Somerset and Devon?

'You see, Hilary, the King is now triumphant everywhere. There is peace with Flanders and peace with Fulk of Anjou. Normandy is safe. There is only the matter of the succession since the White Ship has cheated Henry of his only son. The point is that there are no foreign broils to confuse the issue. Either he wants to prosecute Abelard or he does not. There is really no foreign reason why he should. He can do as he likes.'

'Quite so,' said Hilary, but he was aware that Stephen was wrong. The continuing sore of a secret Saxon heir preyed on the minds of the King and his ministers, and had proved a perfectly adequate spur to prosecute Peter Abelard. As he spoke, he could see the gates to Westminster appear around the corner in the distance, and the squat towers of the abbey rising over them. Whatever happened behind those busy, fearsome gates, with the banners streaming above them, they would know their fate.

Hilary and Stephen were led down stone corridors to a small cloister at the heart of the abbey, then out across a large courtyard and through a large arched door. Inside was the biggest hall that Hilary had ever seen before, with a huge wooden roof too far and gloomy to quite make out. The furthest end of the hall was equally deep in gloom, a mixture of fog from the river and smoke from the tallow candles they burned here even in the day. It smells like power, thought Hilary to himself. For a moment it seemed to him also to smell a little of sulphur. What evils wafted from this labyrinth of corridors? Would he ever emerge again?

It was full of people, all apparently waiting for something. There were groups of soldiers and monks at opposite sides and other merchants and minor aristocrats. They assumed the positions of people who had been there for months. An air of lassitude and hopelessness pervaded everything. A man got up in the distant shadows and beckoned towards them. As Hilary's eyes adjusted to the light, he recognised the churchman waiting for them at a huge stone desk from the chapter house the day before.

'My dear Stephen of Boxley. Good of you to come. Pray approach.'

'Thank you, my Lord Bishop.'

'I will take you through now. The Archbishop is waiting.'

They followed at a respectful distance through another arch, down a corridor and into a long room. It was hard to make out the figure on a great chair in the distance, dark in front of the light from the window and sitting at an odd angle behind a stone desk. When he got nearer, Hilary could see an old man in clerical clothes and a deeply lined face. He seemed to have his head bent partly to one side as if listening carefully. Archbishop Ralph looked older and more infirm closer up. One hand motioned to them in a reassuring way.

'My lord Archbishop, may I introduce you to my colleague, Stephen of Boxley, and – I believe you are Hilary of Orléans, an associate of Master Peter's, is that right?'

'I am, my lord,' said Hilary. Was this the moment when he should bow and kiss the ring of the Archbishop? Beside him, Stephen bowed low. Hilary did likewise and, as he did so, the morning sunlight fell across the desk and he could see the Archbishop's curiously lopsided face. One side smiled in welcome, his eye twinkling with wry amusement. The other side his mouth was stuck in the same miserable grimace as before. On one side, a useless arm was propped helplessly on the desk.

'Welcome, welcome,' said the Archbishop. 'Pray come closer and sit here where I might hear you better.'

At first, Hilary could not make out what he had said. He slurred his words unnervingly. Was he drunk?

'Leave us, please,' said the Archbishop, and Hilary saw two even more shadowy figures, two senior chaplains, come out from behind the desk. They gave him a look of suspicion and dislike as they walked past.

There was silence as the Archbishop seemed to be struggling to speak. Finally he relaxed. 'My colleagues believe – I will not say who but I have come to agree with them – that this trial will do us no good,' said Archbishop Ralph. Hilary was quickly becoming more adept at understanding what he was saying. 'It is a tick... tick... ticklish matter, I fear.' Here he took a deep breath. 'I am grateful to you for coming here.'

'It was our pleasure and our duty,' said Stephen, bowing his head again.

'The scholars rioted in Cheapside after the end of our proceedings last night,' said the Archbishop, wringing his hands. 'Really, this cannot go on.

Stephen nodded.

'I am glad you agree,' said the Archbishop, smiling with half his face. 'Now, I believe that God himself, Christ and all this angels, will probably know whether Master Peter Abelard is a heretic. I personally am not qualified to know. Personally, I don't want Abelard on my conscience.'

Hilary's hopes began to rise. He felt light-headed, and hung on the Archbishop's halting words, holding his breath. An uncomfortable silence fell on the room as the Archbishop attempted to continue. He seemed to have deteriorated considerably since the day before.

'Then we ....' Hilary could not make it out.

'What did he say?' he whispered.

'He said we are agreed,' said Stephen.

Archbishop Ralph held his good hand upwards and pointed down to the table. 'Yes, as you say, we are agreed.' He smiled at an uncomfortable Stephen. 'The trial will not continue today, and we will release Abelard into your custody. If that is acceptable?'

There was another silence. 'That *is* acceptable, I hope.'

Stephen of Boxley seemed to wake out of some kind of reverie. 'Oh yes, I am most grateful, my lord.'

'The only question that remains is how we can square this with the King's Justice. Between you and me, I only agreed to these proceedings because Alberic of Reims somehow managed to find his way to Basset and this obviously solved some other problem of his. I believe Abelard had been involved in some way in the White Ship disaster.'

'Quite innocently, my lord. We had been due to sail with William the Aetheling.'

'Then you are favoured by God, I see. But was there not some other matter? I forget now.'

'Yes, it is true, my lord. I became involved, again quite innocently, in the murder of one John of Muchelney.'

A spasm of what looked almost like fear crossed the Archbishop's face.

'Ugh,' he said. 'How many more times must I hear that name? I am heartily sick of it. We have spent too long on this matter already. Young man, I suggest you say no more about it. These are deep matters. I will deal with Basset.' The mention of John of Muchelney seemed to have made the Archbishop impatient to end the discussion. The Archbishop rang a small bell on his desk. Two chaplains entered the room and he conferred with them.

'I fear the King's Justice has left for Winchester,' he said, with some apparent satisfaction. 'But we will have no more of this trail. It brings no credit to us. Let Basset do his worst in some other jurisdiction. It shall not be in mine. We will release Master Peter into your joint custody. But there is one condition, and I emphasise this.'

'My lord, I am deeply grateful,' said Stephen. 'Also I believe very wise.'

'I don't want your congratulation,' said the Archbishop. 'Now listen to the condition. It is important. Abelard must be out of London by nightfall. And do not let him return, or return yourself. Do you understand, Hilary of Orléans? That is my condition and also my strong advice to you.'

Hilary followed Stephen, bowing out of the chamber with a lightness of heart that he had not enjoyed since the start of his terrifying adventure. The condition was easily met. He would get out of London like a scalded cat. There had been no pardon, and no offer of help with a pardon in France, certainly no promise not to effect slaughter in the West. But the escape from the Tower for both of them seemed enough to lift his spirits.

They were met outside by the doleful expressions of the two chaplains and by a number of monks.

'Hilary of Orléans? Will you please follow me,' said one of them.

Once more, they processed through the rat run of stone corridors and spiral staircases, and finally out from a small side entrance in front of the great hall. To Hilary's surprise, the courtyard outside now seemed to be full of soldiers, with banners flying and metal glinting in the pale light. It was hard to make out what the melee was all about. The arrival of the King or something more sinister?

'Hilary, I think I can see Master Peter, over there by the cross.'

Hilary's gaze followed where he was pointing and it was the expression on Abelard's face, more than anything else, that made him suddenly doubt the sincerity of the meeting he had just come from.

Abelard waved cheerily and he walked towards him. Sure enough, two soldiers saw him and marched alongside.

'Hilary, I fear I don't like the smell of this,' said Stephen of Boxley next to him. 'Perhaps you had better leave quickly while you still can.' He indicated the direction of the river steps behind the palace. Hilary's mood was plummeting. How could he have felt a moment's hope when it was obvious such levity had imperilled their lives all over again? How could he have been so trusting as to tempt fate in this way?

'It is too late. The die is cast,' said Hilary. He was now surrounded by soldiers.

'Hilary! Well met, my old pupil,' said Abelard cheerily when they reached him. 'I would grasp your hand, but as you can see...'

He raised his hands together and Hilary realised they were shackled. 'I am afraid I have led you out of the pot and into the inferno.'

Hilary felt himself held from behind and his hand were shackled too. Stephen was led away protesting by another soldier. Of course, the Archbishop must have known, maybe he could have seen the reception gathering out of his window, had he looked. He need only to have turned around and peered down. Perhaps he could hear it throughout their conversation. All those words about leaving London by nightfall were all elaborate nonsense. They may indeed be leaving London, but in quite different circumstances to what they had expected.

Hilary cursed under his breath and cursed the duplicity of archbishops. How could they live with themselves with such compromises with temporal power? How could this stuttering, divided man be at ease with what remained of his conscience?

'Where are we going?'

'I believe we are on our way to Winchester to see our old friend Basset again,' said Abelard. 'I am hoping we might make a detour to your home village to pick up my books.' He grinned bravely.

Hilary looked at him, unsure whether this was a joke or simply delusion.

'I despair, Master Peter. Is there no end to this nightmare? Nothing ever seems to quite go as people say. When they say I am to be incarcerated or tortured, they let me go. When they say I am to be released, they put me in chains.'

'There is an end, Hilary,' said Abelard, as the soldiers began to move out of the courtyard and the horses began to kick up the dust. 'But I sometimes wonder whether it is a very attractive one.'

The cart in which they travelled, their hands chained together, was increasingly uncomfortable as the roads deteriorated. The hours passed by interminably, with one identical village after another passing by on the Great West Road.

'You should have gone before now,' said Hilary. 'Now you may be caught up in whatever fate my enemies have ordained for me.' The cart gave a lurch into a particularly big pothole. There would be no escape from the Harrying of the West. The Alfred Jewel would lie forgotten in the brickwork of St Andrew's Church for centuries.

Hilary had already noticed that his normally ebullient friend was less than his usual optimistic self. His escape from humiliation at the hands of the heresy tribunal had not cheered him. Nor had the thought of the rage that would now be coursing through the veins of Alberic of Reims once he realised that his old enemy has slipped through his fingers. On the other hand, it was hard to be optimistic about what Ralph Basset had in store for them.

'Master Peter, you stood by me all this time when my life was in peril. The least I could do was to stand by you.'

'You are very good, Hilary, and very kind. I fear I have not entirely appreciated that enough before.'

The journey seemed to stretch endlessly ahead of them, especially if Abelard was going to continue in this kind of mood. Hilary felt he could cope with his old teacher's arrogance, but not his sudden modesty.

'You see, Hilary, I realise now that I am at fault. It was my pride that first brought me into conflict with Alberic of Reims and which also directed my conduct during that trial over the last few days.'

'Master Peter, you were extraordinary...'

'No, Hilary. It was my pride that allowed it to happen in the first place, just as it was my arrogance that led me to the disaster with Heloise, which has destroyed both our lives. I believed that I was so brilliant I could have everything – not just fame and students, but women too. These last few months have brought that home to me in the most decisive manner. And you who have no pride – well, I could learn from you. I *have* learned from you.'

'You are not being fair on yourself. I would follow you anywhere, Master Peter.'

'And I would follow you, Hilary. I *have* followed you.' He gave a wry grin and looked around at the five soldiers mounted around them, trudging along the same road, laboriously through each swollen pothole and broken stone gully. 'Unfortunately for you, it looks as though you are going to have to follow me this time.'

'Be of good cheer, Master Peter. I would rather share a cart with you than a dinner table with Alberic of Reims. Or

Archbishop Ralph for that matter.'

Another squalid village, with broken roofs, was visible from the cart as they trudged slowly by.

'What distresses me the most is that our mission remains uncompleted,' said Abelard. 'We know this shadowy Ranulf de Aquis shot Rufus, as part of a bid for the throne by Henry together with these Saxons, though we know little enough about them. We know there is a Saxon heir who has stayed hidden until now, though we know little enough about him. We know the fear of him is about to bring destruction down on the West, and we are now powerless to prevent it – though goodness knows, we might have done had William the Aetheling not embarked on the White Ship. Perhaps, after all, these things do not matter after all in God's design for the universe. But what we do know now is why Master Hubert died.'

'You speak of Alberic's admission in court.'

'Indeed. That day when you and I were dashing through the catacombs at Notre Dame, Alberic had been there too. He encountered Ralph Basset who was there to meet Stephen de Garlande, the Chancellor of France, and in the strictest secrecy, to discuss the Saxon threat. Master Hubert must have discovered this too, and guessed – as I guess now – that the meeting had something to do with John of Muchelney and the letters you carried around your neck. I imagine he asked one too many difficult questions. Maybe he threatened to tell what he saw. Maybe he worked out why they were so worried about these letters from an obscure Saxon abbot, so worried that it could even bring the pestilential rivalry of the kings of France and England to a temporary halt. The last thing they wanted was the Saxons back in Normandy and England. Either way, they had him killed – and in such a way as they could pin the blame on you when you returned.'

The horror of it overwhelmed Hilary for a moment. He knew, of course, the basic facts, but hearing it all set out like this sounded such a waste. Hubert, Abelard and himself, sacrificed in some ridiculous diplomatic charade. And now the full rage of the new regime in England would fall on the unsuspecting villagers and freeman of Western England in a bid to root out the Saxon plotters.

'We have not even discovered the identity of these Saxon plotters, have we? We know John of Muchelney was a Platonist, that that is precious little.'

It was then that Hilary remembered that he had never spoken about his encounter with the crippled soldier at St Erkenwald's shrine.

'Master Peter, I have an idea about that. While you were preaching outside St Paul's, I met an old Saxon soldier who used that phrase to me. The one that John of Muchelney used. *Hit waes geara iu.*'

Abelard seemed to recover some of his *sang froid* almost immediately. 'He did? How interesting. Did you ask him what he meant?'

'Of course I did and, as you said all that time ago, it was a kind of password for Saxons harking back to the days before the Conquest. But listen, Master Peter. He came from Glastonbury. Do you know what that means?'

Abelard thought for a moment. 'I confess I do not, Hilary. Enlighten me.'

'Glastonbury is a great abbey in the West, where John of Muchelney came from too. They say it was founded by Joseph of Arimathea himself. It is in that marshy region of the far West where King Alfred himself escaped from the Danes and where he planned their defeat. Now Muchelney, where my friend John came from, is a small outpost of Glastonbury Abbey, also next to the marshes. I had not understood that before.'

'You will have to explain some more, Hilary. I do not follow where you are taking me.'

'What I am suggesting is that maybe there has been something going on in Muchelney, or near Muchelney and Athelney. Maybe they are the ones that sent John of Muchelney with the letter, keeping King Alfred's name alive...'

'In the very place that Alfred made his own – you may be right, Hilary.'

'You remember the ink with which John's letter was written.' It seemed strange setting out reasoning to the Indomitable Rhinoceros. Even stranger, perhaps, that he seemed to be listening to it.

'I do. Old fashioned. Weak. From somewhere not quite connected to the world as it is today.'

'Exactly. So perhaps it was these people who killed William Rufus. Perhaps that is what John of Muchelney's letter was trying to convey.'

Abelard stared into space as the cart wobbled along. 'Hilary, I believe you are right. I was not aware of this place. Well done, Hilary. This may be the answer. Still,' he said with a sigh. 'It may be academic now. I no longer have high hopes of extricating ourselves from the clutches of Ralph Basset. Still less of preventing Henry's army from marching West.'

This was a dark cloud indeed for Hilary. His old teacher had always been so confident at every eventuality. Even being pursued through the catacombs under Notre Dame, his confidence had never really faltered. It was as if the huge trauma he had undergone just two years before was only now beginning to drag him down.

'Be of good heart, Master Peter. We have dodged far more difficult situations than this one. And you have taught me for most of my life that the truth shall set us free. The truth about the death of William Rufus is no small thing. It does not leave us powerless.'

'But we do not yet know the whole truth, Hilary.'

Hilary stared at him helpless for a while, horribly aware that it was his own appeal to Abelard's spirit of adventure – his yearning for the truth at all costs – which had tempted him down this disastrous path. He remembered the screams in the night in the Tower of London. It was true that Basset could make short work of them if he wanted, no matter what the truth was.

The motion of the cart was soporific and he fought against sleep. Even in the discomfort of this very basic conveyance, it seemed overwhelming. He saw the shiny helmets of the soldiers who rode with them, and they seemed so implacable, the way their horses put one foot in front of the other no matter what he wished for. Men like these had forced their way into the Royal Treasury in Winchester, despite the courage of William of Breteuil, early the morning after Rufus had been killed.

To think that, only weeks before, he had imagined he somehow had the opportunity and the power to rescue the West of England from military devastation – that he had carried the Alfred Jewel back in his own hands, hoping somehow to use it for some kind of reconciliation. And to think he had criticised Master Peter for his pride. What overweening pride had flung him into this delusion? What miserable failure to remember his mere humanity? Remember man, he repeated to himself: *dust thou art and unto dust thou shalt return*. And unfortunately, rather sooner than later.

After a night in Guildford, it began to rain. Cold water ran down his neck. Abelard slept under a leather cover, but this time Hilary stayed awake, the drips of water running off his nose. He saw the soldiers wipe away the rain from their eyes, and stumble on through the puddles and potholes of the road to Guildford and then the ancient track along the downs he knew as the Old Road to Winchester.

Some way beyond Farnham on the third day, the weather brightened a little and they stopped at an inn for the ritual of dinner. A soldier brought out a simple platter for them. Another stayed guarding the cart while his fellows ate and drank. This time a small group of villagers surrounded the cart slapping their arms to keep warm in the damp, frosty air.

'Where are you from, gentlemen?' asked one of them. His clothes suggested that he was a ploughman.

'We both come from Paris,' said Hilary proudly, aware again of his own vanity. He checked himself. This was no moment to be vain, not before his encounter with Basset and his torturers. 'But on this journey we have travelled from London.'

There was an excited whispering among the villagers and anxious and nervous glances down at the chains that so obviously bound them.

'Is it true what we have heard?' said the ploughman. 'That the King's son has been drowned and there is no heir?'

'Yes, it is true,' said Abelard. 'A tragedy.'

The villagers talked nervously among themselves. 'Then I fear for us, I do, Sir. There will be war when the King dies.'

'Nonsense,' said Abelard with a conviction that implied he had begun to regain some of his spirits. 'Matilda will be Queen. His daughter will inherit.'

'That's right,' said one of the women with spirit. But there was a miserable shaking of heads.

'No. We have had no queen in England since Cordelia. Those men around her – they will not accept it. I fear the future, Sir.'

'I am afraid you may be right,' said Hilary. 'I wish it were not so. Tell me, what is this place called?'

'Ovington, Sir.'

'Is there not a river crossing here?'

Before anyone could answer, there was a shout from the inn as the soldiers emerged, a little worse for drink, and the villagers dispersed nervously. Hilary and Abelard looked at each other, aware of their own small part in the greater tragedy that might one day overtake an England ruled by Matilda.

Hilary looked ahead down the road as the cart began to move. The rain was still holding off, and he could see, beyond the thick woods, a shimmering glint of light which implied that they were approaching the river Itchen.

By the time they reached the river side it was clear that crossing was going to be difficult. The river was high and fast, and the ford accessible only in the middle. It seemed unlikely that all five soldiers and the cart could cross at the same time. The cart would also need to be lightened to pull it quickly across or it might be damaged by the heavy water, thought Hilary to himself. Sure enough, the soldiers discussed among themselves, dismounted and ordered them out. It was strange there were so few people around on in the middle of the day at such a busy crossing.

A moment later, they were being led across the river on foot. It was achingly cold, and in a moment they were wading up to their knees.

'This is bracing,' said Abelard. 'Still, it is good to have my legs as wet as my top half.'

Then, suddenly they understood the reason why the ford was deserted. As they reached the opposite bank, there was a shout. An arrow came from nowhere, straight into the throat of the soldier nearest them. He made a terrible sound, between a scream and a choke and blood spurted over Hilary's arm.

It all happened so quickly. The soldiers on the other bank noticed nothing until their colleague hit the water with a terrific splash.

'Drop down,' said Hilary. 'Quick!'

There was another splash as he and Abelard hit the freezing water at the same time and struggled out of the way.

The other soldier next to them was drawing his sword when a second arrow shot passed them, missing him by inches. On an instinct, Hilary lunged at his legs and the soldier fell heavily into the water with a clang of metal on metal, searching about for where the attack had come from. He reached out at Hilary from the deep water. Abelard pulled him back beyond the reach of the sword, but the solder was getting heavily to his feet.

His colleagues had been waiting to draw the horse and cart across the ford on the other side. As they began hurriedly to wade across to help, a small group of agile outlaws emerged from the woods, wearing leather and hose, shouting blood-curdling slogans. Hilary realised that more of them were in the water. One outlaw was upon them. He put a dagger through the neck of the soldier who was advancing on Hilary. There was another spurt of blood, and Hilary waded forward. Two archers knelt at the water's edge, and he and Abelard could see the other soldiers stumbling out back onto the opposite bank.

'Master Peter, I think we should wade out as fast as we can.'

But as they reached the opposite bank, a hand grabbed Hilary by the shoulder from behind. He turned quickly. Behind them was a burly man with a red beard and a sword.

'*Hit waes geara iu,*' he whispered with a big smile. 'Please come with me, gentlemen.'

They were led stumbling in their chains into the bushes, dripping wet, and found a group of horses had been tethered there. The man indicated a large rock. Hilary's teeth chattered with cold.

'This will take a moment. If you could put your chains there.' He swung an axe. Hilary looked away. There was a crash and Abelard's chains fell away. A moment later and Hilary was free too.

'I confess, getting rid of those chains does put an entirely different aspect on the situation,' said Abelard as he was helped onto one of the horses.

The other outlaws were also mounting and a few moments later they were away, racing across the field. The trees flashed by. Leaves splashed into his face. Hilary hung on for dear life, unable to process quite what had happened to them or what was happening now, glad only that he had managed so much practice with horses in recent months.

A little while later, on the other side of a small forest, the sky beginning to darken in the winter evening, they joined a small track apparently heading northwards, and stopped. Three more men, dressed the same in leather were waiting for them in the shadows under the trees. When they were just yards away, and he was dismounting from his horse, Hilary looked up and gasped. The third man was dressed unlike the others, in a grey tunic with a surcoat bearing a blue motif. His deep blue eyes and the shape of his head looked horribly familiar.

Shaking with horror, Hilary fell the rest of the way off his horse. Abelard was at his side in a moment.

'Do you see who it is?' whispered Hilary. 'It is my nemesis. This is the end, I fear, Master Peter.'

The Man in Gray stepped forward. 'I apologise for startling you. I realise I must look familiar. You are Hilary the Englishman, I believe. I have followed you off and on now for more than a year.'

His voice was low and aristocratic.

'You murdered John of Muchelney,' said Hilary defiantly. 'You tried to take me too. And now...'

'My friend, please be not too hasty in your conclusions. I was following your friend John that night after he had left Beaugency, and warned him that he was being watched. I tried to take his package from him but he refused. When I realised he had died, I believed I should relieve you of the burden you had taken on unknowingly and followed you hard – on to Paris and finally to Marseilles.'

'Wait, wait,' said Hilary. 'You are telling me you wanted to *protect* me? Why were you there in Paris when the whole cathedral, the whole city, seemed to be after my blood? Did you also kill Brother Hubert?'

'All I can say is that I understand your suspicion. Brother Hubert was killed by powerful people in Paris, partly to engineer your arrest – and because he was too curious. My object was to protect you. Alas, you were always too fast for me. Even in Marseilles, when I rode through the night to intercept you.'

'You are telling me you wanted John of Muchelney's letters and papers purely to protect me? Surely they were valuable in their own right?'

'Certainly, I wanted them delivered. I wanted to keep them out of the hands of the English and the French. The French were as determined as the English to make sure no Saxon regained the throne of England. No, it is true, I doubted your ability – your willingness to do so. I see now I was wrong.'

Hilary stared. 'I don't believe it. I went through all that – for nothing? I could have just handed it all to you?'

'Oh, not for nothing, I assure you,' he said. There was an awkward silence. 'But now it is our turn to return the favour. We are finally discharging our duty towards you.'

Abelard now rose and looked him full in the face. 'What is your name, sir?'

There was a silence among them. The other outlaws looked at the Man in Grey expectantly.

'I believe it is time to tell them, sire,' said the huge red-bearded man.

'I agree. My name is Aelfred. I am the son of Guthwine, the son of Leofwin.'

The silence continued.

Despite himself, Hilary fell to his knees on the long grass. Even Abelard bowed his head.

'You are the heir. You are the Saxon claimant to the throne of England?'

'I am indeed the heir,' said Aelfred. 'But that is all. I claim nothing yet. The time has not yet come, though I fear it may not be far off. So please rise, Hilary. I am not yet the King and you have already travelled around the world on this task, which you never asked for. You will not bow to me.'

Hilary rose, and brushed down his knees. He was still wet from the river and the old grass stuck to him.

'You are the nephew of the last Saxon king, is that right?'

The man with red hair interrupted, as if this was too personal a question for the Saxon prince.

'My lord is indeed the grandson of King Harold's brother. That makes him the royal heir.' Another silence fell.

'You realise King Henry is about to march West in search of you?' said Abelard.

'I do,' said Aelfred, 'and we are unprepared to meet him. Especially now.'

'You know that many people will die?'

The Saxon prince bowed slightly. 'Master Peter, you are correct, I fear. And they will not find me. I am discharging my duty to you both before riding West myself. I know you are seekers after truth and I propose not just to tell you to truth, but to show you. That is, if you will come with me before these forests are full of the King's men searching for us.'

Hilary still stared. For more than a year, he had imagined this man as the symbol of everything evil. Now he looked at him, young and determined, not as richly dressed as William the Aetheling had been, but somehow almost as dignified. The two rival heirs to the kingdom of England – he had met them both, and a similar light seemed to shine from them both. Or was he dreaming?

'I fear we have no alternative but to accept your hospitality,' said Abelard.

'I am glad you understand that,' said Aelfred. 'But to establish my character and goodwill, my men have brought you this.'

He indicated a large pannier on a nearby horse and one of the men in leather fetched it over. He heaved it up and opened it with difficulty. Inside were some weighty tomes and some scrolls of parchment and a pen. Abelard walked towards it as if in a dream.

'I don't believe it. My books! I am most grateful to you, sir. I was afraid I would never see those again.' Happily, he flicked through the familiar volumes which had lodged in the barn in Nether Wallop since the summer.

'How did you know where to look?' asked Hilary.

'We still have people everywhere. It seems a pity that, despite their bravery over the generations, we have made so little progress.' He shook his head sadly. 'And now, if you will be so good as to mount again, we ride north. In five days time, you will know all that I know.'

He swung himself up onto his saddle and raised his hand. Abelard tied his books lovingly onto his horse again. The other men in leather stowed their weapons and mounted as well. Soon they were riding along the farm track in the gathering darkness. Perhaps this time, thought Hilary, we will get to the truth.

Hilary could barely stay awake enough to remain in the saddle as they rode for what seemed like hours into the night. Hedgerows and wooden churches began to blur together in his mind. He was aware only that the road was rising. Finally they were climbing a steep slope. Ahead of them in the dark, a flaming torch marked some ancient entrance way.

'We are expected at least,' said Abelard from behind him.

As they approached the torch, it was clear that it was fixed to the gatepost of an old fort. The huge wooden gates were broken and leaned awkwardly against each other, leaving space to ride through by bowing the heads. As soon as they were inside, the torch was extinguished and, in the moonlight, Prince Aelfred held up his hand. We must have arrived somewhere, Hilary said to himself with relief, nearly falling from his horse with exhaustion.

'We will be safe here,' said the Prince. 'Perhaps if you would be so good as to follow my steward into this hut, he will make sure you have what you need to sleep.'

Hilary could see a dilapidated hut of ancient construction, and beyond it so many others in various stages of decay. Mud, wattle and horsehair stuck through the slats of the walls of the building. Then he looked across the eerie moonlit landscape of huts again with a sudden sense of recognition.

'I know this place,' he said suddenly. 'Are we not in Danebury?'

'I congratulate you, my friend. This ancient town has been abandoned for many years now. That is why we borrow it when we need to. We are in Wessex now. It is my forefather Alfred's old kingdom. Yet we must still be careful. We borrow only what is discarded already,'

'I can't believe it,' he told Abelard. 'This old hill town has not been used since before the Conquest, before my grandfather's day. It is near where I was born. I never thought I would see it again. We used to sneak up here sometimes when we were children or searching for lost cattle.'

'Nevertheless, this straw is very welcome,' said Abelard, stretching himself out on the floor of the hut. 'It is also dry, which is a blessing. We shall find the truth soon enough. I do not yet see how we can avert the coming disaster.'

7/Athelney

Danebury hillfort, 16 January 1121

Before the wintry dawn punctured the sky, Hilary found himself awake. It was just possible to see across the hut and he rose from the bedding of straw and pulled on his sandals, and tied them around his shins. Outside, the air was frosty and hurt his cheeks. He was cold in the ecclesiastical garb procured for him by Canon Stephen, but he stood up on the old battlements where he had played as a boy and breathed it in. He had believed that he would never breathe the air outside again, yet here he was.

In the distance towards the east, the sky was just beginning to be lighter. Hilary walked the other way, down the slope, over the old fallen defences, towards the field strips stretching out into the distance below. His feet crunched on the frozen stalks, but he knew the way. It was not yet lauds. There was still time to reach his village before it had woken up for the new day. He could hear his breath rasping heavy in the cold as he reached the bottom of the hill, and headed off on the old path which he knew so well.

It was only a walk for the length of a mass, but the dawn was emerging clear and fresh by the time he could see the village, nestling so silently and secretly down in the valley. He felt a pang seeing the roof of his mother's farm in the distance, but turned his face away with determination. The door of the church swung open easily, and there was enough light through the slit windows to find the cleft in the wall by the tiled floor where the stone was loose. It took a moment to find the black cloth and to retrieve the Alfred Great Jewel from its hiding place, replace the stone, say a quick prayer at the familiar altar and stride out back across the Wallop River.

The sky was light now and people were stirring in the fields as he reached the first slopes of Danebury, pushing past the overgrown defences again as he climbed. He had reached the top, in a cacophony of brambles and reeds when there was a shout from just above him, and the fearsome sound of a metal being drawn from scabbard.

'*Hit waes geara iu,*' said Hilary.

There was a silence, a crunch and then a helping hand back into the old fort.

By the time the day had truly begun, not long after Hilary had reached his hut again, the expedition were all up. Soon, their horses cantering back down the hill and onto the road that he knew was the old road to the West. The light of the sun peeped over the horizon behind them as they hurried on along long stretches of Roman road, through forests and markets, and dozing villages, past oxen and cattle on the road.

By nightfall again, as the sun set before them, they stared at the great stone boulders of Stonehenge.

'I wish I could have stayed and sought out my mother again, or my brothers,' said Hilary sadly, realising he had missed the opportunity in their headlong flight westwards. 'Still, it is too late now.'

'It is never too late,' said Abelard. 'That is what I have learned these last few years. Never too late to get what you long for. Let us hope not, but sometimes you have to change yourself to get it. Now, Hilary, what manner of men built this temple? Those who did not know Christ, I will warrant.'

'It is a place of death,' said Aelfred. 'We will not tarry here.'

There was a glint among the stones as they approached them. Hilary spotted it. Then he saw that Aelfred and his companions had stopped on their horses.

'Let go the donkey,' said Aelfred quietly. Abelard turned round to see the donkey carrying his books settle down to munching the thistles beside the road. 'We must look to ourselves now.'

Even as he spoke, the glint had turned into four glinting helmets emerging from behind the biggest stones. Then ten.

'Archers,' said Aelfred. 'We will not charge them.'

Hilary looked about them. It was quiet except for the wind on the plain, and the lumps of the old barrows in the distance.

'Dust behind us!' shouted one of Aelfred's men. The red-haired giant, moved his horse next to that of the Saxon prince, retrieved his helmet from his saddlebag and put it on his head. Looking back up the hill they had come down, Hilary could see horsemen and spears in the distance.

'We go south, towards Sarum and into the forest,' said Aelfred calmly. The red-haired man, raised his hand and led them quickly off the road and onto the plain. As they did so, the first arrows fell short from the direction of Stonehenge. 'Come my friends, we appear to have been betrayed.'

'It might be a mile. It might be two miles,' said Abelard quietly. 'I believe we can make it.'

As his horse began to accelerate, as fast as possible on the uneven ground, it crossed Hilary's mind once again that he should have stayed in his village and never emerged. A moment later, he felt guilty for it. The trees were ahead of them now, and the banners billowing from the soldiers on the road. More arrows fell. A knot of fear gripped his stomach.

'I never seem to get any better at this,' he said to Abelard on his right, who was sweating in his own saddle.

'Concentrate, Hilary. Keep your head down and save your

breath.' In the distance, the mounted soldiers were now following them across the plain. The archers were moving more slowly on from the henge on foot, every now and then stopping and loosing off a deadly stream of arrows.

The darkness and relative safety of the forest was right ahead now. The undergrowth was becoming impassable. 'Time to dismount,' said Aelfred. 'Lead your horses into the trees. Go ahead, go on. They will not follow us into the forest. And if they do, we will turn and cut them down.'

Sweating despite the cold, Hilary climbed off his horse, patted its black sides and took the halter. Abelard was just behind, looking sadly back in the distance to catch sight of his books. The other rebels were urging their mounts onwards. Hilary looked back. He saw Aelfred standing, completely unafraid, staring at the advancing soldiers. He saw him turn back towards them and, as he did so, another flurry of arrows fell amongst them, and one of them hit the Prince bang in the throat.

There was a splash of blood and he fell heavily to the ground. Hilary watched powerless and in horror. With a shout, the red-haired giant dashed to the spot, cradled the Prince in his arms, and bowed his head. Hilary could see he was weeping. The other rebels had dashed over to the spot as well.

The giant rose with a roar. 'Get back, you fools. We go on, he said to me. Go on. We go on.' He charged past Hilary, tears rolling down his cheeks, back towards his great horse and the looming trees. Hilary followed. The Man in Grey had turned out to be angel not devil, and in the short time he had come to know him, he had loved and revered him, and already he was gone.

Deep in the forest, the rebels wept, leaderless but safe, rallied again by the red-haired giant and succeeded in rejoining a rutted track early the next morning. They passed through the towns of Shafetsbury and Crewkerne and then north again through the increasingly hilly unkempt county of Somerset. Some days later, the huge edifice of Glastonbury Abbey appeared behind the strange conical hill which lent the place some of its magic. Hilary stared fascinated at the great arches. It was evening and the light from the candles flickered through the windows. It was vespers and the monks were at prayer. The January wind blew and Hilary wrapped himself closer in his cloak for comfort.

'It is as you thought, Hilary,' said Abelard after a brief conversation with a monk. 'Glastonbury is the mother abbey of Muchelney. Now we shall see.'

'But what is the point, Master Peter? We cannot now prevent the destruction of the West – what can we do?'

'We can finish this, you and I. We can make an ending.'

By the time night had fallen, the horses stopped by what seemed to be a small wharf. Ahead of them in the gloaming, a dark lake spread far into the distance, as far as they could see. There was no negotiation. A small boat and crew lay beside the wharf. Hilary, Abelard and the red-haired giant clambered down into the gunwhales and sat amidships as four rowers began to haul on the oars. Two others hoisted a lateen sail which filled with the damp air.

'You may be cold, my masters,' he said. 'Pray take these sheepskins and wrap yourselves. We will be here for some time.'

It was a dreamlike journey with only the creak of the oars and the faint splash as they moved out of the water, and nothing to be seen except the rising mist from the lake, the darkness around them and the black waters below. The silence continued as they sailed deep into the lake. There was no sign of an edge to it except the darker outline of hills to their left, and Hilary began to lose track of time.

Sometimes the oarsmen forced their way through a miasma of clogging reeds, while the red-haired giant stood in the bows, strong and erect. The mystical quality of the journey made him feel deeply every new twist, and Hilary felt an overwhelming compassion for the man, lost without his prince. Abelard stared into the blackness next to him and Hilary knew he was determined to press on and find out what was at the other side. Searching his own heart, Hilary knew that he was determined too. This was the very heart of the truth. Some hours later, the hills disappeared to their west and the boat turned south through a series of black marshes, with dense reeds and willow and alder on either side of the banks. It could have been any time in the night when there was a rattle of the oars pulled back on board, and a light bump, as the boat came against a small wooden jetty. The red-haired giant rose and motioned to them to follow. There followed a long causeway, mounted on wood tree stumps, stretching – it seemed in the dark – almost infinitely into space. Hilary took care to place his feet on the slats, many of which were broken, and was able to turn when the causeway bent unexpectedly and to avoid the reeds and the black water. There in the distance, guiding them in, was a small light, from the glowing embers of a brazier. When they reached it, they found it marked a large wooden door in a long pallisade. A bell was tolling faintly in the distance.

'Welcome to the abbey of Athelney, my masters,' said the red-haired giant, banging twice on the wood with his knuckles.

There was a long wait, and then the rattling of mechanics and the sound of a large wooden bolt being drawn back. The door opened to reveal an ancient monk in a brown habit.
'Is it done now?' he asked. 'Is it over?'

The old man shook his head and replied in Saxon.

'What did he say?' whispered Abelard.

'He said, 'It is only the bell for prime,' said Hilary under his breath. The door closed behind them, and they were led through ancient, crumbling fortifications and finally in there a stone arch. Inside the entranceway, standing shivering on the worn flagstones, Hilary and Abelard were led to a small room and seated at a wooden table. Shortly afterwards, lit by a single oil lamp, they were brought some bread and beer and left alone.

'How long is it since we had a proper meal?' said Hilary by way of conversation. The oil lamp cast strange glimmering shadows on the sandstone walls.

'A long time for me. I came straight from the Tower for our meeting at Westminster,' said Abelard. 'I haven't really eaten properly since before we reached Barfleur. I believe my stomach has lost the habit of eating.'

Silence fell between them. Hilary realised they were both considering the same question.

'We could leave, but I believe we should stay and see what answers this place reveals,' said Hilary. 'Do you agree?'

'I certainly agree. We have come so far. The truth is here – I can feel it.'

'Master Peter, this must be Athelney. You realise we are in an old monastery built on the site of King Alfred's old hiding place. It is cut off from the world. Anything could happen here.'

'Yes,' said Abelard, making another bite of the loaf before him. 'This is the source of those papers around your neck and also the source of the mystery, I believe. But why have they left us alone?'

'Something else is happening – that is why. Something else. Finish your beer and then we can find out. I don't want to stay here until someone remembers us.'

As he stood up, Hilary felt for a moment how strange it was –

he who had followed his old teacher so miserably through the catacombs at Notre-Dame, who had fought bitterly against going to Jerusalem, should now be dictating the terms of their adventure. Their relationship must have changed – *he* must have changed.

The door to their small room opened with a creak. The narrow corridor outside was completely black and one side was open to a tiny cloister.

'Fetch the oil lamp, Master Peter, if you will,' said Hilary and, a moment later, the strange yellow light was throwing their elongated shadows onto the ancient walls. There were other rooms jutting out at right angles, some of them abandoned to rubble and cobwebs. It was not clear where they might seek human company, or if everyone was asleep.

'Wait,' hissed Abelard, covering the lamp. 'Look!'

Sure enough, under the door ahead of them, there did seem to be a flickering light.

They approached with trepidation. The door was huge with great ancient nails holding it together, as if it had been patched many times through the centuries. A strange humming noise came from within. Hilary gave it a small push and it slowly began to open. There was a smell of incense from inside and he pushed further. The two of them slipped inside and blew out their lamp.

The small room was surprisingly full, but nobody took any notice of them and it was clear, from the cowled heads leaning forward in prayer, that they were engaged in some intense activity. Monks around them kneeled in prayer under their brown hoods. Two large candles filled the room with eye-watering smoke. A few were chanting some kind of service or incantation, but the focus of their attention was a huge bed at the heart of the room.

In the middle of this rough wooden platform, white faced and inert, propped up on a bedstead, lay an ancient man, wizened with age. His bald head poked out of the coverings as if he had long since shrunken inside them, and his laboured breathing filled the room. One hand was extended out of the bed clothes and was placed on his chest, holding onto a small crucifix. The most distinctive thing about him was the huge scar on his face across his right eye, which was missing.

Hilary gasped involuntarily.

An ancient priest, also in brown robes, was leaning over him, anointing his forehead with oil and intoning the words in Latin of the last rites. Hilary glanced at Abelard to see if he understood, but he was staring fixedly at the man on the bed as he prepared for his final moments.

They remained like that for what seemed like hours, listening to the gentle chanting and the rasping breath, just audible from the direction of the bed.

Finally, as dawn seeped into the sky outside the windows, and the first cockerel began to crow, the breath stopped. The old priest bent down to listen more closely. He rose slowly to his full height. 'The King is dead,' he said sadly.

There was a snuffling in the room and it was clear that at least one of the monks was weeping in the silence. The old priest bent over again and closed the dead, staring eyes of the old man. 'The King is dead. His heir is dead too, and England is gone.'

'Please follow me,' said the priest, his white beard bedraggled from more than one night awake, his brow furrowed in thought, his faded habit dragging along the ground. He had found them back in the cold stone corridor and Hilary and Abelard walked slowly in single file, down the worn flagstones, the early light beginning to flood in through the small windows.

A few monks were filing out of the chapel, having finished lauds, and the sound of their chanting came closer. There were not very many of them, and those that were there seemed stricken in age and infirmity.

Waiting until they had all gone, and checking back down the corridor, the old priest led them laboriously inside the chapel and headed for the altar. It was a small and rectangular building, and the thatch above them had holes that let in the damp and the birds too, judging by the droppings on the floor. The old priest removed the crucifix and white cloth that covered it and revealed a large oaken chest underneath. He bent down and drew out a huge iron key from somewhere in his habit and, with some effort, unlocked the box, opening the lid and staring inside. Then he stood up straight again and addressed them.

'You understand what you have just seen, my masters? Do you understand what has ended? I, Aelfgar of Athelney, have served the King for most of my life, and all my time here as Abbot. You did not know he still lived?'

'There had been rumours,' said Hilary, thinking of the strange omission of any obvious king in the copy of the Bayeux Tapestry he had been shown by Heloise. Some other people must known that Harold had survived to escape the battlefield at Hastings. That was why Prince Aelfred was so determined to describe himself only as the 'heir'.

'He came here as an old man, and I was proud to receive him and care for him. He is the last King of England. The last of the line.' He stared misty-eyed into space. 'He has lived this year for a hundred summers. I believe he was kept alive by the determination to hand on his crown to a worthy successor. That successor is dead.'

'Is there not a claimant to the throne at King Henry's court?' Abelard asked.

The old man grimaced. 'Edgar who they call the Aetheling. The nephew of the Confessor. A mere creature of the Normans. And Prince Aelfred has now died at the hands of the Normans. No, King Harold was the last. But he believed to the end that, if he handed on the Great Jewel, then the Saxons would rise up and reclaim their kingdom – and reclaim the old liberties of England. I believed that too.'

A silence fell between them. Hilary slowly took in the implications of what he had heard. The last thing either the French or the new Norman regime in England would want was a new Saxon dynasty emerging, nominated by the old regime. No wonder they had pursued him. No wonder they had combined forces to thwart the efforts of John of Muchelney. They may not have known that Harold still lived, but they knew about Aelfred and his existence frightened them.

'May I ask you, Father Abbot, why you have brought us here?' said Hilary.

'I am glad you asked me, my son. It is because we wanted you to witness the start of the new age, the crowning of the new king. We have followed you since you first encountered us in the person of our servant John. You have proved yourself an adept and skilful messenger. I also believe you have been to Jerusalem. Am I correct?'

The Alfred Jewel burned in Hilary's side, through his knapsack and belt.

'I ask you now, my son. Do you have the Jewel? Will you bring your burden now to an end?'

Hilary glanced at Abelard. He was looking at him, one eyebrow raised in question. Hilary reached into the purse around his neck and drew out the small object, still wrapped in the old black cloth in which he had first drawn it from its hiding place on the roof of Saewulf's chapel. He unwrapped it slowly. Tarnished and battered, Hilary could see once more the ancient piece of jewellery, made of gold, very old and very beautiful. Its metal had long since ceased to reflect the light. He rubbed it, and a glint appeared.

'Take it,' said Hilary. 'I have carried this quite long enough.'

Aelfgar took the jewel, weighed it in his hands. He peered closely at it, and pressed it into his cheek with a tenderness that moved Hilary as he watched. Then, holding it in one hand, he looked from Hilary to Abelard and back again.

'You have done much, my son. I will ask you one more favour, one more task for the true King of England, who I served. Take this to Count Fulk. Give it him from Abbot Aelfgar. There is no message. He will know what to do. If he chooses, the succession is still his.'

Hilary and Abelard stared.

'I fear, Father Abbot, that you may be mistaken about me. I am not a Saxon. My grandfather came to England with the Conqueror.'

'I know who you are, Hilary the Englishman. I know your mother came from Saxon stock. I know that her father was English and that his father before him was English. No, it was your colleague I address. I know you too, Peter Abelard. I know what you can do. I know you can go safely and with authority across the cities of Europe. I know you can speak as an equal to Count Fulk when he returns from the Holy Land.'

Hilary looked at his friend. He seemed lost for words.

'Father Abbot,' said Abelard with decision. 'If I was to refuse...?'

'You will not.' Abelard thought for a moment. The tension was palpable.

'In that case, I will take the jewel. But I make no promise, Aelfgar. I will do with it what God and my conscience dictate.'

It was clear that Aelfgar took this as acceptance. He carefully wrapped the ancient jewel and handed it to Abelard, reverently.

'I can do no more than trust, Peter Abelard. I trust in you and I trust in God.'

The jewel was stowed in Abelard's purse, and the two men had fed again. They were accompanied silently down the causeway to the boat and rowed back across the lake, which was shrouded in morning mist, and no less mysterious than it had been in darkness. The morning light tasted fresh and alive. Hilary slept as the soporific sound of the oars lulled him to sleep.

The small wharf by Glastonbury Abbey was alive now with traders and mariners. Hilary recognised the distinctive lilt of Breton among the fishing boats landing their catch. He could see a Portuguese boat landing wine and Welsh boats landing skins. It was not difficult to secure a passage to Brittany. There seemed no point now in risking a return to London. Within the time it takes to say mass, they were afloat again, heading through the network of channels across the flooded landscape of Somerset, heading for the sea.

'May I see it again?' said Hilary as he sheltered with Abelard in the stern.

'Careful, Hilary. We do not wish this to be seen,' he said, unwrapping the cloth and allowing Hilary to peer in at the ancient relic. The tarnished gold was beautifully moulded, around a picture of a nobleman in deep blue. Around the outside it was written AELFRED MEC HEHT GEWYRCAN.

'Alfred ordered me to be made,' Hilary translated quietly. It hardly seemed right to touch it. This jewel had been used at the coronation of Harold, the crown placed on his head in Westminster Abbey exactly fifty-five years before, and at Edward the Confessor's coronation at Kingston, and Aethelred's coronation, Edmund Ironside's coronation and all those other kings stretching back into the dark centuries, right back to Alfred himself.

'Do you know what I think we should do, Master Peter?'

'I submit to your decision, Hilary. The cause is dead. We have failed to prevent the Harrying of the West, which may even now be under way – though I believe they will have found the body of Prince Aelfred and they must have known who they killed. We can but hope.'

'We need to end this yoke, not just for us. As you say, this cause is dead. Handing the jewel to Fulk can bring nothing but bloodshed now.'

'I agree, Hilary. If God wills that Fulk or his descendents should occupy the throne of England, then he will arrange it. He needs no help from me. This jewel will not decide it. It can do no good.'

'That is what God wants. You must use your conscience, Master Peter.'

They looked at each other with decision. Then they rose and leaned over the side. It was gone in a second into the uneven wake of their small ship and the gulls that followed them.

Postscript

'We did the right thing, I believe,' said Abelard as they stood on the dockside of St Pol, the smell of tar and fish around them. 'What is more, I have a feeling – I put it no stronger than that – that Fulk's descendents will indeed rule England, but perhaps not in my lifetime. It is, in any case, nothing to do with us. It would be overweening pride to say otherwise.'

Hilary stared at the sea. It had been a long time, but his ordeal did finally appear to be over. There had been no news of slaughter in the West.

'I suggest we take a ship along the coast to Honfleur, and make for Paris,' said Abelard. 'I will see my patron and set things right for you. He knows who killed John of Muchelney, and probably Hubert too. There can be no reason to suggest otherwise now that Harold and Aelfgar are dead. I will explain this to him. You might perhaps return to teaching.'

Hilary grinned at the way his old teacher reverted so controllingly to type. This was the moment.

'Master Peter, I am grateful, but I cannot come with you.'

'I assure you, Hilary. Stephen de Garlande will arrange everything if I ask him. I have decided many things during your adventure. I have been the author of my own misfortunes. My pride has got the better of me. I will return to St Denis and attempt to restore my relationship with the monks there, but I believe my life is to teach. God wants me to teach and I can do that – not in Paris perhaps, but somewhere else, and I would like you to help me. If you will.' Hilary stared into the middle distance, aware that he was being honoured by his old teacher – to lecture alongside him in a new school. And with the Indomitable Rhinoceros as his partner, they would not lack lucrative pupils.

'Master Peter, I am grateful. Deeply grateful – and I can never repay my debt to you for these years. I would be hanging on a gibbet or rotting in a dungeon if it was not for you. But there is something else I must do.'

'Hilary, I can think of no greater pleasure than to be in your company and you have rescued me too. You have helped me see the truth – about myself. But will you not reconsider? If not now, then later?'

'No. I have a different future planned for myself.' Abelard's gaze softened a little.

'If you mean the girl in Argenteuil, she may have taken her vows by now. They may have made sure of it.'

'I am aware of that. I must still try. I never promised her, but I promised myself.'

'And how will you live? What will you do?'

'I am not sure yet. I've learned from you that my conscience is important, and so is hers, even if she made some vows. I may have to take her home to Nether Wallop, the village where I was born in England.'

'Then my blessings on you, Hilary. God speed to you, and may the fates start smiling on you. God knows, it is time, for both of us.'

Two weeks later, after an exhausting and dusty journey on the road to Rennes and Chartres, Hilary stood at the gates of the convent of Argenteuil. He breathed deeply for a moment to control himself. The convent had hardly changed in the months since he had been there last, but there were buds on the trees and the snowdrops were making way for primroses.

Still, it was time now to find out. He banged on the door. It opened a crack and the old retainer he had met that stormy night in November stood before him.

'If you are a guest, pray go straight to the hospital. This is a closed order,' said the old man.

'I am not a guest,' said Hilary, taking a deep breath. 'I have come to see... to fetch Isabella de Payens. I am... to be her husband, in this life and the next. Please tell her that Hilary of Orléans, Hilary the Englishman, is waiting to see her.'

Historical note

Abelard was right. The grandson of Count Fulk of Anjou succeeded to the English throne as Henry II, but more than a decade after Abelard had died.

Hilary of Orléans, also known as Hilary the Englishman, did exist. He is known to have taught alongside Peter Abelard at his new school during the 1120s. At least six of his poems can still be read, mainly love poems addressed to nuns and boys. His poem 'The boy of Angers' is still published in modern collections of gay verse. Abelard was one of the most extraordinary teachers and debaters who ever lived. His whereabouts after his castration at the end of 1118 remain a little hazy, but he is usually thought to have been in St Denis until his final break with the monastery in 1122. Of course, we know differently.

Most of the other characters in this story also existed, including Heloise, Stephen de Garlande, Arnulf of Montgomery, Ralph Basset, Suger, Hugh of Champagne, Fulk of Anjou, Walter Tirel, Purkiss the Charcoal-burner, William the Aetheling, Alberic of Reims, Archbishop Ralph, Duke William of Aquitaine, the first troubadour, and Hugues de Payens, who did indeed co-found the Knights Templar in 1119. There is no evidence that King Harold survived Hastings, though a persistent tradition at the time suggested that he did. John, Hubert, Stephen, Isabella and Alys are all my inventions, but the Bayeux Tapestry is in fact ambiguous about Harold's fate. The White Ship did in fact go down on St Edmund Martyr's day 1120.

As for the Alfred Jewel, that was discovered in a village outside Bridgwater, in the Somerset Levels – where Abelard threw it – nearly six centuries later, in 1693. It can be seen now in the

British Museum. Nobody has been able to say for certain how it was originally used. Coronation regalia is one possibility. The Levels have now been largely drained, of course, and Athelney Abbey is now just a mound in a field outside Taunton. I am particularly grateful to my taxi-driver, Colin Wilkins, who was able to find it for me.

The conclusions about the mysterious death of William Rufus are as I set them out in the story, though the idea that the Saxons were involved in the plot is my suggestion. I have otherwise followed the reasoning in Duncan Grinnell-Milne's excellent 1968 book *The Killing of William Rufus*. Abelard's experiment in the New Forest is described in more detail by Grinnell-Milne when he tried something similar himself.

I have been unable to discover so far whether Hilary managed to extract Isabella from the convent at Argenteuil.

I am enormously grateful to the many people who have helped and advised me with this book, perhaps most of all Kirsty Crawford, without whom I never would have finished. The good bits are all down to her brilliant and incisive pen. But also especially Zoe Weeks and Gill Paul, who both read it through and made notes, and of course my agent Julian Alexander, all of whom gave me invaluable guidance, and Sarah who kept me encouraged. I'm afraid the mistakes are all mine.

Appendix

(The original is in the Bibliotecque Nationale in Paris)

To an English Boy
By Hilary the Englishman (Hilarius of Orleans)

Hail to you, the handsome boy, who'll never ask
For anything, no gift, no gain, no task,
In whom integrity and beauty bask,
Who captures all who see behind your mask.

Your golden hair and face I can't resist,
Your conversation, but why make a list?
There is no flaw in you that I have missed
Except your vow that you just won't be kissed.

Nature wondered for a moment, to employ
Its forces to make you girl or boy –
But while deciding which gender to deploy,
You leapt out male to give us all some joy.

Later, when she began to make you wake,
She marvelled that she could such a creature make.
Yet poor nature had made one mistake:
She still had forced you to mortality take.

Yet any other mortal can't compare
With this unique son and nature's heir.
Her beauty chooses now to live in you, in there –
Within your flesh as white and light as air.

Believe me, if Jove was ever to recover,
Then Ganymede would hardly be his lover.
You would be helping him discover
Wine by day and kisses under cover.

You're loved by every boy and girl the same,
They sigh to hold your unrepeated flame.
Those who call you 'English' are to blame:
Change the vowel and use the 'angel' name.

Other titles by David Boyle

Building Futures
Funny Money: In search of alternative cash
What is New Economics?
The Sum of our Discontent
The Tyranny of Numbers
The Money Changers
Numbers (with Anita Roddick)
Authenticity: Brands, Fakes, Spin and the Lust for Real Life
Blondel's Song
Leaves the World to Darkness (fiction)
News from Somewhere (*editor*)
Toward the Setting Sun
The New Economics: A Bigger Picture (with Andrew Simms)
Money Matters: Putting the eco into economics
The Wizard
The Little Money Book
Why London Needs its own Currency
Eminent Corporations (with Andrew Simms)
Voyages of Discovery
The Human Element
On the Eighth Day, God Created Allotments
The Age to Come
What if money grew on trees (*editor*)
Unheard, Unseen: Submarine E14 and the Dardanelles
Broke: How to survive the middle class crisis
Alan Turing: Unlocking the Enigma
Peace on Earth: The Christmas truce of 1914
Jerusalem: England's National Anthem
Give and Take (with Sarah Bird)
People Powered Prosperity (with Tony Greenham)

Rupert Brooke: England's Last Patriot
How to be English
Operation Primrose
Before Enigma
The Piper (fiction)
Scandal
How to become a freelance writer
V for Victory
Lost at Sea
Cancelled!

See also our website at <u>www.therealpress.co.uk</u>

Printed in Great Britain
by Amazon

84320873R00253